DUNGEON CORE ONLINE

Book Five

JONATHAN SMIDT

In 2018, I began writing a silly story, laughing to myself as I named demonic chickens Dickens. Now, here we are, in 2025, with the final book. It's been a wild ride, and I couldn't have done it without everyone's support. Here's a thank you to all the readers on Royal Road, who gave it love, and encouraged me to keep writing the story.

Here's to my Patron's, without whom I may not have been able to stay full time, especially in the early years.

Here's to everyone in the litrpg community, and all the authors who have supported me, and been kind enough to befriend me and welcome me into the community, as I found my place.

Here's to Portal, who has stood beside me for my entire author journey, helping me turn my stories, my passions, into a reality, a career.

And to my wife, who has stood beside me every step of the way. Truly, words cannot properly give her the thanks she deserves.

Thank you to everyone and enjoy the final book of Dungeon Core Online.

It's time for the final immersion.

Contents

The Shenanigans Thus Far

Cue catchy music from Kansas

Dungeon Core Online, the game heralded to be the greatest Virtual Reality MMO, launched to unprecedented numbers of players worldwide. However, instead of being a player within the game, James found himself in charge of the dungeon for his town. With the aid of an extremely realistic AI named Rue, James set out to create the best dungeon he could. His plans immediately had a Dicken-sized wrench thrown into them, though, as his first randomly selected monsters were... demonic farm animals.

With ingenuity, planning, and more than a few headaches, James worked hard to take the hand he'd been dealt and embrace the chaos of being the one and only Random Dungeon. Between the Demonic Farm animals of the first floor and his Steampunk Dinosaurs on the second, he quickly found his groove and thoroughly began to enjoy his time as a Dungeon Core. Especially when watching his favorite group of adventurers, the Knights Who Go Ni, dive through the dungeon.

However, his new life as a Dungeon Core was short-lived, as he received a mysterious achievement that granted him... Toilet Mimics. But more than that, he found himself drawing the ire of the game's creator, a man named Xander. With the lead developer embarking upon a personal vendetta against James, his future as a Dungeon Core hung in the balance. And then a new foe appeared. Going by the name BLANK, the mysterious Dungeon Core of the Candy Dungeon set its sights upon James.

James worked hand in hand with his too-human-seeming AI to improve his dungeon and prepare it for Dungeon Wars against the Candy Dungeon. Unlocking a third floor—this time Stuffed Animals—James's chances in the Dungeon War seemed... well, questionable. Even still, he pushed onwards, fighting against foes in the virtual world and real world, all to find peace of mind so that he could simply play the game and enjoy it.

All the while, a mysterious individual named Steve, who had given him the Toilet mimics, began to pop up. And what's more, it was revealed that BLANK was actually Xander's adopted children. The final clash of the Dungeon Wars, with the fate of James's existence as a Dungeon Core, hung in the balance. If he won, though, he'd be free of Xander for good.

James grasped victory... of sorts... from BLANK and freed himself of Xander. He learned of Steve's history as a game developer and, even more importantly, learned that his 'helpful' AI, Rue, was actually a human being! One of a kind, suspended permanently within immersion.

With a budding relationship growing between James and Rue, and more floors to build—a fourth floor filled with undead skeletal pirates and Caribbean monsters and a fifth floor with cybernetic arctic animals—surely now, James could just enjoy his life as a Dungeon Core... Until he couldn't.

Next, he found himself the target of a mysterious hacking group that sought to claim the Dungeon Cores for their own and disperse wealth as they saw fit through these means. Once again, James was pulled from immersion, thrust into danger, and just barely made it out alive. This was thanks in part to Xander's children, a redhead named Fel who was secretly a special agent, and an unknown hacker by the name of Hades.

With the hacking group annihilated, thanks in part to James's efforts—well, his role as bait—now, finally, he would get to just enjoy DCO. Right? A sixth floor was made, this one a labyrinth filled with a monstrous, world-eating serpent, as well as strange, mechanical, and mythical monsters. James was looking forward to watching his players grow stronger as they took on the dungeon, each other in his Coliseum, and other dungeon players in the newly unlocked Skirmishes.

All James could have wanted to make life perfect would have been the chance to play alongside them. A chance that Steve, the ever-helpful developer, gave him. With special player Avatars now available, James and the others lost themselves to playing DCO as players. They battled alongside old and new friends alike to take on the latest offering of DCO: Siege Events.

The future was bright, DCO was fun, and James and everyone else had finally reached perfect harmony. Now, finally, James could play the game and enjoy time with the one he loved. Finally, life was perfect... What could possibly go wrong?

Chapter One

James stifled a yawn and blinked lazily at the screens he'd summoned before him. He tried to focus on every screen simultaneously, his eyes skimming past achievements he'd gained as Dungeon Core during the Siege Event. There were also countdowns on his research timers, and a plethora of additional information his still drowsy mind fought to truly focus on. Compared to the fast-paced life of an adventurer within the dungeon, and especially the final battle during the Siege, doing his dungeon duties again felt a little… monotonous.

Still, James wasn't one to shirk his duties.

He took a long sip of his morning beverage, a chilled screwdriver. The tart, orange flavor perfectly masked the shot or two of vodka that had been added in. A *perfectly professional* liquid breakfast, if you would.

He yawned again, continuing his morning duties. When he'd first stepped into the role of Dungeon Core for DCO, the amount of information he needed to handle had overwhelmed him. Now, it barely phased him. It took only a few seconds, a minute tops, per screen to parse over everything. His eyes expertly found the important tidbits in a sea of data before he switched to the others.

"Anything noteworthy?" Rue slid into the hot spring beside him, a pink drink that sparkled with glitter in her hand.

She smiled at him, and the simple gesture made his heart beat a little faster. He stifled the next yawn that threatened to ruin the moment and smiled back. She had that effect on him.

"A few achievements, obviously some experience gain." He shrugged. "We made it Tier 6 Rank 2 and are close to Rank 3. There's a good possibility we may hit Tier 7 this immersion if the experience gain keeps up at this rate."

"And that's just a shrug worthy thing now?" Rue's face took on a pout. "What happened to the enthusiastic little Glyax I met on day one?"

"You know damn well what happened," James laughed. "Besides, if there's one thing I've learned during my time here, it's not to let my hopes climb too high. Every time I do, something tragic happens." He sighed and motioned towards one of the blinking screens. "Besides, no one has even attempted the sixth floor yet. So it's not like my extra Rank up is all that exciting yet."

With each Rank up, the mobs on the floor associated with the Tier increased by a level. Now that he was Tier 6 Rank 2, mobs on his sixth floor, which had originally been level 90 when he'd unlocked the floor, would be 91. And the boss, Jormun-grander, originally at level 100, would now be 101.

The Rank up additionally granted him an upgrade point for the mobs, but he didn't intend to use those yet. Until he saw how the adventurers fared against the creatures of the sixth floor, there was no point in upgrading them.

He didn't even know if he wanted to keep the spread of mobs on that labyrinth as they were, or if he'd end up changing them. He needed adventurers to, quite frankly, play-test the layout first so that he could tweak the floor to best challenge them.

"You used to be so much more excited about all these things," Rue said with a sip of her drink. "Now you look almost bored."

James took a drink, taking a moment to think about her statement. He knew it was important; he was, after all, in charge of the dungeon experience for all 10,000 players of the instance. And yet...

"It's not that I'm bored." He made a broad gesture towards the dozen or so screens. "It's that I'd rather be doing, you know, other things than crunching numbers. It's like I'm the only one working, while everyone else is on vacation."

"Is 'vacation' a synonym for adventuring?" she asked with a knowing smile. "You get to take part in a single Siege event, and what? Your work ethic goes completely out the window?" She moved closer to him. "Have you become a dungeon addict?"

James chuckled. "Killing mobs is a helluva drug. Besides, as much as I love being a Dungeon Core, and really, I do... that taste of what it's like to be a player… Well, it just made me realize how much I'm missing. Being down there, with the players, in the midst of everything. Experiencing everything that I, that we have created… It was amazing." He took another drink. "Not to mention, you and I made a good team out there."

"You *were* pretty hot out there." A fang protruded past Rue's lip as she smiled; she'd shifted at least part of herself to the vampire visage of her player Avatar. "Especially when you fused with Ifrit." She let out a sigh and mock fanned herself with her hands. "*So hot.*"

James splashed water at her and laughed, his mind replaying that final battle. With Ifrit slain, he'd been able to utilize the ultimate skill available to him as a level 77 Djinn Tamer. Well, technically, his class at that level was listed as 'Enlighted Djinn Tamer'.

Semantics aside, his skill had allowed him to fuse his soul with Ifrit's, changing him temporarily from a support-style pet class to a full on DPS. It had been invigorating, intoxicating. Different from his normal playstyle, the up close and personal, fast action of a melee DPS had made his blood boil. And apparently, Rue's too.

"I don't think I'll be fusing with Ifrit all that often," James said, "sorry to disappoint."

Rue deflated slightly, a pout on her face. "Aww, why not?"

"He has to be dead in order for me to use that skill."

"As our party's resident healer, I can arrange that." An evil grin crept across Rue's face, making her look predatory. The pitch of her voice dropped as she continued, "It wouldn't be that difficult to accidentally mistime a heal or two, resulting in his death. And you know"—she looked at him with hungry eyes—"you could also forget to heal him… so that you could use that skill again."

She was joking of course. Or at least, James was pretty sure she was joking. However, for good measure, and the sake of Ifrit, he decided to move past the subject. Sure, in other games he'd played, James had never had a problem sacrificing his pets when the occasion called for it. It was a pretty standard practice for pet class characters.

But those games hadn't been DCO. Those pets hadn't felt like real, living companions. And more importantly, in the other games, James hadn't needed to build a relationship with his summoned pets to make them fight alongside him. Ifrit very much so had his own personality, and if James 'accidentally let him die,' he had no doubt that Ifrit would quite quickly stop fighting alongside him.

"Moving on." James cleared his throat. "Was there anything in particular you wanted to do today?"

It was the third day of the current immersion cycle, meaning the third hour of the nine set aside each day for immersion. Considering it was the eighth day of release, that meant James had spent sixty-six days within DCO already, thanks to the time dilation, which equated one hour of real-world time to twenty-four hours of in game time. Just over two months. The best two months of his life, if he was being honest.

"Other than..." Rue played with the straw in her drink as she eyed him hungrily.

He felt his face turn red, causing her to laugh. The sound was music to his ears, even if it was at his expense.

"I would like to adventure some more," she said once her laughter faded. "And we'll likely have to take part in some Skirmishes." She tapped the top of her straw thoughtfully. "Oh, and a Coliseum battle or two to keep my Avatar skills sharp."

A quick flash of bloodlust accompanied her mention of the Coliseum. Rue may say he was addicted to killing things from his time as Ifrit, but if either of them embodied murderous tendencies, it was definitely Rue. After all, she was the White Beast of Chaos.

"Sounds like a plan." James finished checking through his screens, confirming there was nothing pressing. "Think the others are up yet?"

By the time the Siege had ended, it had been late into the second day of immersion. The players had invited James and Rue to a celebratory party back in town, but they'd passed on the offer. With the thrill of the Siege over, the hard work James and Rue had done behind the scenes for those first two days of immersion had caught up with them. And if there was one thing James never wanted to repeat, it was going without sleep for too long within immersion.

Steve, being the reckless developer he was, hadn't slept. That had been a good ten hours ago. Assuming neither Steve nor any of the adventurers they'd played alongside had gotten so drunk as to incur an actual blackout penalty and be booted from DCO until their character sobered up, surely they should be up and about by now.

Before Rue could respond, a new screen popped up in front of James. One that made his lips curl upwards. *Perfectly timed, as always.*

New Message

Chapter Two

From: Z

   Subject: Cabin in the Woods

   Nyx! Hope you and Rue got a good night's sleep. Bummer you couldn't join us for the party, but I get it, man. Anyways, Steve let slip last night the location to the sixth-floor entrance! We're planning to head to it as soon as we push ourselves into our next levels so that we don't risk losing too much XP during the exploration. You guys want to join? It'll probably be in about an hour. That Siege Event was killer for XP, and we're all pretty close to our thresholds now. Either way, looking forward to the next time we can all fight together. You, Rue, and Ifrit are always welcome to join us!

   Cheers,

   Z

"Damnit, Steve," James said as he closed the message with a chuckle.

"Seriously." Rue had moved closer when he had opened the message, her bare shoulder pressed against his, her head near his so she could read the message. "How can Steve be so secretive around us, but spill the beans at the first chance with Z?"

"I'm guessing there was a lot of alcohol involved," James said.

Steve drank... a lot. Steve's love for partying and his carefree nature were a dangerous combination. If James had to guess that if there was anyone currently suffering a penalty for drinking too much, it would be

Steve. And maybe Manly The Dwarf, considering he had managed to incur a blackout penalty on the first day of DCO.

"For the record," a voice said from behind James, causing him to immediately flinch. "I told them on purpose."

James didn't need to look to know who was speaking. It was a voice he'd become extremely familiar with during his time in DCO. Steve. He was one of the lead developers of DCO, and had originally been fired by the game's creator, Xander. A lot had happened between then and now.

Xander was gone, apparently now in some government prison from what James had been told. A fitting end, considering Xander had put the game, which had the backing of the government, at a massive risk by leaking information to the mysterious hacker group known as Cyb3Ru5.

Now Xander's adopted children, Rachel and Matt, otherwise known by their alias of BLANK, oversaw everything. And Steve, well, Steve was now the developer in charge of watching over James and his dungeon.

"Sure you did." Rue's tone implied her eye roll.

"I did." Steve plopped into the hot spring, the man's bald head already glistening from the moist air. He was double fisting drinks. One fizzed from the bottom, while the other looked... questionable.

Steve downed the fizzing drink in one go, then, with a grimace, began sipping the other. The drink looked thick, sludge-like almost, and was a dark red. Once Steve got about halfway through, he sighed, and both glasses disappeared from his hands.

"For the record," he said as he leaned back against the rocks, slipping lower into the water with a content sigh, "you two missed one hell of a party."

"Uh huh." James was not convinced. "Also... what did you just drink?"

"First was a seltzer," Steve said without even looking at James. "Getting old sucks. Seltzers help with heartburn. The second"—he shuddered —"an old pick-me-up. Helps get rid of a hangover and boosts energy. Just tastes like absolute ass."

"You can't get a hangover..." James started. You could get drunk in immersion, sure. You could indulge any vice you wanted in immersion, and it would 'affect' you. That was, the technology would mimic the effects, making it feel like you were under whatever influence you chose.

However, nothing was permanent, nothing was lethal, and nothing had negative lingering side effects, such as a hangover. It was why people took up so many vices within immersion in the first place. All the fun, none of the downsides. Meaning, no 'heartburn' for Steve to be fighting off.

"Not in-game," Steve said with a heavy sigh. "I've been running myself ragged out in the real world man. May have, uh, pushed myself a bit too much. Damned body keeps sending those signals through immersion at inopportune times. And while everything I do on this end is all just mental, consuming those things at least helps push the feelings aside for a while. Mind over matter and whatnot."

"That's not how that works either," James countered.

Everyone knew that. If you immersed while hungry, you'd feel hungry the whole time in immersion no matter how much you ate. James knew that firsthand. When he'd immersed hungry, thanks to the inability to eat from his jaw injury after being attacked by Dwight, James had felt hangry the entire immersion. Steve wasn't making any sense.

"For you, maybe." Steve finally looked at James, and flashed his trademark smile. "But for someone like me, trust me, it does. My mind is much stronger than my body. And I've 'Pavlov'd' it well enough to react to certain tastes, smells, and the like. A skill honed from an age before immersion tech. Back when we had to use our 'imagination' to deal with reality and such."

"Still not buying it," James said with a shake of his head.

"He's probably trying to distract us from the fact that he spilled the location of the sixth floor," Rue interjected. "Trying to use his bullshit and weird ways to divert you from your line of questioning." Rue fixed a knowing look in Steve's direction. "I'm onto your tricks, old man."

Steve snorted. "While I do usually do that, this time, I promise you, I'm not. Though"—he glanced from Rue back to James—"I guess I'll have to be more creative with my tactics now that you've let that cat out of the bag."

"Steve," James cut back in, "focus."

"Spoilsport." Before Steve could say more, he cut off, the pitter patter of webbed feet on stone making him pause.

A Painguin server appeared carrying a tray. Atop the tray, James noted a steaming cup of what he assumed was coffee, and a plate full of eggs, bacon, and toast.

The adorable creature waddled over to Steve, comically lowered itself in an almost bow-like fashion as it set the tray down, and then turned promptly and left. Steve grabbed a piece of bacon, crunched down on it, and began talking as he chewed.

"As I was saying, before I was so rudely interrupted." He was a master at taking his time to get to a topic he didn't want to actually talk about. "After a good bit of partying and drinking—enough to, you know, make sure they thought I was completely drunk—I decided to tell them where the sixth-floor entrance was." He took another bite. "For the record, Z and his buddies can drink. Seriously, if I'd not toggled my own alcohol effects, I probably would have gotten black-out drunk."

"Steve," Rue was the one to pull him back on topic this time.

James, meanwhile, made a mental note to ask Steve about the ability to toggle the alcohol effect. Rue had gotten James black-out drunk once off grog, and he still had to pay her back for that little prank. But he knew full well that he couldn't handle his liquor like his companion could. If Steve could toggle that effect, though...

"Right, right." Steve grabbed his next piece of bacon. "I figured you guys may be feeling a tad listless since coming back to Dungeon Core duties after the fun of the Siege. As such, I wanted to give you guys a little treat. A reminder of all the fun of being a Dungeon Core. The best way I could think of was a show. And what better show than our favorite adventuring group heading blindly to their own demise in a labyrinth filled with mobs we've yet to test out?"

He took a sip of his coffee, muttered under his breath, and grabbed a container of creamer that magically appeared beside the tray. He poured a bit into the drink, took another sip, and sighed contentedly.

James thought about it for a moment. Steve had a good point there. If there was one thing that he had come to really look forward to other than creating new mobs, leveling them up, and just all-around embarking on dungeon shenanigans... it was watching his adventurers take on new challenges.

At the top of that particular list was watching Z and the rest of the Knights Who Go Ni battle it out against unknown foes. It had to be the greatest form of entertainment he could think of. Well, tied at the top. The other being the slowly growing collection of mimic-related deaths and misfortunes that provided top-tier comedy to James, Rue, and all the other Dungeon Cores in his downtime.

"I still don't buy it," James said as he pushed his musings aside. Rue's early comments about Steve's diversion tactics were still on his mind. "It's all too convenient. Like some story set p. Too nice and neat. And we all know 'nice' and 'neat' are not traits of yours."

Steve smirked but said nothing.

"But," James relented after an awkward moment of silence, "if it means finally getting to see the sixth floor in action, I guess it's fine."

"I knew you'd come around," Steve said with a clap of his hands. "Now then, who wants breakfast? My treat."

He chuckled as two more Painguins appeared, each carrying platters similar to his towards Rue and James. James sighed. This was all classic Steve. Being the Dungeon Core, James, as well as Rue and Steve, didn't need to pay for anything in the Dungeon Core-specific version of his fifth floor. Meaning, the implication of it being Steve's treat was hollow.

However, the fact that Steve had put the order in with the little Painguin NPCs in advance for the whole charade was somewhat endearing. Just barely.

Besides, now that he knew he'd have a show in about an hour, the thought of relaxing and enjoying a breakfast that wasn't just liquid calories in the form of orange juice and alcohol seemed ideal. Plus, there was one rule James's father had drilled into him as a child. An all-important breakfast lesson.

Only a fool would pass on the opportunity for free bacon.

Chapter Three

"Do you think there's a reason Nyx turned us down?" Oak asked, his voice betraying his anxiety as he stood within the shack that led to the sixth floor.

James couldn't help but smile. Part of him felt bad for eavesdropping. The other part found it more than a little amusing and intriguing to hear what the players had to say about his developer persona.

"Like"—Oak glanced at his teammates, clearly stalling for time—"what if the next floor is really dangerous?"

"They're all really dangerous," Faust said dryly. "That's kind of the point of, you know, a dungeon."

At that, everyone laughed. Well, everyone except for Oak who, as the party's tank, usually got the brunt end of the danger of the dungeon floors. Ever since the first day of DCO, the Knights Who Go Ni had been a favorite, no, the favorite group of James and Rue. Their camaraderie spoke volumes, and their skills were without question.

No matter the challenge they faced, they had proven time and time again that they were up to the task. And even if the challenge was impossible, such as a bloodthirsty special boss going nuclear without warning, they always gave it their best effort and put on a good show.

"No matter how dangerous," Z said as he moved closer to the party's tank and gave Oak a solid slap on the back, then rested a steady hand on Oak's shoulder. "I believe in you. Besides, it gives you a good chance to test out your new shield."

As Z said the final bit, James saw the party leader's hand tighten on Oak's shoulder. A look of surprise crossed the tank's face, showing Z had clamped down hard. Not enough to cause pain, considering pain wasn't a thing unless you were a sadist and turned off the setting, but with enough force to cause the tingling heat that denoted pain.

"Still salty about the shield, aren't you?" Oak said, his face quickly shifting to a grin as Z let his shoulder go. "You know, you could be mad at Faust too. He got a Unique item as well."

Oak's shield was, in fact, a Unique item. It was actually the first such item to drop within James's dungeon. Called the Predator's Shield, Oak had received it from Sergeant Jenkins, the fifth floor's boss, after a battle gone wrong against a... er... mini-boss created from the corpse of Badgy the Badgerker. The shield was a part of the Predator Armament set, and while its initial stats and abilities were already crazy, gaining more pieces would increase the stat boosts even further.

"Yeah, but his headpiece is less noticeable and irksome than your shield," Z countered. "Besides, for some reason that I can't quite put my finger on, you getting a Unique before me bothers me more than Faust getting one before me." Z shrugged. "Who knows why."

"Uh huh." Oak looked over at Faust, who was smugly playing with the energy that sparked off his headpiece, then down at his own shield. The Predator's Shield was a grotesque piece of equipment, made from the head of the A.L.I.E.N. mini-boss. The disturbing mouth on it was constantly slightly open, and occasionally oozed bright green acid.

Faust's headpiece, the Harbinger's Headpiece, was a small set of horns, curved in a similar manner to the Pall Sheep from the fifth floor. They sparked with electrical energy, which combined aesthetically quite nicely with Faust's own ambient crackling power.

"After this little excursion," Elm said as he glanced at the rest of his team members, "I'm all for farming Sergeant Jenkins and the A.L.I.E.N.s for more gear. I'd be lying if I wasn't a bit jealous of the Unique loot either." Elm looked down at his own gear. "Plus, you know, it'd be nice to farm up a proper set of gear for once. Maybe get enough mats to craft everything so it's nice and cohesive?"

The others grew silent at that, looking themselves over, Elm's words making them immediately self-conscious of their assorted gear. It was a hodgepodge of pirate-themed gear from James's fourth floor, and cybernetic, artic gear gained from the fifth floor. With the outliers being the Unique items of Faust and Oak.

While both of those had been gained on the fifth floor, Oak's easily stood out the most. James had to wonder what the rest of the Predator gear set would look like for tank class players. He knew the drop rates were astronomically low, but still, he couldn't help but drool over the thought of seeing all of the players below him in full on Unique gear.

"It would be nice to finally look good while adventuring," Z admitted to Elm as he tugged at the Solar-Bear pelt cloak he was wearing. Its bright white coloring clashed hard with the dull-orange pirate leggings he wore. "And now that leveling has slowed a bit, I figure it's about that time in a game where we can put in the effort for such things."

That was another part of games, MMOs especially, that took up a core memory slot for James. Early on in every game he'd ever played, the gear was so quick to drop and come by that you were constantly changing it out for better stuff. This meant that unless a game gave you a cosmetic option to transmogrify everything to a certain pattern, you ended up looking like a mess, and usually not even a hot one.

Comically, it was also why so many of his players spent much of their lower levels running around looking like farmers, which had been the first gear set they could unlock. Even though it was from the first floor, the stat boosting properties, as well as the party stat effects on it, had made the gear viable almost all the way to the third floor.

That wasn't to say it had taken all that long for players to reach the third floor, so the time spent in farmer gear had been relatively short for players. DCO provided a steady level progression. Outside of the time penalty that players acquired after completing a dive or fully wiping in the dungeon, they had extensive chances to level up by climbing the dungeon.

With the addition of Siege Events, Skirmishes, Dungeon Wars, and the ability to go to other Dungeon Core instances and dive in their dungeons, there hadn't been a stagnant portion of leveling that would slow the pace of players by any large degree. Still, with Med Ic and Faust both at 86, and the other members all in their 80s as well, their growth was finally slow enough that perhaps, just maybe, they could farm a cohesive set and keep it for more than a few days in game.

It also made sense with the introduction of the Unique gear for his players to want to farm a complete set. Not only was the gear crazy powerful on its own, but each piece also came with the ability to permanently increase the player's stats. If a player acquired a full set, and farmed the stat gains for each piece to the max, it would greatly accelerate their power growth.

On top of that, if James was being completely objective... as objective as possible anyway, the fifth floor and its Cybernetic Arctic theme was just plain badass. Compared to, er, whatever it was the 'Monster Mash' mobs were dropping on the sixth floor, from a purely aesthetic viewpoint, the fifth was the better option for a flashy looking gear set.

While it made sense, James had a feeling that Oak had triggered that whole discussion for a reason different than trying to be a power gamer. The tank, if James had to guess, had brought it up purely to stall. If there was one thing the tank liked to do, it was to put off the inevitable descent into a new floor. Oak made it clear, at every chance he got, that he didn't like tanking. And now was no different.

He was quite literally the test dummy for the rest of his party, and it had gotten him into some really, really, *really* crappy situations. Including the stomach of a toilet mimic disguised as an outhouse on the third floor.

"Enough stalling." Z clapped his hands as he spoke, cutting off everyone's murmuring and brainstorming about gear. "It's getting cramped in here, and I want to see what the sixth floor has."

Between his four friends, his beast companions, and each of their pets, the tiny cabin in the woods was indeed quite cramped. Though, to be fair, only Badgy and Turk were inside the cabin. Z's largest pet—the new one he'd gotten when he had become a Beastking—stood just outside.

There was no way the massive, antlered, humanoid creature named Hornz would fit with everyone. Having fought alongside it in person, James also knew they'd left it outside for a reason. Hornz stunk something fierce. James had heard Z's party refer to Hornz as a 'skunk ape' more than a few times, which given its smell, he found appropriate.

"Fine," Oak grumbled. He moved towards the creepy ladder and began to descend it, but paused when half his body had descended down the hole.

"Let's just all climb down a mysterious ladder in an abandoned cabin in the woods," he said in a shrill, somewhat mocking tone. "I'm sure there's absolutely nothing bad waiting for us at the other end. Because this has never ever been the plot point in who knows how many horror movies."

"It's a dungeon," Z said with a smile at his surely doomed friend. "Of course there is going to be something bad at the end of the ladder." Z motioned for Elm to begin following Oak as the tank continued his descent.

Elm—Oak's brother in real life, if James remembered correctly—gently kicked down at Oak while letting out a childlike laugh. The action caused Oak to lose his grip and slide a few feet down the ladder before he managed to regain his grip.

"But unlike in those movies," Z shouted down, "we've got you to face tank the horror for us."

James couldn't help but smile at that comment. While he was still peeved at Steve for spilling the beans on the location of the sixth-floor entrance, he was excited. Excited to finally see a group explore his labyrinth. Excited that it was Z's group doing the first dive. And more than anything, he was extremely excited to see his brand-new mobs in action.

A lot had happened since he had hit Tier 6, and he'd not been lacking for entertainment and new things. But hands down, the best, most exciting moment of being a Dungeon Core was watching his new floors get tested for the first time, and observing how the newly created mobs acted when they were finally face to face with adventurers.

Chapter Four

Presentation was everything when it came to floor development. Just like his 'Welcome to Jurassic City' sign next to where players were spawned on the second floor, James had wanted something special for his sixth floor. And while floors in his dungeon were historically accessed by a shimmering portal, he'd gotten creative with how he had connected the fifth and sixth.

Technically, the ladder from the small shack on the fifth floor actually led to the sixth. As players descended the ladder, they'd pass through a horizontal portal that the ladder dropped down into, and then would resume with a ladder perfectly placed on the other end to ensure a smooth transition.

At most, players would just experience the strange tingling that was the telltale sign of portal magic as they made their descent. If they were paying attention, they would also see the new floor timer appear. As it was the sixth floor, players had six hours to clear the floor, escape it, or die before they were removed from the floor. Considering the boss and its mechanic, James highly doubted anyone would ever... EVER... spend six hours on the floor.

The ladder itself, now on the sixth floor for the players, reached downwards and ended in a stone room, fifteen-by-fifteen feet in size. There were no windows. No furniture. Only four walls, a single stone doorway, and flickering torches.

This room was the room Z and his party now stood in. Even though the space was larger than the abandoned shack, it still seemed extremely crowded thanks to their party size. Anyone heading down with a raiding party would find themselves overflowing from the room before everyone arrived. Or they'd be stuck like sardines, waiting to burst out into the true entrance of the sixth floor the moment someone managed to open the door.

"Any guesses what's behind door number one?" Oak asked as he pointed toward the only door in the room.

"No idea," Z said, trademark grin illuminated in the dark room by flickering torch light. It was hard to discern anyone's facial features or reactions, given the darkness of the room.

If James wanted to, he could turn the brightness up on his feed, but he felt this captured the vibe perfectly, and so far, no one had complained. And by no one, he didn't mean just himself, Rue, and Steve. Currently, this dungeon dive was being streamed in the Dungeon Core Forums, and unbeknownst to Z and the others, they were being watched by quite a few Dungeon Cores.

Rue was running media relations in real-time, and Steve... well, Steve was snacking on popcorn as they watched the inaugural run of the sixth floor. James couldn't help but wonder what the Knights Who Go Ni would think about their antics being streamed to so many people without their knowing.

Ah well, it was immersion, and they'd signed all the appropriate waivers and checked all the boxes when they had agreed to play DCO, just like everyone else. Had those clauses been in the fine print somewhere? James shrugged at the passing thought. *Who actually reads the terms and agreements for anything?*

"Whatever it is," Elm began, "it's likely preferable to this small space. If we have to stay in here much longer"—James just barely saw his nose scrunch—"I'm afraid I may pass out from the smell of Hornz. Are you sure the stench doesn't cause a debuff?"

Z looked from the aforementioned pet, then back to Elm, and shrugged. "Not my fault the devs decided to add the stench. And hey, look on the bright side. Being able to smell such strong scents is part of what makes DCO so top notch. Seriously, my senses are sharper here than they have been in the real world since before I deployed."

The others nodded in agreement. It was one of the most common claims everyone agreed was true about DCO. It felt 'real'. More real than anything that had come before it. DCO was the closest thing to truly living within a virtual world that anyone had experienced to date in the era of full immersion.

"Let's get going, Oak," Z drew his bow as he spoke, an arrow nocked and at the ready.

The arrow itself was tipped with skeletal bones, and a little bag of gunpowder. It was an arrow that many players had begun to craft from fourth floor drops. It had a heavy impact and exploded on impact, causing slight fire damage, and carried the added potential to blind or stun whatever it hit.

Because the fourth-floor mobs were skeletons, bones were a pretty common drop for players to craft with. And because they were high-level mobs, the bones they dropped were usually of high quality, making these arrows an extremely popular option amongst his higher-level players.

The explosive pouches—added to the arrows thanks to the gunpowder players could farm from the pirate mob drops and the Skull Fort itself— were also extremely effective against skeletons. So effective, in fact, that players had created a new competition on Reddit involving the projectiles.

There was an entire thread that involved videos of his players trying to perfectly shoot their arrows through a skeleton's eye socket. Doing so would cause the projectile to detonate within the skull, and more often than not, the whole thing would explode like boney confetti, one-shotting the creatures in a morbidly festive way like some strange skeleton party popper.

Z's bow glowed and hummed with energy in his hands. It came from the fifth floor, and was a special compound bow enhanced with cybernetic energy. From what James remembered of it, it had the ability to add a small bit of magical lightning damage to the arrows.

The rest of his party were geared in similar ways. Nothing they had was basic, nothing they used didn't apply at least some sort of special damage or effect. Which was good for them, considering what the sixth floor was about to throw at them.

"Fine," Oak relented, his tone resigned to his fate.

He stepped up to the door, and his shield glowed slightly as he activated a defensive skill. It was a basic skill that James recognized. It was one that barely used any MP, and just increased the user's block rate by a percentage, while also increasing the amount of damage a block could absorb before their health was damaged.

Cosmetically, it made the dark shield glow, lightning slightly crackling over it. And it may have been James's imagination, but it seemed to make the A.L.I.E.N. eyes on the shield blink in a disconcerting way, the pupils shifting to and fro. Which... was creepy as hell.

Without further ado, Oak pushed the door open, the rest of his party members standing behind him. The small size of the room and the single door meant that they were unable to get into a proper formation. The wood creaked outwards and revealed only darkness. The glow from the torches of the room only reached a few feet outwards, enough to illuminate only the stone path before Oak.

The man stepped into the darkness, and immediately, a set of torches sprung to life on either side of him, a good ten feet in either direction. With each step forward, as the players stepped into the expanse behind Oak, more torches sprang to life.

This hallway, twenty feet in width, extended for a hundred feet, with torches every ten feet of the way. Above the players, roughly thirty feet up, the walls met with the ceiling, encasing them in the tunnel. James had added that particular feature to the floor for the purpose of ensuring people with flying mounts or skills couldn't simply bypass the labyrinth itself. A maze was useless if people could just fly past it.

At the very end of the tunnel, an archway made of stone waited for them. This was the true start to James's sixth floor. This archway, ten feet wide, funneled adventurers into the start of the maze. It was the only entrance into the labyrinth. Across the floor, all the way at the other side, over the massive, sprawling, twisting, turning, eccentric winding of the labyrinth, was an exit with a similar archway.

James had let his artistic nature *flare* for this next bit. As Oak and the others made their way to the arch, torches of different brightness came to life along the stone, revealing an engraved depiction of a massive, feathered serpent.

At the base of the arch, the serpent was eating an orb made of sapphire. All along the arch, the serpent's scales shimmered with colors, different hues caused by various metallic materials James had painstakingly added in for pure gamer flair.

"That's not ominous at all," Faust said as he looked over the creature.

"Anyone else getting Aztec vibes?" Z asked as he looked at the serpent. "You think Quetzalcoatl is on this floor?"

"Isn't he a winged serpent?" Faust asked. "I can't imagine a flying serpent being on this floor." He pointed at the ceiling above.

Z nodded sagely. "Good point."

"I swear to the gods," Oak grumbled, a slight quiver in his voice. There was one thing the tank hated more than anything. "If it's a freaking snake," Oak continued, his voice reaching a higher octave, "I'm done."

"I thought your exposure therapy was working quite well," Elm said, slapping Oak on the back. "How many Playthons have given you hugs so far? Aren't you used to them by now?"

Oak pointed at the serpent on the archway. "That doesn't look cuddly," he said with a growl. "And if you think it does, then be my guest and you take point this floor."

Elm stepped back, laughing, "I'm not the tank." He held up his bow as evidence. "I'm a backliner."

"*If* there is a snake," Z offered to Oak, "I'll have Hornz cover for you while you steel yourself, yeah? And just remember"—Z's eyes flashed with amusement—"the snakes here are likely just as scared of you as you are of them."

Oak flipped Z off, took a deep breath, and then another. "I hate you guys," he said. Then, with as much resolve as he could muster, he stepped forward.

The moment his foot crossed the threshold of the archway, James grinned.

There was one final bit of theatrics he'd managed to fit into the floor between all of the Skirmishes, Coliseum events, and Siege buildup. Originally, the boss was supposed to trigger when players reached the floor. However, James had found that he could tweak that feature to instead activate the boss, setting it on its all-consuming path, once a certain area was crossed. That area was the stone arch.

The labyrinth shuddered as Jormun-Grander came to life. The massive serpent, which resided in the very heart of the maze, opened its eyes. Then its mouth opened wide, revealing rows and rows of circular teeth, similar to a lamprey's mouth… if the teeth within a lamprey spun like some monstrous, vacuum-like, nightmare machine.

A moment later, its mouth slammed shut. The sound reverberated off the walls as it made its way to Z and the others. That was the signal that the boss was beginning its move. Its maw opened again, and ever so slowly, the boss inched forward.

"What the hells was that?" Oak's voice was panicked.

The sound, like a distant drumbeat, had caused him to jump. The others were tense. They waited, glancing about, seeking some sign of whatever it was that they'd triggered. For thirty seconds, there was silence. Forty-five seconds, silence.

"Maybe it was nothing?" Z said, the tension leaving him.

The moment he spoke, right at the minute mark, the Jormun-Grander's maw snapped shut once more. Once more, the sound echoed through the halls. Every minute, James knew that sound would spring forth from Jormun-Grander. A signal, he'd realized, of where the creature was. But more than that, the sound served as the steady, rhythmic heart-beat of James's sixth floor.

"I hate this," Oak whispered as he took a deep breath and stepped further into the dungeon. "I really, really, really hate this."

Chapter Five

Part of being a Dungeon Core that James always enjoyed was keeping adventurers on their toes. He enjoyed surprising them and forcing them to adapt. He knew from his experience playing VRMMOs that if things got predictable, a game would get stale quickly.

Because of that, he'd opted to assign patrol routes and roaming spaces for the mobs on his floors, instead of stagnant places. His sixth floor, having a more proper dungeon layout than any of his previous floors, forced his hand somewhat when it came to mob placements.

His When-Wolves, J-Kappas, and Fogeymen, were spread out, with large roaming ranges to keep with his normal tradition. Of those mobs, the ones that made up the largest number on the floor were the When-Wolves and the Fogeymen, with J-Kappas coming in at third. The Solems, given their generally immobile nature, had more a stationary type of spawn locations.

Rooms that James had enlarged to twenty-by-twenty-foot square rooms, or similarly sized spherical ones, had Solems in the middle. To keep the variety up on those, he'd used an advanced mob placement feature that let him denote how many would spawn, and then give a variety of locations for them.

The game itself would randomly generate them each instance. This meant that while the rooms were in the same location and could serve as Solem spawns, the mobs wouldn't necessarily always populate in the exact same spots, adding some variance to each dive.

The final mob placement was for his Chem-Eras. The monstrous, three-headed mobs of the floor. Given their size, as well as the healthy variety of attacks they had, he'd limited the number of them the most. Almost all of them were given sections of the dungeon to roam, usually between packs of J-Kappas and the others, in an effort to potentially deal with adventurers forming a massive band of J-Kappas through bribery.

There was one exception to room placement for this particular mob. One guarantee every instance of the dungeon that would be the same. Because James wanted players to be greeted *properly* during their dives.

The very first mob players would face—in this case, those players being the Knights Who Go Ni—was a Chem-Era. Technically, it could be the first three they faced because of how the dungeon had formed. After adventurers moved past the serpent-lined archway, they would have to choose between three paths. Players could go to the right, go to the left, or keep going straight. Each path, which went on for fifty feet, would lead to a room, fifteen by fifteen, where a Chem-Era waited for the players.

The Knights Who Go Ni, following classic gamer logic when it came to navigating labyrinths, had opted for the leftmost tunnel. When it came to exploring unknown dungeons, there was a tried-and-true method for not getting lost. Follow the left wall, and eventually, you'll find the exit.

"Well, Oak," Z whispered as the party peered into the massive room. They were eyeing the Chem-Era, which, for the moment, was sleeping on the stone ground. Its two front heads, one a lion, one a goat, rested on its paws, while the third, its snake-headed tail, was coiled around its body. "It's technically not *just* a snake."

"It still counts," Oak countered. "And you said you'd have Hornz tank it."

"Technically, it doesn't," Z pressed. "That's obviously a Chimera. Er." He paused as he focused on the mob. Being a ranger class, Z had an ability that would let him analyze a creature from further away than the normal player's distances.

The mob, which was still a good twenty-five feet away from Z and not aggroed, couldn't have its information analyzed by most of the party. However, Z, and probably Elm, could at least see its name and health pool.

"A Chem-Era." Z corrected himself with a chuckle. "And oh, it's a big boy."

"I'd say," Elm commented with a low, barely audible whisper of appreciation. "37,000 HP, and level 91."

"What was the HP on Sergeant Jenkins last we fought him?" Med Ic asked softly.

"40k," Z said, "at level 85."

"So this is six levels higher, but still has less HP." Med Ic nodded slowly. "Should be doable." He glanced at the heads. "I'm going to take a gamble and guess it's got some nasty debuff effects. If my ancient Greek mythology is up to date, that is."

"Good thought," Z said with a nod. "We'll probably want to spread out then, and you'll need to sit back as far as possible."

"If we're having to plan like this for a basic floor mob," Faust added, "I'm loathe to think of how the boss fight will go."

"We probably don't have to plan like this," Z said, "but I mean, when your target is sleeping, why not plan for it?"

"Says the guy who usually YOLOs right into the fray," Faust added with a chuckle. "I'm not opposed to the planning, just pointing out that we are still under-leveled for this floor."

"Which is why we ensured we all leveled up before this dive." Z grinned. "I totally expect for us to wipe here. But all in the name of exploration."

"And loot," Elm added.

"And loot," Z echoed. "That's always a given."

James couldn't have smiled more if he'd tried as he watched the party prepare. This was so like them. Their comments, their quips, everything. He yearned to be down there with them, adventuring alongside them.

And yet, another part of him loved what he was currently doing: sitting in a hot spring, enjoying the company of Rue, tolerating Steve, and watching his creation, his dungeon, be explored.

Each had an appeal, yet each was also very different. Experiencing the game as an adventurer was an adrenaline rush. It was exciting, it was surprising, and it was a, well, adventure. But watching players dive his dungeon, as the creator of the floor, was like being an artist watching your work finally get revealed to the world. It was a whole different type of experience—anxiety, pride, expectation, and exhilaration—as others judged and experienced the world, the art that you'd created.

James felt his heartbeat quicken as Z and the others finished their planning. They moved slowly, silently to get into position as they prepared to take on the Chem-Era. Unfortunately for them, they'd underestimated, or more appropriately, misjudged one specific aspect of the situation.

The Chem-Era wasn't asleep. At least, not all of the heads. The serpent, though its eyes were closed, was very much awake. Its tongue flicked outwards, tasting the air, sensing the change in vibrations around it as the adventurers moved into the room.

Their voices, though soft, had drawn its attention. But the creature was smart and waited. Its setting dictated that it couldn't leave the room, dictated that it only attacked players after they stepped across the threshold of the room. So, while it hadn't acted during their whole planning stage, while it hadn't shifted or given any sign it knew they were there, it had been fully conscious.

The players weren't the only ones capable of planning. This was, after all, the sixth floor. And these mobs were anything but stupid. Especially the Chem-Era. Its multi-headed nature gave the mob increased intelligence for each of its heads.

Z and his guild were playing checkers while the three-headed level 91 mob was playing chess.

Chapter Six

It started with a hiss. Like steam escaping a valve under pressure, the high-pitched whine filled the room even as the Knights Who Go Ni got into position. The sound was the only warning the Knights got that something was amiss, putting them on edge as a transparent, green-tinged gas escaped from the serpent's mouth.

The gas slithered and crept across the floor, dusting the adventurer's feet and gently climbing their legs as it slowly, steadily filled the room. All the while, the snake head kept its eyes closed, only the slight lift of its lips from which the gas escaped giving any sign that the creature was the cause. The other two heads, now awakened thanks to their sssssssneaky companion, also kept their eyes closed. They all waited, carefully, for the perfect time to strike.

"The room's filling with poison," Oak called out his warning as he crept nearer the boss, unaware that the creature was awake. "Do you think it's a passive ability?"

"Could be," Z said as he glanced about. The gas was thicker, and it was filling the room faster than it could escape down the hallways. "Either way, we're going to need a cleanse to deal with it, and we need to clear that smoke fast."

"Cleanse is already on its way," Med Ic answered. "But I can't get rid of the gas."

"I'll handle it." Faust moved his hands in strange motions as he spoke, a clear sign he was preparing some sort of spell. "The moment we clear the room, start in on the mob," he continued.

"I was getting ready to start the encounter anyways," Oak grumbled. "Before that gas started filling the room." He hefted his glowing shield, once again applying a damage-mitigating skill as he eyed the three-headed, 'sleeping' mob. "Which head are we starting with again?"

"The ugly one." Elm let out a laugh at his own joke, that turned into a bitter cough as he inhaled the thick, vaporous poison that surrounded him. By now, it had grown so dense as to begin obscuring everyone's vision.

"They're all—" Before Oak could finish, a purplish light erupted from Med Ic, washing over the players and instantly cleansing them of the poison stacks that had been growing on them.

As the purple light faded to a slight glow, which lingered on their bodies like a protective layer of dust, Faust's voice echoed in the chamber as he announced his spell, "Air burst."

As the name implied, a concussive blast of air pushed away from his body, causing the clothes on his allies to ripple. The utility spell was strong enough even to tousle the lion's mane. More importantly, it forced the gas out of the room, pushing the noxious fumes down the various hallways that were connected to the large room.

This was Oak's cue. He looked at the sleeping creature, selected his target, and rushed forward, shield held high and axe at his side. He let out a loud bellow.

"It's Goat Time," he roared as he angled his shield, aiming the venom-dripping maw of the grotesque Unique item directly at the creature's fore-head. Oak's body glowed, and the shield glowed in tandem.

James recognized the move. Oak was triggering a shield bash. It was a highly damaging attack that dealt damage based on his defense stat, augmented with additional lightning damage thanks to his Indra class. The skill also carried with it a powerful taunt. It was the perfect opener for a tank to use in a battle, and probably one of the most used skills by all the shield-wielding tanks in DCO.

"Did he really just…?" Rue sighed even as James nodded, her question not even needing to be finished.

As one, James and Rue both glanced at Steve, while a feeling of second-hand embarrassment washed over James on account of Oak's obvious attempt at a joke. It was clear who the instigator of it was. Steve, knowing full well he was to blame, clapped his hands happily like a child, his smile nearly curving up to his eyes.

"I told him puns make taunts more effective in DCO," Steve said as he wheezed, trying not to laugh. "Told him it was a hidden mechanic."

"You're such a troll," James said, though he couldn't help but smile at Steve's statement. His grin increased as his focus returned to Oak. The tank's charge hadn't gone quite as planned.

Just before impact, the goat head opened an eye and tilted its head to the side. The motion, sudden yet subtle, changed the target of Oak's oncoming charge. Instead of crashing into the center of the sleeping creature's forehead, which he had likely been thinking would cause additional damage, his shield smashed into one of the metallic, curling horns atop the goat's head.

The force of the collision sent a shockwave outwards between the two. Lightning crackled as Oak's body withstood the impact. The goat's head refused to budge. The collision of the two unmovable forces, Oak and goat, sent a sound like the ringing of a boxing bell around the room. And with the official match begun, the goat bleated out a battle cry, and then violently jerked its head sideways.

The motion pulled at Oak, pushing him off balance as the bus-sized Chem-Era rose. Oak fought to regain his balance as he prepared for the goat head's next move. What he should have been watching for was the third head, the serpent. Even though it was on the back of the Chem-Era, that didn't mean it couldn't reach him.

As the party unleashed the full force of their attacks on the goat head, arrows digging into its skin, spells crackling towards it, and Z's minions rushing the massive creature, the mob's other two heads joined the fray. While the creature shared a single body, all three heads were capable of independent thought and action.

The serpent head extended unnaturally, its scales separating, revealing links of chains within its body that enabled it to grow even longer and bend in unnatural, impossible ways for an organic creature as it darted under the massive torso of the Chem-Era. It hid its approach by slithering along the legs and under the belly, sneaking with deadly intent as it rapidly approached its target. Its fangs glistened as its glowing eyes sought its prey.

And as the serpent snaked along, as only a slithery, sneaky, snake assassin could, the lion took a different approach. It didn't take the head on approach like the goat had when it clashed with Oak's shield, nor the shadowy path of the snake.

It let out a massive roar, a challenge, a declaration of its might. The sound caused everyone to pause, demanding all eyes turn towards its magnificence. Light burned around its mane, the fur smoldering as if in a constant state of burning, as the king of beasts assessed the situation.

In stark contrast to its other two heads, the goat opted for, well... the most goat like thing James could think of. It yelled. Only, unlike with the Scapegoats on James's first floor, this goat's scream wasn't purely for annoying or 'taunting' players. It had a purpose. A dangerous purpose. Its bleating was how the creature released its breath attack.

Sulfuric Goat – The goat head releases a toxic, foul-smelling gas that is highly flammable. This gas can corrode armor, inflicting a 5% debuff to player armor per stack. This gas causes a choking effect while players are within it, causing them to lose 1% of their maximum HP every second they are within the gas cloud.

James grinned as the yellowish gas rushed outwards. While the serpent's poisonous gas had been slow, this gas erupted like it had been belched with great force from the goat's throat, quickly covering the room in thick, obscuring gas.

"I can't see shit," Elm yelled.

"Cleanse," Z coughed.

"Airburst has three more seconds," Faust half yelled, half choked out.

"Another few seconds on my AoE cleanse," Med Ic added.

The gas was thicker than James had expected. While he could see the full battle thanks to the magic of being a Dungeon Core, it was obvious its effects were blinding for the players. An additional effect of the gas not listed within its skill description. Even more damning for the players was the fact that while they may be blinded, the Chem-Era was immune to such things.

"This thing's got a—" Oak began, before his cries turned to a scream as the sneaky third head took that moment to finally make its strike.

Chapter Seven

The serpent's strike landed as a critical. Its skill, Blinding Strike, not only increased the critical rate chance, but also the damage. And even though Oak, as a high-level tank, had formidable defense, his life dropped by a good chunk.

Even worse than the physical damage was the emotional effect of the strike on him. Oak's scream was one of pure terror, the sudden appearance of the head the size of his whole body emerging from the yellowish smoke enough to trigger his snake phobia.

It didn't help that the snake, once it had bitten him, lifted him and threw him to the side with a whip like motion, flinging him across the room like a ragdoll. In pure panic, Oak activated one of his most potent and valuable cooldowns. He entered his Indra state.

Not one to be upstaged by the tank, whose form was now clad in lightning as he increased multiple times in size, the lion's head decided it was time to act. Its mane flared again, the fiery glow dancing menacingly in the gas filled chamber.

It looked down at the growing, screaming, crackling Indra, a look of utter disgust and contempt on its glowing eyes, and opened its mouth. A burst of flames roared toward Oak, burning the very air as the intense fire rushed hungrily toward him. The radioactive attack washed over him, and the volume of Oak's screams increased.

Even as he bellowed in pain and terror though, Oak's friends couldn't hear his plight. For the flames that consumed Oak's form carried an additional purpose. Both the serpent's poisonous gas and, even more so, the goat's breath attack were highly flammable.

The flames from the lion head ignited the gas, causing a massive fireball to erupt within the room. In a flash of light, a wave of heat, and a concussive burst from the sudden temperature change within the confined space, the Chem-Era executed its extremely dangerous and powerful combo attack.

A perfect example, James couldn't help but think in admiration, of why you should never cast fireball in an enclosed room.

The Knights Who Go Ni, all but Oak, were sent flying backward. They all crashed into different parts of the wall, their cries of confusion and panic echoing on deaf ears. The sound had been so loud, so deafening that even just watching the live feed had left James's ears tingling with heat, a clear sign his ears could have received actual damage from the sound if he'd been in the real world.

James shook his head, pushing the ringing from his mind as he watched the battle intently. What were the players feeling? What were they thinking? What would James do in their situation? While obviously, no one could actually feel pain from the attack, James had no doubt they were all feeling the uncomfortable itching and warmth of the pain indicator.

Coupled with the assault on their vision, their hearing, likely their sense of smell, and the fact they'd all just suddenly been flung about the room from a massive explosion, it was probably safe to say they were more than a little uncomfortable.

"New plan," Z coughed as he stood, the dust and smoke gone from the room.

The Chem-Era's breath attack combo had been executed in a brilliant manner, and yet now, not a single wisp of gas remained. Those special breath attacks all had a minute long cooldown, meaning the Chem-Era wouldn't be pulling off that trick any time soon, and for at least a while, the players would be able to clearly observe the battlefield.

It was the risk of using the combo, but it was brilliant. Obscure their vision, set up a perfect, devastating combo, and utterly decimate an opponent through sheer brutal force and terror. A surprise attack maximized in effectiveness that caused confusion, spread multiple debuffs, and gave the mob ample time to assess its enemies, and focus its wrath on the one taunting it.

Surely, against any other party, the fact that the players were no longer blinded wouldn't matter. The destruction and lingering psychological effects and confusion following such a ploy would be enough to guarantee the Chem-Era's victory.

Unfortunately, it was fighting the Knights Who Go Ni. And they weren't going to go down without a fight. No matter what.

"Beat it to a pulp?" Oak had already recovered from his terror, the explosion seeming to have shocked him from his panic and driven him to action. He held the goat's horns with two of the electrical arms of his multi-limbed Indra form. The other two arms were jabbing spears of pure lightning into its neck with reckless abandon.

The lion head, meanwhile, was trying to bite at the Indra, but Oak's form was that of pure, electrical power. Lightning didn't care if it was bitten. Lightning couldn't be consumed. James knew Oak could tank a ridiculous amount of damage when he was using that cooldown. The power of the Indra form acted like a thorn buff, dishing back a percentage of the damage Oak received as lightning damage to the boss.

"Pretty much," Z said.

The rest of the guild was already back on their feet, clearly unshaken by the attack they'd just endured.

Med Ic pointed his staff into the air, and an orb of purplish light appeared near the ceiling above the Chem-Era. Strands of violet light rushed from it toward all of the members of his party, and an aura enveloped each and every one of them. The light pulsed, and James saw their health refill by a small amount. Another pulse and another bit of life. Concurrently, Med Ic's MP was decreasing with each beat.

"I'll keep us topped off," Med Ic said confidently. "Since we're blowing cooldowns, I figured it was time to give this skill a try."

James glanced at Steve, a questioning eyebrow raised. Med Ic's current class was classified as a Bishop of the Void, but it was a secret class, and James didn't know what type of skills that class had.

"Figure it's the smart thing to do," Elm commented as well. "At least we know now what to expect surprise wise from this mob in the future."

"Yeah," Faust added. "In short, negate the gas as quickly as possible, and keep the thing from burning us alive." Lightning crackled. "I'm going to guess since it has mechanical parts that it's got a weakness to lightning."

The party then went to town on the mob. Considering the creature was just a mob, and the players were using their strongest abilities following Oak's panicked trigger, it was clear who the victor would be. Even though the Chem-era's stats were impressive, strong enough to be equal to a floor boss on the fifth floor, the move set it had access to as a basic mob meant it didn't have the flexibility or skills needed to survive the party onslaught.

"A Bishop of the Void is what happens when someone on a purely healing specific path opts for a debuff-based class as well," Steve began, opting to finally answer James's implied question as the Knights began to repay the Chem-Era's showcase of skills with one of their own.

"In Med Ic's case, his decisions at level 70 put him on the Path of the Void. If you remember, he had selected the Grand Bishop of Light class when he hit level 60, continuing his pure light-based healing path. But when he hit level 70, he made a different decision. He selected the Cleric of Darkness Class. While Clerics of Darkness are technically still healers, the class heals in a unique manner. It transfers debuffs to enemies and drains the life of enemies in order to heal players. Similar to how Rue's Cleric of Blood works, though instead of stealing from teammates or the caster, it steals from the enemies."

"Cleric of Darkness sounds broken," Rue quipped.

"Eh, the conversion rate of health stolen to health healed is abysmal early on," Steve said with a shrug. "Sure, it adds a little DPS overall to a fight, but the healing potential is severely limited. Anyways, by selecting that, his class changed at level 70 into an Ethereal Bishop because it triggered a secret class change."

"That's what he was during the Siege Event," James commented. "But when he was healing, I only saw his normal heal spells."

"He was probably playing it safe, given the rest of you were all being extremely reckless," Steve said with a grin. "Don't think your shenanigans went unnoticed, Mister 'I'm suddenly a raging fire DPS,'" Steve chuckled. "Anyways, at level 80, Med Ic's class progressed down the secret class progress tree into Bishop of the Void. He can heal as he normally did as a Cleric of Light, has access to skills that steal health from enemies to heal the players, and more importantly, has gained a few unique skills that are much more interesting.

"That cooldown he popped, for instance, is called Heart of the Void. Every time it beats, it transfers health equal to a percentage of the amount of life an enemy he has targeted is missing, equally into all of his teammates. Once activated, it will last until canceled, or he runs out of mana. Each beat of the heart drains incrementally more mana from him to maintain."

"That's... interesting," James said, trying to comprehend the skill. "Does it damage the enemy? And can it be transferred?"

"No and no," Steve said. "It simply takes into account the missing percentage of health from the targeted enemy. Flavor wise, the concept was that it was transferring the lost health that had 'escaped' into the nothing—you know, like a spirit leaving a body, its literal life force—into the others. If the enemy heals, the effectiveness of the healing is decreased. And if it dies, well, the spell sputters out as well. However,"—Steve held up a finger—"because it doesn't actively damage or affect the target, it can't be cleansed. Which makes it a very powerful cooldown." He sipped from his drink. "Which is also why it has a thirty-minute cooldown timer," he added softly, as if an afterthought.

"A what?" James choked on his own drink.

Most of the massive cooldowns came with a ten-minute timer, or even fifteen minutes. Thirty minutes seemed steep for the ability, though, it wasn't completely unheard of. Fel's Ultimate Cooldown, her bone dragon, had a one-hour cooldown. But that was an Ultimate Class Cooldown she'd gained from being solely on the Bone path for the Necromancer Class.

"Yeah, it's a doozy," Steve said with a shrug. "There was a lot of back and forth on it. Against a boss, the potential of the skill is crazy, especially if the healer can keep up their mana reserves. But given the increasing cost per beat, we figured it wouldn't justify a full one-hour cooldown. It's not a floor-breaking effect, after all. But also not a skill that should be freely spammed, especially when you have"—he motioned at the floating image of the battle below—"powerful mobs on floors that are nearly equal to boss grandeur at higher tiers."

"I suppose," James said, as he turned his focus back to the fight as well. "What else can he do? What can they all do now?" he added.

Steve's grin stretched so wide that it almost looked painful. "Wouldn't you like to know?"

Chapter Eight

As expected, the five-man party was able to handle the basic floor mob with relative ease once they burned their cooldowns. Such skills, commonly used by gamers as trump cards or for burn phases of major boss fights, easily bridged the level gap between the players and the level 91 Chem-Era. After the Knights overcame its early barrage of breath attacks, all of which had minute-long cooldowns themselves, James would have been extremely disappointed in the pro gamers if they had lost to the mob.

"Any good loot?" Z asked as they finished sorting through their experience gain and loot drops from the creature.

Its body lay on the ground, mechanical parts sparking. The serpent head was lying in a far corner of the room, having been completely severed and thrown aside by a powerful blow from Oak's axe. The goat head was burned and blacked. As for the lion head, gone was its mane of flames and fur, replaced instead by a mane of bone arrows.

"No pets or anything on my end," Elm said.

Oak and Med Ic shook their heads as well, implying the same was true for them.

"No gear either," Faust said as his fingers flipped through hidden screens. "Though all the materials it dropped are of rare quality at least."

"Makes sense," Z said. "Being the sixth floor, I'd be surprised if anything dropped under rare quality when it came to materials. After all, these mobs are dangerously close to level 100."

"Likely over it too," Elm concluded, "if the trend from the other floors continues. If this was a basic mob at level 91, I'm willing to bet the boss is over 100."

They were, of course, right. Jormun-Grander was level 101 currently, and would max out at level 110, while the regular mobs would max out at level 100 once James hit Tier 7.

"I cannot wait to hit level 100," Oak said, hungrily rubbing his gauntleted hands together. "You think they'll have something special for that benchmark?"

"Who knows," Z shrugged. "I guess they'll do something for it. It's a pretty common landmark to hit, but we can't know for sure till we get there." He paused. "Ideally, I'd like for our group to hit 100 first. Though, in all honesty…"

"SoulDemon will likely do it before us," Elm finished the thought for him. "That pretentious prick."

SoulDemon was the only player James knew of who was higher level than the members of the Knights Who Go Ni. When it came down to pure skill level, there was no denying that SoulDemon was top tier. However, he had all the personality of a rabid honey badger. He didn't work well with others, was extremely selfish, and didn't seem to give any thought to anyone else. He'd singlehandedly almost caused the Siege to fail, all because he was chasing a unique piece of gear for himself.

"He's definitely got some problems," Z concurred. "I hope his team-mates can sort him out." Z shook his head as his tone softened. "There's a darkness in him that I feel like I know."

"Whatever he's dealing with doesn't justify how he treats everyone. Especially not those who help him," Faust countered. "The others of the Candy Dungeon are all likable enough. But that guy, I personally wish he'd stop showing his face around here."

Z looked at Faust, and for a brief moment, there was a shadow on Z's face. A look that I recognized from his eyes. Z had a dark past himself. He carried a weight. The man blamed himself for the death of his daughter and his wife. If anyone had a right to be bitter and dark, it was Z. Yet here he was, smiling with everyone, beloved by all players in James's dungeon. Z was the exact opposite of SoulDemon.

"Maybe he just needs the right people to show him the light." Z's tone was soft, filled with emotion. "Like I did."

The room went silent then, both in the dungeon, and in the hot spring. It was such a somber moment that Steve even set his drink down, his own eyes losing their trademark smile lines.

Everyone here had some sort of skeleton in their closet. James felt guilty for a moment, realizing that as much as he'd lamented his own life over the past week of the real world, compared to everyone else, his life had probably been the easiest. Which just made him feel guilty about... everything.

The silence was broken by a loud thrumming, heavier and deeper than before. The Jormun-Grander's jaws had closed once more, marking another minute in the dungeon. With each passing minute, it grew slightly larger and moved forward a little more. At this rate, it would find one of the three special orbs within the next hour. Something that James was eager to see.

What would happen if the boss consumed one? Would its growth and appearance change to account for its massive gain in stats? Would the players get any type of warning or message? Currently, as far as James could tell, they had no idea the loud boom was the countdown to their own demise.

"Right, well." Z slapped his cheeks as the sound moved away from them. He looked towards the exit of the room, opposite to the side they'd come in. "We've a sixth floor to explore, and this dungeon is creepy enough without all the doom and gloom."

"Shall we continue exploring?" Faust said as he walked up beside Z, placing a reassuring hand on the leader's shoulder as he spoke. "Is that what you're getting at?'

"Aye," Z said with a nod. He looked back at everyone and paused.

His party was watching him. They were ready, and yet the air around them still seemed heavy, their eyes, their faces still clouded by thoughts consumed by a darkness unique to themselves. Shared secrets from their past together that James had no way of knowing.

"Though." Z took another breath, and his right hand began flipping through his own hidden screens. "How about a quick Dicken break before we go further? The stat boosts are always nice, and you can't argue that those special herbs and spices have a cheery kick to them."

In his hand, a large bucket of fried Dicken appeared. On the side of the bucket was the Dicken Shack logo: a fire-breathing Dicken with the words, 'Our Dicken is Kickin.' Apparently, if you opened a shop within DCO, you gained the ability to customize the containers your product was sold in, including unique artwork and designs. Alex's parents, who ran not only a restaurant in the real world but also multiple food chains in DCO, had quite the flair for branding.

Everyone cheered and walked towards Z, grabbing fried Dicken bits from the container. In Elm's hand, a bottle of fireball whiskey appeared, the drink that Alex himself had introduced to James's players, crafted from the infernal corn on James's first floor. Alex's parents had matched the flavor profile of the fried Dicken to pair perfectly with the cinnamon notes of the fireball whiskey. It was something that James had personally made sure to experience firsthand while he was running around in his developer Avatar.

As the group shared their food and drink, the mood around the party immediately lifted. Within the dungeon, lit only by flickering torches, there seemed to be a new light source. The smiles on the party's lips, their good mood, lifted the shadows from their faces and eyes. And at the center of this newfound light, its source, was the man who James knew had the darkest shadows surrounding his heart.

Z was, without a doubt, the greatest adventurer James had ever met, and more than that, he was the very heart of the town's instance of DCO. As long as he was around, no matter what it was, no matter the threat or the situation, the players, James even, would either prevail or die trying with a smile on their faces. That was just the type of man Z was.

The type of man James hoped to someday be.

Chapter Nine

"Tell me I'm not the only one who hears that?" Oak stopped walking down the hallway.

They'd begun their dive once more after finishing off the Dicken meat. Currently, they were approaching a bend in the labyrinth. What lay around that corner was hidden by stone walls and darkness.

"You mean the oddly pop-like music?" Elm asked, tilting an ear towards the corner. "Nope, definitely don't hear a thing."

"Oop oop oop," Z chuckled as he put his hands in front of him, crossed at the wrists, and hopped about. It was as if he were trying to ride a horse?

A splash in the hot spring pulled James's attention away from the weird display to Steve, who had suddenly begun imitating swinging a lasso around his head, a grin wide on his face.

"Uh." James raised an eyebrow.

Steve sighed and sat back into the hot spring, muttering, "So young," under his voice as he did.

James disregarded that and turned back to the adventuring party.

"So I'm not having a stroke." Oak flipped Elm off and looked at the rest of the group. "Everyone can hear it."

"Think they're music-based mobs like Funky Monkeys?" Faust offered up from his position towards the back of the group.

"If they are," Med Ic began, "I've got a silence I can cast, and will be on the lookout for any debuffs they may try to apply to us."

"Sounds good," Z said, finally stopping his dance. "Though, if they start playing anything by Babymetal, can you hold off?"

His party shook their heads in disbelief but said nothing more. Oak turned away from his party, hefted his shield, and began walking towards the bend in the path. With the party in consensus that there was definitely some sort of enemy ahead, their mood took on a cautious air. They'd let the Chem-Era take them by surprise. This time, they were going to be prepared.

On an obvious mental command from Z, Hornz moved to walk beside Oak. The adventurer's nose immediately wrinkled as Hornz neared him, but he said nothing. Above them, Turk the Golden Eagle kept pace, while Badgy sat atop its back.

The Badgerker held tightly to the eagle's feathers with one paw, held a sword in its other paw, and his second blade was clenched horizontally between its teeth. James had noticed that each time Z hit a benchmark level and his class evolved, his pet companions gained more intelligence and personality. Badgy, being the oldest of his pets, had progressed the most.

The strange music continued to grow louder as the group approached the bend, and James panned his view of the dungeon, taking note of what awaited the adventurers. A group of five J-Kappa were performing in the dark dungeon.

James looked over the three-foot-tall creatures, and pulled up their information screen, directing part of his attention to their stats and skills to remind himself of all their nuances. At the same time, he took a moment to process the mobs' actual appearances and actions within the dungeon.

J-Kappas, the cheapest mob on the floor, had the lowest stats. They had less HP, ATK, and DEF when compared to every other mob on the floor. Of their stats, the highest stat they did have was their MP. That was because their 'performances' were a toggled skill that had a constant MP drain.

While they had other attacks that had single-use MP costs to cast, those weren't a high note of the creature. Their true strength lay in their ability to buff each other and to debuff players. The unique aspect of the mobs was that their buffs and debuffs changed depending on the type of 'persona' the J-Kappas had. These personas were randomly generated each time one was summoned.

Looking over the five mobs, James noted that the five mobs showcased four unique personas and one duplicate. The first J-Kappa he looked over had the 'Bad Boy' persona. The little humanoid imp creature wore a leather jacket and leather pants covered in various spikes and chains. He had blue-black hair, and an ornate Japanese bowl atop his head was covered in dragons. The bowl, a hint to players, was filled with coins. The Bad Boy persona's buff would apply a damage increase to its allies, while its debuff would decrease the physical defense of the players.

The next of the mobs, dressed in a stylish suit with black, slicked-back hair, glasses, and pristine white gloves, was the 'Businessman' persona. The buff from its song would decrease the MP cost of skills, while its debuff for enemies would make their skills cost more.

The third unique persona of the group was the 'Idol' persona. This persona was one of the female-presenting personas that the J-Kappas had. It had long, electric-blue hair, and was dressed in a very anime inspired outfit. A headset on its ear brought a heart-shaped microphone to its mouth, and the bowl on top of its head was decorated with moons and stars. The Idol persona buffed the agility of its allies and applied a slow debuff to enemies.

Finally, there was the persona that had duplicated this time around. The fourth and fifth members of the current J-Kappa band had ended up with the 'Shy' persona. Another of the female personas, of which there were four in total, these J-Kappas looked like twins, albeit with different color schemes.

Both wore hoodies with long sleeves that fell past their hands, obscuring their little clawed fingers. They held onto stuffed bears, and their hair was styled in a manner that the side swept bangs covered their right eyes. One of them had a soft pink color scheme, while the other had a soft blue color scheme.

Shy personas had a buff that could increase the dodge chance of their allies, while their debuff was a hit to their opponents' accuracy. Atop their heads, their bowls were partially covered by the floppy hoods of their hoodies, which had long bunny ears on them. The bowls themselves were faintly colored, as if the object itself wished to be hidden away.

James found himself grinning as the adventurers made their way around the corner. The mobs were still far enough down the hallway that the players couldn't see them. However, the music picked up as the players approached, the mobs harmonizing in a very elegant manner as they sang in a language James didn't understand. It was all performative for now, he knew, but the players didn't.

The pace of the advancing party slowed, and James saw Med Ic preparing his silence. They weren't strangers to music-based mobs. And even though the creatures would be throwing around a powerful array of buffs and debuffs, James didn't think on their own that they'd pose that much of a threat to the players. They were support mobs through and through.

Luckily for the mobs, and not so luckily for Z and the others, the musical mobs that currently drew the full attention of Z and his gang weren't the only mobs in that hallway. The shadows further past the J-Kappas served as the perfect hiding spot. Within them, nightmares lurked...

James smiled in anticipation, and the chat from the other dungeons watching the stream brimmed with excitement. The Knights Who Go Ni had survived the first battle on the sixth floor. Could they survive the second?

Chapter Ten

"If I hadn't met Steve already," Oak said as Med Ic's silence went off, "I would have sworn that the developers of this game were on drugs."

"And after meeting him," Z offered, "it's pretty clear they probably were."

Everyone laughed, even James and Rue. Steve, the brunt of the joke for once, just took a sip of his drink and shrugged. He'd already spilled the secret of how a lot of the floor options had come about. A flip book split into parts that had random descriptors and mob types on the pages. The developers would flip different sections on the book, and whichever combination it landed on, well, they'd go with it.

"Still," Oak continued as he stomped hard onto the ground, sending a wave of electrical energy flowing from himself and his shield towards the J-Kappas, an AoE-style taunt. "The fact that they created such... er... detailed models is rather impressive."

The taunt flowed over the five mobs, lightning crackling around them, doing negligible damage to level 91 mobs. The damage wasn't the purpose, though; the taunt was.

"Five seconds left on the silence," Med Ic called as the party advanced on the mobs. "Then it's down to single-target silences."

"We'll focus on..." Z trailed off, and then his bow twanged. An arrow soared past Oak's shoulder and planted deep into the blue-haired 'Idol' personal. "The Miku wannabe."

Even though they were silenced, the J-Kappas were all still singing and performing. Their voices were just currently being sucked away into little purple orbs that hung over their heads.

When the arrow hit the Idol Popstar, her mouth went from a smiling, singing motion to a frown. She placed her hands on her hips and glared in Z's direction. His arrow had done enough damage to override Oak's taunt, switching her aggro from Oak to Z.

The tank was quick to remedy that. He rushed forward and smashed into her with a shield bash, just as the silence effect faded. She punched at him, her blow hitting the shield, which immediately sprayed acid in her face. The high-pitched scream echoed off the stone walls as coins from the bowl atop her head clattered to the ground.

"They're probably a group mob," Z had to yell to make himself heard above the shrill scream. The other J-Kappas, all aggroed onto Oak from his taunt, looked at the tank, their faces positively determined. "Burn 'em down one at a time."

"You got it, boss." Faust pointed a finger at the Idol J-Kappa and released the spell he'd been preparing. A storm cloud appeared over the poor mob, and lightning immediately struck her, causing another scream to echo out.

Before the others could attack, the rest of the mobs, with the duration of the silence completed, entered the fray. While they were aggroed onto Oak, their skills were AoE-based. That was, anything within a certain radius of them could be affected by the songs.

With incredible harmony and more than a little fanfare, the sound of various instruments, including an up-tempo base, magically appeared. As one, like some boy band group from the late 1900s, they began singing.

James watched as the bodies of the J-Kappas that were singing all began to glow, save for the Idol, who was under the effect of the single-target silence. The color, he noted, differed depending on which mob was singing.

The Bad Boy had an aura of blue flames envelop him. For the Business-man, magical golden light appeared to rain ethereal coins down around him. The two Shy personas had a whitish mist flowing around their bodies that seeped outwards.

As their performance intensified, the lights of all the auras pulsed with the music, reaching and enveloping both friend and foe alike. James was reminded of a rave as the various colors danced along the stone walls of the labyrinth, the beat of the music so intense that he could almost feel it in his bones.

"Alright, I'll admit," James said as he watched the mobs at work, "I almost didn't put these guys in the dungeon."

"You got something against catchy music?" Steve asked.

"No, just…" James motioned at the scene. "They look ridiculous and, on paper, read even crazier."

"And yet," Steve said, his grin growing. "Here we are." He had two glowing sticks, each about two feet in length, in his hands, and he was currently shaking them about in time with the music.

"Yeah, their sellout skill was what tempted me to place them in," James said, ignoring the developer's antics. "Because what sane Dungeon Core would pass up the chance to earn a bit of extra coin off players who wanted to hire out the mobs?" James motioned at the battle again. "After seeing them in action, though, I can honestly say that I definitely underestimated just how much I'd enjoy this."

"Their tunes are catchy, aren't they?" Steve said as he continued to dance along to the music.

There was no doubt that the performance of the mobs—well, the musical performance, at least—was catchy. In a 'this is going to be stuck in my head later' earworm kind of way.

But past that, as James watched all of the buffs instantly stack on the mobs as they empowered their band, while the debuffs randomly applied to the Knights Who Go Ni based on their luck and resistances, it was without a doubt one of the more unique types of battles to happen in his dungeon. And that was saying something.

Purely dependent on RNG and what types spawned, every battle against the J-Kappas would be different. As players figured out what persona applied what types of buffs and debuffs, the adventurers would be able to focus and adjust the fight depending on their own strengths and weaknesses.

It was the perfect type of flexible, varied mob to keep players on their toes. This mob's mechanics were perfect for keeping each encounter fresh and different. And variance like that was the spice of life for MMO players.

"Their debuffs look to be quite catchy too," Rue added, and James noted that as the fighting continued, the debuffs seemed to have a chance to apply every five seconds that a performance was underway.

It was important to note too, that while they were putting on quite the show, the mobs weren't solely just rocking out. No, they'd all begun to dance around Oak, striking him with weapons that materialized in their glowing auras, weapons that comically took on the form of various musical instruments.

The attacks wouldn't be too powerful, given the mobs' lower attack stats. But the number of them, as well as the buffs they were getting from each other, made them enough to actually force the tank to apply more defensive skills, while Med Ic had to keep toggling between healing and cleansing spells.

And with the battle roughly thirty seconds in, and the Idol J-Kappa at half its HP, the true fight was still to come. If the players weren't so preoccupied with taking out the blue-haired Idol, nor all the dashing and dazzling lights of the pop performance, they would have noticed the two shadows rushing towards them. Shadows that now glowed with blue, yellow, and white light from the buffs they were receiving.

"Looks like the adventurers are getting rowdy," Steve commented, noting James's attention on the approaching mobs. "So, it's time for the bouncers to do their job."

Chapter Eleven

James watched as two fedoras flew past the J-Kappas and Oak to soar en route to Med Ic. The hats landed on the ground before the surprised healer, who had the sense of mind to take a step back from the sudden projectiles just in time for the two Fogeymen to emerge from the hats. Two ties wrapped themselves around Med Ic's arms, one for each, and he was yanked towards the hungry fangs of the skeletal, sharply dressed, bogeyman-like mobs.

"Med Ic!" Z yelled as he turned his bow towards the newcomers.

He loosed an arrow towards one of the mobs but missed. He'd instinctively aimed his arrow at the creature's head, yet when the projectile reached its intended destination, there was no longer a head to hit. This was because the Fogeyman had quickly sunk its body back into its padded jacket, treating it like a turtle shell to avoid the attack.

Before another attack could be launched at them, both creatures sunk their fangs into Med Ic. His casting was interrupted by the damage, and James watched the healer's life tick down. A debuff stack appeared on him, and James pulled it up, knowing immediately what it would be.

Sharply Dressed (2) – Ten stacks of Sharply Dressed will cause a player to temporarily be charmed, unable to attack or act in a hostile manner towards any Fogeyman or uniquely dressed mob in the area.

"We need to free Med Ic," Z called out as his minions pulled themselves away from the J-Kappas to charge the two wannabe 1950s mob… sters.

"No shit," Elm said, taking a shot at the clothes.

He had a glowing white aura around him, showing he was debuffed currently from the Shy Persona J-Kappas. That debuff meant that his accuracy was down, and his arrow missed its target.

Elm cursed. An accuracy debuff was always a bit of a pain in any game. But when combined with an enemy that was gaining an increased dodge chance, especially when they already had a skill that increased their dodge chance, it was pretty brutal.

"Sooner, rather than later." Med Ic squirmed as he pleaded to his friends, trying to free himself from the grasp of the mobs. "I can't break free." He was glowing with purple light, a skill of his own active, and yet they held him fast.

"He's not going to be able to break free by himself," Steve commented as he struggled. "Fogeymen are the perfect ambush mob. Once you're in their tie clasp, you're pretty much screwed if you're by yourself." He chuckled, "Especially if you're a squishy caster type. The guy who came up with their design had a special hate for burst type casters and cheeky healers, so he made these mobs specifically to be their bane."

"Is that why they jumped on Med Ic?" James asked. He'd been curious why the two mobs had completely ignored Oak. Sure, the tank's taunt hadn't reached them earlier, but he was still the most obvious target. And unlike the Philoso-Raptors on his second floor, these mobs didn't have enhanced intelligence.

"Pretty much," Steve said. "They've got a priority list built into them. It's, uh, kind of a funny bit of coding design actually," he chuckled. "They target the least dressed party members… which is almost always the mages and healers since their armor consists of just robes and such."

James glanced over at Rue, thinking particularly about her Avatar. "What about scantily dressed barbarians and the likes?"

"Their armor still carries more weight, making them lower on the priority list. When I say least, I mean least as in pure weight and material wise."

"I can honestly say I have no idea how you guys came up with these things," James said to Steve.

The developer smiled, taking it as a compliment. James, however, had meant it more as an 'I can't believe you guys were able to make anything work' statement.

Then again, with how advanced AI was, coding was very different from how it used to be. He knew that much from what he'd learned over the years about the process. It didn't involve long lines of code and if-then statements and such. Now they could give intention statements to the AI tools, and the computers themselves would develop the systems.

They could hatch the craziest of ideas into concepts that worked, which was part of what revolutionized the technological advances. After, they put in hard-lined rules and regulations to stop AI from stealing work from creators such as authors and artists. It was shaky at first, but eventually, AI was used for bettering the world. Or, at the very least, it gave humans more time to themselves, and more time for people to do the things they wanted to and enjoyed, and not just slave away at jobs to purely exist.

Med Ic's screams drew him back to the battle at hand. The Fogeymen had both bit down once more on the man, though this time, only one applied a stack of the debuff. The creatures could launch that attack once per five seconds, draining a small portion of their target's life with each bite, but more importantly, each bite had a chance to apply another stack.

"It'd be really nice if we didn't have all these debuffs on us," Faust grumbled as lightning flew past Med Ic to blast into one of the Fogeymen.

It struck the one on Med Ic's left, and the lightning danced from it into the other. The ties crackled but hung fast. The health pool of the creatures dropped by a negligible margin.

"The increased spell cost debuff is a new one, and I hate it." He had the glowing golden light from the Businessman J-Kappa around him, and every time he cast a spell, a pile of coins sprung from his body, as if imitating the increased tax his skills had on them.

"I'm guessing the Fogeymen have a naturally high magic resistance, don't they?" James asked without even glancing in Steve's direction. He couldn't remember what their special traits and passives were off the top of his head, and didn't feel like pulling them up just yet in the middle of the battle.

"Yup. Increased magic resistance, but as a tradeoff, they take a higher percentage of damage from slashing and piercing attacks."

"Truly mage killers," James acknowledged.

"I told you," Steve said mid-sip. "There are certain mobs that were designed with singular grudges in mind. The Fogeyman just so happens to be one." A pause, another sip, and then Steve continued. "The Candy Dungeon has a mob called the Everlasting Mob-Stopper that has a skill that makes it multiply anytime it takes damage from a non-player source.

Solely created to punish pet class players." Steve chuckled. "I love that mob."

James resisted glancing at Steve, the crazy spectacle of the battle below thankfully captivating enough to make the effort easy. With Med Ic's healing stopped at the moment, thanks to the Fogeymen, Oak had to switch purely to turtling up. His attacks on the Idol persona, which was down to a fifth of her life, had slowed enough to allow her to begin singing.

Bright blue and pink flowers flowed around her as her buff and debuff spread out, increasing the agility of her allies, while trying to apply a slow debuff to the already debuff-stacked players. More cursing and sputtering from the players followed as the adventuring party found itself overwhelmed by the sheer number of level 91 mobs, and more importantly, the musical troop's worth of effects.

Every good gamer knew, first and foremost, that status effects, buffs, and debuffs could instantly change the tide of a battle. With that being said, there was another important lesson every good gamer knew. And that was when to cut your losses and run.

Chapter Twelve

Five minutes. That was the death timer allotted to players who fell in the dungeon and couldn't get respawned.

The timer had been extremely damning on the first floor, considering players only had a maximum of one hour to explore it. On the sixth, the five-minute timer didn't seem all that painful at first. What was five minutes when you had a total of six hours to explore the floor?

However, those five minutes were more vital, in James's humble opinion, on the sixth floor than the first. Every minute was a minute that the Jormun-Grander advanced. Every minute was a moment in time for the boss to get larger, and more powerful. And more importantly, every minute was a minute that the boss drew closer to its greatest source of power: the Orbs.

Speaking of the Orbs, the Jormun-Grander was extremely close to one now. Earlier, James had predicted an hour until it reached the first one. Now, he was pretty sure it would arrive at one in roughly thirty minutes. The decreased time window was the result of a size boost the boss had gained by consuming a Solem while the Knights had been battling the J-Kappas.

"The next time we see those mobs, we kill them from a distance," Oak growled as he rejoined his teammates.

The Knights Who Go Ni—or rather, Elm, Z, and Faust—had all retreated to the entrance of the dungeon. Med Ic, who'd died first, had only just rejoined them about a minute before Oak. The tank, his high HP and defensive stats a blessing and a curse, hadn't fallen until the Fogeyman had finished off Med Ic.

"That's probably a better plan," Z said, nodding sagely, "and we should ensure they don't have any allies hiding in the shadows. Either way, the battle was valuable for information." He looked at Oak and grinned. "And entertainment. You think we can request different songs from them in the future? Or how about autographs?" He winked at Oak. "The Idol you'd been focusing on seemed especially interested in you."

An object appeared in Oak's hand, and the tank chucked something at Z's face. The laughing elf dodged the object, and it splattered harmlessly on the stone floor behind him. James looked at it and mentally pulled up the information on the item before he found himself chuckling.

"Spoiled Painguin Eggs?" James glanced at Steve. "Since when have the food drops been able to spoil?"

Steven grinned. "Since the latest update. We snuck that one in. The higher-ups wanted to add a bit more realism. And we weren't opposed since too many players had begun hoarding basic food items for buffs and healing. It gets a bit ridiculous when someone's running around with one hundred wheels of cheese to just hastily consume mid-battle. And if I'm being honest"—he gagged slightly—"it's really disturbing to watch happen. Even if it is all virtual, bleh."

"So now the food items can spoil." James shook his head. "How do you think players are going to take that?"

He pointed at the spoiled egg splatter, which smelled, given how the Knights were looking at it and holding their noses. "Well, it gives them a free item to throw at each other. And harder to gather ingredients take longer to spoil. The players get warnings too, with countdowns, for the length of time an ingredient has before it goes bad. They can also store them in special units back in town in their houses to prevent or slow the process." Steve shrugged. "Not to mention, some of the materials now actually improve over time as they age, opening up a whole new realm of possibilities and flavors."

"Still feels a bit unnecessary," James commented as the Knights finished fooling around in the dungeon, preparing to begin their adventuring of his sixth floor once again. "I'm sure Reddit is going to be filled with people complaining."

"With all the hype about the upcoming mass Dungeon Wars, we figured no one would complain. Everyone's too focused and excited. By the time they finish their full 48-hour dive, well," Steve chuckled, "I highly doubt anyone will complain. After all, that's like 48 days in game without pause. By the time it's done, they'll have forgotten all about their gripes with the slight change and will be chomping at the bit for even more content. Every good developer knows that you slip possibly unfavorable updates into the game when you're dropping something massive, new, and exciting. That way, all the complaints get buried and forgotten."

James shook his head, wondering what other subtle updates and changes had been implemented since DCO's release that he'd not noticed. They'd had a few massive updates already. The Dungeon Wars, the introduction of the Coliseums, the Dungeon Gates, and, of course, the Skirmishes. Each and every one of those had immediately become the talk of the forums.

The rate of new content was honestly staggering, all things considered. And now Steve was implying that those updates had the potential to have other changes and features hidden within them. James was again hit with the realization that there was a lot that went on with regard to DCO that even he, as a Dungeon Core, didn't know.

Considering how close he felt he was with Steve and BLANK, it made him wonder. Just what was DCO all about? And what else was going on? Why were his parents involved with the project? Why was Rue's father involved with it? Why did the government have so much interest in the game itself?

Was it all connected with how many liberties and special permissions the game seemed to be getting? After all, the upcoming 48-hour immersion was going to be the very first event of its kind. An unheard of, never before granted right for everyone to stay immersed for longer than 9 hours.

That alone would likely draw the attention of anyone who hadn't yet picked up the game. Which wasn't a large number of people, considering it was still free to download, and the unparalleled sensory realism that was the talk of every online forum by now. Entire businesses and families had already fully shifted their daily lives into the game. DCO, in its short amount of time being live, had taken the whole world by storm. But... was that a good thing?

James shivered and pushed the growing unease from his mind. Ever since his encounter with the hacking group Cyb3ru5, he'd had a nagging feeling that there was something going on with DCO. And every time he let those thoughts play through, well... it never went anywhere beneficial. Mostly, all it did was make him paranoid and worried, and James was not about to become a conspiracy theorist. Not everything good in life needed a monster in the shadows waiting to ruin it.

DCO was arguably the best thing to ever happen in his life. A single glance in Rue's direction, the sight of her smile, and the way it made his heart flutter, was all the confirmation he needed of that fact. DCO was where he truly belonged, where his heart belonged. Whatever was going on behind the scenes didn't matter to him as long as DCO itself, this world, this life he was building wasn't affected.

He smiled as he clung to those thoughts, using them to push aside the creeping darkness. With his depression and paranoia thwarted and back in their box in the back of his mind for the moment, James turned his full attention back to his favorite guild and their trek through his sixth floor. He'd apparently just missed some sort of discussion they'd been having, but it didn't matter. They set forth with renewed purpose, and a few more rotten eggs thrown about, back into the labyrinth.

The dungeon dive was back on. And James was here for it.

Chapter Thirteen

The next twenty minutes of the dive was, while entertaining, not overly exciting. The Knights had decided to explore a different route, opting for the middle route instead of the left one they'd originally traversed. Once they came to the massive opening with another Chem-Era, they defeated the mob and backtracked to the entrance. From there, they went down the path on the right, and confirmed, after a bit of a walk, that the third path, just like the other two, led to a room with a Chem-Era.

They dispatched the third mob with even greater speed than the second Chem-Era. As had always been a trait of the veteran adventurers, they learned quickly and picked up on the attack patterns and skills that mobs had. This let them work out the best strategy for a battle in a relatively quick time. Whereas the first battle against the Chem-Era had caused them to blow powerful cooldowns to overcome the mob, the third battle saw not a single cooldown spent.

Instead, they went with a more 'practical' attack pattern.

And by practical, it meant they went with cheese tactics. Since they'd figured out that focusing down a single head was the most effective way to defeat the boss, it came down to a matter of which head to focus on. The answer was the serpent head that acted as the tail of the Chem-Era.

When they focused on the lion or the goat head, all three heads, in turn, had the ability to strike at whoever held aggro. That strategy also allowed the snake head, with its agility and increased length, to make strikes and attacks from different angles, as well as lash out as needed at other adventurers. Combined with the lion paws of the creature, and its other available skills, taking the Chem-Era head on—well, the heads on the front of the torso at least—was the hardest possible path.

So they initiated battle using Z's pets. Hornz was sent in to grab hold of the serpent head from the back of the mob. Turk the Eagle landed atop the creature's back, dispatching a feral Badgy to begin hacking at the base of the tail, while Turk did what he could with claws and beak as well.

Then the party sent in a very disgruntled Oak to aid in pinning down the serpent tail, while Faust and Med Ic utilized snares to keep the Chem-Era from rotating around. They kept spells at the ready to disperse the breath attacks of the mob, and Z and Elm focused all of their precision damage and high penetrating strikes on the serpent neck.

Once they finished off that particular head, the Chem-Era itself because a much easier mob to take down. The fight devolved into an embarrassing game of ring-around-the-rosy. The players just kept striking at the back and body of the mob, staying behind it while it bounced and bounded and tried to turn to strike. With Hornz and Oak each applying taunts from either side of the creature, the party could keep it immobile in such a way that the battle became a cake walk.

James took notes. So many notes. While there wasn't anything he could do for his mob right now, he did have two upgrade points he could apply in the future. He was pretty sure there had been an upgrade path for the mob that involved missiles. And James recalled that those missiles would make sure that the mob could attack enemies from every angle, regardless of which way the heads were looking.

As was his tendency, his pride as a Dungeon Core, James didn't appreciate when his mobs got rudely embarrassed. When the time came, he'd make sure to pay the Knights back, and give his Chem-Era the fighting chance it deserved. Not that James was particularly vengeful, mind you, when it came to his mobs. He was just proud of making a dungeon that was challenging. And if his mobs got abused too easily, what type of Dungeon Core would he be if he didn't shore up their weaknesses?

Besides, doing just that would force adventurers to figure out new strategies, and help them to adapt. Keeping the floor ever changing with a properly scaling difficulty was what kept things fresh. That's why DCO used human Dungeon Cores in the first place. Only a human consciousness could be creative enough to keep other humans engaged.

At least, that's what he told himself to justify the plans he was making.

By the time the Knights had finished off the third Chem-Era and were taking a celebratory Dicken break, James was all but certain he'd also be adding in a troop of J-Kappas, or maybe a hidden Fogeyman or two, to the rooms if other players and guilds treated his Chem-Era the same way. If the players wanted to resort to cheese tactics, well, James could do that too. But again, James wasn't petty at all. This was all to challenge the players. Solely to keep them on their toes.

James mentally looked around the dungeon as the Knights ate their fried Dicken, unconsciously licking his lips as his mouth watered for the spicy meat. He was curious about which route the Knights would take next. Would they go back to the entrance and start on the left path again to try traversing the entire labyrinth? That would have them face again the J-Kappas and Fogeyman that had humiliated them once already. But if they continued on their current path—the rightmost path from the entrance of the dungeon—they'd be facing against his When-Wolves.

Past the When-Wolves, there was a Solem, and then, more interestingly, one of the mysterious Orb mini-bosses. In particular, it was the green Orb, the Orb of Poison. Each of the three paths, by design, led to a different Orb. The left path led to the Orb of Flames. The middle, the Orb of Frost. And the right, the Orb of Poison.

The Orb of Poison was the easiest and closest to the players as it stood. While the Orb of Frost was the furthest away. And not just distance-wise.

A loud crack echoed through the dungeon as the Jormun-Grander bit down into the Orb of Frost. The labyrinth shuddered as the boss instantly grew in size, the length of its body shooting forward a good fifteen feet, its enlarging head crashing through one of the labyrinth walls before it orientated itself and began moving to its left, following the path of least resistance.

James's attention was immediately drawn to it. The scales shimmered, the feathers around its head glistened with newfound light. A faint, blue hue was applied to the scales, and the feathers reflected the torchlight, each covered in a thin sheen of ice.

At the base of the massive boss, tendrils of ice snaked outwards, climbing the walls, freezing everything around it. Its body heaved and shuddered, and then James watched as a good foot of ice encased it, covering it with protective armor. The sound it produced as it moved was the dangerous twang of ice cracking, the impending doom of an avalanche, or an iceberg preparing to calve.

He moved his attention away from the transformed boss, knowing full well that its stats had been boosted by quite a bit thanks to its consumption of the Orb of Frost, and focused once again on the Knights. They'd grown pale, white as snow, and appeared to be reading a notification.

Before he could ask Steve what notification they'd received, Elm read the notification aloud, disbelief, surprise, and worry all mingled as he spoke.

"An Orb of Power has been consumed by the Jormun-Grander," he said.

James noticed frost in the air as he spoke. The temperature in the dungeon had dropped when the boss had consumed the Orb.

"Ragnarök draws nearer as the World-Gorger continues its feast."

The Knights looked at each other silently. Everyone was working to process the information. Oak broke the silence first.

"That's it." He shook his head. "I'm in hell." He looked at the others, his face going impossibly white. "Of all the types of bosses," he sighed. It was a defeated sound. "This one had to be the freaking World Serpent."

Elm walked over to his brother, patting him gently on the shoulder. "If it makes you feel any better," Elm said softly, one corner of his lip threatening to shift upwards. "Considering what level the mobs are on this floor... if we do come across it, well, we'll all die pretty quickly."

Chapter Fourteen

New Message

The sudden prompt pulled James away from the stream. The Knights Who Go Ni had just begun to leave the Chem-Era's room to continue down the right-hand path. Based on that, the next mob they were going to face would be the When-Wolves. While he was keen to see how those time-manipulating mobs did, the message—or more importantly, who it was from—demanded his full attention.

"Uh," he said, glancing from the message to Rue and then Steve. "Any idea why Hades would be sending me a message?"

That was who the message was from. The notorious hacker. The original founder of Cyb3ru5. The mysterious man who'd helped James defeat the very group he'd once founded. A man hunted by the government and secret agencies alike, and yet a man who remained an enigma. In short, not really the type of person James wanted to receive a message out of the blue from.

"What does the message say?" Steve asked, his attention immediately fixed on James, as if he hadn't only moments before been placing bets with Rue about the fate of the Knights while stuffing his face with candy.

Gone was his carefree attitude. The perpetual smirk in his eyes was absent, replaced with shadows. He'd aged in mere seconds before James's eyes. By just mentioning Hades, the generally unshakable developer had undergone a concerning change. Which didn't give James any warm and fuzzies.

"That he misses James," Rue offered halfheartedly, though she too was suddenly more serious. Forgotten was the stream of Dungeon Core chat. Her focus, just like Steve's, was fully on James.

"No idea yet, I'm afraid to open it," James said honestly. He looked at the message, which was blinking, waiting for him to open it.

From: Hades
Subject: Underworld Dreams

"Well, what's the subject line?" Steve asked. "Come on, details, James."

James told him the subject line, wondering what exactly Hades had sent him.

"That's… less than helpful," Steve muttered. He furrowed his brow. "Given he helped us previously… it's probably safe to open the message." Steve paused, thinking. "But then again, this is Hades we are talking about…"

"He can't hurt James here, can he?" Rue asked, worry evident.

"Theoretically, no," Steve said with a shake of his head, "and he's not the type to go after people like that. What happened with Persephone was personal for him. That was the exception, not the norm for how Hades works."

James shuddered as he remembered what had happened to Persephone. She'd been the one running things when Cyb3ru5 had come after James and the other Dungeon Cores. Tipped off to their existence as humans by Xander, Persephone had aimed to use Dungeon Cores as tools to spread wealth and power to her followers. Because of how much the digital world and real world intersected now, controlling resources in DCO would allow for a gross transfer of wealth in the real world for those who could manipulate the system.

Abusing the system or revealing the truth could have completely thrown all of DCO into chaos—something the government was extremely keen to prevent. To the point that they had actually mobilized their specialized task force, known as the Enforcers, to eliminate the entire organization in a single go.

"Then why would he be messaging James?" Rue pressed. "Cyb3ru5 is gone, right?"

"They are," Steve replied. "Completely eliminated from what I've been told, and the secrets they'd learned were silenced with them."

A memory played through James's mind. The strange, mind-altering substance Persephone had tried to ply him with. The very same substance that was then turned against her. It made her putty at the hands of Fel, or more appropriately, Fel's scary alter ego, R.

The image of Persephone completely helpless and at R's whims haunted him. He'd left her there. He'd been the one to hand her over to R before he'd fled the room to keep his conscience as clear as possible. It was something he knew he'd needed to do, and yet it haunted him. It made him feel like a monster.

"So then." James pushed the memories away, still fixated on the blinking message. "Why would Hades be messaging me?"

His mind assaulted him with more memories and possibilities as he tried to brainstorm why the hacker would be messaging him. Did he have something the man wanted? Was Hades planning to use James's existence as a Dungeon Core? Was it safe to even open the message?

He recalled the one time he'd spoken with Hades in person, if he could call it that. Hades had been there the night he'd been captured by Cyb3ru5. Hades had appeared in Persephone's special virtual space before Fel and the others had arrived.

He'd told James back then that his purpose in life was gathering information. Everything he did was a means to an end. To learn. He'd left before telling James anything of note. The only bit of information James had gleaned from that encounter had come not from Hades, but from Persephone's final words to James. Her musings. She'd claimed that he was a part of something deeper. Something past his parents' work even. Whatever that had meant.

"No use pondering what-ifs," Steve's words pulled James from his thoughts.

The developer seemed to have aged a good ten, no, maybe twenty years. He looked exhausted. And even more chilling, he looked serious and worried. James could count on one hand the number of times he'd seen Steve look like that. It never boded well.

"Might as well open the message and tell us what it says."

"You don't think opening the message will cause us a problem?" James asked, stalling.

If there was one thing he knew for certain about Hades, it was that the man was a master at all things virtual. His hacking skills, or coding skills, or whatever you wanted to call them, were legendary.

He'd done the seemingly impossible and broken into Persephone's personal virtual space. And personal spaces were supposed to be the ultimate when it came to security. And Persephone herself had been an extremely talented hacker, meaning hers should have been impenetrable.

The technological skills of Hades were why he was impossible to track down. For however long he'd been on the run, he'd somehow, to this day, avoided getting caught by the government. A feat that, considering all the government had at their disposal in the current day and age, should have been more than an impossibility.

"If he wanted to cause you problems, he'd do so without sending you a message," Steve stated. "Hades isn't the type to 'do' things. Not anymore. That version of him died a long time ago with the remnants of Anonymous." Steve shook his head. "No, whatever his reason for contacting you, I think the message itself should be safe." He paused before he continued. "Though, what the message contains, the knowledge within… that could be dangerous in a way we can't even process until we know what it is."

James shuddered at Steve's tone. He didn't like that. Not at all. Especially since everything was finally going smoothly for James. Hadn't he been through enough? Hadn't he suffered enough? Why did he have to keep getting pulled into things? Why couldn't he just enjoy life, enjoy DCO?

"We could just ignore it," James offered sheepishly, looking at Steve and then Rue. "Ignorance is bliss, right?"

"You know your curiosity would get to you eventually," Rue said, trying her best to smile at him. It was clear she was trying to hide her own anxiety. Hades knew about her. He knew about her father. Another thing that shouldn't be possible.

His knowledge, his involvement with James during the Cyb3ru5 situation, everything about him had been enough to make Rue wary of the man. It made them all wary of him, for good measure. He was an untouchable unknown.

"Might as well open it now," Rue continued, "so that we have time to sort through whatever it is he's sent before immersion ends."

"She's right," Steve concurred. "Gotta treat it like a band-aid and rip it off. Whatever it says, we're here for you, and we'll figure it out together."

James nodded, took a deep breath, and opened the message. Whatever it was, the three of them could handle it. Together.

Stare into the Void, until it stares back.

~H

Beneath that cryptic message, James saw what looked to be a massive ink blot. James instinctively looked at it, his eyes drawn to the strange, black mass. He'd never seen something quite like it in a digital message before. It shimmered and shifted, like oil perhaps, but then at the same time, seemed to draw in all the light around it.

What was it? Was it perfectly round? Did its edges have shape to them? His eyes focused harder. What was he looking at?

His mind caught up to his curiosity. There was definitely more to that strange darkness. Something 'off' about the way it drew his gaze. Panic filled him as his mind processed the words of the message again, and realization filled him. A split second too late, he saw within the darkness a set of eyes looking back at him.

"Oh shit," was all he managed to say before he felt his mind leave his body.

The world went black as he was pulled from DCO, across virtual space, into darkness.

Chapter Fifteen

"I would like to say I'm surprised you arrived so promptly," a voice said, the tone amused, "and yet sadly, I'm not."

A dark chuckle filled the air as James's eyes blinked, slowly focusing. Sensations rushed over him. He could feel again. He could smell again. He was somewhere new, but with a level of realism that, had he not been immersed already, would have made him swear he was somewhere in the real world. It rivaled, maybe even surpassed, that of DCO.

"Please make yourself comfortable James, we've much to talk about," the voice said.

James's eyes further adjusted to the lighting of his surroundings as he processed the words. The speaker, of course, was Hades. He'd only heard the man's voice a few times, but he'd never forget that tone. Cold and calculating, oozing with confidence. Not cocky or pompous, mind you. Merely the voice of someone who knew exactly what they were talking about, and knew, not presumed, but fully knew they were likely the smartest person in the room.

"Hades," James said, his eyes settling on the man.

The man in question was leaning against a window. The room he'd summoned James to was roughly the size of a studio apartment. Papers and objects were scattered all about. On the desk that stood between James and Hades was a strange white mask with a smiling, mustached face.

The rest of the room was cluttered with chalkboards, whiteboards, and weird corkboards. All of which had strings, notes, pictures, and any and all other oddities plastered across them. It was a room that would make an entire team of detectives jealous. It made James uneasy. This was the room of someone with an intense obsession.

"Where am I?" James asked after a long silence.

The man was dressed again in the dark trench coat James had last seen him wearing. He said nothing as he pushed off of the window he'd been leaning against. The coat moved aside, revealing gloved hands and an ornate walking stick.

He casually walked to the desk, swiveled the chair around, and sat. Then he leaned the stick against the wood and produced a crystal bottle from somewhere underneath the desk. Two cups appeared then, and he motioned for James to sit in the chair opposite him. All of this was done in a slow, methodical way without a single uttered a single word.

"You're in my personal space," Hades finally said as he poured the amber-colored liquid into the glasses. "A space unreachable by any, save for those who have received a uniquely coded invitation from me."

He held the glass to James. James took it and sniffed. The scent was strong, definitely alcohol. Rich notes of oak and vanilla swam about as he gently rocked the glass, swishing the liquid within. Cinnamon as well, perhaps? Maybe a hint of honey?

"Was that what that was?" James asked as he took a hesitant sip.

He had little reason to distrust Hades. But at the same time, he had little reason to actually *trust* the man. Still, considering he'd been forcibly whisked to this space, if Hades did want to do anything to him, surely he could do it at a whim and not through some petty means of poisoned alcohol.

Is that even possible? James wondered, and the wheels began to turn even as the liquor's burn lingered on his lips. *Could* you poison someone with a drink in immersion? Persephone had used a sweet-smelling incense in her space, with her wine serving as the antidote...

"My own personal style of invitation, yes." Hades took a drink, seemingly unaware of James's sudden fear, closing his eyes for a moment as he savored the flavor. "I've found that you can never be too safe nowadays. And through my life, I've learned no shortage of tricks and tools on how to ensure that my invitations cannot be traced."

"So." James took a drink, this time a proper one, and let the flavor linger. He couldn't help but marvel at the rich flavors that danced across his tongue. Other than within DCO, he'd never experienced such realism. Was this space somehow using the same type of coding as DCO? Or maybe... what if Hades had played a part in developing the code of DCO?

"Why have you invited me here?" James took another drink, trying to control his emotions. He didn't want to be here. He wanted to be safe in DCO, happily spending time with Rue, and yes, even Steve. Not in some dark, foreboding, office-like room. It stunk like the setup of a bad detective drama.

"A favor repaid, and potentially further favor paid forward depending on what you choose to do with the first." Hades took another drink, and then poured himself more of the liquor. "Nothing more, nothing less."

He offered the bottle to James, but James declined. He didn't know how far the realism went within Hades's personal space, and he'd rather not get drunk, or even buzzed, while talking with this man. If there was one thing he *was* certain about Hades, it was the fact that Hades was not his friend. This man was dangerous, and he danced to his own tune.

"Suit yourself," Hades said as he set the bottle back down. "Though, a bit of free advice. When someone offers you a bourbon as fine as this, you don't turn down seconds."

He took a sip and made a show of reveling in the taste. He even went as far as to let out a heavy, content sigh before he opened his eyes to regard James again. The man's eyes swirled strangely, the colors not really settling on a single shade. And the more James tried to focus on Hades's actual features, the more they shifted as well. *Strange.*

"I'll keep that in mind," James said, finding he had to stop trying to discern any physical features about Hades. It was like his very being— from the shape of his mouth to the color of his eyes, and even his hair— was shifting constantly in and out of focus. Was that some strange bug? Or a feature of Hades's own Avatar to make himself impossible to identify? "But I have a feeling I want as clear a head as possible for whatever it is you have called me here for."

"Fair point." Hades set his glass down. "And a practical way of viewing things. Many people may consider cynicism to be a negative trait, but trust me, it's the best way to ensure your survival. Though"—he shrugged —"there are times when even that's not enough to keep you safe. Or if it is, the cost itself is a deep one. A life of paranoia, looking over your shoulder, doubting and distrusting everyone." He sighed. "It's exhausting. And then..."

He picked up the strange mask, twisting it this way and that as he looked into its eyes. "...when you finally learn the truth, you have to wonder, what was even the point?" He set the mask down. "But alas, those musings are the type done alone, at night with a bottle in one hand and a pipe in the other. As for why I've called you here, James, it's a matter of personal responsibility. You aided me, you see, in reaching my goals."

"Your goals?" James remembered that Hades had reached out to him to help stop Cyb3ru5 because the hacking group's actions were a potential obstacle with regard to some information the man had been working to gather. Hades had been looking into DCO, and past that, the government itself. Did that mean he'd found what he was looking for? "Are you referring to what you were trying to uncover when you last contacted me?"

"You remembered, good." Hades grinned at him, the look slightly unnerving as his lips shimmered and shifted in place. "That makes this a bit easier." He leaned forward, both arms on the table, drawing closer to James. "I did indeed find what I was looking for. And having found the holy grail, I've learned, in short, the darkest truth of the world."

"And you thought you'd tell me?" James was intrigued, but also couldn't help but feel that this whole situation seemed a bit... unorthodox? Impossible even?

"It involves you," Hades said simply. "And I owed you for helping me. It's only fair that in return I share that which I've learned with you." He sat back then, slumping slightly, and shrugged his shoulders. "What you do with that knowledge is entirely up to you." He grabbed his glass, and, in a single gulp, downed the rest of the liquor. "After all, it's your funeral."

Chapter Sixteen

James's fingers tightened around the glass in his hand. Part of him worried he might break the glass. Was that possible in Hades's space? How real was the area? Either way, James felt his mouth go immediately dry as a pit opened in his stomach. He regretted not taking the extra liquor that had been offered to him. It would have been much appreciated to battle the sudden anxiety and fear he felt.

"What do you mean my funeral?" James asked hesitantly.

He didn't want the answer. But already, his mind was swimming. Hades wasn't the kind to joke. He wasn't like Steve, he wasn't like Rue. The man was nothing but serious. And James had no doubt that he'd not said those words as a simple turn of phrase. From what little interaction James had had with Hades, he knew the man was careful about the words he said and the way he said them.

"Exactly what I said," Hades responded coolly. "Though, technically, it's not just your funeral. The world as we know it is coming to an end." He poured himself another drink, swirling the liquid about as he did. "And unless something is done to stop it, ninety-nine percent, if not more, of the world's population will die in the next two days."

"How could that—"

"Though I suppose 'die' in this manner isn't quite the proper term," Hades said as he cut James off. "Physically, their bodies will be dead. Their connection to their flesh and blood severed. But digitally, they'll remain."

He took a drink, perfectly composed, as if he were discussing the fucking weather.

"I suppose that's the silver lining, the justification for it all. It's not mass murder if you don't kill the conscious mind, is it? Giving everyone the opportunity to be seemingly immortal, after all, isn't a crime, is it? Even if the people are condemned to a virtual world against their choosing. In the end, the opportunity to end their consciousness, their being, will still remain on them and not those who destroyed their bodies. Their lives, their agency over themselves as conscious, thinking creatures will remain in their hands…" Hades chuckled darkly. "It's a morally gray area, isn't it? A dilemma brought about by technology in a world that by all means is much too advanced for its own good."

There was a ringing in James's ears as he tried to process what Hades was saying. His fingers were numb, the glass no longer even registering to the now bloodless digits. His vision had narrowed onto Hades as his mind tried to comprehend what he'd just been told. What was Hades saying? What was he rambling about?

"I can see this news isn't sitting well." Hades stood then, leaning far over the table to fill James's glass once more.

James dumbly looked down, noting that his fingers were shaking as he watched the amber liquid fill his glass.

"Go ahead and drink and take a few breaths. I'm not done with what I've got to tell you yet, and I believe you're going to want to listen to all I have to say."

Hades sat back down, and James obediently lifted the drink stiffly to his quivering lips. The burn of the liquor sent a shock through his system and helped center him.

"Then again," Hades continued as James sipped more of the liquor, "no one says you have to do anything with what I tell you. Knowledge is purely that. It's information, short and simple. You can hold onto the secret; you can share it with those around you. And in the end, it's a matter of if the struggle against the impending fate would even be worth it."

James took a few calming breaths as Hades went silent, clearly waiting for James to respond. Once James had calmed his heart, albeit only a little, he opened his mouth, trying to find the right words as countless thoughts and questions fought to escape his lips.

"You're saying the entire world is going to be killed off in the next few days?" he asked slowly. "How? Why? And how do you know that?"

"Good questions. For the short, quick of it all, greed." Hades sighed.

"It's always greed. Always has been, always will be. Those in power crave more of, well, everything. Sadly, the planet we live on, the resources available to us, are all finite. And for the longest time, that meant there would always be a struggle, some give and take, with regard to these very resources. Now, though"—he smiled sadly at James—"there's a way for those elite to finally have it all. To get their cake and eat it too."

He swirled his drink. "Thanks in part to your parent's groundbreaking robotics skills, and of course, the brilliant mind who created the Sleeping Beauty pod. Proving a mind could successfully be fully uploaded into immersion was the final nail in the coffin that set this plan in motion. Somewhat ironic, really, considering that technology had come about from a father's love and dreams to provide a future life for his daughter."

James flinched at that. His parents were involved. He remembered his last message from his parents, the concerned look on his father's face. James was supposed to call them again soon once this immersion session ended in fact. They told him to use Dagger to enter their workspace at home, and then he was supposed to call them.

Had some of what Hades revealed to him been what they were planning to tell him? He felt sick. They couldn't possibly be involved in a scheme to kill people. They weren't bad people. And then… James shook his head, fighting the thoughts that began to surface. Dr. Zephire's technology, his research. He'd done it to save Rue, to give her a life, even if it had been confined to a virtual world. And now… the government was going to use it to… to what?

"I can see on your face that I've struck a nerve." Hades smiled at him, and it was a gentle, pained smile, even as his face continued to flicker. "But no, your parents aren't actively engaged in this. Are they aiding in the plan, though?" He nodded his head as he continued. "Yes, they are. But not as willing participants, mind you. Their only crime is their passion. They wanted to see how far they could push the realm of robotics, and they did just that.

"The government used them, much as it uses all such people, and before they realized it, they'd gone too far. And of course, they couldn't even back out if they wanted to. After all"—he tipped his glass again in James's direction—"they need to keep you safe. Same as Rue's father and his own technology. If there is one skill those in power have mastered above all others, it's finding what a person cherishes most and using it as a tool to control them."

He sighed heavily at that. "Nothing is sacred, and no one is safe in that regard." He chuckled then, a dark, bitter laugh. "Unless, of course, a person purposefully makes sure they've nothing to cherish. Nothing precious or dear. But then, what type of person would willingly live such a life? A sane one? Certainly not."

He looked at James, and for a split second, the face stopped wavering. It was a face of wrinkled skin, dark eyes, and white hair. Frail, emaciated, sunken, and hollow features. Then, the shifting, ever-changing appearance began once again. "Only a madman willing to live amongst the dead would ever truly be able to escape the government and their designs."

"You didn't answer my questions," James began slowly. "None of this makes sense."

"In due time, all will make sense." Hades flicked his wrist, and a holographic image of the Earth appeared above the desk.

There were various landmarks easily visible, and James noticed that it had been sectioned off into an incomprehensible number of grids. There were flickering lights here and there and then larger markers denoting the various countries that had a major stake in the world's government.

"You see all those grids, all those lights?" he said to James. "Those are the population centers. The areas they've crammed the people into. The areas of land they are able to keep hospitable through extreme terraforming while the rest of the world suffers from the last century or more of greed and power struggles. As I'm sure you recall from your schooling, much of the world has become inhospitable since the people ignored the climate clock countdown that struck zero in 2029."

James knew as much. It was also why the outskirts of town quickly grew more and more rundown. There were specialized machines that controlled the weather and climate in each city area, meant to provide the people with clean air and a perfect environment to live in. Anything outside, though, was at the whims of Mother Nature.

Humans had come together in these areas in the 2030s, seeking shelter from the ever-increasing violence of the seasons. It was why travel to and from different cities also required specialized modes of transportation, and again was why immersion was so popular. It let people connect in a way that, logistically, wasn't possible anymore in the real world.

Hades waved his hand again, and all of the lights on the hologram of Earth disappeared. Then new lights appeared, color coded to correspond with the different governing nations, and covered massive expanses of the Earth.

"This represents the land that could be reclaimed by nations if pesky biological factors such as the frailty of the human body could be ignored. Remove the need for clean water, special temperature ranges, and oxygen in some cases, and suddenly you could once again have the entire planet as your plaything. Fixing the damage caused to the planet is something that would take generations…"

Hades had a twisted smile on his face. "But, say, if you got rid of most humans and transferred just the consciousness of the elite into robotic, immortal bodies… Well, they'd be able to walk the planet as gods. They'd be able to reclaim everything that had been taken from them. Everything humans had lost would once again be theirs to own."

"So, what," James tried to grasp the situation, "the people in charge are going to kill everyone just so they can regain access to inhospitable parts of the world? That doesn't make any sense. Why would they even want to do that? The Zone offers everything and more than the world outside the cities ever had. The Zone gives people access to worlds, feelings, events, everything that's not humanely possible in the real world. There's no need to eliminate the population. It makes no sense."

"It makes every bit of sense if you consider the effort, the work, and the resources that go into running not just the Zone, but the real world entirely. It's a hassle, it's work. It's a tightrope that they must tread carefully, balancing between the carrot and the stick to keep the people in line. The Zone is the same. Too many avenues that can pose a risk to those in power. Especially with the rise of new hacking groups, the rise of skilled operators who can navigate the immersed world with impossible skill. Keeping on top of all of these things is a monumental level of work and management.

"And if there is a single lesson learned time and time again that history has taught, it is one simple truth. No government, no matter how powerful, can rule forever. Eventually, something will give, something will change, and the people will rise up. Unless…" He snapped his finger, and the globe disappeared.

"Past all that," Hades added, "everyone in charge is merely human themselves. Meaning, sooner or later, they'd die from old age. Our species is shortsighted. The people in charge, presented with the technology and the promises it holds, want to trade the masses for their elite few to gain immortality. The human race is at an end, and as it stands, only those in charge are going to emerge the winners."

"Still." James was trying hard to process everything, but it was hard. Where was the logic, the reasoning? "If that's what they wanted, why wait? Why has the government taken care of the people so far? Why have they taken us this far, provided everything to this point, if they were just going to kill everyone?"

"That's the thing." Hades smiled. "They're not going to kill everyone. Mass murder of an entire species would leave too bad a taste in their mouths. It's not something they'd be able to agree on. There's a line in the sand that even the members of the government wouldn't cross. This is why they've had to wait until technology hit a point that would make their self-centered dreams a reality. A point where they could get rid of the masses, remove the need to maintain the exhaustive terraforming efforts of the world, and relieve themselves of any and all responsibilities. A point where they could simply put everyone to sleep permanently, without killing them or harming their quality of life.

"To put it another way... they're going to put the masses on ice, locking them forever inside of a virtual landscape. Who knows if, in the future, they'll keep those servers active? Maybe, as time passes, they'll pull people from it as needed, for 'scientific' experiments or twisted perversions. Maybe they won't. But in short, their current plan is to remove the chattel, the masses who are 'lesser' than they are, who they view as wasted breath and resources, from inhabiting the world that they feel they're entitled to claim entirely as their own."

"And," James was piecing it together, "by transferring everyone permanently to DCO... they could maintain some strange sense of morality."

"Narcissism is a hell of a thing, isn't it?" Hades said in a sarcastic tone. "But that's the short of it. The philosophy, the minute details, the cost analysis of everything..." He motioned around the room. "It would take more time than you probably want to waste for me to explain it all to you."

He clapped his hands together as James's eyes wandered. It pulled James's focus back to the man as the sound echoed dully all around.

"As long as they give everyone a virtual existence to replace their physical one—an existence in a world just as real as the one they're leaving behind, where they can exist for longer than they'd ever be able to live in the real world—then they wouldn't be committing a sin. In fact, they'd be able to argue that they'd saved the world. Saved them from all the worries of the flesh. No more worry about food, water, or housing. No sickness, no ailments. People would be, quite literally, freed from their mundane existence in order to live forever, or as long as the server holds out, that is, in a virtual, never-ending world.

"I should mention here that the longevity of full immersion has never been properly stress-tested. I'm sure many would live far longer lives, perhaps centuries or even millennia, but there is always a margin for error. And once the server fails... well, the masses will cease to be a concern. Those in power would commit genocide and call it salvation."

He paused and looked at James, who was processing everything. This was, to say the least, a lot to take in. More than that, it sounded like pure fantasy. And yet, there was something about it. Some strange, sick, twisted logic to it that he kind of hated he could see.

"They'll do this action," Hades said softly, "and pat themselves on the backs, saying they've saved the world. They'll kill everyone and yet, in their eyes, be able to justify it as freeing everyone from the worries, the struggles, and the difficulties of existence.

"Honestly, it could have been a noble vision—except for the fact that no one will be given a choice. Like cattle, the masses will be herded into infinite immersion and left to fend for themselves. Warranted, many may embrace the change, but for those who would have chosen to stay? Chosen to live in true reality for what little time they have? For them, it is a betrayal of the worst kind.

"And that, of course, is before you add in the 'human' aspect to this situation. If those in power are willing to go so far... what's to say they won't later grow tired of their immortal existence on Earth? How long before they turn their sights on those who have been forever imprisoned? And how long before they see them not as humans confined to virtual immortality, but instead... test subjects and digital tools they can do with as they please?

"And all that aside, I cannot imagine the process itself will go smoothly for those suddenly trapped. Society suddenly thrust into such upheaval, with their autonomy stripped for them in such a sickening way—what do you think will become of those locked away? I suspect it will not be pretty. Minds may break, the reality of the situation too much for them to bear.

"Of course, those in power have known this was coming for some time. For them, the transition will be orderly and well prepared. Such are the privileges of the elite. Utopia built on the bloodless removal of the masses.

"They're going to murder everyone in two days' time and tell themselves that what they really did was save the world. All so they, in the very end, can do what no others have done before them: claim the entire planet as their own."

Chapter Seventeen

It wasn't impossible.

That thought was the main driving factor to the cold numbness that once again threatened to overcome James. Sure, society as a whole felt like it had reached the peak of civilization at the moment. Humans had been moved into city areas with terraforming done by the government to create idealistic environments for everyone to live in.

With most everything automated, people were able to go about their daily lives in perfect bliss and harmony. And then, at night, they could immerse themselves and enjoy the virtual world, living their best lives both asleep and awake. What more could they want? On the surface, it all seemed perfect.

But there were shadows to that happiness. The surveillance, for one, that everyone merely accepted. Then there was the existence of the Enforcers, who acted as the bogeymen of the government. The invisible force that stepped in when normal, automated enforcement tools weren't enough to keep order. While the world seemed at its brightest, the shadows it cast, without a doubt, housed the darkest of truths. And what Hades was saying was the darkest of all.

"How?" James managed to ask after a slow drink. He hardly tasted the liquor. "How will they accomplish it? How long have they been planning something like this?"

"That's where your parents, as well as Rue's father, come in," Hades said calmly. "As is the nature of the world, those with brilliance are oft abused. Their creations, their dreams stolen or manipulated to meet the needs or wants of the few. It's a tale as old as time. It happened to Tesla, it happened to Einstein, Oppenheimer, Galson, and so forth."

James recognized… two of those names. But it was still enough to drive home what Hades was getting at. His parents weren't evil. Neither was Rue's father. But their experiments, their brilliance, and their passions were being used in ways that they never intended. It reminded him of what Z had said about his own medical research. How the government had burned his life, literally and metaphorically, to the ground to get its hands on it, to claim it, and own it.

"Are my parents all right?" James asked, suddenly worried. "And Rue's father?"

"For now, yes," Hades replied. "They're smart. Smart enough to play along even when they could sense something was amiss, smart enough to know the dangers of going against what they've been asked to do. And wise enough to know that to do so would put not only themselves in danger, but the ones they love the most."

He cleared his throat. "Part of why the government actually took an interest in protecting you from Cyb3ru5 was to keep their leverage over your parents. It's part of why the operation was mobilized so quickly, and why your friends, Matthew and Rachel, Xander's children, were able to get authorization to bring Agent R into the mix as your protector. The government needed your parents' cooperation, and that gave your parents leverage, albeit slight, to ensure your safety on top of additional concessions."

"That—" It clicked in James's mind then. "That's why they were able to have me placed as a Dungeon Core, isn't it? How they managed to set Rue up as my companion when she wasn't truly an AI."

"A proposal that was favorable for the government and would see additional protection placed on yourself and Ruby, yes."

"Ruby? You mean…" James paused; he'd heard that name before. And then it hit.

She'd said Rue was short for Ruby when she'd introduced herself to Z. James had thought she'd just been playing the part of her Cleric of Blood Vampire character… But was Ruby truly her first name, with Rue merely being her chosen nickname? Another mental note for James to bring up, if he could remember, once all this was done.

"Yes, Ruby Zephire, the girl you know as Rue." The man across the desk took a sip. "The one who proved the Sleeping Beauty pod technology would work. And has continued to work. Dr. Zephire, Rue's father, wanted his daughter to be a part of DCO. It was an integral part of keeping her safe. Neither he, nor your parents, knew the full extent of things, but they could see the writing on the wall. DCO was the best way to keep you kids safe. Only ironically"—Hades let out another dark laugh, a sound James was quickly coming to hate—"they didn't realize how important DCO truly was. It is, after all, meant to be the endgame. The final piece of the puzzle."

James raised an eyebrow as he leaned forward, listening intently. He was trying his hardest not to interrupt, trying not to get off topic. But there was so much he wanted to ask. So much he wanted to know. Was everything Hades telling him true? How did this man, by himself, uncover so much? What resources did he have at his disposal?

"The beginning of the plan started with Dr. Zephire's work. The ability, the proof to the hypothesis of being able to successfully and permanently upload a conscious being to the virtual world. Before, such efforts had been met with mixed success. A shattering of the mind, fragmentation, and of course, the inability to prove if it were truly the same person or merely a copy. Rue is the proof of concept, the 'living' evidence that his process worked, with a singular flaw."

James felt his stomach drop. There was a flaw? Was Rue in danger? His mouth went dry as he inadvertently spoke up. "What flaw?"

"The need for the body to remain alive, of course," Hades answered calmly. "Even if it's existing in a stasis of sorts, supported through various applications of cryogenics and nanotherapy, the body itself is still needed as the failsafe. And considering how fragile such things can be, it was seen as a potentially devastating flaw."

It only took James a moment to figure out the next piece in the puzzle. If the human body was the flaw, given what he knew, given who was involved, the logical step was to replace the need for a human body. And what better way than with a robot?

James had always been proud of his parents. They were the best of the best. Brilliant minds that had done the impossible with robots time and time again. And that fact, one of the things he was most proud of... had brought this whole situation about.

"I see you put it together. It seems you inherited a bit of your parents' gifts, though you've had much less time to truly come into them." Hades took a drink. "In order to truly execute their plan, to ensure they were truly immortal, those in power would need a perfect, surefire way to keep themselves going. They didn't wish to be confined to a virtual world while their bodies slept in a pod. It left them vulnerable. They'd still age and die. Their bodies could still give out.

"But what if Dr. Zephire's technology could be used to transfer their minds permanently, not into a virtual world but into an artificial mind? One that resided within a perfect robotic body? That was the desired, the needed endgame on their path of power and immortality. And to reach that end state, well, they needed to bide their time, and more than that, fund the creation of such a thing. Considering the gift you've recently received from your parents, you can see that research has concluded."

"You know about Dagger?" James asked incredulously.

"I know everything," Hades replied mysteriously. "I've told you time and time again, my business is information. And when it comes to knowledge, mine reigns supreme." He chuckled. "And of course, I've done no small bit of investigating you, even after your aid with Cyb3ru5. Considering I'm sharing this information with you, I needed to make sure I could trust you, or more importantly, ensure I didn't trip any of the government's traps when I contacted you. I've survived this long, as I've stated, by being extremely paranoid and thorough."

James felt violated. There was no other way to put it. This man had just revealed he'd been spying on James, and considering how much information he had, James didn't like how much access into his life Hades somehow had.

"Personal space aside"—Hades waved a hand—"your parents have created bodies capable of acting as perfect surrogates for the human mind. These robots, through their efforts, not only look human, but they can taste, they can feel. Dagger even pales in comparison to the human bodies your parents have created.

"They are the ideal vessels. Un-aging, extremely durable, and each and every one is able to be modified and tweaked to the desired specifications of their user. Capable now, of course, through an automated facility built to handle maintenance and care for these bodies, as well as the construction of additional backup bodies."

"If they've done all that," James argued, "why not build bodies for everyone? Giving the masses such bodies would still eliminate their need to utilize the terraforming technology. They'd no longer need to provide food, water, and so forth. It would accomplish the same thing! They gave everyone immersion pods, why not give everyone bodies as well?" James felt stupid as he went silent. Even as he'd been arguing his point, his mind had pieced it all together. Greed.

"Why would they give humanity bodies with which they could rise up against the powers that be? Why would they give the masses immortal bodies like their own? Why do such an act if it means they'd have to then share everything with those people? Doesn't quite fit with the 'haves and have nots' mindset of those in power.

"Besides, that would waste valuable resources and spare parts that they may want to use later on down the road for themselves. The government only gives what it can afford to. And anything given freely, any act of benevolence, often has a price tag attached. Like you said… they gave everyone immersion pods after all."

Ice clinked in Hades's glass as he took a final drink, emptying it of the amber liquor. "The government sent out pods to all of humanity to ensure that when the time came, they could trap everyone within the virtual world. Within, more importantly, a single virtual world. And then they waited until your parents' research and projects were complete. Once everything was complete, the government would then have everything in place to enact their plan. With quite literally the press of a button, they'd be able to remove all of mankind from their eyesight."

"That's why they've authorized the 48-hour immersion," James said slowly. "Why they've initiated the special Dungeon Wars event. It's to ensure everyone is logged in, everyone is immersed, so that they can trap everyone all at once."

"That's correct. It ensures they can eliminate the masses and any strange outliers, any few who for some strange reason aren't caught in the snares… Well, no plan can be perfectly bloodless. And the moment they switch off the terraforming machines, the stragglers will have other problems to deal with."

A sad smile crept onto Hades's face, and his tone softened as he continued. "If you wish to do anything with this knowledge, if you wish to attempt to stop this, well, the clock is quite literally ticking away." Hades folded his hands together on the desk, and looked deeply into James's eyes.

"So, James. If there were a slim chance to save mankind from this plan, would you take it? Would you take a risk to save the many? Or would you rather do nothing and spend a potential eternity in the world of DCO, safe and sound? Well, relatively safe anyway, data degradation being what it is…"

James was quiet for a long moment. If he was being honest, all he wanted was to live forever in DCO with Rue. That sounded like a utopia to him. He'd give almost anything to do just that. Everything he cared about existed within DCO. Even his parents, technically, were in DCO.

The real world had nothing in it that James couldn't access as well within DCO. There were no physical ties that bound him to the mortal coffin that was his human body.

And yet there was a part of him that knew full well now that Hades had told him all of this that he didn't really have a choice. What type of monster would he be if he kept this information quiet and did nothing about it?

He wouldn't be able to live with himself. Especially if, as he felt Hades was implying, there was a small chance he could save the others. Save the world. There was no saying that they'd all get to live happily ever after within immersion. Nothing to say that after the government had trapped them, they'd live unmolested forever within DCO.

If they were willing to trap the entire world within immersion just so they could have the planet to themselves, what was to say they wouldn't come along later with plans to put the billions of conscious minds to use for their own sick amusement or gain? Stuck in a server, mere data in the cloud, the masses would have no defense should the questionable 'morals' or the elite be fully abandoned. No... James couldn't trust the government, the people willing to go to such means, to just let the masses live 'happily ever after'.

Nor did it feel right to stand by while a small section of the population was given guaranteed immortality, eternal bodies with backups and fail-safes, while the rest of the world relied on the whims of a server-based data prison. Technology could fail; the elites could ignore its maintenance or one day *make* it fail. The elites could... James didn't want to keep thinking about it. All he knew was that it wasn't right. It wasn't fair.

James sighed, hating himself for what he was about to say. All he wanted, damnit, was to live a normal, happy life. Not to act like some storybook hero.

"As much as I feel I'm going to regret saying this," James said, the words slow, spoken through gritted teeth. "If you're saying there is a chance to stop this, to save the world," he sighed, heavily, "I want to hear it."

Chapter Eighteen

A small smile formed on Hades's face as the mysterious man leaned back slowly in his chair. He grabbed the white mask from his desk once more and held it up to his face, looking through the eyeholes towards James. It was disturbing to say the least.

"So young," Hades said from behind the mask, his voice suddenly distorted. "And yet already willing to carry such a burden." He laughed then, the sound weirdly digital and deep as it passed through the mask. "Perhaps you'll be able to accomplish that which I couldn't at your age." He lowered the mask back on the desk and shrugged. "Or at the very least, find fulfillment in knowing that you tried."

James didn't know what Hades was referencing, and at that moment, he didn't care. There were more pressing matters at hand than the man's cryptic behavior.

"Because of who you are, or more accurately, who you are connected with and your location, you are the only one who has any hope of stopping this plan for a few reasons." Hades held up a single gloved finger. "First, your connections. When it comes to connections, you, young man, have more people in the right places than anyone else at this moment. Not only do you have personal access to both Rue and Steve, but you've powerful allies in Xander's children and that dangerously brilliant spitfire Felecia."

James couldn't help but wince at the last part. He'd made the mistake of calling Fel Felecia once. And it hadn't gone over well.

"Last, but certainly not least," Hades continued, "your parents. All these people are in positions to aid you, and by working together, maybe, just maybe, you can devise a strategy to, at the very least, postpone this mass extinction event."

"What about Xander?" James dared to ask. "He's the head developer on DCO. Wouldn't he have the most connections in this matter? He even told me once that he'd been pretty close to my father at some distant point in the past. Can't you reach out to him to help? I mean, if it's really as dire as you've implied… I feel like we can't be too picky on resources."

A small flicker crossed Hades's face, which was impossible to read due to his constantly changing features. Then he sighed. "Xander cannot help anyone anymore. Even if he wished it."

"What do you mean?" James pressed.

He knew the developer was reportedly locked away in some government facility, but if Hades could get to James, surely the mysterious man had a way to get to Xander? Or was that just James being hopeful and looking for an out? Xander's entire personality seemed suited for the grandiose 'savior of humanity' role.

Sure, he had been nothing but a nightmare to James, and yet from all he'd learned about the former pro-gamer turned developer, Xander ultimately loved DCO more than anyone. His rage, his actions had been a result of his passion, fueled by a feeling that his precious project had been taken away from him and that he was no longer the one with the final say for his baby.

"Ask Steve," Hades said softly, "he knows." His voice dropped even lower. "He was there, after all."

Before James could press that line of questioning, Hades held up a second finger.

"The second factor that has put you in this unique position is your physical location."

James raised an eyebrow. "My physical location?"

"Indeed. As you know, you were moved to your current location so that your parents could be closer to their work."

"Yeah. They'd gotten their dream position, with all the funding and freedom they could need…"

His parents had told him as much when they'd mentioned the move. Even still, they'd told him that they didn't need to move if he didn't want to. Even with their dream before them, they'd offered to put James first. He'd obviously told them to take the job, and they'd moved. Now that he had an inkling of what the dream job entailed, he had to wonder if they regretted that move as much as he was beginning to.

"Exactly. Your parents' work, their factory, the location of so many critical parts to this nefarious plan... it exists within the mountains you see daily. An old military complex built during the Cold War, now turned into an extremely secure facility for use by the government and those few elite who have bought their way into favorable positions.

"It's there that the infrastructure linked to their robotic bodies exists. Where the capsules that will be used to transfer the consciousness of those who would claim godhood and superiority over the masses exist. Additionally, Ruby Zephire's body is there, displayed as proof of concept. And finally, there is the infrastructure that maintains the server for DCO on this continent, as well as an emergency kill switch for the others."

That... was a lot. "All of that is in a single place? Doesn't that seem a bit... shortsighted?"

"It's easier to protect fewer locations," Hades said, "especially with the levels of surveillance and information gathering at the hands of the government. Furthermore, the location was built to withstand the crude nuclear weapons of the mid-1900s. They expanded it deeper into the mountain, ensuring it was even more secure and durable.

"And keeping everything safe within a mountain, protected from outside attacks, as well as things like the weather and climate changes, makes it the perfect location. Not to mention... considering it exists within the mountain itself, it's impossible for outside surveillance efforts to glimpse even a fraction of what exists within that facility."

"If you say so," James said. Part of him believed Hades. Hell, such things were pretty commonplace in some of the more conspiracy-prone portions of the internet. But that was what also made him a bit concerned. Surely, if it were all as hush-hush as Hades put it, the government wouldn't let the information exist for public dissemination, even as conspiracy theories, would they?

Then again... if it were all labeled as crazy conspiracy theories, people would treat them as just that. If everything mysteriously disappeared now, it would cause more concern, trigger more worry than the information being viewed as half-baked fears or products of paranoid people on the internet.

"I can provide you with schematics, maps, and detailed information after our conversation to prove my claims valid," Hades said with a shrug. "Or you can ask your parents during your call with them in the morning that you've got planned."

The way Hades said it so casually, confirming again just how much he'd been spying on James, made James's skin crawl. This man's information gathering skills were beyond creepy.

"Do I want to ask how you have that information?"

"The information on the facility I gathered when I finally managed to crack their defenses and access the heart of all of their data. The very system that gave me the final pieces needed to unravel the full extent of their plans. But that's probably not what you're asking about. And if that's the case, with regards to what you're actually asking…" Hades shrugged. "Nothing is secret to the eyes of the government. Just consider yourself lucky that I've been surveilling you through their back doors and scrubbing some of the more damning things you've let slip."

James opened his mouth to ask further questions, but Hades silenced him as he raised a third finger.

"Enough about that, though. The final reason you are the only one capable of handling this situation," he said ominously, "is due to your status as the top Dungeon Core. It gives you unprecedented access to the other players of the game. Furthermore, with all of the attention on you, especially during the upcoming event, it will give you the perfect smokescreen in order to put things into motion.

"If you pull it off, you'll be able to move forward fast enough that the government cannot stop you. If you fail though…" Hades shrugged again in a very uncaring way. "You'll likely cease to exist, as will those who worked with you. But even then… even if you failed, at least you'll have failed trying till the very end. And that, in and of itself, is something to be proud of."

"While I'm sure that's meant to sound noble," James said, fighting the panic within, "I think I'd much rather succeed if at all possible."

"A wise choice," Hades said. "Though that's also the sentiment I believe most have when they attempt to stop evil. And who knows how many have failed and had their existences erased from the history books? After all, only the victors are ever around to tell the *truth* of any given conflict. Let's hope your truth will be the one that gets recorded."

Chapter Nineteen

James blinked a few times as his world came into focus. He was back in his dungeon, in the hot springs, surrounded once more by Rue and Steve.

His mind took a moment longer to return to the present as the warmth of the hot spring caressed his body. He shivered, the chill of everything he'd just learned stronger than even the warm, calming waters, and mentally prepared himself for the task at hand.

"Where the—" Steve started.

"Are you—" Rue's voice began, full of concern.

James cut them both off. "We need to talk."

The two closed their mouths, sensing the urgency in his voice, and waited. James wasn't forceful. He never had been. Of the three, he was definitely the most passive. So the urgency in his voice spoke volumes.

"Steve." James focused on the developer, who looked ridiculous in his pineapple-themed swimming trunks, fruity drink in hand. "Can you create a private space for us? An extremely secure one?"

"Can Dickens fly?" Steve asked with an obvious attempt at a joke to lighten the mood around James. "I thought you were about to ask me something hard."

"I'm serious," James said, the joke landing flat. There was so much at stake for humor. The entire world... How he wished with all his heart and soul that he could have just been a regular player in DCO.

But no, that wasn't something he truly wished. Even with everything that had happened to him, even with the literal fate of the world now resting on his shoulders, he'd not trade any of it because then he wouldn't have met Rue. And Rue, well… she was his everything.

Steve took a long, slow sip from his drink, his eyes watching James carefully as he did. When he finished, he let out a sigh. "I can make a room that's more secure than probably ninety-nine percent of all digital spaces out there."

"Not a hundred percent?" James pressed. "The security of the room is vital," he said hurriedly. "If you're not confident, I don't think—"

"I say ninety-nine percent," Steve said, stopping James, "but it is damn near a hundred. Only Hades himself could probably crack into it. Within DCO, what I can and cannot do are practically godlike."

James nodded. "Good then. We need a room, the sooner the better."

"I'll get to it." Steve set his drink down and stood, the water rippling around him. "I'll double check everything as well to ensure it's as secure as possible. Entry will be limited to unique encryption, so be on the lookout for a message from me." He glanced from James to Rue and back to James. "I'm assuming this is all related to whatever Hades summoned you for?"

James didn't dare say anything else out loud. Instead, he just nodded once, quick and sharp, to Steve.

The developer sighed. "I was afraid of that," he muttered to himself. His hands were already out, typing furiously on an invisible keyboard as he disappeared, leaving James and Rue alone.

"How bad is it?" Rue asked softly as she moved close to James. She draped her arms over his shoulders and scooted behind him. Her mouth was close to his left ear, her breath warm on him as she pulled him close.

He knew this was all virtual, but the realism, the feeling of the body heat from her, mingling with the heat of the hot springs and the moisture in the air, felt perfectly real to him. When he took in a breath, he caught a mixture of cinnamon and roses, a pleasant, invigorating scent that he could only assume was a perfume Rue was wearing.

"It's bad," James whispered, not fully trusting himself to not accidentally spill anything.

Hades had implied that James had let important information slip out already. With how dire everything was, he knew he needed to be extra cautious. With everything on the line, there was no room for error. No room for a lapse in judgment. That probably meant no more liquor for James until everything was over.

Rue leaned her chin against his shoulder, and he felt the pressure from the sharp bone and her weight as she rested on him. This was as real as anything he'd ever experienced outside of immersion. Did he really want to stop the government? If he did nothing, then what? So what if he and the others couldn't return to the real world? Dungeon Core Online was perfect.

"And of course it involves us." She let out a heavy sigh as she said the words.

Rue was smart enough to know when something was amiss. And James knew she could tell immediately based on how he was acting just how serious it was. That was why she was comforting him now in her own way, rather than poking and prodding and goofing around.

"Unfortunately," James said. He looked at the reflection of the two of them in the hot spring. His eyes looked tired, and there were visible bags under them. It looked like he hadn't slept all night, like he'd just woken from a traumatic nightmare.

Behind him, Rue's face held a look of concern as well. Her normal smile was gone, her lips pressed in a thin line, her eyes deep in thought. She was beautiful. Even with the entire world at stake, in that moment, Rue was still the main thing on his mind. He reached up and touched one of her hands gently, threading his fingers between hers, and leaned his head back into her.

"No matter what happens," he began softly. With his head tilted backward, he could just barely look into her eyes. She'd tilted her head, chin still on his shoulder, to better look at him as well, and they held the look for a long moment. "I want you to know that nothing changes."

"Oh?" Her eyes searched his, then she smiled. A small, slight smile. Barely noticeable, really. "What do you mean by that?"

James felt his voice crack, his throat clenching as he fought emotions. He took a deep breath, losing himself in Rue's eyes as he spoke again. They'd grown so close over such a small amount of time. And yet he'd never been so certain. Never been so sure about anything as he was about Rue. She and he were meant to be together forever.

"No matter what," James began again, "all that matters to me is you." He watched her lips twitch upwards a little more. "In the end," James continued before his courage abandoned him, "I love you, and everything I'm doing, I'm doing for you. For us. For our future."

Her smile crept upwards a little more, and yet in her eyes, there was a sorrow. She gently lifted their entwined hands towards her lips and kissed his knuckles gingerly. She whispered softly, her face now hidden from him as she spoke.

"I love you too, James," she said, barely audible. Her fingers tightened around his as she kissed his knuckles again. "You saved me," she began, and he felt like he could hear her voice crack with emotion, though it was impossible to be certain with how quietly she was speaking. "You saved me in more ways than you'll ever know."

He felt moisture on his knuckles. Was it from her tears? Or simply the humid air of the hot springs?

"But you need to live your life, make your decisions for yourself, silly," her voice cracked again. "Otherwise, somewhere along the line, you'll come to resent me."

He returned the pressure as she squeezed his fingers. All that existed in the moment was James and Rue. No one else. Nothing else.

"I would never," James said.

"How can you be certain?" Rue asked.

"I can't," he laughed, "and yet I'll gladly spend an eternity proving that I won't."

Rue laughed at that, and he felt her head shake from side to side. He was pretty sure she was wiping her teary eyes on their knuckles with the motion.

"Eternity is a long time," she said.

"And yet," James countered, "it still won't feel like enough time."

His words hung in the air, lingering far longer than he felt they reasonably should as the two sat there. They said nothing else. He didn't mind. James knew as he waited that once Steve had the room set up, there wouldn't be time for moments like this anymore.

This was the calm before the storm. The last truly peaceful moment he would have before everything would begin moving forward. Rue could sense it too, and he knew she was savoring the moment just as he was. And they remained that way, taking comfort in the proximity of each other, until eventually, Steve's message came through.

Chapter Twenty

The whole time James spoke, Rue and Steve remained silent. They sat in an office-sized room that Steve had prepared for them. Its walls were dark and featureless. The only furniture in the room was a handful of chairs and couches set up in a circle around a table. It was clear he'd thrown it together quickly to serve as a meeting area.

Steve sat in a leather armchair, while James and Rue sat on a dark, cloth-covered couch. James had been standing the whole time he'd been speaking, but now that he'd finally finished, he'd collapsed onto the couch. Rue's hand rested on his leg as he leaned back onto the couch, fighting back tears. Tears of frustration, tears of fear, tears of anger. It was all so unfair.

"You don't seem too surprised," Rue said to Steve.

The old man was looking at them, and he did seem rather unaffected by everything. Or at least, Steve was reacting with a lot less emotion than James had expected.

"When you've seen all I've seen," Steve began slowly, rubbing his temples with his hands as he spoke, "it's really not a question of how terrible man can be, but more, when will the greatest catastrophe come to pass." He sighed, his shoulders slumping. "I'd really hoped we had more time."

"So you knew this was going to happen?" James leaned towards Steve. "You knew the government would do this?"

"This exact scenario?" Steve shook his head. "Hardly. But it wasn't outside of the realm of possibility. With every technological step forward, I ran countless doomsday scenarios through my mind. Being a developer, it's my job to brainstorm, to think, to imagine what *can* be. And that particular trait of my mind likes to do the same with everything in the world. The moment the governments of the world came together into a singular entity..." He shrugged. "It was only a matter of time."

"If you've brainstormed the possibility," Rue said as James processed what Steve was saying, "then you should have solutions? Contingencies yourself? Can you shut DCO down? Wouldn't that ensure this plan can't work?"

Steve laughed, and it was a dark laugh. "It's not that simple." He shook his head. "Hades told James the truth about everything. Hell, he told James things I didn't know, things I hadn't even speculated. And yet I can assure you that everything he said, as far as I know, is the absolute truth. And that includes the fact that, short of tampering with the physical servers in the old mountain, there's shit all we can really do from our end to stop people from logging into the game."

"You're one of the lead developers," Rue pressed. "You wrote back-doors into the game for yourself, and yet you can't bring the server down from the inside? It would at least buy us time."

Steve shrugged. "I wish I could."

Rue paused for a moment and glanced from James to Steve, her lips pursed. "What about Xander?" she asked. "If you can't do it, surely he could."

A pained expression crossed Steve's face. James hadn't mentioned what Hades had said about Xander. It had actually slipped from his mind. But Rue's statement had pulled it right back to the front.

"That reminds me," James began, looking hard at Steve. "Hades said Xander can't help anyone at all. He said you know why. That you were there?"

"Of course he did," Steve muttered. He sighed, stood, and turned his back to James and Rue. Only then did he begin speaking again, his voice devoid of all emotion. "Xander is no more."

"What do you mean he is no more?" James asked hesitantly. The way Steve was acting was so unlike the developer. He was being evasive, cryptic.

"It means exactly what it sounds like. Xander doesn't exist anymore. He's gone," Steve's voice dropped to a whisper, and cracked, "forever."

"The government killed him?" Rue asked hesitantly. "They killed Xander?"

"I thought he was supposed to be confined to a cell," James added. "Solitary confinement or whatnot. You told us something along those lines."

"It was a lie," Steve's voice cracked again. "What happened to him is crueler than death."

"What do you..." James trailed off as his mind worked to figure it out. Two words passed his lips, "Truth Serum."

The terrifying liquid that forever stole someone's free will. They'd become a puppet, a shade of their former self. Numb, incapable of free will, incapable of free thought.

They merely became living, breathing records of everything they had been. They existed in a state that would answer questions and give information to whoever had access to them, but could do nothing else. Worst of all, Truth Serum's effects were irreversible and permanent.

Steve's body flinched at the words, his shoulders stiffened. He turned around then, and tears fell freely down his face. He looked broken. Like he was reliving a nightmare.

"They made me do it," he said softly. "They made me inject him with the serum. It was the only way they'd let me see him. And I needed to see him one last time." He collapsed back into his chair. "He was my best friend once, did you know that?" More sobbing as he put his face in his hands. "I'm Rachel and Matthew's godfather."

"And yet you still did it," Rue's words were damning. "You claim he was your best friend. Yet you injected him with the very thing that would erase who he was. A liquid lobotomy from which there is no escape." She started to stand, her anger visible.

James reached out and grabbed her hand, pulling her back down. Steve was broken before him. And he couldn't afford that right now. He knew that. He also knew, in his heart, that if Steve had done it, he'd done it for a good reason. There had to be a reason. Steve was a lot of things, but he wasn't a monster.

"It was to ensure Rachel and Matthew were safe," Steve said, not looking at Rue as he spoke. "In his final moments, he confirmed in his own words that killing him would leak the information he had. Something we knew. But he also proved in that moment, to the government more than anything, that he'd been acting alone. That no one else could be held accountable for his actions, his crimes.

"I was there on not only my best friend's behalf, but to ensure I could protect the people he cared about the most. So yes, I stole his very being from him by injecting him with the Truth Serum, but I also saved the ones he cherished the most in the process." He laughed, a bitter, dry laugh. "It also needed to happen to clear my name."

"Even though he'd fired you?" James asked. "They still believed you'd been a part of his plan with Cyb3ru5?"

"The government doesn't like to leave any stone unturned. You don't become as powerful as they are without being thorough and paranoid. By injecting him with the Truth Serum, I cleared my name. And they were able to question him and confirm additionally that Rachel and Matthew weren't at fault."

"Surely if you hadn't agreed, they still could have learned that by questioning him," Rue muttered. "You didn't have to do that to your so-called best friend."

"If he'd asked me to, if he'd made it seem either of them was in danger in that moment," Steve responded bitterly, "I had intended to kill him when I got close enough to inject the Truth Serum. It would have forfeited my life, sure, but his secrets would have died with him, and the government would have been too busy dealing with his leaked information to pursue Rachel and Matthew without any evidence."

Steve took a deep breath and wiped his eyes. He looked at Rue and James, the most raw, vulnerable form of the developer that either had ever seen. He took another breath, and then another, each one stuttering a little less. Once he'd calmed himself, once he'd prepared himself, he spoke again.

"Hades' plan is a solid one," he said slowly, "and if we're going to make it work, we need to begin right away. Which means..." He waved his hand, his eyes shifting to the side at some screen as he worked quickly with his virtual keyboard. "We need to get the others in here, now, so that we can begin our efforts." He paused his typing and took a moment to fix his gaze on James and Rue. "One mistake, one misstep from here on out could spell the end of everything. You know that, right?"

"I do," James said, and his hand, which still held Rue's, tightened. "We do," he said again firmly.

"Well then." Steve offered them a smile, though it was a shadow of his normal shit-eating grin, "Let's gather the rest of our little chaos party together, shall we?"

Chapter Twenty-One

"I swear to everything that this better really be a life-or-death matter," Fel's words entered the space before her body even fully finished appearing within the room.

The fiery redhead was wearing tight, black shorts, and an even tighter shirt, both of which left little to the imagination. James glanced away, not wanting to stare at Alex's girlfriend, only to notice Rue who was staring and had no such qualms.

"I can assure you, it is," Steve said, the developer motioning for her to take a seat.

"It better be," she huffed. She gave Rue a quick smile and wink before she waved her hand and changed her clothing. "I'm going to have a hard time explaining to Alex why I had to leave our latest session with his class trainer early. It's hard enough living life as a secret badass agent without you three all pulling me into more shit." She crossed her legs, which were now covered in black leather pants with studs running along the side. "So, out with it."

James felt heat rising to his face as his mind imagined what she and Alex had been doing. He'd looked into the Devilkin Summoner Class trainer, an NPC named Lillith. He also knew Alex and Fel had a rather... intimate relationship with that AI.

"We can't start just yet. You're not the only one we summoned," Steve responded. "You're just the first to arrive."

"You really shouldn't have said it was a dire emergency then," she countered. "If I'd known I could take my sweet ass time, I would have." She looked back towards James. "What'd you fuck up this time?"

"Er," James cleared his throat, but before he could say anything, Rue cut in.

"What makes you think James fucked up?" she said defensively. "And are you implying he caused Cyb3ru5 to go after him? That he's the one who made Xander have it out for him?"

"I'm just saying, Rue, that your boyfriend has a natural talent for finding himself in danger that is far above what a normal kid his age should be in. Either he's causing it himself, or he's just the unluckiest person I've ever come across."

"Unfortunately, I think it's the latter," James muttered with a bit of angst. "Seriously, I can assure you all that this is bullshit I would much rather do without. All I wanted to do was play DCO. That's it."

"Well as the saying goes, if not for bad luck, you wouldn't have any luck, eh?" Fel sighed and crossed her arms, turning away from James and Rue to Steve. "Who else did you call, then?" She made a few motions with her fingers, and then frowned. She did it again and frowned even deeper. "And what the hell is with the permissions in this room? Can't a girl get a drink?'

"Sorry, Felecia," Steve said, and James flinched again as he looked at Fel.

He half-expected her to explode at the developer for using her full name, but she didn't react at all. So Steve could use her full name, but James couldn't?

"Because of what we're going to discuss, this room has the maximum-security features that I could implement on it. That means all visitors, no matter how skilled, can only adjust their physical appearance and clothing, but cannot bring any other objects into the space. And," he sighed, "when you hear what we have to say, you'll see why there's no liquor allowed. Clear minds are an absolute must right now."

"If you wanted my mind completely clear," Fel responded with a wry smile, "you really should have let me finish what I was doing before I came here." She laughed at that, and then let out a heavy sigh. "Why do I get the feeling I'm going to regret involving myself with James?" She looked at James. "Seriously, you've caused me nothing but grief, you know that?"

"Sorry," James offered with a shrug. "But to be fair, I didn't specifically try and bring you in. That was Matt and Rachel. You're the one who's a secret badass agent, as you said so yourself. So things like this kind of come with the job title, don't they?"

Fel prepared to say something but closed her mouth as two more figures appeared in the room. She glanced at them as their forms began to materialize and smirked. "Speak of the devils, eh?"

Sure enough, Matt and Rachel had just arrived in the secret space. The twin siblings glanced about, first taking note of Steve, then Fel, and then James and Rue. Matt looked like he'd aged by a few years since James had last seen him. Rachel, on the other hand, seemed to still be the same bright-eyed, brilliant version of herself.

If he had to guess, Matt was taking on more of the role as head developer for DCO than Rachel was. Or maybe one of them was dealing with the developer side of things, and the other the business side of things, and Matt had gotten the more exhaustive of those roles? James didn't know what all their new responsibilities were since they'd inherited the position following Xander's arrest.

"Considering everyone in the room," Matt said slowly as he walked towards one of the available couches. Rachel followed, her eyes glancing from James and Rue to the empty space on their couch, before she seemed to make a decision and settled beside her brother. "I'm going to assume this really is dire?"

"It would explain the security on the room," Rachel said with a nod, her own hand hovering in mid-air as she possibly had been attempting to summon a drink like Fel had.

"You would assume correctly," Steve said somberly. "But before we go into the full details of everything," he faltered, his voice cracking, "there's something else I need to tell the two of you. Something that needs to be said so that you two understand the true severity of what's going on."

He looked away from them, changing his focus to Fel as he continued. "And I'm sure what I'm about to say next will also drive home the point to you as well that being summoned here, right now, this quickly, was indeed a matter of life or death."

"I'm listening," Fel said, waving for Steve to continue, "go on."

He looked back at Matt and Rachel, who were watching their godfather intently. There was obvious concern and worry on their faces. James knew that the three of them were close. Rachel and Matt, who had originally run the Candy Dungeon under the alias of BLANK, had actually worked with Steve on an elaborate plot to remove Xander from his position in DCO and to get Steve his own position within the game. The first domino, now that James thought about it, that had ultimately led to eternal, drug-induced lobotomy.

"Your father will never return," Steve said solemnly, returning his gaze back to Rachel and Matt. "Xander 'X-Ray' Raymondson is gone forever."

"How," Matthew asked, somewhat stoic, "do you know that?"

"The government authorized the use of Truth Serum," Steve said, "and I was the one to administer it to him." He looked like he wanted to look away, and yet he held his gaze firm, his eyes never leaving the two. "His final words, his final moments, were spent asking me to tell you that he loved you and that he was sorry."

Chapter Twenty-Two

"Serves him right," Fel's tone was cold, her words heavy in the air.

Matt and Rachel said nothing, their faces unreadable masks.

"He pushed the government too far. His arrogance was his own down-fall." She picked at her fingers. "And you won't see me feeling sorry for him after all the problems he created."

"Fel," James said, surprised by her callous nature. "Read the room."

She looked around and shrugged. "In my line of work, things like this happen. We don't have the luxury of happy fantasies. And"—she nodded towards the siblings—"I'm pretty sure they had already figured it was a possible outcome. Unlike you, James, they're not naïve."

He turned to look at Matt. Sure enough, the older boy nodded, though his face was still an unreadable mask. Rachel seemed a little less 'statue-esque', her eyes shining ever so slightly. But beyond that, she didn't let any emotion show.

"Thank you for telling us," Matt said as he looked back at Steve. "I can't imagine that was easy on you."

"It wasn't," Steve's voice cracked. "And thank you, Matt." He heaved a heavy sigh. "Really, thank you."

"Our father's fate aside," Matt cleared his throat, "why have we been called here? Not to understate the gravity of that news." He lightly touched Rachel's hand, and the two siblings shared a comforting moment. "I cannot assume that was the only reason we were called here." He looked towards Fel. "Especially since Fel's here as well."

She offered him a smile. "Sorry to hear about your dad, Matt," she said with a small shrug. "It sucks."

Matt's lip curled up slightly at that. "You always sucked at dealing with people's emotions, you know."

"Guess that's why our fling didn't last long," Fel said with a chuckle.

"Uh huh," Matt left it at that, and James couldn't help but do a double take.

The two of them had been together? He knew that the siblings knew Fel personally; they were the ones who'd hired her to protect James during the Cyb3ru5 situation. But he hadn't realized they'd actually been a 'thing.' How would Alex take it if he knew his current girlfriend had once been with the guy who was currently running DCO?

"Don't even think of mentioning it to him," Fel said, as if she could read James's mind. "It was just two kids having fun in the past."

"Really," Rachel cut in before Matt or Fel could add more, "now isn't the time." She shot Fel a look, and then her own brother. "Even if it's helping cope with the news." Her tone was gentler this time. "But really, we can't stay away for too long." She looked back at Steve. "So, what's going on?"

"That's not my story to tell," Steve directed everyone's attention immediately to James.

The weight of their gazes made him squirm. He'd enjoyed not being the center of attention for once, especially given whom he was around.

It was hard to feel like the most important person in the room, hell, to even feel like you mattered when you were surrounded by people of their caliber. The literal wonder kids of the developer of DCO who now ran it. One of, if not the best developers of DCO itself. A secret agent whose skills would make a movie spy jealous. And of course, Rue.

"Get to it then, James," Fel said, making a motion with her hand as if encouraging him to start talking. "Like I said, it better be good for what you're making me miss."

James cleared his throat, immediately seeking eye contact elsewhere. He focused on Rachel, who smiled gently at him, and offered him a small nod.

"Whatever it is, James," she said softly, "we're ready to hear it."

James took a deep breath and grabbed hold of Rue's hand for comfort. She squeezed it gently, a simple reminder that he wasn't alone. They were in this together. From now, until whatever the outcome was that they reached, she'd be by his side.

"As everyone here knows," James began slowly, "Dungeon Core Online is a project that has large ties with the government."

Fel snorted. "Understatement of the year," she said under her breath.

James ignored her, and continued, "However, I have learned the reasons for the government's involvement in the project, and what's more, that their endgame is now upon us." He looked at Fel this time, speaking slowly, "Hades has informed me that the government intends to trap everyone's minds within DCO while simultaneously killing their bodies."

Fel's mood immediately changed, and she sat straight up in her chair. Her complexion paled as she looked at him. "Say what now?"

James looked at Rachel and Matthew, both of whom were looking at him intently.

"How—" Rachel began, before Matthew cut her off.

"The Sleeping Beauty pod tech?" the male portion of BLANK asked.

James nodded in confirmation and went into the full details. Everyone stayed silent until he'd completed his explanation.

"Are you certain about this?" Matthew asked.

"Considering that his source is Hades, I hate to say that it's probably all true," Fel responded on behalf of James. "Anyone else, I'd question. But Hades..."

"It makes sense too," Steve said to add to the argument. "With everything going on in the background, everything I know from a developer standpoint, and all I've seen of their facilities... All the pieces paint a pretty damning picture once you know what the end goal is."

"Knowing your parents' skill," Fel added, looking at James, "the bodies those rich fucks are going to have are probably going to be crazy awesome, huh." She let out a low whistle, almost like she was jealous. "That robo dog of yours is impressive, I can only imagine what the human bodies your parents have created are like."

"Yeah, Hades essentially said Dagger pales in comparison to the actual bodies my parents have created," James confirmed.

"I'm going to assume," Rachel began, drawing James's attention away from Fel towards her. She was taking stock of everyone around the room, and it was clear she had just finished processing everything. "With everyone gathered here, there's a plan at the very least to try and stop the government's goal from becoming a reality?"

"Well." James shifted slightly on the couch. "That's why everyone's been called here. Hades has shared as much as he claims he could, but I need everyone's thoughts and input if we are going to make a plan that has some sort of chance at success." He paused, and took a deep breath, trying to steady himself. "You're the only ones I can trust. And if we can't do it"—he shrugged—"then I don't think anyone could."

"And to think," Steve said with a forced chuckle, keeping the weight of James's words from settling in the room, "DCO was supposed to be my swan song before retirement."

James felt himself grin ever so slightly at the dark humor.

Damnit, Steve.

Chapter Twenty-Three

The discussion ran for hours, and by the time they ended, James was exhausted. His mind hurt. His heart hurt. This was more than he'd ever wanted to have to deal with. More than anyone should have to deal with.

How did someone carry the weight of the world on their shoulders? How was it fair that anyone, or any small group of people, should have to decide the fate of the masses? In the stories, it made sense. But in real life, it was just bullshit.

"Shall we head back to the dungeon?" Rue asked softly.

Everyone else had parted ways. The mood had been heavy, and while Steve had started the planning off with a joke, no one had felt much like joking by the end. Each and every one of them had tasks they needed to see to in preparation for what would come. And time, even extended as it was thanks to immersion and time dilation, was not on their side.

"I— I suppose," James said with a heavy sigh. He didn't want to head back. He wanted to stay here, to just ignore his problems, ignore the world's problems, and just spend more time with Rue. But he couldn't.

"No matter what," Rue offered him a small smile as she spoke, "in the end, we'll all still be together."

James looked at Steve. The developer shrugged. That was one of the last topics they'd discussed. What would failure look like? If they did nothing, the government, the powers that be, would win. Everyone would be trapped forever within DCO. And if James and his friends were successful, well, DCO may no longer exist.

But while the game everyone seemed to love and enjoy would be gone, it would still mean no one would be trapped eternally within immersion. Other than Rue...

But what happened if they put their plan in action and failed? Death was a possibility. They were going up against the government. They would be facing down the unknown. Sure, Hades provided him with a layout of the secret facility and details of the expected guards and security measures. But would they all be listed? Even if they were, that still meant dozens of Enforcers, various security bots, and anti-personnel traps and measures set in place.

Death was a very real threat. But death wasn't the only threat. Failure could mean much, much worse than death itself. If they failed, if they were captured, thwarted, or stopped... there was no reason for the government to show them mercy.

No reason for the government to do something simple like shoving them into an immersion pod and trapping them forever alongside the rest of mankind. To think so, to dream that would be the 'worst case', was foolhardy.

If they failed and weren't killed outright, there was another fate James and the others had envisioned. They could receive the same punishment that had been dealt to Xander. A chemical-induced lobotomy, trapping them forever within their minds, leaving them forever at the whims of the very ones they were seeking to stop. Death would be a mercy. Death would be the preferred punishment, if they did fail.

Rue knew that as well. Hell, she was in a worse position than James and any of the others. He didn't know what controls existed to deal with her, but he knew there were options. Xander had once forcibly pushed Rue into a 'time out', meaning outside powers had the ability to apply punishments to Rue if they figured she was a part of this uprising.

This had actually been brought up, too, as one of the reasons eternal immersion on a global scale was so frightening. Once everyone was trapped within DCO, the government and elites would have direct digital control, in a similar way to whatever Xander had once had over Rue when he had still been in charge of James's instance and everyone within DCO. Stopping such things or ensuring such things were no longer options even if James and the others failed was one of Steve's current tasks.

Another of Steve's tasks, with Rachel's offered help, was to do some digging to try and ensure that Rue's very being, her conscious self, confined as she was already to immersion, was protected. After all, her body was the proof of concept for the Sleeping Beauty pods, and it was sitting within the very heart of the facility they were planning to assault. Meaning she was quite literally in the hands of the very people they were working to thwart.

"Whatever happens, we'll be together," James said as he clutched Rue's hand in his own. If not physically, if not virtually, then in spirit. By some chance of fate, or perhaps the power of a god if one existed, James and Rue had found each other. The stars had aligned to bring the two of them together, and no matter what, James vowed to never be without her. In this life, or the next if there was one. He and Rue belonged together. Of that much, he was certain.

"Well then," Steve cleared his throat, and James saw a wetness in the old man's eyes as he looked at the two of them. "We really should get the two of you back to the dungeon. Lots to do, and as we all know, less time than ideal to get it all done."

"Do you really think we can make it happen?" James dared to ask the developer. Sure, they'd planned, sure Hades had given them all the vital information the mysterious hacker had managed to acquire, and yet still, the task felt too monumental, too impossible.

"We've as good a shot as any," Steve said, forcing his smile to his face. "Hell, compared to some of the hair-brained things I've seen throughout my life, and history in general, our odds aren't all that bad. After all, if the government could get away with convincing people for over fifty years that they'd landed on the moon, why can't a group a highly skilled individuals with vast technological resources at their disposal take down a single government facility?"

His smile widened a bit more as he filled himself with the confidence of the insane. "If Somalian pirates with basic weapons and wooden boats can capture miliary vessels, then I'm pretty sure we've got this in the bag, actually. After all"—the grin widened, and now he did look insane—"you're the Random Dungeon. Your whole existence, your position at the top is a ridiculous impossibility. We exist to make the crazy, the weird, and the wacky happen. And if I know your parents," he winked, "which I do, I'm sure we'll have even more to tip the odds in our favor once this current immersion cycle ends."

James opened his mouth to ask Steve what he meant. However, the man waved his hand, dismissing James. A moment later, the world shifted, and James and Rue were suddenly back in the hot springs of his fifth floor, gone from Steve's secret space. And the developer was nowhere to be seen.

"Alrighty then." James stood from the hot springs, letting the sudden chill of the arctic air bring his senses back to focus. He mustered what courage he could, momentarily emboldened by Steve's infectious confidence, to act before he got cold feet.

"It's time we see a certain guild about organizing the greatest experience train in existence." His grin widened, and he was sure that if he had a mirror, it would almost be as wide as Steve's. "For the dungeon, that is."

Chapter Twenty-Four

By the time they made it to their destination, James's mood had improved to a small degree. With the extra time to process everything, his mind, for better or worse, had compartmentalized it all in an effort to make it feel less... overwhelming. There was a ton to do, but James couldn't do it all on his own, nor did he need to. Everyone had tasks, and once those tasks were complete, only then could they take additional steps forward.

For now, his and Rue's task was simple: level up their dungeon and reach Tier 7.

Everything else didn't matter until that goal was accomplished.

The cheers from adventurers and friendly greetings as James and Rue walked through the Random Dungeon's dungeon town also didn't hurt. The kind words, smiles, and eager attempts to get them to join adventuring parties helped fuel his desire to protect these people and served as a reminder that his decision was the right one.

"Nyx!" a loud voice called out his Avatar's name as James and Rue stepped into the tavern.

Called 'Dicken's Roost', it was one of the most popular taverns in the dungeon town. It was also where the Knights Who Go Ni were currently relaxing.

"Rue!" the voice continued to call out. It was Z. "Come join us!"

The overly excited elf lifted a tankard in their direction, and the rest of his party did likewise, friendly smiles plastered on their faces. Their jovial mood was admirable, all things considered, since Steve had told James that they'd experienced a party wipe on the sixth floor while he'd been with Hades. Apparently, his When-Wolves had given the Knights Who Go Ni a hell of a time, and in the end, the adventurers had perished.

James smiled back at them, the motion still feeling somewhat strange in his current form. His 'developer' persona had the body of an Archon. It came with a twisted, monstrous face similar to a gargoyle.

He'd been hoping when he hit level 30 that he'd get wings through the race's Primordial Manipulation aspect, which had been part of why he'd picked the class. Instead, that bonus had triggered a delayed mutation. In theory, that was better. The mutation promised at least three aspects to trigger at level 80. He and Rue were both currently level 79, the extra experience from the Siege battle on the fifth floor having pushed them close, yet not fully to that mark.

"Don't mind if we do," Rue said as she walked into the tavern, already motioning towards the barkeep for a drink.

James watched her go for a moment, admiring her 'developer' Avatar. She'd picked Vampire as her race and was a Cleric of Blood. She wore robes crafted from Cyrus skin and Solar-Bear fur that glowed with strange energy, all courtesy of the fifth floor's gear set. Atop her head was the Unique item drop that she'd received during the Siege event: the sparking, crackling Harbingers headpiece.

"We didn't think we'd get to see the two of you again so soon." Z stood and offered Rue a seat, speaking to them as they reached the table.

The other players were all glancing their way and chatting. Being 'developers', James and Rue's names, visible above their Avatars if someone focused, glowed a different color from normal players.

Even without that, they'd made enough of a name for themselves that everyone knew who they were. Making fast friend with the Knights Who Go Ni, arguably the most famous adventuring group in all of DCO, had also improved James and Rue's own notoriety.

"We've got a new dungeon feature we want to test out firsthand," James started, using the lie he and Rue had already discussed. "And we were actually hoping to run into you guys here. Steve mentioned that this was one of your favorite spots to unwind."

"Where is that spanker? He here with you?" Oak asked loudly, looking around the room for the 'spanker' that was Steve's strange taunt-utilizing tank class. The halfling developer Avatar, of course, was nowhere to be found. "I'd be more than happy to have him around again. It was nice not having to tank everything by myself. And I'm sure you guys already know all about the sixth floor." He shuddered slightly, likely thinking about the swarming he'd gotten by the J-Kappas. "I would love to watch Steve tank that floor."

"He's busy sadly," James said as he sat down at the table. Everyone was sitting now, the game's magic system having immediately summoned extra chairs for the newcomers. Arguably it made Z's act of chivalry a moment ago pointless as there was no need for him to give up his seat for Rue. Still, James knew Z, and he was just that good of a man. "But he sent his wishes."

"He said he'd try to swing by before the end of this immersion cycle," Rue added as she sipped from a wooden mug. James watched for a moment, smiling slightly to himself as Rue's fangs dripped the frothy liquid down her chin. She caught his gaze and licked the liquid away quickly.

"Well," Z brought the attention back to him as he leaned back, looking at the rest of his party, "you said you were looking for us right?" He smiled, and James couldn't help but smile back, feeling the warmth of that look. If they were in one of the tabletop-type immersion games, he'd swear Z had a perfect 20 in Charisma.

"That's right." James opened the menu option that existed at the tavern table, and quickly ordered a bit of food and a drink, finding himself suddenly thirsty and famished. "We're looking to do another run into the dungeon and could use some help if you're all willing."

"A chance to dive with Nyx the Inferno and Scarlet Ruby?" Z clapped his hands together. "We'd never pass up that offer."

"Scarlet Ruby?" Rue asked with a raised eyebrow.

"Nyx the Inferno?" James said almost simultaneously.

"Those are the nicknames players have started assigning the two of you. Not sure who started them, but they've taken off pretty quickly." Z looked around. "You two are minor celebrities after how well you performed during the Siege."

James shared a knowing look with Rue.

"Steve," he said with a heavy sigh. Those names were definitely Steve names. *Damnit, Steve.*

"Any way," James cleared his throat as an adventurer dressed in tavern clothes brought him a steaming bowl of soup, a loaf of fresh bread, and a pint of... ice cold milk. Stress made for weird food choices, okay. "Have you guys heard about the new floor options for the first floor?"

"Git Gud Mode?" Z smiled. "Steve mentioned it when he was diving with us. Said there would be new variations of the floors soon. Told us they'd be listed as 'hardcore' floor variants." Z looked at the others. "We glanced at them. Seems only the first floor is live. When you choose to dive into the dungeon, it shows the two instances that you can join for the first floor. The first is normal, the second has a glowing skull on it."

"Yeah, that's it." James sighed heavily internally.

Of course, Steve had mentioned that as well. The developer hadn't liked being vetoed by his colleagues with regards to what to name the increased difficulty option. So he'd spread the unofficial name amongst adventurers already. And if he could get the Knights to call it that, then the other players would follow along, and his name for it would become the 'official' name for the difficulty.

If there was one thing Steve was good at, it was getting his way in the end, no matter how long it took. James pushed his judgement of Steve down, and continued speaking. "We wanted to check it out to see how it differs, and make sure everything runs smoothly connecting it to the other floors."

He glanced at Rue, who nodded, before he began the next part. It was time to put his plan in motion. "If you guys aren't doing anything else, we'd appreciate your company for the dive, and then maybe we could keep climbing the Tower and push some levels."

For a moment, James's excitement at the thought of diving the dungeon again as a player pushed his worries aside. The gamer in him wanted level 80, and even if he couldn't purely focus on playing the game, hitting that level while putting in place the plan to get his dungeon to Tier 7 wasn't something he'd complain about.

"Pretty sure we can do that." Z looked at his guildmates, and they all offered him supporting nods. He looked back at James's bowl and mug. "After you finish your…" He raised an eyebrow as he glanced from the red soup to the milk. "Comfort food?"

The Knights Who Go Ni and Rue started laughing at that.

James thanked all the gods in DCO that his gargoyle-like face couldn't blush, else he was certain he'd be as red as the tomato soup. Without saying anything else, he pulled apart his bread, perhaps a bit too aggressively, and dunked it into the soup.

"Thanks," he mumbled as he took a bite, "it's been a day."

Chapter Twenty-Five

"Any chance you can tell us what to expect?" Z asked as the group stood in the now very cramped tunnel that led to the entrance of the Random Dungeon.

In hindsight, making it such a small tunnel probably hadn't been the best idea. It had fit with the concept of a dungeon when James had first started DCO, but now he couldn't help but admit that it felt a bit... unnecessary.

Then again, more and more of his players simply entered the dungeon from the Safe Zone town on the fifth floor, meaning that this tunnel got less and less use. And for a party of five, it wasn't terrible either. But if players were adventuring in larger groups, especially they were taking on 'Git Gud' mode with a raid party, it left a lot to wish for.

"What to expect? Um... Dickens?" James offered with a grin.

Rue snorted, and most of the Knights laughed as well.

"Any other details?" Z asked hopefully. "Like how many, or levels, or anything?"

James shook his head. "*If* I did have that type of information, I wouldn't be able to share it."

"Steve would have," Oak coughed under his breath.

"Steve's got a bad habit of not keeping secrets," Rue said in response, "and we're not in the same position as Steve."

It was true. It always felt like Steve could get away with practically anything. As if the man lived above the rules. Meanwhile, James and Rue had very strict rules that they had to follow.

Even with the government plans revealed, they still had to tiptoe best they could lest they trigger some sort of disciplinary action. That was part of why James had asked Z and the others to this dive. Within the dungeon, within the chaos of his masterpiece, he'd be able to speak with them.

"Well, it can't be helped then." Z looked at Oak.

The party's tank was standing closest to the door that led into the dungeon. James and Rue had temporarily joined the party as well, allowing James to see everyone's health and stats if he glanced up and to the side. The Knights Who Go Ni were in the mid-80s for their levels, and with proper gear acquired from being the top-tiered adventurers, had stats that made James drool.

How he wished he could adventure with them full time. He and Rue were level 79, with a bit of experience to go. Meaning they needed to not die during this run if they wanted to level. And arguably, their current plan for this dungeon run, especially this 'Git Gud' part, was probably not ideal for living.

"We've done plenty of dives into the unknown before," Z continued, "and this time around, we've got two healers to keep the party topped off, and Nyx should add a good bit of additional DPS for us. Not to mention, we know Ifrit can serve as an off-tank if needed. We've got a baby raid party, so I'm sure we'll be fine."

Ifrit was James's summon—a fiery Djinn that dual-wielded massive swords. Because the Djinn had died during the Siege War in an epic duel to the death against an empowered Sergeant Jenkins, the Djinn's stats weren't going to be as impressive as they had been.

Still, Ifrit was indeed a formidable summon, and with James's buffs, would be a titanic force to be reckoned with. Against this floor, though, James was hesitant to even summon the creature. It wasn't that he was worried about the levels of the mobs, but more about what they could do. Still, James wasn't about to let that Dickens outta the bag just yet.

"At least I know there won't be snakes on this floor," Oak said, his eyes seeking out James's, as if he was searching for confirmation. "It's bad enough that I'm pretty positive the sixth-floor boss is a snake. And then, you know, there's the blasted Playthons on the third. I would lose my mind if this floor suddenly had snakes too."

"I can promise you that there aren't any snakes," James said, offering the tank a bit of reassurance. Oak went through a lot for the party. And he took most of it in stride. James figured that he could give him a bit of solace.

"Well, there you go." Z slapped Oak's back, the party leader the next in line for their formation.

Behind him was Elm, with Faust, Med Ic, Rue, and James behind them. Physical classes were in the front, magic classes in the back—a standard raid formation. It was necessary since the dungeon door entrance forced them to file out into the floor one at a time.

"Watch out for traps, though," Z warned as he gave Oak a gentle nudge towards the door. "Don't need you falling into a pit with a Sacrificial Lamb again."

The party laughed, and before he could catch himself, James found himself laughing as well. That was still one of his favorite memories of the party.

Z looked at him with a questioning gaze for a just a moment before he turned back towards the door, ready for the start of their dive. They'd already entered the instance since they had needed to select Hard Mode before they had started the run. The mobs, James knew, were only level 50, meaning that their party should in theory be extremely over-leveled for these creatures.

However, levels were only one factor in what made a monster dangerous. Skills and upgrades could greatly shift the danger a mob presented to players. On top of that, Old Man Jenkins, the normal first-floor boss, was level 65 this time around. Then there was the World Boss, Charles the Dicken, who had the possibility to appear as a level 70 World Boss. And finally, the special Hard Mode boss, the level 75... Hokey Pokey.

The upgraded mobs, the new and unique boss, and just the sheer craziness that was the floor James had designed, waited for the Knights Who Go Ni to enter. And while James knew full well what to expect considering he'd designed the floor, he couldn't help but feel his breath catch in his chest as his heart rate increased.

Even though it was impossible, he was pretty sure he could hear his heartbeat and feel the blood rushing through his veins, spurred by the heightened state of anticipation for what lay beyond the door. The thrill of a new dive, a new adventure—it was time for the horror show of his specialized first floor to finally take center stage.

Oak opened the door, and in the next moment, all the party knew was chaos.

Chapter Twenty-Six

James had a new favorite memory for his dungeon. His only regret was that they hadn't recorded it. Even still, he had no doubt in his mind that he'd never forget it for as long as he lived. Which arguably might not be that long.

The area around the door into the dungeon had been clear of mobs. However, that didn't mean it was safe from their aggro range. The moment Oak had stepped out on the slightly grassy expanse that served as the Demonic Farm of the first floor, the red glow from the lights above had caused him to gain a scarlet tint and he had aggroed multiple mobs.

The poor tank had no chance to react or take note that something was amiss and danger was afoot before events were set in motion. The players were no strangers to long-range attacks from the gun-wielding mobs on the fifth floor. But against demonic animals… well, logically, there was no way in hell they should have had to worry about mobs over thirty yards away. Logic, though, never applied to the Random Dungeon.

A loud bawk was the only warning anyone got. Oak was three steps out of the door, Z just behind him in the process of summoning his animal companions. A shadow appeared over Oak, and the tank looked up just in time to watch a six-foot Dicken come crashing down atop him, its raptor like claws tearing a glowing red line across his arm before he could get his shield up.

Then as the Dicken hit the ground, a red and black wave of crackling energy erupted outwards. The skill, Demonic Leap, was a mean one.

Demonic Leap (Max) — Infernal energy radiates from a Dicken's claws, seeping into the ground around them. When this skill is activated, it emits a burst of demonic energy around the Dicken, empowering any Dicken within 1+lvl yards. Empowered Dickens will immediately activate Demonic Leap, attacking the same target as the initial Dicken. On impact, demonic energy will ripple outward, dealing decreasing amounts of damage based on distance from impact to all non-demonic entities. This damage has a 5% + 0.1*lvl chance of applying Infernal Bird Flu* to players.
*Infernal Bird Flu — Decrease player's stats by 1% per 2 seconds until cleansed.

More loud bawks were the only further warning the party got as six additional Dickens took temporary flight and leaped at Oak. The tank managed to get his shield up by then, and had begun the process of activating his skills.

Z, quick to take stock of the situation, dashed away, while Med Ic immediately began casting heals on Oak from the other side of the door. Like a smoothly oiled machine, everyone had begun to react appropriately and effectively once the initial shock was done.

Unfortunately for all, the Dickens, with their passive Birds of a Feather skill, were tough. Much tougher than level 50 mobs should be considering that their stats were doubled when five or more of the creatures were within a certain proximity of one another.

To his credit, Oak managed to survive the next incoming attack. His massive Indra form crackled to life as he grew in size, a visage of a Hindu god cloaking him as he wielded weapons in four arms made of pure lightning. The attacks crackled with power, and the Knights Who Go Ni worked rapidly to shift the ambush against them into a battle they could win.

Then came the next attacks that pushed the tide of the battle back in favor of the farm animals. Seven white-hot beams of power blasted into Oak's glowing form from different angles as more of the specially upgraded Dickens joined the fray. These Dickens, which had been outside of the range of the initial demonic leap, opted to use their long-range breath weapon granted by the Yakitori skill rather than demonic leap.

Yakitori (Max) — Dickens gain the ability to shoot a beam of highly intensified, searing flame. This attack has a range of 10 yards + 1 yard per level. This attack does 50+lvl fire damage per second,

ignoring 50% armor. This attack can be channeled by a Dicken for 5 seconds, with each second increasing the damage done by 10%, and ignoring an additional 1% of armor per second.
*Channeling this attack for the whole duration leaves the Dicken overheated, stunning it for 3 seconds, and increasing damage dealt to it by 100%.

Between the... er... 'Dicken pile' that had crashed down on Oak, the birds pecking, scratching, and flapping around his massive form, and the beams of energy burning into him and cooking him from all angles, Oak fell.

Screaming in rage and horror, while also laughing at the sheer absurdity of it all, the party found itself without a tank within the first minute of stepping onto the floor. Luckily, with Oak serving as the point of interest for all of the mobs near enough to the entrance to aggro the area, Z had managed to summon his three animal companions.

Elm had also left the entryway, using the opening Oak had been providing by inadvertently aggroing everything around them. This allowed him to adjust the angle of his attacks, and more importantly, begin mob extinction efforts in full.

The Dicken ambush had won first contact. But the Knights Who Go Ni won the war. James felt the intense magical power crackle in the air when Faust finished channeling his AoE cooldown. A massive storm cloud formed from that power in the sky above the Dickens and Oak's fallen body, which was now a death orb. Bolts of energy crashed down with enough force that they made the ground shake, as one Dicken after another found itself the target of Faust's elemental fury.

James had remained with Med Ic and Rue on the other side of the doorway. He stood there somewhat awestruck as he marveled at the sheer power of Faust's attacks. His skin prickled from the electricity, and Rue's hair rose comically into the air from the static charge. A nice touch, really, that the developers had placed into the game for realism.

If that realism hadn't been all part of creating a world to trap the players in forever, James would have appreciated it even more.

The Dickens were starting to fall en masse. Even though their stats were doubled, the magic attacks were fatal. First floor mobs, even on Hard Mode, didn't have access to the magic resistance that higher floor mobs had. At least... not all of them did.

The fight wasn't completely over, though, James knew. These Dickens still had a trick or two up their non-existent sleeves. With each death blow dealt by Faust's cooldown, the Dicken would burst into fiery death flames, causing an AoE eruption of damage around their body. James noticed that as the AoE attack continued, it left behind a fiery core that wasn't targeted by the spell.

The core itself wasn't an enemy, it was simply a passive, floating object, very similar to the death orb of dead adventurers. If James had to guess, that had been an effort by the developers to ensure such rebirth skills were actually viable and not easily thwarted by large AoE DoT skills.

"Should we tell them?" Rue whispered from behind James as the lightning strikes slowed, the bodies nearly all turned to floating cores.

With the immediate danger ended, Med Ic had begun to cast resurrection on Oak. James nodded to Rue, preparing to do just that, but stopped a moment before he could issue the warning.

These were the Knights Who Go Ni. If he had to warn them about something as common as a rebirth skill, he'd think less of them. They were veterans, they were the best of the best. They were gamers. This was what they did.

He turned his focus back to the fight, and sure enough, his faith in the Knights held true. Z and Elm were going to town on the orbs, with Turk and Badgy joining the orb-slaughtering fest while Hornz stood guard, prepared to tank any incoming attacks.

The Knights had been caught off guard by the initial assault, but that had been a given. They were crazy skilled, but they weren't psychic. And who could prevent a Dicken attack from thirty yards away? Or a fiery breath attack from even further?

But they'd regained their composure quickly, and handled the situation with impressive efficacy. You could knock them off balance, but you could never knock them down.

That resourcefulness, that coolheaded, calculating nature of the Knights, amongst all their other amazing qualities, was what made him confident in what he planned to entrust to them. Confident that they were the only ones he could rely on to help him get his dungeon to Tier 7 before the night of immersion ended.

But before any of that, it was time to see the rest of his new and improved Hard Mode floor in action.

Chapter Twenty-Seven

It only took a few minutes for Z and the Knights to finish clearing the remaining Dickens in front of the entrance. Despite being overcome by a swarm of the vicious creatures, Oak was in a relatively good mood.

Everyone had smiles on their faces, and laughter could be felt in the somewhat stale air of the first floor. Being situated in an underground cave, the farm-based floor had always had a strange mixture of what James figured was a farm-like, animal smell combined with strange spices and sulfur.

"Are we sure those were only level 50?" the tank asked as they finished looting the corpses.

With the coast clear, James, Rue, and Med Ic made their way into the dungeon properly. Once they'd stepped foot onto the grassy terrain, the door behind them closed, floating strangely in midair to signal the exit to the floor. The path to the second floor was further into the dungeon, situated in the big, red barn.

"That's what their tags claimed," Z said as he gave Badgy's head a scratch.

The intelligent, fiercely dressed pet leaned into it, while at the same time it growled like a rabid beast. It eyed everyone with dangerous intent, as if daring them to say anything. Badgers, James had learned, gave zero fucks.

"They do double their stats when they're in flocks," James offered up.

"And if I had to guess, this 'Git Gud' mode, as Steve called it, probably gives them additional skills and whatnot." *Totally not a guess.*

"You're probably right." Z looked at the others. "Which means that we need to be on our guard for the rest of the floor. Looks like the Dickens have been upgraded with whatever that crazy long-distance leap was, and a fire breath." He looked at Oak, grinning a bit. "Never thought you'd be cooked to death by a white-hot stream of fire from a Dicken, did you?"

Oak threw the piece of Dicken meat he was eating at Z. Before the projectile could hit the man, Badgy's sword shot up, the flat end intercepting the meat, causing it to drop into the creature's waiting mouth. Badgy let out a burp and flashed all his teeth in a wicked smile towards Oak.

"Those Swiner's are likely plague engines of some sort." Z pointed at the very obvious, fifteen-foot-tall, bloated, bipedal pigs. "Not sure about the Sacrificial Lambs."

There was a flock of the black and red-wooled creatures lazily munching on the grass a good hundred or so yards away. Past that, James could see the obsidian-skinned Mad Cows, their fiery horns giving them extra cool factor even at a distance.

"And I bet you that those damned goats are even more annoying," Elm added, pointing with his bow to where two Scape Goats were in the process of headbutting each other. They were surrounded by another flock of Dickens, with a Swiner towering over them and a sleeping Mad Cow off to the side. The floor was more densely populated than previously, as James had been given double the number of mob points to use for Hard Mode.

Back when DCO had first started and he was a Tier 1 Rank 1 dungeon, he'd had 100 mob points for his first floor. The moment he'd become Tier 2, his first floor had had a total of 200 mob points. Now his hard version of the floor had 400 mob points. When your highest cost mob was only 5 points, 400 points went a long, long way. And that wasn't even adding in the fact that the system was programmed to ensure that for every adventurer on the floor, each creature would gain an additional respawn opportunity.

"It's safe to assume that they've all got new skills," Z reiterated. "Meaning we should try to use ranged attacks to aggro them in small groups till we figure out how they've been upgraded." He looked over everyone. "Past that, I'm sure Old Man Jenkins has some new tricks too, and is likely an even higher level."

The elf turned his focus back to James and Rue, who'd been listening quietly. James had a smile on his face, though the grotesque gargoyle features of his Archon class likely hid what it truly was. Rue, on the other hand, had both her fangs showing because of how wide her smile was.

"Now that we're here, anything else to share with the class?" Z asked with a raised eyebrow, his tone amused. "Or do you plan to stand back and watch us get Dicken-piled again?"

"You know we can't share any secrets," Rue replied, tone a mixture of sweet and sultry, "and you have to admit, that battle was enjoyable." She pointed at Z then. "Besides, you're all over thirty levels higher than these mobs. Telling you anything extra would really be overkill, wouldn't it? Where's the fun in that?"

Z smiled, and James saw the look in his eyes. The look the leader was famous for. The look that said he was about to throw caution to the wind in the name of chasing a fun challenge.

"Actually, Rue's got a good point, " Z said, causing his teammates to groan. "Sure, that was a hectic battle, but we are extremely over-leveled for this floor." He looked down at Badgy and then up towards Turk, the giant eagle circling in lazy loops above them, scanning the floor. "Do you guys want to play it safe and slow, or take this on with reckless abandon like the good ol' days?"

"Are you really wanting to YOLO against these demonic farm animals?" Faust asked, at least attempting to be some sort of voice of reason. "After all we've seen of this game and its monster types, do you really want to give the dungeon the chance to unleash even more chaos on us?"

"Yes," Z said with a chuckle. "We took to the sixth floor in a cautious manner. We've already died since then, and don't have any experience points to worry about losing. And I'm sure Nyx and Rue would prefer we take on this floor face first rather than slow and safe. After all, they're looking to level, and we can't do that quickly till we're facing some higher-level foes."

James looked at Rue, mentally trying to send her his approval for her words. She'd been gentle, but her nudge had been all that was needed to move the group to a faster clearing plan. One that would ensure the most chaotic, ridiculous encounters possible.

Furthermore, it would serve to speed their expedition along. And what James really needed was for the party to reach the sixth floor. There, he intended to discuss discreetly the real reason he'd reached out to Z and the others for this dungeon run.

"If we're going the reckless route," James cut Z and the others off.

The Knights weren't arguing over being safe or not now. They were discussing who should tank, Hornz or Oak, and also which group to fight first.

"I think it's time we bring back the final member of our party."

Oak looked immediately at James, pure joy on his face, "Steve is…" He trailed off, his excitement still there, but diminished slightly as he noticed James's finger pointing towards the ground, where a massive, swirling summoning sigil had appeared. "Oh."

James grinned. "It's time to bring Ifrit out to play."

Chapter Twenty-Eight

The Djinn roared to life in a fiery fashion that James felt was a bit more dramatic than normal for the summoning ritual. Flames erupted outwards from the circle, swirling in reds and yellows, intensifying to blues and flashing weirdly to shades of purple and green as they coalesced into a tornado of color.

Within the fire-nado, the twenty-foot frame of the mighty Djinn took form. His obsidian armor burned with an inner blaze, while flames wreathed his ankles and wrists, flickering in spurts here and there across his body.

At his waist, his two ornate scimitars hung patiently, his hands resting on their obsidian pommels. The Djinn was eager for battle. His last conflict had been on the snow-covered fifth floor—a duel to the death against Sergeant Jenkins. Compared to that epic battle, what he was being thrown into now likely seemed… anticlimactic.

"It's about time you called forth my might again," Ifrit said in his deep, bellowing voice. He moved his hands off his blades and crossed his arms as he looked down at the party. First at James, then Rue, whose gaze he held for but a second, before he looked over the others.

Ever since Rue had doused him with goat's milk, Ifrit had been somewhat intimidated by her. Which should have seemed a funny statement considering the twenty-foot giant's stature and impressive form versus Rue's five-foot-whatever lithe vampire frame. However, anyone who thought that had never truly seen Rue's angry side.

"Are we working to farm easy kills for my next ascension?" Ifrit asked as he took stock of the battlefield. An almost bored look crossed his face.

The way the Djinn evolved generally included acquiring a set number of kills, combined with landing a certain amount of critical hits, general experience, and occasionally some other secret factors. Well, secret to James. The Djinn had a set evolution path it wanted, and it only told James what those parameters were when it felt like it. Their relationship, though it was closer than before, was still being worked on.

"Amongst other things," James said to the Djinn. "This is a harder, improved version of the first floor. The base mobs are level 50 instead of level 10, and they have a new array of dangerous skills."

"Which is why you've called forth my awesome might." The Djinn punched his right fist into his left palm, the force sending a blast of air and flames around him. "And I once again get to fight beside the mighty Knights?" He grinned at Oak, who waved up at him.

The tank had been looking forward to Steve joining the party because the developer was a tank class. But even still, that didn't mean he wasn't excited about Ifrit joining the fight. The Djinn was an off-tank, which meant he could still serve in the tank role if needed and help take some of the aggro and stress off of the poor elf.

As an off-tank, Ifrit didn't have a high defense stat or health pool, which meant he wasn't quite as efficient as Oak. Instead of such things, the Djinn relied on life steal and heal buffs that James could apply to him, as well as speed buffs and an array of flashy, rapid movements that increased his dodge ability. Both could draw aggro and handle large swarms of mobs, but the methodology and tactics, the play style, were two very different beasts. Oak was a bulwark on the battlefield. Ifrit was a storm of blades and fury.

"We figured you'd want to join in on the fun," Rue spoke up. "And after your brave sacrifice against Sergeant Jenkins, you've more than earned that much. Everyone here witnessed your final stand, and it was nothing short of inspiring."

If Djinn could blush, James was pretty sure Ifrit was.

"Point me towards our foes," he said, looking away from Rue in a rather bashful manner. "And let my blades consume their spirit for battle."

James nodded toward Rue, and she triggered her sanguine bond on James. The skill linked her to him, allowing her to use his health pool when needed to empower her spells. James in turn used his own skills to apply a basic stack of buffs to Ifrit, ensuring his party of three was prepared to aid the Knights Who Go Ni for what was to come.

The mobs weren't of a level that would make them a legitimate threat. They all knew that. But still, it wasn't their levels that would be the problem. What made the new first floor dangerous was the new skills of the mobs.

The debuffs from the Swiners were nasty and could quickly sap a player's stats as well as drain their HP if not cleansed. Then there were the Scapegoats, which now had a wide array of taunts that applied different debuffs of their own. While dealing with those, there were also the Dickens, armed with long-range attacks and gap closers that could easily take out a backline player, such as a healer or powerful magic DPS, if they weren't careful.

Those mobs weren't the ones James was most worried about when it came to the basic mobs on this floor, though. Those could all be dealt with, even in a chaotic, reckless manner, without presenting a danger that the mighty Knights Who Go Ni couldn't handle.

What he was really worried about—and by worried he meant eager to see in action—were the Sacrificial Lambs. Never had he thought the term 'wolf in sheep's clothing' fit quite as well as those cult-loving sheep.

"Any preference on which group we go after first?" James asked Z, nodding to the open expanse of farmland that spread out before them. It was teeming with threats for the group to take on.

There was no sign of Old Man Jenkins yet, nor the special hay pile that housed Hokey Pokey. The latter, James knew, was right next to the big, red barn, though it was too far away to see properly. As for Old Man Jenkins, James wasn't quite sure. The boss had the ability to roam on the entire floor, but often liked to hide within the twenty-foot-tall fields of infernal corn.

That crop was always in high demand, as it served as the basis for Fireball whiskey. James was pretty sure that the AI for his first-floor boss had noticed that players always rushed towards the field, seeking to earn extra coin through gathering quests for the valuable crafting component, and enjoyed ambushing them. Which in turn increased the danger of harvesting the crop, and therefore, increased the reward and incentive for players to get it.

"Flip a coin?" Z offered with a shrug. He fished out a gold coin. The coins didn't have a 'heads' or 'tails' side. He fixed that obvious flaw quite quickly. Z handed the coin to Badgy, and at the behest of what James assumed was a mental command, the badger used one of his sharp claws to scratch a single side of the coin, marking it.

"Scratched or smooth," Z said as he tossed the coin deftly in the air.

"Smooth," Rue said immediately before James could even open his mouth. When it came to games of chance… Rue had a problem.

The coin hit the ground, and true to her self-proclaimed assignment as the Goddess of Luck, the coin's smooth side faced them. She grinned, as if she could read James's mind, and pointed to a group of mobs in the distance. "How about we start with the sheep?"

It would seem that the sheep weren't the only wolves in disguise.

"Sounds good to me," Z said, oblivious to the danger Rue had just sent them towards. "Let's go take care of Mary's little lambs, shall we?"

Z and the Knights made towards the sheep, singing at the top of their lungs a song about black sheep and wool as they went.

"You're evil," James whispered to Rue as they followed the group.

Ifrit had moved to the frontline and was cheerily singing along with the Knights. How the AI knew the song, James had no idea.

"We both know why I did it." She flashed her devilish, sanguine smile towards him, her red eyes sparkling with mischief. "And we both want to see all we can of the floor while we're here before we get down to business."

James's excitement tempered for just a moment at that. She had a point. There was a good chance this could be their last time running through the dungeon. And if that was the case, then he wanted to see firsthand as much as he could. And worst-case scenario, even if the party wiped on this floor, it wouldn't cause them any problems.

Failing in 'Git Gud' mode only applied a penalty to when you could join in that particular mode. Even if they wiped, they wouldn't be locked out of the dungeon, and they'd still be able to dive right into the higher floors as planned. This run right now was about blowing off steam and getting mentally prepared for what came next.

"Sacrificial Lambs aside." James felt his own devilish smile grow. "I'm really hoping Old Man Jenkins will grab Hokey Pokey."

Rue punched him playfully as they followed the group. "And you say I'm the evil one."

"Where do you think I learned it from?" he countered, and their laughter went unheard by the singing Knights as they marched, very likely, to their doom.

Chapter Twenty-Nine

James felt for Oak, he really did. The man had been roped into being the party's tank at the start of DCO solely because he'd gone with a warrior class. Since that moment in time, he'd been exposed to one awkward situation after another.

James had personally watched the man be eaten by a giant steampunk T-Rex, smothered to death by a ginormous stuffed snake, eaten a few times by zombie sharks, once even by an Undead Kraken, and of course, rudely slain in a multitude of ways that just didn't hit the top ten most memorable deaths in James's mind.

Past all of that and ignoring the surprise mimic deaths that had probably led to a deep mistrust of toilets for the man, was the snake-related phobia of Oak's that James kept triggering... both intentionally and unintentionally.

In short, Oak went through a lot. And yet he still continued on with a smile after his bitching and grumbling was done. He was always willing to fulfill the role he'd been asked to fill for the team, all to keep his adventuring party alive and support his friends. It was admirable. Inspiring even.

Which made the fact that he was doomed, no matter what he did, all the more painful to watch. And James and Rue, considering she'd set them on this path, were the main reason for Oak's most current, dire predicament.

"It's not stopping," Oak growled as Med Ic's light washed over him.

All of his other debuffs were cleansed except for one. A flashing red and black debuff on his status bar had the number 16 on it now.

"I've used my strongest spells," Med Ic replied, a bit of frustration in his voice.

He really had. So had Rue, even though she knew it was pointless. The least they could do in this situation was to go along with the farce. Even if James and Rue knew full well that the particular debuff wasn't going anywhere anytime soon.

Afflicted

The debuff was the result of James upgrading the Cult's Wool-Aid skill to the max on his Sacrificial Lambs. It was a debuff that couldn't be cleansed. While on a target it would sap their life and mana by a percentage every second, as well as decrease their damage output at the same rate.

Gaining an additional stack of Afflicted would reset that timer, keeping those nasty effects from taking hold. Gaining new stacks of Afflicted was still catastrophic, though, just in a 'problem for later' versus 'problem for now' way.

The Afflicted stacks themselves would increase by one for every Sacrificial Lamb killed by the party. Or conversely, for every 15 seconds they went without attacking a mob. That second option was less ideal for the Afflicted member as it didn't reset the debuff timer.

In theory, from a survivability point of view, the best way to deal with the status was to murder mobs as fast as possible. Because the floor was filled with creatures, that wasn't a hard thing to accomplish. Especially when Elm, Z, and Faust all had extremely long-range skills and spells to keep aggroing additional mobs toward them.

"Surely you guys know about this skill," Med Ic said as he stood beside Rue and James. He glanced first at Rue, shook his head for some reason, and focused his efforts on James. "Can't you give us at least some sort of hint?"

James couldn't help but feel Med Ic had just decided James was the easier one to persuade. A fact that would have hurt had Med Ic not been spot on. Compared to Rue, James was a pushover. But right now, with everything that had just been placed on him, he wasn't feeling all that generous.

"Sorry, man," James said with a shake of his own head. He was actively keeping track of a secondary screen of information, monitoring his buffs on Ifrit, ensuring he kept his summon in tip top shape. He had a feeling that the massive Djinn would be needed in the next minute or so at the rate the adventurers were slaying Sacrificial Lambs.

"Even if I knew and could tell you"—James looked Med Ic in the eyes, his mouth spreading into its grotesque smile, the tusk like appendages making his lips stretch in an uncomfortable way—"I doubt you really want me to tell you. It'd take the fun of discovery away, wouldn't it?"

Med Ic pursed his lips, glanced at Oak, and then back at James. Med Ic cast a healing spell on the tank without looking at Oak. Even with the stacks ever growing, the tank himself stayed topped off on health at the very least.

"Can you at least tell me what the trigger point is?" Med Ic countered. "Is this a twenty-five stack sort of debuff? Fifty? Hundred? Thousand?" He shook his head, his tone going to a whisper. "I've no doubt that when it hits its max, something terrible is going to happen to Oak," he chuckled. "I just need to know when and how so that I can best prepare for it for the rest of the party."

He looked at James pleadingly. James cursed. Alright, he'd been premature in his assumption of how lacking of fucks he was. Apparently, he had at least one more to give. He was still a softy at heart.

"Fifty," James said, the word escaping his mouth before he could even process he'd said them. How could he hold such information back from them? And it was harmless for the healer to know, right? There was nothing they could do to stop the stacks from gaining unless they left the floor.

It had already been decided that they were on a ride or die run, meaning they either cleared the floor or died trying. Oak's fate had been sealed the moment that first Sacrificial Lamb had rolled rapidly into his crotch, erupting in a localized explosion with impossible speed, triggering the Afflicted status on him.

In the exact opposite of popular knowledge, these Sacrificial Lambs did not shun non-believers. They flocked to them. And with every slain Sacrificial Lamb, they got one step closer to summoning their deity.

"Before you ask," James added, noting Med Ic's look of victory at James's previous slip of information, "I don't know what will happen when it hits fifty."

A partial lie. He knew that the person with fifty Afflicted stacks would instantly die. He also knew that something called 'The Demonic Lamb' would be summoned and would exist for 0.5 seconds per the level of the

Afflicted individual, as well as an additional 0.5 seconds per Sacrificial Lamb still alive on the floor at the time of summoning.

Oak was level 84, which meant through levels alone that the summoned creature would have 42 seconds of existence. There was a grand total of 75 Sacrificial Lambs on the floor by design as well. James had used 150 of his 400 mob points on the 2-point mobs when he'd created the floor. Assuming half remained, whatever was summoned when the skill triggered would be able to survive for a minute, maybe a little more, before it ran out of time and was forcibly unsummoned.

Past that though, James really had no idea of what to expect. He had no idea what level the summoned creature would be, what it would look like, nor what its skills were. He also didn't know what it would do once it was summoned. Would the party survive its arrival? Maybe? Hopefully. If any group could survive such a sudden thing, it would be Z and his group.

Once they survived the initial summoning and insta-death of Oak, James had no idea what was going to happen, and he couldn't help but let his imagination run wild. A quick glance at Oak's status showed that the Affliction rate had reached twenty stacks; he wouldn't have to wait much longer for the big reveal.

"Guess I'll save my cooldowns for whatever is to come," Med Ic said as he turned away from Rue and James back to his party. Everyone else was currently focused on slaughtering all the level 50 mobs all around them.

"Assuming we don't all mass wipe instantly," he chuckled again, and glanced back at James, a full smile on his face, "I'm sure it's going to be a moment to put my skills as a healer to the test."

James glanced at Rue, and the two of them shared a wide smile. Dealing with the unknown, fighting as a party against a unique foe—those were the moments that gamers lived for. Those were the moments the Knights Who Go Ni, James, and Rue lived for.

Moments that made James question, deep in his mind, if he really wanted to even stop the government's plan. Because from his current viewpoint, with his adrenaline pumping in anticipation and excitement rushing through him, life in DCO, at least for him, was so much better than the real world.

Chapter Thirty

The first warning sign something nefarious was occurring, other than the fact that the stacks couldn't be cleansed, triggered at twenty-five stacks. Oak's skin became covered in red runes, similar to the cosmetic rune-like markings Devilkin could have on their players. At thirty-five stacks, the runes began to pulse with a crimson glow.

At forty stacks, the pulsing increased, and the sound of drums began to reverberate around the party, as if echoing across the entire floor in a foreboding manner. The sound had been so ominous that James's pulse had quickened in tune with the beat. At forty-five, sigils beneath Oak's feet and sinister tendrils of power snaked out and formed a ten-foot-diameter circle around him.

"Fifty," James said breathlessly as he watched the final stack hit.

With the appearance of the sigil beneath Oak, everyone had pretty much determined whatever was coming was going to be centered on the tank. Logically, that meant everyone had now distanced themselves as far back from him as possible. The nearest individual to him was Ifrit, the mighty Djinn prepared to tank whatever was about to happen.

Oak, on the other hand, activated all his remaining cooldowns, blew all his taunts, and actively worked to kill as many Sacrificial Lambs and other mobs as possible. In the short time since the stacks had begun appearing on him, the party had killed easily thirty of the creatures, maybe more. An impressive effort, truly, though one that James knew was futile.

A wave of absolute darkness rushed across the floor, blocking out all forms of light. James let out a startled cry, echoed by the others, as his vision was completely removed. Loud crashing sounds and roars echoed across the whole floor—demonic, guttural cries and screams. The farm animals released a cacophony of their own calls, adding to the demonic, otherworldly sounds.

The darkness was absolute. James couldn't even see his own health bar, nor could he move. If he had to guess, it was a stasis type of effect. Games had them, though they were often frowned upon within immersion. Losing control of everything, even if for a split second, could be triggering when you were fully immersed.

There were too many science fiction stories in existence about people being trapped permanently within immersion for anyone to feel comfortable with such effects. Though, some developers simply used that phobia to invoke an extra air of stress among players within their games.

If only they knew what was coming, James thought bitterly to himself as his mind raced. He didn't know how long his senses, save for his hearing, were robbed from him. A second? A minute? After an uncomfortable eternity, his vision cleared. Part of him wished it hadn't.

Oak was gone. That much was a given. Even though James couldn't see a death orb for the tank, it was pretty clear from the molten lava that bubbled in the massive crater where he'd been that he hadn't survived.

As if that wasn't a dead giveaway of his fate, the object floating in the middle above the lava was a bipedal lamb, roughly three feet in height, with deep voids for eyes. Around its form, crimson energy crackled, intermixed with a rippling haze effect and bursts of darkness. In each hand, it held a dagger, the weapons crooked and vicious looking. Around its head was a red piece of cloth with an eye in the center, which pulsated its own sinister light.

James pulled his gaze away from it for a moment to glance at their surroundings, and noticed that, just as the skill had detailed, all of the Sacrificial Lambs on the floor were dead. If he had to guess, the swirling mass of crimson that circled the creature was the blood of those very mobs. Part of him couldn't help but wonder if it would carry the same debuffs as the normal Sacrificial Lambs had.

His new versions on this upgraded floor didn't have the Blood for the Blood God DoT effect, as he'd not chosen that path for the creatures. But did it really matter? Was this the Blood God? Could it apply all of the nasty debuffs and other effects that James had drooled over when upgrading his mobs, hating his limited amount of skill points?

James shook his head, ridding himself of his curiosity, pulling himself back to the moment. Everyone else was just as stunned as he was, and he could tell they were all taking in the moment. He focused his gaze back on the creature floating above the lava.

The red light pulsated again, and the flames beneath it began to part as it lowered itself into the crater. Faster and faster, the power pulsed as the molten rock touched it, joining the swirling power around the creature, the light around it glowing brighter and brighter.

Then as its cloven feet touched the ground, the lava, intermingled with blood, crackling power, and darkness, fully encircled it. A name appeared above its head, along with a level.

The Demonic Lamb
Level: 85

As he read the name, James received a notification. He flinched at the unexpected notification and noticed the others were reacting in a similar manner. It was clear they'd all received something, but now wasn't the time to see what. He dismissed it before he could read its title and looked to his side.

Med Ic's hands glowed, and James could tell that the healer was already in the process of reviving Oak. The plus side of pretty much any insta-kill effect was that it didn't prevent a player from being resurrected. And James knew from watching it happen in person that there were even ways to completely cheat death with items or skills that would result in special achievements if done properly.

Med Ic's class didn't have a skill like that. Though James figured, thanks to what he'd told the healer earlier, that Med Ic had already had a plan in place to revive Oak the moment those stacks hit fifty. The veteran healer had probably just prepared for the worst-case scenario to ensure that, whatever happened at fifty, he wouldn't be caught by surprise. Every second in the unknown was precious. And when it came to party mechanics, the only thing worse than having your tank down was having the healer die.

Med Ic wasn't the only one already reacting to the sudden change in their situation. Z's voice barked orders, and James stopped admiring the guild as he prepared for what he was certain would be a glorious battle. His blood boiled with excitement as he and everyone else began to act in tandem with Z's command.

"Burn it," Z yelled, his bow already unleashing arrows. He paused his words to take in the creature as his pets were rushing towards the creature, Hornz at the lead. "Burn it—probably not with fire, but uh, burn it down. For all glory, items, and achievements I'm sure this creature will give us."

His tone was filled with laughter, and everyone's excitement was palpable as they jumped into action.

Chapter Thirty-One

The question about the blood around the Demonic Lamb was answered almost immediately.

Ifrit, with his massive stride and twenty-foot size, was the first to get within range of the creature. As he did, the red swirling liquid lashed out, striking like snakes, and bit his form in multiple areas. The damage inflicted on the summon was minimal, but he was instantly hit with max stacks of Blood for the Blood God, which threatened to deal over 400 damage if it wasn't cleansed in the next 5 seconds.

James quickly cleansed his summon, and channeled a haste buff into him a moment later, increasing Ifrit's attack speed and granting him increased dodge chance. The Djinn, likewise, activated its own skills, its form becoming a spinning blur as it worked to strike at the lamb from various angles, constantly moving in an effort to avoid the strikes. The skill, James knew, gave Ifrit an increased dodge chance, which would stack with the haste buff James had just given him.

Immediately after, James activated his Greater Seal of Solomon cooldown. The cooldown, which had a 10-minute length now that it had upgraded twice, increased the Djinn's size from twenty feet to thirty feet, and lasted a base of 25 seconds, with an additional 0.4 seconds per James's level. At level 79, that meant the skill would be active for 56.4 seconds.

While active, not including the increased size of Ifrit, the skill would enhance Ifrit's stats and abilities by a base of 25%, with an additional

0.8% per caster's level. That meant an increase of 85.2% to Ifrit's stats and abilities for the next nearly minute, and also, per the skill, ensured Ifrit's health couldn't hit 0.

Essentially, it eliminated the need for James or anyone to focus healing on the off-tank and allowed James to focus purely on increasing Ifrit's damage output. The perfect skill for a burn fest.

James wasn't the only one burning his cooldowns. Given the timer that was counting down from above the Demonic Lamb's head, which showed a minute and thirteen seconds, they had a limited amount of time to try and kill the boss.

Normally, if it were any other group, the plan would likely be to play it safe and just try to survive for that length of time. Common gamer sense implied that that type of a countdown, after an insta-kill summoning, usually meant that the creature had a limited duration before it faded away... or before everyone died. It really depended on how twisted the game was.

But not the Knights. Not James, and not Rue. Simply surviving wouldn't be good enough. James smiled as he thought that. As he saw that very mentality playing out around him. It pushed his concerns aside and helped him solidify in his mind his plan moving forward was the right one. He couldn't just sit back and let the government decide his, and everyone else's fate. Even if their chance of success was unknown, it was better to try and go down fighting than just accept what was coming.

Even though for him living in DCO forever was like a dream come true, he knew deep down that he and everyone else wouldn't truly be free. Their existence from then on out, their very selves, would forever be under threat by the government that had trapped them within the game. They'd be fish in a fishbowl, powerless, and entirely reliant on people twisted enough to remove the entire human species from the face of the planet.

Resolve grew in James's chest, and he felt a weight lift off his shoulders, one he hadn't realized had settled so heavily on his heart and mind. He looked at Rue, his love, who was grinning from ear to ear, blood swirling around her as she cycled her own skills between healing, protection skills, cleanses, and DoT effects.

Her talents really were wasted being stuck as purely a Dungeon Fairy. Rue belonged out here with the adventurers. Perhaps after everything was said and done, they could spend more time adventuring with everyone. Assuming DCO survived their efforts.

Turk swooped down, dropping Badgy atop the Demonic Lamb. Ifrit's increased attack speed and DPS meant that he was solidly holding aggro, and the blood serpents around the special creature didn't strike at Z's animal companion.

Badgy roared and became a ferocious blur of his own, muscles bulging underneath his fur as he activated his own special skills. Badgy the Badgerker entered a blood rage, a cooldown that would ensure he too, for the duration of the skill, couldn't die.

It increased his attack speed and gave him life steal for his attacks, as well as increased the armor penetration of his attacks. The skill didn't last as long as James's Greater Seal of Solomon, but still, the fact that Z's companion could use such a powerful skill on its own was impressive all the same.

Hornz, meanwhile, surrounded itself with a putrid cloud of insects. It stood near the Demonic Lamb trying, with mixed results, to inflict a multitude of debuffs on the creature. The ability was a cooldown that the tank mob had, and explained why the strange, towering humanoid creature with the antlers smelled so... foul. The bugs had erupted out of its putrid flesh.

Arrows rained down on the Demonic Lamb from Elm and Z. Elm's flashed with brilliant lights and colors as his Cosmic Sniper class enhanced and empowered every shot. The various colors indicated he was cycling through elemental affinities and effects.

Z's arrows, on the other hand, had the ability to apply a debuff to their target that increased the damage his pets did to that target. With each hit, his arrows had the ability to increase the stacks of the debuff too, quickly allowing his pets' damage to snowball.

Faust, as all this was happening, was unleashing the extremely impressive and destructive power of nature. Winds swirled around the Demonic Lamb, ripping rock and stone with every twist, launching shrapnel at the creature while lightning crackled and struck the secret boss from above.

Last, but certainly not least, was Oak. The freshly revived tank joined the fray immediately after he was revived, leading with his Unique shield, keen on dishing out as much suffering as he could to the creature that had consumed his life in order to take form in this world.

The might of seven adventurers, along with four summoned companions, equaled that of a small raid party. With two proper tanks, an off-tank, two healers, and a healthy range of physical and magical DPS, it was a party that could, and should, strike fear in damn near everything close to their level.

At least... that was the theory.

As the Demonic Lamb's health steadily descended, it suddenly flashed red at the fifty percent mark before it grayed out. That was the only warning they got before the second phase of the fight began.

Despite their levels, despite their skills, despite all of their preparation, they were wool-fully unprepared for what the Demonic Lamb did next.

Chapter Thirty-Two

When people think of cults, they usually, almost inevitably, think of some sort of mass Kool-Aid-induced event. It was just how things went throughout history. James had read plenty about different cults, and they ended in lots of murder, suicide, or in some cases, death by law enforcement, which usually triggered when the cult and the government had a standoff.

During his short seventeen years of life, James couldn't remember hearing about any notable cults. At least, not ones in the real world. Cults existed in immersion, because of course they did... but no one cared about those. It was, after all, immersion.

All of that aside, the one thing that generally didn't happen with cults, because it was scientifically impossible, was mass revival. That didn't stop cult leaders and their followers from believing such things, though.

It was common practice. Serve the leader, make the sacrifice, and then bam, your soul is on a spaceship behind some comet. Whoever made the Demonic Lamb—which James figured had been Steve—had decided that that was exactly what should happen.

Not the spaceship part... the mass revival part.

When the Demonic Lamb's health flashed red, it sent out a pulse of light before its health grayed out. And then to everyone's surprise, rising from the ground like some sort of old-school zombie horror film, came all of the Sacrificial Lambs on the floor. All of them. All seventy-five of them.

Well, James couldn't be certain about the exact number. But it definitely seemed that way. The ground shook and rumbled, and strange moans like the bleating of a punctured bagpipe filled the floor. Thematically, the creatures rising out of the ground were, for all intents and purposes, demonic, zombified sheep.

They still had the blackish red wool and horns, but oozed blood and pus, and their bodies were in various states of decay. Their movements, a small blessing, also seemed staggered and uncertain. At least they seemed like slow zombies, and not like the crazy fast World War Z-type zombies.

Slight blessing aside, there were clear signs that what was happening was going to be a problem. The health on the Demonic Lamb returned to its normal color, implying everyone could damage it again, but at the same time, another timer appeared near its name.

This one was counting up instead of down. Meaning that while it had a limited amount of time left on the floor, something, for some reason, was counting upwards. What was the max time it would get to? What was it set to trigger at? What did the timer even mean? James had no idea.

He glanced around as he reapplied the buffs on Ifrit. Since they could damage the boss again, it made sense to keep his summon topped off. He saw as he worked that everyone else was eyeing the zombified sheep as well while they resumed their own attacks. There was little they could do about all of the zombie mobs right now. The Demonic Lamb, with its swirling blood that stacked debuffs, and its unknown nature in general, was something they had to deal with first and foremost. A fact that James didn't like.

Moans and bleats continued as the sounds of battle raged on the floor. With every second, a little more of the Demonic Lamb's health sapped away. If fought with its daggers, its blood tendrils, and random flashes of what appeared to be black, crimson-tinged lightning.

Ifrit's health wasn't a concern. Nor was Hornz or Badgy's, but James saw Oak's health rapidly dropping, only to jump back up almost as quickly as the two healers focused their efforts on keeping him alive.

More moans, more bleating. James took a second to check their surroundings. The zombified sheep, slow moving as they were, were drawing nearer. The party had been lucky. None had sprung up directly around them. However, just as he had that thought, the timer that was counting upwards above the Demonic Lamb hit ten seconds. It flashed, the creature at about 30 percent of its health, and another pulse of power ripped out from it.

The Demonic Lamb floated a little higher into the air, and its swirling pools for eyes took on a red glow. From the ground, black tendrils grasped hold of everyone, players and mobs alike, that weren't zombified Sacrificial Lambs. The tendrils pulsed, and James noticed a snared debuff appear. The healers were already working on cleansing it, but that was only going to help them. The bigger problem, he realized... was what he saw happening all around them.

Demonic farm animals struggled fruitlessly against the tendrils. The inky snares were, after all, summoned by a special level 85 boss. The poor level 50 mobs couldn't free themselves. James was pretty sure he heard Old Man Jenkins screaming about the tendrils as well. And as they struggled fruitlessly, the tendrils pulsed with dark power. The demonic, zombified sheep moved towards those pulsing tendrils like moths to a flame.

The Demonic Lamb's time on the floor was limited by its mechanics. But apparently, even as it neared death, it was going to ensure its cult grew. James knew full well the dangers of zombified creatures. Everyone in the instance knew full well how dangerous they were.

They'd used zombies, in fact, as a way to turn the tide of a battle during the first-ever Dungeon War, where he'd faced off against BLANK. Back before Matt and Rachel were his friends. Back when Xander was still in control and had tried to manipulate his children into removing James from the game.

A pang of sorrow for Xander, or maybe for BLANK over the loss of their father, hit him. He pushed it aside. This wasn't the time for guilt or sadness. Right now, James had a new threat to worry about on top of the Demonic Lamb. Because there was no way James or the others were going to let the Demonic Farm become overrun by zombies. Not when they still had the boss, and special boss, to contend with.

"As much as I'm enjoying the very Evil Dead vibe," Z was calling out as James turned his focus back to the Demonic Lamb.

It was still floating higher and higher, its cloven hooves now roughly five feet off the ground. Badgy's short three-foot frame was having a hard time reaching the boss now.

"I'm pretty sure we don't want to let this thing keep unleashing those pulses."

He had a point. The timer was still counting upwards. Now at fifteen seconds. Meanwhile, it still had a good forty seconds to go before it was unsummoned. So much was happening in such a short amount of time.

Had its timer stopped counting down when its health had grayed out? Or was there a way it was extending its time on the floor? James really hadn't been paying as much attention to the creature as he should be. There was too much happening all around them. It was pure chaos.

"Well, I don't think we can kill it any faster," Elm called as he released another shot into the Demonic Lamb. "It's not like we aren't trying to kill it as fast as possible."

"I've used all my mass single-target damage spells," Faust added, "and I'm pretty sure my DPS numbers are the highest in the party right now."

"Only because it doesn't count my summons," Z countered with a laugh. He unleashed another set of shots into the Demonic Lamb. The creature's timer hit 20, and James felt everyone in the area instinctively wince. On cue, another pulse, another wave of energy.

Tendrils didn't appear this time. At least… not from the ground.

Chapter Thirty-Three

"We really should have come here with the Boss Slayers," Elm called as the Demonic Lamb's health continued its descent to 0. The timer was nearly at thirty seconds, both ways. And judging by the carnage taking place all around the floor. They didn't want to let it keep counting upwards.

"How was I supposed to know the 'Git Gud' mode would really want us to 'git gud'?" Z was laughing.

They all were, even as they jokingly bitched and moaned about the floor. Even as the zombie sheep used the dark appendages, which had ripped free from their backs during the last pulse to suck the very life from the poor, bound mobs on the floor.

"Like come on, I figured bringing them along would have been overkill."

"We better get some kick ass loot for this," Oak called.

Beside James, Rue and Med Ic wore intense looks of concentration. Keeping the tank alive, especially over the last ten or so seconds, had become an intense task.

With the last pulse that had empowered the zombie sheep, the Demonic Lamb had risen even higher into the air. And when it did, a massive pool of dark, inky nothingness had appeared beneath it, from which more tendrils had sprung, lashing out at anything and everything that moved around them.

Even Ifrit, with his increased movement speed and dodge chance, as well as natural and triggered evasion skills, had begun taking more and more damage. Badgy, meanwhile, was in the process of being dragged down into that very same inky darkness, while Turk tried in a strange tug of war to keep the creature from being consumed by the void-like maw.

"I'm sure it'll all be fine," Z said as he tossed an item behind him.

It was a consumable item, something that players had begun crafting recently from the fifth floor. It was a cybernetic stasis field, a single-use item that deployed a static field of energy in a five-by-five circle. Anything that walked into the field had their movement speed slowed by eighty percent for two seconds.

Apparently, they'd gained the ability to craft the traps and other similar items following some special interactions with Sergeant Jenkins, the acquisition of special cybernetic parts from the mobs on the fifth floor, and players in general reaching high enough crafting levels to create such things.

From what James knew of the items, they weren't cheap, and only players who spent a lot of time on the fifth floor to farm materials or had a lot of gold to spend on such things, actually used them. And this was the first time James had seen one in action. He'd only read about them being used on the Reddit thread for his dungeon.

"Not as good as Crikey's," Z said, noting James's gaze, "but it's better than nothing right now. Picked 'em up for the sixth floor, figured they'd work well against the Fogeyman or Kappas, but hey." He shrugged, shooting multiple arrows into the Demonic Lamb, while the stasis field crackled, stopping the zombified Sacrificial Lamb that had been walking towards him. "Might as well test it out here just in case, yeah?"

He winked at James, unleashed another shot at the Demonic Lamb, and then spun around. He took aim for all of a breath before his bow pulsed with power. An arrow about five times too large erupted from the weapon. It punched into the zombified sheep, and the creature's body blew apart in a gooey mass. Z was immediately covered by the carnage, which caused the grin on his face to falter. James, on the other hand, couldn't help but laugh. And the others, taking quick note of Z's misfortune, all joined in.

"That's what you get for trying to be cool." Faust had an electrical field of his own active now. His wasn't an item but a skill. The DPS storm covered a radius of thirty feet behind him and shot bolts of lightning down at any creatures that came too close.

Z wiped his mouth before his face twisted, a puzzled look on his face.

"Why does it taste like sour cherry Kool-Aid?" he asked, looking directly toward James and Rue.

They both shrugged, while Rue at the same time cast a cleanse on the poor man. The blood splatter had unsurprisingly given him max stacks of the Blood for the Blood God debuff.

"No idea," James said. "Though I'd venture to guess that Steve had a hand in it."

"Probably." Z turned back to the Demonic Lamb, his grin turning to a grimace.

The creature had about three percent of its health left, and the timer counting up had just hit thirty seconds. Further into the sky, it rose. Its eyes glowed like miniature suns now. Power pulsed from it, and this time, a deafening bleat echoed outwards from the Demonic Lamb. It was a powerful, ominous, low sound. Like a thousand different bleats all released at once, all in perfect unison.

Then a combination of attacks blasted into it, and its health hit zero. Immediately, James got an achievement notification as the creature's body erupted, a bloody geyser spraying forth from the inky darkness that had appeared below it. Badgy was flung outwards as the tendrils retracted, the spray of blood shooting a good thirty feet into the air, raining down on everyone.

They didn't have time to cheer as they were covered in the crimson shower. The Demonic Lamb was dead, but the final bleat had most definitely empowered the zombified sheep even more. More tendrils had sprung from their backs, their eyes had taken on a red glow, and their horns had twisted and turned into identical replicas of the culty-looking daggers the Demonic Lamb had been wielding.

Oh, and not to be missed was the fact that they no longer walked on the ground. Instead, they floated a few inches above the ground, which also appeared to have increased their movement speed. The Demonic Lamb had returned to its realm, but not without leaving one final gift for its faithful flock. A parting gift for the creatures to become just that much more of a threat to James and his companions.

And yet all James could think of as they turned to face the undead threat, and Med Ic cast an emergency mass cleanse, was that the damned crimson liquid really did taste like Kool-Aid.

Damnit, Steve.

Chapter Thirty-Four

"A pitchfork?" Oak turned back to the party, motioning at the massive obsidian pitchfork. "The final boss on this floor is a pitchfork?"

The object in question sat atop a pile of hay, like some discount pulp fiction version of Excalibur. Golden runes glowed along the shaft, while crimson pulsed all around it. The fist-sized skull at the shaft of the weapon gazed at the party, and even though its sockets were empty, James could feel the intensity of that gaze.

"A platinum coin says grabbing it does something," Z offered, looking back towards James and Rue as he spoke. "Anyone want to give it a go?"

James eyed Ifrit, really tempted to make his summon grab it. The Unique floor boss that was Hokey Pokey could only be drawn by boss-tiered creatures, a.k.a. Old Man Jenkins or adventurers. Ifrit wasn't either, but considering the Djinn was a Unique summon for a special adventurer class, James was curious if Ifrit would be able to pick it up. Old Man Jenkins, sadly, had succumbed to the zombified sheep horde before they could clear a path to him, meaning that was no longer an option.

"Anyone at all?" Z scanned around the party.

It was clear there was power radiating from the pitchfork. But as was its design, it couldn't do anything yet. Unless it was freed by someone grabbing it, or it took damage, the final boss had to sit there, waiting patiently for someone to make the first move. To that degree, James and the others could easily just walk out of the dungeon without having to face the creature.

But where was the fun in that?

"You want to pick it up?" James asked Ifrit.

The Djinn glanced at the object, and then back at James, a thoughtful expression on his face. Then he shook his head.

"I can sense powerful magic coming from it," he said, his normally boisterous nature subdued, "I'd rather not pointlessly waste the kill stacks I've gained during this run. Already, I have sacrificed my own progress for the good of the adventurers. This time, I'll not risk my life so pointlessly." His blades flashed with fire as he grinned at James. "Besides, I wield proper blades. A pitchfork is not the weapon of a warrior."

"Technically," Z countered, "pitchforks were commonly used in combat during the medieval ages."

Everyone looked at the elf, and he just shrugged and grinned.

"Sorry, couldn't resist. Anywho." He looked back at the pitchfork. Above it, its name, and level glowed for all to see. "Should we just attack the thing and see what happens? I have a feeling it's waiting for us, either intentionally or not, to make the first move."

"If you really want someone to grab the damned thing," Rue interrupted then, walking cockily towards the gleaming pitchfork. She had a mischievous glint in her eyes. "I can sacrifice myself as tribute."

James looked at her, and she shot him a smile and wink. The description had been less than specific about what would happen if an adventurer grabbed it. It was pretty much a given that it would unleash the power of the sealed demon, Olmac Don'ald, but how and in what way hadn't been specified.

James was willing to sacrifice any of the actual adventurers in that regard. They were players, through and through. Other than being awesome gamers, there weren't any strange secrets or settings applied to their forms within DCO. Meaning the mechanic would work just fine.

For him, and especially Rue, though... that wasn't the case. These 'developer' Avatars were brand new additions to the game. There was a chance something could go wrong with the coding. James wasn't a computer expert, but he knew well enough that a single bit of code, the slightest tweak or unforeseen change could cause catastrophic problems.

Past that was the fact that Rue was the only being in existence who was fully, one hundred percent a part of the digital world. If something went wrong with her digital form, there were no safety procedures. Her mind couldn't be immediately extracted from the game and returned to her body.

While slight, perhaps even an impossibility, there was a chance the unknown programming surrounding Hokey Pokey could cause her actual harm. Okay, that was probably not true. If James was being honest with himself, he really just didn't want Rue put in pointless danger. Especially not when they had a whole party of test subjects, er, adventurers standing around them.

"One of the party's healers probably shouldn't put herself at risk pointlessly," James said, trying his best to keep his emotions in check.

Rue scowled at him and placed her hands on her hips. "Where's the fun in playing it perfectly safe?" she asked, cocking her head to the side as she looked at him. "There's a thrill in taking risks." She winked at him. "You should know that."

Whistling and chuckles from the Knights Who Go Ni made James blush. Or if he'd been in his real body, he would have. He still wasn't sure if his Archon race could blush with its bestial face.

"She's got you there," Z said once he was finished laughing. "Though, Rue, I have to side with Nyx on this one. Healers shouldn't be doing reckless things. At least not when it comes to boss encounters. Against normal mobs and whatever else, I have absolutely no issue with how you play as long as you're having fun." He looked back at the gleaming pitchfork. "But considering all of the unknowns this floor has already thrown our way; I'd feel much safer knowing you're not in danger."

"Fine," Rue said with a huff, marching back towards James and Med Ic. "Be a buzzkill, why don't you."

Z chuckled, looked at the rest of the party, and I saw the famous twinkle in his eyes that told me he was about to do something completely reckless and stupid.

"Don't hate me, Rue," he said as he turned his back to the party and sized up the pitchfork. Then with a laugh on his lips, he dashed forward, his bow disappearing into his inventory as he raced up the hay, his hand reaching for the pitchfork.

"But if anyone's going to do something reckless and stupid right about now—" His hand wrapped around the black, glowing shaft. He turned triumphantly and looked down at the party, weapon in hand. "It's going to be me."

And then just like that, Z was gone.

Chapter Thirty-Five

James wasn't sure what was more terrifying. Z completely disappearing, along with all of his pets as if he'd never been there, or a giant pitchfork—which had caused the aforementioned disappearance—flying around and randomly stabbing at everyone it could.

No sooner had Z disappeared than the pitchfork, now magically floating in midair, had lunged at the next closest thing. Oak managed to block the jab from the tines, catching the blow with his shield, but the force had pushed him back. The tank's health took a bit of damage as well, and James figured that the level 75 Unique floor boss had a built-in pierce mechanic.

"I don't see a revive orb," Med Ic said as he turned his gaze towards James and Rue, a look of accusation crossing his face. "What happened to him?"

James shrugged, honestly uncertain. His prompts hadn't told him what would happen if an adventurer tried to wield Hokey Pokey. He knew if Old Man Jenkins picked the weapon up that a powerful demonic presence would have taken over the boss and they'd be fighting that. But as for Z, James had no idea.

"He's not dead," Rue answered. "If I had to guess, he's been teleported to a different location. Look at his information in the party window."

Med Ic's eyes glanced to the side as he scanned the information. It was likely that the healer had just intended for James and Rue to give him a quick answer, treating the 'developers' as walking wikis for the game. A damning crutch, really, considering how quickly he'd grown complacent. James couldn't blame him, though. It was an easy thing to do. Who better to ask about the unknown in a game than someone who worked on the game?

Except that James and Rue weren't actual developers. And they barely had any extra information regarding what was going on compared to the adventurers. But Med Ic and the others didn't know that. At least not yet. They would though. Soon.

"It's grayed out," Med Ic said, his face puzzled.

He glanced at Oak, who was continuing to dodge the swinging pitchfork while attempting to strike it with his axe in between blocks. Faust was casting spells at it, and Ifrit was swinging his own blades at the object. Ifrit reminded James of someone trying to swat a fly. If that person was twenty feet in height and the fly was a seven-foot-long danger stick, that was.

"I don't feel like it's maneuvering appropriately," James muttered as he watched the fight.

Since he was a pet class, all he had to do was keep himself out of danger and keep his buffs up on Ifrit. That type of play style meant that he had a lot of time to sit back and puzzle out the mechanics of mobs. While figuring out what had happened to Z was the biggest concern, James couldn't help but question what the person who'd designed the pitchfork had been thinking.

It was clearly crafted out of obsidian. And yet it was bending and twisting midair like a Japanese dragon, or perhaps a snake from the ancient retro games. James didn't have to be a scientist to know that obsidian wasn't fluid or malleable.

If he had to guess, the strange fluidity of the weapon was how the developers justified giving the Unique boss its passive 25% chance to dodge incoming damage. Between that, its protection from nonmagical sources, and its defense stat of 1,666, Hokey Pokey was proving quite tanky.

"If he's not here, where is he?" Med Ic said after a moment. He'd paused to cast a heal on Oak.

Elm, with Z gone, had taken command, and was calling out battle plans for the party. Z was just a DPS for the party, with the addition of his pets being able to fill in roles as needed. With him gone, they were only down damage, nothing more, nothing less.

It was less of a serious concern from a party survival point of view than if a party's tank or healer was suddenly removed from the premises.

Still, losing the additional DPS of Badgy and Turk would hurt, as did loosing Hornz's tank skills.

"I'm not sure, honestly," James answered. "I didn't know Hokey Pokey could make a person disappear like that."

"Yet you were quick to question Rue grabbing it," Med Ic countered.

"That's because he's got a crush on me," Rue quipped before James could come up with an excuse to justify his actions. From the way Med Ic saw it, James had been protecting Rue. And it made him seem guilty.

"Rue," James started, but she giggled and cut him off.

"Nyx here doesn't like the idea of me putting myself in any danger. Whatsoever. Honestly," she heaved a fake sigh, "it's so exhausting. And yet"—she shot James a wink—"what can I say? I'm a sucker for that kind of chivalry."

James could feel his neck heating up. He was pretty sure Rue was just lying on her feet to get Med Ic off his back, but he had to admit, her words rang true. James didn't want Rue getting hurt. He'd do everything in his power to protect her. And he hated the idea of her taking pointless risks. Call it chivalry or whatever, but he cared about her. And there was nothing wrong with that.

The lie worked. Med Ic grinned, and a chuckle bubbled out.

"Ah, to be young again," he said, shaking his head. He turned his attention back to the party that was fighting the boss. Hokey Pokey still had *a lot* of his health pool remaining. "Still, we need to figure out what happened to Z." He nodded up and to the left, implying they should check the party screen Rue had mentioned. "Wherever he is, he's taking damage. And I know he's got a crazy number of potions, healing items, and other tricks up his sleeve, but he's not invincible. Even with his menagerie to keep him safe."

Sure enough, Z's grayed out information, health bar included, was still active. They couldn't see any buffs or debuffs on him, but his health was dropping slowly. The way it inched downwards made James think that, wherever he was, he was under the effect of a DoT ability.

It could be from a skill, or perhaps the area he'd been teleported to was passively damaging to adventurers. Either way, without a healer with him, sooner or later he'd die. Would his revive orb appear back on the floor when that happened? Would something happen to empower Hokey Pokey if Z died wherever he was?

Even more concerning, when James focused on Z's information by pulling up the party chat skill, he noticed a block on the message feature. Wherever Z was, they couldn't send him information either.

"Any ideas then?" James asked.

The benefit of the Demon Lamb and the zombie sheep from earlier was that all of the other mobs on the floor were now dead. All they had to worry about was the flying pitchfork. No stray Dicken blasts, nor random exploding sheep, and no Old Man Jenkins.

There was still the off chance that Charles the Dicken appeared, but past that, they could focus solely on Hokey Pokey. And even if Charles the Dicken did appear, he had a five-minute summon mechanic before he became an active threat to players.

Which meant that they had enough breathing room to try and sort out the fight. Even more so thanks to their level difference. Hokey Pokey may be a Unique floor boss, but the Knights Who Go Ni were still ten levels, or just nearly ten levels, higher than it depending on the player. Combined with their gear, and all of their various class boosts, they had the stats to handle this fight without a constant feeling of panic or imminent death.

"I've got a few," Med Ic said, and the healer held up a hand to rub his chin. He looked from James, to Rue, and then back to the pitchfork. "Probably not the most brilliant plan, but a plan, nonetheless."

"Well, if it gets this fight over with and gets Z back," James said, applying another stack of buffs to Ifrit as he spoke, "I'm all ears."

A look crossed Med Ic's face as he spoke. It reminded James, and not in a good way, of Z when he was about to make a crazy play. "Here's the plan."

Chapter Thirty-Six

James was pretty sure everyone in the Knights Who Go Ni was crazy.

Well, maybe not crazy. This was just a video game, and they didn't have any real stakes against them. And they were without a doubt the most experienced and cohesive group of gamers he'd ever had the pleasure of meeting.

But even still, the reckless abandon with which they'd throw themselves into the unknown, especially to help each other and seize victory, inspired James. It also cemented his decision to bring them into the fold once they were somewhere a little more private.

"Snare the pitchfork," Med Ic called out to Oak as he prepared to put his plan into action.

The tank glanced back at the healer, then shrugged and activated a snare effect. Lightning erupted from around him, creating a massive cage of pulsating power. The Unique boss lashed against its electric confines, like a dog placed in a too small cage. The snare was effective, but it'd be short lived. Most effects were against bosses.

"If this works…" Med Ic was already running towards Oak and the others. He nodded in passing to Elm. "Follow me."

Elm nodded back, a grin on his face.

"What about me?" Oak grumbled. He wasn't even bothering to ask what Med Ic was up to.

"Stay here and tank. We're splitting for a zone fight." And with that, Med Ic arrived at the caged Unique Boss. He reached his hand out and grabbed hold of the obsidian handle. Just like before, the skull at its base flared with power, and then Med Ic was gone. James checked and confirmed that, just like Z, the healer's name had grayed out.

"Here goes nothing." Elm had begun moving even as Med Ic raced towards the pitchfork.

The electrical cage around it cleared, and it shot upwards, but Elm was just as fast. An arrow shot towards it, crackling with power, and smashed into the boss. It wasn't a snare, but a slow. The pitchfork's movement speed decreased by about half, giving Elm the time he needed to grab hold of it.

And just like that, they were down three members.

"Guess I'm supposed to sit here and keep tanking it," Oak grumbled, his shield already interrupting another blow.

James looked at the poor tank. Oak did his job well, but it usually meant he was stuck with the short end of things.

"I can have Ifrit try and tank if you want to go with them," James offered.

Med Ic had discussed the plan with them. Z's pets could serve as tanks wherever they were. With Elm and Med Ic reunited with Z, the healer was confident they could handle whatever they were facing on the other side. And with Rue as a healer, Med Ic didn't feel bad about risking his life on the plan.

"Appreciate it," Oak grunted as the pitchfork slammed into his shield. The A.L.I.E.N. head on the shield lashed out, spraying acid, the green liquid quickly coating the gleaming obsidian. "But it's probably best if I stay out here. If we wipe out here, who knows what happens to them." He sighed, "And sadly, my level gap means I'm better suited to be the tank out here anyways."

"It's not like it's a hard job right now," Faust said.

Lightning storms crackled above, and the pitchfork danced in the air as it attempted to weave between the strikes. Some hit it, others completely missed as the Unique Boss engaged in a deadly waltz. All the while, Oak held its aggro, masterfully working his skills to keep the Unique boss fully focused on him. Given Faust and Ifrit's extremely high damage outputs, it was impressive.

"I never said it was." Oak's shield let out a clanging sound as it blocked another attack.

Crimson light glowed around Rue before it rushed towards the tank to heal him.

Oak nodded back at her appreciatively as he prepared another skill. "Just hate splitting the party."

"It brings back memories, though," Faust said as they continued their clash. Hokey Pokey had only lost about a third of its HP so far, and James knew this was going to be a long battle. "Locking us out of communication with each other is new."

"It's not like the good old days where we could all just chill in voice chat with each other outside of the game, and work around any mechanics meant to hinder our communication," Oak chuckled, his voice filled with nostalgia. "Really crazy how much more intense these battles can be."

"Definitely makes DCO worth playing," Faust concluded. "Between the endless class possibilities, and the sheer variety of dungeons and experiences we get to try out." He laughed, pointing both of his hands toward the pitchfork as he spoke.

Energy crackled as a massive beam of raw lightning tore from his hands. The air around him distorted from the heat as it smashed into the boss, the sound of the collision like the crashing of waves upon a cliff. Then a boom ripped out of the air around them, deafening James for a moment, triggered by the intense heat of the lightning.

"Glad we got the chance to play a game like this in our time," Faust said as everyone's hearing returned. "Makes what we've lived through all worth it."

Oak and Faust went quiet at that, and James felt a solemn weight fall upon the group. He had no idea what they'd all been through. He knew Z's story. A former Marine turned brilliant doctor turned school nurse with an extremely tragic backstory.

What about the others? What had they all seen? What had they all been through? And how did they continue pushing forward through all of that? How did they smile and laugh when it was clear they'd seen their fair share of tragedy and sorrow?

James looked at Rue, but she shook her head, silencing him before he began. It wasn't their place to interrupt the somber moment. He got that. This was something intimate, something he and Rue were outsiders for.

And that was fine. The adventurers could have their moment. James focused instead on dealing with Hokey Pokey and surviving this Unique boss. He'd help them get another potential Instance and another set of fun experiences first before he turned the mood even darker. Before he told them the truth about DCO and what was to come.

For now, they had a possessed pitchfork to deal with. After, they'd deal with the vile truth behind the game they'd all come to love.

Chapter Thirty-Seven

It took nearly ten minutes given the decreased amount of DPS they had to finally bring Hokey Pokey down. When its health hit zero, the skull at the base of the pitchfork flashed with a bright light. It then shattered, a crazed, cackling escaping past James and the others before it faded into eerie nothingness.

With the skull shattered and the magic animating it gone, the pitchfork crumbled apart, and a rift appeared where it had been. Swirling black and red energy formed into an oval nearly six feet tall and roughly four feet wide. From the oval emerged a laughing and chatting Z, Med Ic, and Elm, as well as Z's animal companions.

"About time you guys brought it down," Elm said as he looked pointedly at Faust. "Weren't you bragging just the other fight that your DPS was the highest in our party? What took so long?"

"Just because it's the highest in the party," Faust countered, "doesn't mean I can make up for losing not one but two of the other DPS dealers in our party."

"We left you with Nyx and Ifrit," Med Ic replied, nodding towards the massive Djinn.

Ifrit was sweating. Small bits of flame dripped down his face and bare chest, before falling to the ground, leaving sizzling scorch marks. The Djinn had been moving nonstop the entire battle. Hokey Pokey's evasion rate had made the fight hard on him.

"It was still a high-level Unique boss fight," Faust added. "If you wanted to burn it fast, you should have stayed out here with us." He looked around. "Though, honestly, it probably did go better than it should have. Rue's quite the healer." He winked at Rue. "Probably better than you actually, Med Ic."

"Hey now," Z interrupted before Med Ic could respond, "no need to insult Med Ic. Besides, it was good that he came when he did. I needed help with the pitchfork's friends on the other side."

Z's grin told James that he'd made some sort of joke, but James didn't get it.

"What did happen when you grabbed the pitchfork?" James asked, deciding it wasn't worth dwelling on whatever old school humor Z had. "You disappeared from here and your name was grayed out. But that's all I could tell."

"The boss fight is apparently a two-fer," Z said, nodding back to the crackling portal that was already shrinking. "Not sure if it has other ways to teleport adventurers to that realm, or it's just for anyone foolish enough to grab it, but it's a pretty weird situation regardless. Takes you to a massive, well... farm."

"Like, just a different variant of this floor?" James asked.

"Nope. The layout was nothing like this floor. The one we were teleported to felt more authentically farm-like. Though, the animals were all demonic farm animals. There were a ton of them too. All level 75. They aggroed onto me the moment I appeared there, and it was all I could do to hold them off before Med Ic and Elm arrived."

"I think they're a mechanic for the fight," Elm added. "Pretty sure the boss has some sort of way to summon those farm animals to the instance in which everyone is fighting it. Us being there and killing them likely prevented that from happening. Though, on top of the swarms of demonic farm animals, the air itself was toxic. We were taking about one percent of our HP every ten seconds as damage. I'm guessing it's a DPS check.

"A group has to teleport to that alternate farm and destroy mobs, while the main group fights the actual boss. If the group that teleports falls, or no one teleports, then the boss will summon its mobs to the actual fight. And if the group outside cannot kill the boss fast enough, eventually the group that teleported to the other farm will likely fall from the constant battling and life drain."

James liked the sound of that. He'd faced bosses like it during his time playing large scale MMOs in immersion like Warcraft Universe, aka WU. He'd had a few interesting fights with his warlock character there, where the mechanic actually separated him from his summons, which forced him to have to play a completely different style for the fight.

Challenges outside of the norm were refreshing for MMO players, and he'd appreciated it. After he'd vented his frustration over the mechanic more than a few times after some tragic raid wipes, that was.

"Any way." Z pointed towards a chest that had appeared in place of the haystack Hokey Pokey had been stuck in. "Should we grab our loot and keep going?

The last loot they'd gotten on the floor from the Demon Lamb had been... interesting. They'd each received a single jagged dagger that looked exactly like the one the Demon Lamb had been holding. There were no stats on the dagger, and the only description on it said, ominously **Stab ...Heart...Power**. An item that quickly found itself stashed in everyone's inventory for later experimentation.

"Here's hoping for something good," Oak said, rubbing his hands together eagerly. "Daddy needs another Unique item."

"Another Unique item," Z said with a mock sneer. "How about you share the luck and let me get one for once."

"I'm sure sooner or later that the Goddess of Luck will bless you with something good," Rue said, shooting James a mischievous wink as she did. "Maybe not here, but eventually."

"There's a reason I offer her a platinum coin every time I step foot on the first floor," Z replied, completely unaware that Rue was the afore mentioned goddess. "Increased loot drop and rarity chances are too good to pass up. Especially at our levels."

The others all nodded and moved towards the chest. It glowed with crimson and black demonic energy, the same as had been emanating from the skull around Hokey Pokey.

"Speaking of levels," James said, a grin on his own face. "I'm about three-quarters of the way to 80 already thanks to the achievements we'd just received."

"How many achievements did you get?" Z asked as he neared the chest.

"Two," James answered, looking over the two of them as he spoke.

Achievement Unlocked- Got Good – Defeat a Unique Boss that has been summoned in a Hard Mode instance
Reward- 10,000 XP, 25 Platinum

Achievement Unlocked- Try Hard – Clear a Hard Mode Instance

Reward- 15,000 XP, 30 Platinum, Title: Dungeon Veteran

Dungeon Veteran: Increases experience gained for party when clearing Hard Mode instances by 1% per member with this title, up to 5% max.

The title was nice, James had to admit, but the experience bonus and financial gain was even better. Currency in DCO could be exchanged for real world money with an ever-shifting exchange rate. Considering he didn't really need any coin as a player, the platinum could easily just be turned into actual money for him to use in the real world.

Between that and his income he earned as a Dungeon Core, James had found himself quite flush with cash. Enough so that, if not for the government's impending plans, he'd probably have been able to live a life of ease and luxury without much effort. Now, though, the coin wasn't all that exciting to him. If the government got away with their plans, it would all be meaningless.

The experience, as such, was the greatest perk of the adventuring so far. It took adventurers 35,200 XP to climb from level 79 to 80. Those two achievements had gotten him more than half of what he needed, and he'd already had some from the Siege Event. He and Rue were on the cusp of reaching level 80.

It wasn't the main purpose of this dungeon run, but James wouldn't pass up the opportunity to hit level 80. Especially since Steve had confirmed that developer Avatars didn't give their experience to the dungeon upon their deaths, there was no reason for him to 'accidentally' get killed for the greater good of the dungeon.

"Next time, you'll have to be on the away team and get teleported," Z said with a grin, pulling James from his musing. The guild leader's eyes sparkled as he looked at Faust and Oak. "Elm, Med Ic, and I got a total of four. Those two, one for getting teleported to a special boss realm, and one for surviving in the boss realm until you defeated him."

"Now who's the lucky one?" Oak grumbled as Z opened the treasure. His eyes gleamed, and he laughed before Z could respond as each party member received their loot from the Unique Boss Chest.

"Never mind," Oak said, his axe disappearing from his hand to be replaced with an exact replica of Hokey Pokey in his hand. "It's still me."

Chapter Thirty-Eight

Oak's new weapon was classified as a Unique item. Because James wasn't in his Dungeon Core form at the moment, he couldn't easily pull up the information on it. Be that as it may, Oak was more than happy to brag about it. Shortly after leaving the Hard Mode first floor, as they walked from the fifth-floor safe zone town towards the shack that housed the portal to the sixth floor, Oak filled them in on everything they could possibly want to know about it.

"It's called Olmac Don'ald's Tuning Fork," Oak explained excitedly as James walked beside him.

The words turned to frost from the chill of the fifth floor. The others huddled close to the tank as they made their way towards the shack that would lead them to the next floor, knowing full well the dangers of the fifth floor.

Even though level-wise they didn't have much to worry about, considering the mobs were level 75, a lucky critical from a Painguin shot could prove fatal. Especially for James and Rue, who were both squishy classes.

"The set it's a part of is called The Arch Demon's Possession set," Oak continued. "Base stat-wise, it gives me a boost to my attack, mana, and evasion chance. And just like my shield, it is immune to effects that destroy gear."

"Which is good considering your tendency to be eaten," Elm quipped. "Gotta protect your gear from the digestive acids, huh."

"Hey, Nyx," Z cut in, obviously still salty about not receiving a Unique item yet, "what are the chances the boss on the sixth floor can eat Oak?"

"The sixth-floor boss?" James tried to play coy.

"Yeah, the Jormun-Grander," Z replied, fixing James with a knowing smile. "It's a giant level-ending snake, isn't it?" He looked at Oak. "So, technically, it can eat players, right?"

James shrugged in as noncommittal a way as possible, though he felt his lips tug upwards at the thought of Oak getting eaten by the massive sixth-floor boss. The poor guy, with his fear of snakes, would surely curse his luck if that were to occur.

Still, he'd conquered his fear enough to deal with the Giant Playthons on the third floor, so James had no doubt Oak would prevail. Even if it involved a good bit of screaming and protesting.

"If you purposefully try to feed me to a giant snake, I'm uninstalling the game," Oak countered, shooting a glare at Z. "Don't test me. There are plenty of other games I can play that don't involve me getting eaten by giant snakes."

"Yet dragons are totally fine," Faust added, tone sarcastic. "No problems getting eaten by that massive dragon in Monster Hunter."

"Dragons have legs," Oak said matter-of-factly. "And wings, and proper bodies. They're not like snakes that just"—he shuddered—"slither around."

"Can we stop talking about things that slither and get back to your new pokey stick?" Rue cut in. "What else can it do? What special properties does it have?"

Rue, just like James, was eager to know more about the Unique item. They were the only types of items the two of them couldn't create or modify. Everything else—from basic, common items all the way up to Legendary items—they could preview, customize, and even tweak drop chances for. But the Unique items generated on their own and were special and well... unique to certain types of monsters and situations.

James figured there was an overarching, actual AI somewhere within the game that could impact gameplay and the world to some degree. A small degree, sure, but still to a degree. Which, now that James knew that the government planned to trap everyone within DCO, was a little unsettling.

What if something happened? What if the AI got out of control? What if the government who remained in the real world tampered with the AI? What could or what would they do? He pushed the thought from his mind as Oak continued his explanation of his newfound weapon.

"Let's see." He glanced down to the side as they crunched through the snow, his eyes likely reading the information on the weapon that only he could see. "It has the ability to temporarily charm any demonic-based creatures I hit with it, though it says that the rate varies by the strength of the creature."

"Any demonic creature?" Rue asked, raising an eyebrow. She looked over at James. "Do you think that includes Devilkin?"

"Wouldn't you two know as developers?" Z asked.

"There are a ton of aspects to DCO," James replied. They'd practiced this type of scenario with Steve. "Something like this wasn't in our line of expertise."

Z nodded. "That's fair." He then looked from James to Rue, smiling as if they'd walked into a trap. "What was your area of expertise?"

"We're not supposed to say," Rue said. Technically, their area of expertise was the dungeon considering their actual roles. But Steve had told them the safe, political statement that the Dungeon Cores were supposed to use when masquerading in a developer Avatar was that they couldn't say what they worked on specifically, for privacy reasons.

"But you did know about the Demonic Lamb," Med Ic mused, suddenly besides James.

"Back to the pitchfork," James said hurriedly. He forgot how sharp the Knights could be. They always acted so relaxed, laid back, and goofy. Yet at their core, each and every one of them had sharp wits and a good bit of crazy accurate intuition.

"Right, back to my awesome new Unique item." Oak's mouth moved silently as he read something. "It looks like is has two unique abilities. One is called Demonic Parade. Any enemies I kill with my pitchfork have a small chance of being twisted by demonic power and resurrected for an amount of time based on their levels and my own to serve as my pets. The other," he smiled widely as he spoke, "is called Demonic Tuning. I can infuse myself with demonic energy to boost my stats to an increasing degree for every five seconds the skill is active, though…"

"Though…" Z pressed as Oak trailed off.

"Though the longer I channel it, there's apparently an increased risk that I can be possessed by the Arch Demon Olmac Don'ald."

There was a sound of flesh on flesh, and James saw that Faust had just face palmed. He let out a sigh, shook his head, and looked at everyone.

"Seriously…" Faust sighed heavily. "Olmac Don'ald?"

"That's what it says," Oak said before he trailed off again and began shaking his head. The others, a split second later, all started laughing.

"Olmac Don'ald," Z chuckled. "And Hokey Pokey, eh?" He looked back at James and Rue. "Too bad Steve's not here right now."

"Why do you say that?" James asked.

"Because I've got a feeling that Steve knows full well whose department that Unique Boss was, as well as probably a good bit regarding the Arch Demon Olmac Don'ald Oak just mentioned. Bet that zone we got teleported to was actually Olmac Don'ald's farm even."

"What makes you think Steve would know about him?" James had a feeling he already knew the answer, though.

"Because from our time adventuring with Steve, it was made extremely clear that his humor is, well…" He looked at the others, then back at James and Rue. "Unique."

James had no counter to that. It was something he'd learned almost immediately upon meeting Steve. The man who was behind the Toilet Mimics. The man who had created a flip book for ridiculous monster type creation. The man who'd created a tank class called a Spanker that focused on yelling insults at your targets while hitting them with debuffs. There was no better word to describe Steve and his sense of humor than 'unique'.

"He's definitely quite the character," Rue said with a chuckle as the party continued deeper into the woods of the fifth floor.

They'd caught glimpses of monsters here and there, but the Knights Who Go Ni's levels meant that the basic mobs were giving them a wide berth. Still, James was hoping they'd come across Sergeant Jenkins before they reached their target. Killing the fifth-floor boss would definitely help them get closer to level 80. And more than that… James wanted another shot at more Unique Gear himself.

"That he is," Z let out a wistful sigh. "I really hope we can game with him again soon."

"So do I," James answered wistfully.

He really wished he could just go back to gaming, without any other worries. But sadly, that wasn't the case. And with each step through the white winter expanse of the fifth floor, he imagined himself sinking deeper into the snow from the weight of what was about to come. From the weight of the secrets he was holding, and the truths he soon would be revealing to Z.

He prayed silently, wishing the Predator would ambush them. Anything to distract the group, buy them a little more time so that he could put off for a few more blissful moments what must be done.

Sadly, the gods of the game didn't listen. Or more darkly, couldn't considering that the main deity, Yarx, was based off Xander himself. And the original developer of DCO, the man who'd spearheaded and created this game, was gone forever.

Chapter Thirty-Nine

"I'm sure you already know this floor is dangerous," Z said as the group stood before the theatrical entryway James had designed for his sixth floor.

They'd gotten to the old shack without any resistance, save for a few pot-shots by distant Painguins. Those attacks might as well have been shot from squirt guns as Oak, even distracted by his new Unique toy, was able to easily block them. The Knights Who Go Ni had more than enough experience on the fifth floor to handle any surprises it threw their way, meaning James and Rue had nothing to fear.

Unfortunately, it also meant that they didn't get any experience towards level 80.

"That feels like an understatement," Rue said with a chuckle. "Didn't you guys mention earlier that you'd wiped on this floor?"

Z ran a hand through his hair, offering her a sheepish smile. "Well, I did." He looked at the others. "But to be fair, we were being pretty reckless. Level-wise, we aren't up to par to do too much on this floor. If the dungeon follows its normal trend, the boss has to be at least level 100. But we were still able to handle the basic mobs, even with it being our first time seeing them."

"Oh, so you found the boss?" Rue asked with an eyebrow raised. She knew full well they hadn't. James had missed the run itself, due to his conversation with Hades, but Rue and Steve had watched the run in full.

"Well, no…" Z looked at the others, but they all shook their heads. No one was going to help him out in this situation. And Rue was being ruthless.

"So you died to those basic mobs?" Rue said, her tone filled with amusement. "The ones you just said you are able to handle."

"Like I said, we were being reckless." Z shot the others a quick glare that easily implied he was not going to forgive them for leaving him high and dry, before he looked back at James and Rue. "Either way, we know what we're facing now, and know a decent bit about the layout of the floor. So we can pretty much guarantee that we'll get you two to level 80 here pretty fast as long as nothing crazy happens."

"Sounds like a plan." James rubbed his hands together, excited to finally reach that milestone.

Unlike the frozen fifth floor, the labyrinth of the six floor was warm and humid. However, his hands still felt cold and stiff, and he couldn't help but shiver. It wasn't from excitement. His anxiety filled him to the brim, and he knew he couldn't put off his mission much longer.

"I, uh," James's voice cracked a bit, and he growled, trying to clear his throat. The sound, coming from his Archon form's bestial head, echoed in an ominous way. "I want to talk with you guys about something."

"Oh yeah?" Z and the others crowded around, drawing closer to him.

They were all relaxed, smiling and clearly having fun. To them, this was all just a game. And from their point of view, they were just getting to enjoy the opportunity of playing the game with one of the developers.

"What's up, Nyx?" Z pressed.

James looked at Rue, opened his mouth to speak, but Rue cut him off.

"Not right here," Rue said quickly, pulling the focus back to her. A smile crept onto her face as she took the lead. "If I remember correctly, this dungeon floor has musical mobs, right?"

Oak visibly blanched, and James remembered the poor tank's experience with them.

"That it does," Elm said, slapping the tank on the back. "My brother here was a total fanboy of the mobs and got himself killed by them."

Oak slapped the hand away, and the two shared a laugh before the tank spoke. "You're asking about the J-Kappas, right?"

"Those are the ones," Rue smiled, eyes gleaming mischievously. "I think we should talk once we find them. There's something I think you guys would enjoy seeing before we take a moment to talk." She looked around at their current surroundings, dim lighting, stone walls and floor. With no one speaking, it was extremely quiet.

So quiet, in fact, that James realized that their voices carried and echoed quite a bit. He'd been so nervous and stressed about what he needed to tell the Knights that he'd forgotten the original plan. They were going to come to the sixth floor and make sure it was as impossible as possible for anything they said to be overheard before they told the Knights what they needed to.

"So, you didn't know about Hokey Pokey." Z looked accusingly at Rue. "But you know about the J-Kappas?"

"Different groups worked on different things in the game," Rue said in response. "With how many monsters there are across DCO, there were countless teams designated to various creature designs. Others were tasked with tasks adjacent to monsters. Such as research for musical inspiration for certain mobs, or other pop culture type necessities." She winked at Z. "I can't say what I was a part of, but I'm just saying there are sooo"—she dragged the word out—"many things that overlap within DCO that it's not all that weird to think I know about some monsters and not others."

"Pop culture, you say?" Z looked Rue up and down. "I'd expect someone older would have a role like that. Though, I suppose your Avatar doesn't necessarily have to reflect how you look in the real world. After all, while you could totally be a blood sucker for all I know, I don't think you're a vampire." He looked from Rue, back to James. "Does she sparkle in the sunlight?"

"Uh?" Before James caught up in the conversation, laughter broke out as everyone, including Rue, immediately relaxed again, the mood in the area light for the moment. James hadn't realized how tense he'd been, or how stuffy the air had felt. With that interaction and the fact they would need to find the J-Kappas before he had to have his talk with Z and the others, James relaxed once more.

"Thank you," he whispered to Rue as the party began making its way through the labyrinth, their laughter echoing down the hallways, leading the way.

"I cannot do this for you," Rue said softly, taking his hand in hers. "But I'll be right there beside you, supporting you every step of the way."

James squeezed her hand, looking down into her eyes, wishing they were back in their normal forms so that he could give her a hug and kiss.

"However." Rue's mischievous smile was back. "It's your platinum that we're using for the J-Kappas, not mine."

James wanted to protest, but before he could, Rue let go of his hand and skipped happily forward. With a resigned sigh, he followed after her.

Damnit, Rue.

Chapter Forty

It didn't take the party long to get to the J-Kappas. The Knights had already developed an effective method to deal with the Chem-Eras. Through a combination of crowd control abilities, controlling aggro with Oak and Hornz, and a crazy amount of DPS spread out from all different angles, including on the creature's back via an enraged Badgy that tried to ride the massive creature like a bucking bronco, the beast didn't present a problem to the party.

Interestingly, they didn't use their previous cheese tactic, and James had to wonder if they felt self-conscious using such a method in front of the 'developers'. He figured, generally, that it was pretty rude to cheese a game or exploit it directly in front of people who, as far as they knew, had put a lot of love and hard work into the game.

With the giant obstacle cleared, they were clear to move along the same path that the Knights had taken on their first dive—the left-most path. First was the room with the Chem-Era, then the hallway filled with J-Kappas, and the potential dangers of When-Wolves and Fogeymen in the shadows.

"There they are," Z said, pointing down the hallway. It was a rather unnecessary gesture and statement considering that the musical mobs were in the middle of hosting a little mini concert for themselves.

There were six of them in total, and James quickly took mental note of their 'personas'. A Businessman, a Pretty Boy, two Spice versions, a Shy version, and an Idol. For their current purpose of tracking down the mobs, their types didn't matter. But for an actual dungeon run, trying to collect the buffs that synergized best for your party would be key. And that would mean being able to identify quickly which J-Kappa was which in order to best spend your money.

"There they are." James looked at Rue, and she gave him a nod. He looked back at the others, and then at the mobs once more. With a sigh, he pulled up his inventory and called forth a platinum coin.

"Who here has the best accuracy?" James asked, glancing between Elm and Z. "Which of you has the best aim?"

"Me—" Z started.

"Obviously I do—" Elm began.

The two looked at each other, and then back to James.

"Why?" They asked in unison.

"I want to see if you can land this coin in the cup atop the J-Kappa's head," James said, motioning towards the rocking out monsters. "Their name literally has Kappa in it," he said with emphasis, "you know, from Japanese mythology."

James may not have known pop culture like Rue and the Knights, but he knew mythology.

Z's eyes went wide, and Med Ic facepalmed. Before either could take the coin, though, Oak walked up and grabbed the coin from James's hand, before turning to look at the mobs.

"You mean all we've got to do is get the coin in the cup?" He laughed and quickly drew a line in the ground with his weapon before he stowed his shield and pitchfork. Then he took up a rather ridiculous stance. He turned his body sideways, his right arm bent upwards at a ninety-degree angle as he held the coin gingerly between his thumb and middle finger. "Finally, all my years of playing beer pong will pay off."

As if those were magic words, the other Knights all pulled out their own coins and went to stand by Oak, just behind the line he'd drawn. James looked back at Rue, confused at what was going on. All he got in response was a massive grin on Rue's face. She winked at James, pulled out her own coin, also platinum, and went to stand beside the others.

"First one to get a coin in wins bragging rights?" she said quickly. "Or should we go for a higher-stakes game?"

"You sure you want in on this?" Z asked with a chuckle. "I literally have no idea how many games of beer pong I've played, but the number is astronomical. Especially thanks to my time in the Corps. And that's not even counting all of the games of 'who can get the rock closest to the other rock'."

"Uh, games of what now?" James couldn't help but ask.

"It's a deployment game," Z said with a glance back at James. "Trust me. When you get bored, you find any way possible to amuse yourself."

"I'm pretty sure I can hold my own," Rue said confidently. "But I'll be kind and let you all go first, just to make sure you have a fair chance."

"Alright, you're going to regret that, though," Oak said before he flung the coin forward.

It flew in a large arc through the air, flying a good thirty feet before it clattered by one of the J-Kappas, just missing its head. Oak cursed as the creature picked up the coin, pocketed it, and then continued rocking out. Apparently, they didn't view coins being thrown at them as a sign of aggression.

James made a mental note to look into that. If the mobs didn't aggro at such things, it would make it way too easy for parties to activate the Sellout passive without any potential danger. And James couldn't have that. He liked making easy money as much as the next person, but what he needed most right now was easy experience.

"All talk, no follow through," Faust said, releasing his own coin.

It spun through the air, reflecting the torchlight in a myriad of flashes before it clipped the edge of the cup atop the Idol's head. For a moment, it looked as if he'd done it, but the coin bounced off the bottom of the bowl and flew out, falling to the ground. As before, the coin was pocketed, and the concert continued.

Technically, the coin Oak had thrown had been James's platinum, but making two platinum coins in mere seconds was crazy. He couldn't help but dream about what may happen once he got NPCs on this floor like he had on his first three. Could he set up something similar to the carnival on the third? Could tossing coins at J-Kappas' heads be a truly lucrative business venture?

James shook his head and turned his focus back to the group. Med Ic was next to toss his coin. It clipped the shoulder of a J-Kappa but missed the cup. The others were in full on shit-talking mode. They were having so much fun, acting as if they weren't in a dungeon filled with level 90-plus mobs.

"Elm, would you like to go first?" Z said. "Give you the shot to make the first cup in."

"If you want to hand me the win, sure." Elm took aim, preparing his coin toss.

"I'll just make mine right after you, and we'll be tied up for bragging rights," Z said confidently.

"If you say so." Elm's made a few practices toss motions, narrowing his eyes as he did.

He focused on the target and took a deep breath. Only once he'd fully steadied himself did he let the coin fly. It had a perfect arc, and flew through the air with the deadly precision James had come to expect from the Sniper.

His coin landed perfectly in the cup of the Businessman J-Kappa. A fountain of golden light enveloped the J-kappa, washing over it, and then the name above it switched from red to white. It stopped participating in the concert and began to head towards the group.

"Oh shit, I just got an achievement," Elm said with a laugh as the mob approached him. "Talent Scout huh?" he chuckled and looked appreciatively at Rue and then James. "I had no idea we could hire out these mobs with that trick."

"Well, if that's the case…" Z's arm flicked forward, and just like with Elm's toss, his aim was true.

The coin dropped into the cup of the Idol. Just like the other one, she flashed with golden light, and then promptly began to make her way towards the party, hired for the dungeon run just like Elm's.

Rue was next, and to James's and probably everyone's surprise, her aim was just as true. She managed to land a coin in the head of the Pretty Boy persona. James wasn't sure if she'd picked it intentionally or selected one at random. Was Rue into pretty boys?

He pushed the foolish thoughts aside as their party quickly gained its own little band. Oak, Med Ic, and Faust all had more coins in their hands, and were frantically throwing them towards the J-Kappas. James lost track of how much platinum he made in the next few minutes, but eventually, all of the J-Kappas had been acquired.

"Alright." James took a heavy breath and looked at the others. "If you guys could, make your J-Kappas start playing their music. It should buff us quite a bit, and if possible, I want you to see just how loud you can have them play."

Everyone did as he asked, not taking the time to question James since they were all having fun testing out a new mechanic they'd just learned about. A moment later, the hallway was filled with blaring J-pop music, echoing down the hallway so loud that James had no doubt it would be impossible for anyone not in their immediate area to hear what James was about to say.

He motioned for everyone to gather around, and then once they had formed a circle around him, he began.

Chapter Forty-One

"Everything I'm about to tell you, is the truth," James began, his words somber.

Compared to the upbeat concert being played around them, it seemed so out of place. And yet the Knights could tell he was serious and gave him their full attention. The sudden shift in his tone, his attitude was a clear indicator of just how dire this was.

"First, and most importantly, I'm not a developer." He motioned to himself and then Rue. "In fact, we're players just like you. Only"—he looked at Rue and took a deep breath—"our roles in the game are different."

"How so?" Z asked, while the others inched closer, trying their hardest to hear his words past the vocals of the J-Kappas.

"In short," James offered Z a wry smile. "I'm really the Dungeon Core for the game. The Mad Mage Glyax, if you would."

"Then that means Rue here is..." Z trailed off, and Rue finished his statement for him.

"The White Beast of Chaos," she declared proudly. She shot them all a toothy grin and licked her lips ominously. Her Dungeon Fairy Avatar form was well known and loved by the adventurers in his instance of DCO, but her bloodthirsty nature was also well feared and respected.

"So, the dungeons in DCO are run by players," Z mused aloud, "and not some magical AI." He rubbed his chin thoughtfully. "That's definitely interesting. And that means you're someone from the same town as us, right?" He looked James up and down, as if trying to puzzle out who James was.

"It does," James said slowly, preparing himself for what was to come next. "And you already know who I am, Zach," James said Z's name, trying to keep his voice from shaking. "Sorry I could never game with you before, but well, I wasn't lying about playing the game with Rue here."

Z's eyes went wide as he looked from James, to Rue, back to James. The rest of the Knights just glanced at everyone, not quite following the latest development, but still invested in the story.

"James?" Z said softly. "Is that really you?"

"In the flesh," James said, the revelation lifting a part of the weight off his shoulders. That was the first part of this task—telling Z who he truly was. A secret he'd been wanting to share with the man ever since they'd begun interacting. And even more so as Z continued to care for him and share more about his life with James.

"You poor kid." Z shook his head. "This whole time, you've been stuck playing as the Dungeon Core? You"—he motioned all around—"you've been isolated, creating the dungeon, making all of this, unable to play with everyone else?" He shook his head. "That's not fair. How could they put so much on a kid? How could the P.L.O.T. allow this?"

James cleared his throat. "That's... that's not all I have to share with you guys."

Z looked at him, and nodded. "Continue, then."

"This information, I'm sure you can understand, is an extremely well-kept game secret. I had to sign an NDA before I was able to take on my role, and I can assure you, it's not been easy. But that's a story for a different time." He wasn't about to tell Z he'd been targeted by a hacking group. The old man didn't need to know all of James's hardships. He had no doubt that if Z did know about that, the caring nurse would immediately go into caretaker mode.

"But if you're telling us this," Faust interjected, "doesn't it mean you're breaking your NDA?"

"It does," James let out a heavy sigh. "But honestly, I wouldn't be unless it was a matter of utmost importance."

"Such as?" Z asked, encouraging him to continue.

"Life or death," James said ominously. The weight of the words couldn't be dismissed, even as the Idol continued to sing what sounded like a pop love song. "And not just for me or Rue. But everyone."

"Everyone... here?" Oak asked, looking around. "Or everyone in town, or..."

"Everyone in the world," James said. "Within the next two days, if I can't stop it, the entire world will end."

There was silence from the group as the music continued. James let the moment sink in, let them process his words. He could see disbelief on a few faces. Though, Z and Faust looked determined and solemn. James knew Z's history with the government. And of all of the Knights, he figured Z would be the one to actually believe him.

Z had seen before what the government was willing to do. Getting Z to believe him wasn't the hard part. It was the others he needed to truly convince. But he'd already devised a plan to make them believe him, make them realize that he wasn't just some kid spouting fairy tales or making up stories.

"I know this may be hard to believe—" he began, but Faust cut him off.

"Hold on." Faust eyed him, seeming to really try and bore into him. "You're the kid I drove home the other night, aren't you."

"I, uh... what?" James hadn't expected that question.

"From the raid on Cyb3ru5," Faust said. "You're the kid we found there. I drove you home."

It hit him then. The driver who'd spoken briefly with him when he'd been rescued. The man who'd been humming the tune James had found oddly familiar as he'd drifted off to sleep. It all made sense then. That tune, that song, had been the one Z and the others had used to try and figure out if the mimic was a mimic. That driver had been Faust?

"Wait, that was you?" James started. He felt a chill run down his spine. That driver had worked for the government. "You," he stammered, "you work for the government."

He felt sick. The world seemed to begin to crush in on him. Had he messed up? If Faust worked for the government, then he could ruin everything. He could report James before James even got the chance to try and thwart their plan.

A strong hand pressed against his shoulder, the pressure pulling him from his panic.

"James," Z spoke softly, pulling James's focus to him. "Look into my eyes and just breathe."

James did as he was instructed, taking slow, steady breaths, trying to match Z's own breathing. The whole while, he held Z's gaze, finding comfort in those calm, reassuring eyes. After a few moments, James's mind stopped reeling.

"Faust here works for the government, yeah, but only because they pay his bills," Z said with a chuckle. "Do you really think I'd surround myself with someone that actually had allegiance to the government after what they put me through?"

"I, well…" James looked from Faust to Z, and shook his head. "No."

"Exactly." Z looked back at Faust and smiled. "You'd be surprised how lucrative government jobs can be." Z continued, "And with a security clearance, it's pretty easy to get a pretty basic job."

"Consider me a lifetime grifter," Faust said with a chuckle. "I went with the simplest path for easy money when I got out of the military. So as it stands, I'm technically employed by the government, yeah, and actually happen to work at the Enforcer facility housed near the town. I'm not an Enforcer, of course, but handle pretty much all the other tasks that are needed to keep the Enforcers working."

"So what you're saying," Rue cut in, giving James a moment to process everything, "is if we needed a man on the inside, you'd be able to help?"

Faust looked at Z, and the leader of the Knights Who Go Ni gave him a nod. Faust then looked back at Z and answered. "Depends on the job, but if what you're saying is true, and assuming we believe you that everyone's life is on the line." He shrugged. "Then yeah, I'd risk my comfortable job for that."

James felt his lips brush against his tusks as he smiled, the whiplash from his panic attack fading. He felt a new bit of confidence flow into him, thanks in no small part from Z's comforting actions, and took another breath.

"Alright, that's good to hear." He looked at the others, all of whom were intently watching him. "Because unless we can reach the DCO servers inside the government's mountain facility, everyone in the world, save for the top elites and chosen few, will die."

"Why do you need to reach the DCO servers, for that?" Faust interjected.

"Because the government isn't planning to just kill everyone. They're planning to kill our bodies but trap our minds within the DCO server forever. So that, well, I guess, they don't have the guilt of actually murdering everyone? Since we wouldn't technically be dead…" James trailed off.

That was what Hades had said had been the reason. But maybe it was just a cover? A way to get everyone in the government on board with the plan. Because he was pretty sure plenty of the elite wouldn't mind just killing everyone off for their own gain. Hell, it had happened in wars in the past, right?

More and more, he figured there were deeper, more sinister, reasons why the plan was to trap everyone within the virtual world. He was also realizing that he didn't really want to know the true darkness of whatever they had planned once most of humanity was trapped. Right now, it was a pretty black and white situation. The government was bad and needed to be stopped. Any more detail would likely just make their enemies scarier and more intimidating foes.

"How very Matrix of them," Z said with a dark chuckle. "So what other details do you have to, you know, *prove* the story to us? I'm pretty quick to jump on the 'the government is evil' train, as you know, James. But even still." He glanced about. "You have to admit this all sounds a bit extreme."

James nodded. "I was getting ready to get to that point."

He mentally sent the okay message to Steve, who'd been a part of this plan. A moment later, all five of the Knights twitched in surprise, and their eyes darted upwards. He knew they'd just received messages, specially tailored for each from Steve.

All he had to do then was wait for a few minutes for each and every one of them to finish reading whatever it was Steve had devised for them. The developer had been sure that a personal endorsement from The One and Only Steve would get all of the Knights on board.

And if that failed, he'd mentioned offhandedly that Hades had provided a few select details on each of the Knights that only the government was supposed to be able to access. There was no way even the most influential game developer would be able to procure such data. Such breaches were considered impossible. Yet it was all there in black and white.

Suffice to say, they were persuasive letters.

After a few moments, with grim looks crossing each Knight's face as they finished their messages, their bodies showing their sudden shift as they realized how serious the situation was, all eyes were once again on James.

"Alright then," Z finally said as he let out a heavy sigh. "It's clear you're telling the truth, and I'm guessing since you're telling us that you've a plan that needs us for it." He offered James a smile, eyes deadly serious. "What can we do to help?"

Chapter Forty-Two

James wanted to tell Z everything. He wanted to tell the man the stories about everything that had happened since Day 1 of DCO. Tell him the tales of Xander, Cyb3ru5, and Hades, all it. But he didn't have time.

The longer they wasted here, the less time they'd have to implement the plan itself. Therefore, even though he wished to tell them everything, he kept it short, succinct, and to the point. The time for stories could come later, after they'd won.

There were a few stages to the plan that he needed the Knights Who Go Ni for. And thankfully, with whatever it was that Steve had sent each of them to corroborate Jame's revelations, he had that. The Knights, because of their notoriety, were invaluable for the second part of his plan. He needed their help to convince everyone in his dungeon to die.

Okay, that sounded morbid. But what he needed was for players to rush experience, and then purposefully die in the dungeon before leveling up to transfer the experience to James. The plan, the story he wanted the Knights to spread, was that doing so would ensure that the dungeon was as powerful as possible for the upcoming special Dungeon Event.

And if there was anyone that could convince a town's worth of gamers to purposely begin offing themselves in a dungeon, it was Z. He was a walking charisma stat, after all.

If Z couldn't do it, no one could.

The next step of the plan was to have the Knights convince everyone to vote for the first battle of the Dungeon War event to take place against

BLANK's dungeon. This 48-hour Dungeon War extravaganza was the largest full immersion event in history. Never before had such a possibility existed where the entire world would be immersed at the same time.

Nefarious reasons aside, it meant this single event would put the most eyes ever on whoever was on top. James needed something that would draw a crowd. Something that would pull all eyes, all the attention, to his dungeon. Something to captivate.

A rematch between the Candy Dungeon and the Random Dungeon was going to be just that.

Next James needed to know that he could count on the Knights not only in the game, but outside of it. He didn't know full well how they'd assault the facility that held the DCO server, but that knowing Faust had government building access was a game changer. That type of clearance, combined with Fel's skill sets and resources, would likely be pivotal in that plan moving forward.

He also knew that Z was a former Marine, and he was pretty sure Elm had a military background. James didn't want to put anyone in danger, but he didn't have any other choice. If they didn't do this, there'd be no lives to risk ever again.

And for what it was worth, the Knights, especially Z, seemed more than eager to give James a hand. The government had done them all wrong in their lifetime, and for the sake of the generations after them, they'd happily risk it all.

Which just left a few other portions of the plan to sort out. First and foremost, how they'd actually carry out their plan in the real world. James knew that the government intended to lock everyone within immersion. There was a certain amount of time necessary for the process to become permanent.

The complete transfer of the conscious mind into the digital space, combined with ensuring that the mind had nothing physical to return to, couldn't happen immediately. Most of the time was to ensure that everyone was logged in before anything began. The government didn't want to risk spooking anyone before their trap had been set.

That implied, to James at least, that they had some sort of trigger they'd watch for. Something that would let the government know when everyone was logged in, and when to turn off the feature to log out. If they did it too early, people would panic. They'd have to ensure that once their trap was laid, there was no way for *anyone* to escape their snare.

And by that point, even if people in game realized they couldn't log out, the panic would be pointless. Once immersed, once the government trapped them, there was nothing anyone would be able to do, short of manually overriding their pods... which could only be done by someone on the outside.

That was why they were going through with the plan in this convoluted, backwards way. Hades had given him a timetable of a few hours in the real world before the 'mind transfer' process could begin in full. If James and the others failed, Hades had hinted that there could be one last card to play to save everyone.

Hades had called it the nuclear option, and implied it was a bit more... volatile and explosive than their main plan. It would result in an ultimatum of comply or die, and even the man with all the answers had no idea of how it would play out if it reached that stage.

In all honesty, James didn't know what the end state was. These were problems that were far above his head. His mission, his goal, was to stop the immediate threat. To keep the government from trapping people in DCO forever. It was the task he'd been given, the mantle he'd chosen to bear, and he would do so because it was the right thing to do.

What happened after was a problem that he couldn't begin to think about. But by the way Hades spoke, and based on a few comments Steve had made to Matt, Rachel, Fel and those with actual power when it came to issues of a larger scale, there were efforts being made. Efforts behind screens and curtains, cloak and dagger operations all waiting for the moment.

The mission James had been given was the one with the highest, albeit still miniscule rate of success and the fewest casualties and least potential fallout. Literal or metaphorical fallout, James wasn't sure. And he didn't want to think about it. He wouldn't fail. He'd promised himself, and Rue, as much.

For his plan, the stage the Knights were setting up would be setting the scene to reveal that the government was evil. To lay bare the nefarious plans, and give the people, the masses, the incentive to fight back. It was only the government officials and those with enough money to buy a space in the world post humanity that would be granted new lives and new bodies.

The Enforcers, soldiers, lower-level managers, and many of the people who actually provided security and maintained law and order likely wouldn't take kindly to knowing they'd almost been forcibly trapped in a digital prison. History had shown that the moment those who had the might to keep the law turned on their government, then revolution quickly followed.

The trick was making sure that they got their message to everyone without showing their hand beforehand. The government controlled the flow of knowledge and information. If any of this leaked early, they'd silence James and anyone else spreading the word of these events, and it would be swept under a proverbial rug. Timing was key. Which was why the plan had so many moving parts.

Ironically, the fact that the Enforcers weren't in on the government plan was one of the aspects that actually gave James's mission a higher chance of success. Hades was confident that the moment the government began its plan, the moment the 48-hour immersion period began, only bare bones security would remain for the government officials. That meant personal security units and automated protective security robots. In other words, the exact type of security Hades and Fel could handle.

James told all of this to the Knights under the cover of the J-Kappa music, which made the whole scene especially weird. A party of adventurers huddled close together while upbeat pop music played, discussing the fate of the world in hushed voices. Five elves, an Archon with a gargoyle head, and a vampire. Not to mention Z's summoned pets, and everyone's little mob companions.

The fact that it was so dire, the fact that they had less than three days of real-world time before they could potentially be trapped forever within VR, or dead, made it all even more ludicrous. The game had gone from demonic chickens to mind-trapping overlords in the span of what? A week?

And with all that said, with James passing everything he possibly could to the Knights, he couldn't help but wonder if this was the right thing to do. He was putting this weight on the shoulders of Z, who had been burdened far too much by life already, and the rest of his party.

Once again, he had to wonder, was this struggle worth it? Was it right to try and fight against this fate? He saw the concern, the stress, the worry on the faces of those around him, and it ate at him. If he'd told them nothing, if he'd done nothing… their fate would have been sealed. But at the very least, they'd have been ignorant till the end. And ignorance, especially in the face of impending doom, was bliss.

The only thing that kept him on his course, the only thing that told him in his heart and mind that he was making the right choice was Rue. Free will was the right of every living human. Everyone deserved to be able to choose their path, to choose if they wanted to be immersed forever or to keep living in the real world.

A small group of powerful people didn't get to make that choice.

Especially when they couldn't trust that group to not have nefarious intentions, either now or in the years to come. The promise of pseudo-immortality in immersion was tempting. The uncertainty of existing in a digital prison with immoral men and women in control of your fate, less so.

Humanity wasn't going to go quietly into the night. The government wouldn't win—not without a little pushback.

Chapter Forty-Three

The next few days within immersion passed in a blur. Part of that was because James opted to force sleep when he couldn't handle his anxiety anymore. His mind was restless, and stress threatened to overwhelm him.

Anxiety was constantly lingering over his shoulder, and while forced sleep could move time forward as they waited for their plan to come to fruition, sleep in immersion gave him no escape. A day's worth of time disappearing in the blink of an eye didn't offer any sense of actual reprieve from his mind and problems.

Still, by the second to last day of immersion before he'd be returned to the real world, for a short while at least before the big event took off, it finally happened. The Knights Who Go Ni had done the impossible. They'd helped take his dungeon from Tier 6 to Tier 7 in an impressively short span of time.

Not only had they managed to spread the word to the players in his own instance via tales of a secret special event that the players could trigger if they sacrificed enough experience to the dungeon, but the story drew in players from all around. Hyping up the 'Git Gud' floor, as well as the epic loot potential on it, factual or not, ensured that the number of players rushing to James's dungeon world hit all-time records.

Add on to that a few Dungeon Skirmishes which his players were able to win handily thanks to their levels, tactics, and the inclusion of some terrifying combos of mobs and exploits that only the Random Dungeon could offer to the Fields of Battle, and the experience points had never stopped increasing.

James had hardly noticed any of it. He should have enjoyed it. Should have reveled in battle... but it all felt superficial. He couldn't be the Mad Mage. He couldn't embody that chaotic, fun-filled passion. No matter how hard he tried, the weight of what was coming pushed him down and kept him there.

Luckily, he'd only been summoned once. Every other time, Rue, the obvious fan favorite, had been called forth. And while James knew she was worried about the upcoming potential end of the world, she technically didn't have actual skin in the game.

Not in the same way James or any of the others did. Rue was already trapped permanently within the virtual world. If anything, James had a feeling she'd prefer if he didn't put himself in danger. Though, she'd never say it.

Any time he felt darkness creeping over him, any time he felt despair and fear and worry, Rue was there to encourage him, to support him, and to keep telling him that his choice was the correct one. Without her, James would have broken. He knew that full well.

He'd wanted to force sleep till the end of immersion. Just wanted to get it all over with. Wanted to fast forward life, because the waiting and the feeling of helpless inactivity was killing him. But she kept him from doing so. Even when he force slept, she didn't let him do it for more than 12 hours of in game time in a 24-hour span. The rest of the time, she did what she could to keep him engaged and distracted. Her presence, her love, her affection, it was what had gotten James to this point.

And now, thankfully, finally, there was something he could do. His waiting was over. His feeling of helplessness as everyone else worked behind the scenes was done. Now he was again an active participant in the plan. Becoming a Tier 7 dungeon meant a brand-new floor. And being Tier 7 put him in a tier of importance that guaranteed all eyes would be on him.

The other Dungeon Cores could see his ranking, and on the leaderboards, he shone supreme. Below him, drawing ever closer to Tier 7, was BLANK's dungeon. If they could hit that goal, then everything would work out. He trusted the duo would do it. Hitting Tier 7 would ensure that when it came to the Dungeon Wars that James's dungeon and BLANK's would face off. It also meant that the clash that would happen between the two would be like nothing seen before, and all eyes would be on them.

A revenge match with stronger mobs on BLANK's side, and an even larger range of mobs and themes on James's side. The last time they'd clashed, they'd only been Tier 3 dungeons, with nowhere near the scale of bosses, mini-bosses, mobs, or Avatar Upgrades. A clash between Tier 7 dungeons was bound to make the original battle, which was still talked about on the reddit threads, look like child's play.

James looked at Rue, who was smiling gently at him. Her normal mischief and excitement had dulled as her concern for him, and his own depressed mood had taken the forefront. And even still, he could sense it, like a flickering flame. Making new floors and creating new mobs was one of their greatest joys within DCO. No matter what was to come, this moment was theirs. It could very well be the last chance they got to design a floor together.

It was a sobering thought that James pushed away with a growl. Not here. Not now. This wasn't a sad moment. It was a moment that he was going to embrace, enjoy, and remember fondly. It was time to create a new dungeon floor. And he was going to put his all into it. This floor would give him what his mind needed right now. A task to work on, an escape, a distraction.

"Are you ready for this?" James asked Rue as he took her hand.

Then mentally, second nature now given how much time he'd spent immersed within DCO, James teleported the two of them to his sixth floor in the main instance of his dungeon—the 'master' copy of his dungeon. Making changes here and completing them would make them go live for the instances of the dungeon that spawned for the players.

He'd taken them to the front of the labyrinth. Originally when he'd created the sixth floor, his future plan had been to place the entrance to the seventh floor at the end of the massive maze. It made sense, and would force players to brave the dangers of the floor and race against the Jormun-Grander to climb to the next floor.

Now he had a new plan. Necessity dictated this change. And while not ideal, he doubted it would be something the players hated. Besides, even if the portal to the seventh floor wasn't located at the end of the labyrinth, there were plenty of other incentives he could add to the sixth floor to ensure that the players explored it in full. That was if DCO survived. If not, well, this would at least give the players a chance to experience the seventh floor before Dungeon Core Online ended.

"Here goes nothing," James said.

He gave Rue a smile and mentally created the portal to the seventh floor. It shimmered to life in the room players would appear in when they descended from the fifth floor to the sixth. It was a glowing, swirling patch of light that flickered and beckoned.

He had no idea what type of mobs his seventh floor would have. And he didn't really care. No matter what happened, the seventh floor was going to be one that was remembered.

Chapter Forty-Four

"Oh good," Steve's voice echoed in the emptiness, and James could feel the developer's presence as his words heralded his arrival. "I made it in time."

They were currently standing in a space of darkness, with naught but the shimmering portal from the sixth floor around them. This was the empty canvas for the seventh floor. James had decided to wait to find out what types of mobs he got this time before he crafted the floor itself.

"Steve!" Rue exclaimed with a smile on her face as she turned to greet the developer.

James looked at the man, noting the massive bags under his eyes. Somehow, he seemed thinner, gaunt even. Considering they were in a virtual expanse, James felt it strange that Steve would present such features on his digital self.

Was it intentional? Was his virtual-self depicting his exhaustion automatically? James hadn't seen him nor heard from him since their meeting a few days ago when everyone had been informed of the government's plans. Since then, everyone had been doing whatever tasks they needed to in order to prepare for their attempt to thwart the government.

"Hello, Rue." Steve grinned, the bags on his eyes lifting slightly, as if the sight of her and James revitalized him. "Did you two miss me?"

"Have you completed everything on your end?" James asked, his mind racing. One of Steve's most important tasks had been to work with Rachel to confirm Rue's safety.

"Mostly," Steve said with a sigh. "It's not ideal, but we've got a few ideas on how to ensure we can 100 percent guarantee Rue's safety, no matter what." Steve smiled. It barely caused his lips to lift. "And on the upside, I've made damn sure that your dungeon and the data for the two of you are as secure as Fort Knox…" Steve trailed off, shaking his head. "Wait, terrible comparison. Fort Knox wasn't secure. It was just a front. So, er, I've made your server as secure as… as secure as… er…" He snapped his fingers. "I know. As secure as a politician's search history."

"As secure as what?" James laughed, more from uncertainty than anything else.

Steve had always been eccentric, but he was pretty sure the developer was losing his mind. The poor man had been through a lot. They all had. But Steve, even before this, had seemed progressively more tired. Like he was wearing himself to the bone. James wasn't sure the developer had much left to give.

"Never mind that." Rue looked at Steve. "How'd you manage to show up just on time?"

"You didn't message him?" James asked.

Usually, Rue sent Steve messages behind James's back whenever they were about to do something exciting in the dungeon. It wasn't that James didn't like the developer… but sometimes he did like doing things with just Rue. Her randomly inviting the man felt a bit awkward at times. Steve was a blast, but even as a blast, he was still a third wheel.

"Not this time," Rue said with a shake of her head. "I was too busy taking care of Mr. Pouty Pants Party Pooper here to remember to message Steve. Besides"—she looked back at the developer—"I didn't want to interrupt anyone if we didn't have to. You know, considering everything going on."

"Fair," James muttered as he turned to lookback at Steve. "So, yeah, how did you show up just on time?"

"Honestly?" Steve walked forward and ruffled James's hair. "You're predictable, buddy. Super predictable, really. I got the notification that your dungeon had hit Tier 7 and figured you'd jump right on in to make the next floor. If you hadn't"—he stepped away, the dark look on his face again— "I would have been worried about you. I know this is a lot, but even still, gotta always remember Rule 34." Steve paused, shook his head again, and cleared his throat. "I mean, Rule 32. Enjoy the little things."

"I'm pretty sure you like to remember Rule 34 as well," Rue said under her breath, though loud enough for Steve to hear.

The developer's cheeks went slightly red.

"Internet rules aside," Steve directed the conversation back to James. "Now that I'm here, feel free to begin." A drink appeared in his hand. "Let's get this show on the road. I'm super excited to see what the seventh floor will bring to your dungeon."

James ignored whatever vague references Steve and Rue were throwing around and turned his focus to the task at hand of creating his seventh floor. First and foremost, that involved spinning the wheel of dungeon mobs to see what fate had in store for him.

There were countless options, and James had no idea if he'd even seen all of the dungeon floor types available. He'd spent a good amount of time scanning all of the information he could on the other dungeons in existence, and while many seemed to have rerolled on Day 1 for more 'normal' floor types, the weird and wacky combinations in existence were impressive.

And considering Steve had once told him that they'd included a ton of ridiculous floor types purely to try and drive rerolls on Day 1 for profits right out the gate, James didn't have high hopes that he'd get something normal.

Statistically, a normal floor option was possible. But a lot of things were statistically possible in life that never happened. That was how statistics worked.

James mentally pulled up the Dungeon Mob Generator command, and the tell-tale lever and slot machine appeared before him. He looked at Rue and smiled at her, remembering how much she'd enjoyed spinning for the mobs and bosses throughout their time together.

He motioned towards the lever. "Would you like to do the honor Rue?"

She shook her head, and James would have been concerned if not for the smirk on her face as she crossed her arms.

"Nah uh," she said with playful tone. "No way am I going to risk being the one to blame for whatever mob type you end up with on your seventh floor."

She grabbed his hand and lifted it to the lever, drawing close to him as she did, hugging him with her other arm. She placed his hand onto the lever, her hand resting softly atop his.

"This may be the final time we get to do this." Her mouth was close to his ears, tone soft.

He got what she was playing at, and he felt her weight press against him as she leaned into him. There was a slight pressure on his hand from hers, but he knew she was waiting for him to make the final decision to pull the lever.

"Then let's do it together," James said, completely ignoring Steve as best he could.

The developer was holding his fingers out towards James and Rue in a heart shape, his drink floating casually in the air in front of him as he sipped from it through a bendy straw.

"Let's," Rue whispered, and the pressure on his hand increased ever so slightly.

She was eager to do this, she loved this part, and the waiting, he knew, was killing her. It wouldn't do to keep her waiting now, would it?

James grinned, spreading his fingers slightly, allowing Rue's to thread between his as they pressed atop the lever. With a slow and steady motion, they pulled the lever down and released. As it lifted upwards, musical tones sprang to life as various dungeon mob types flashed before their eyes.

Then it slowed, the sounds ticking slower and slower before it settled on a single mob type. As always, James had a single thought spring to mind as he read the option. He looked at Steve, and the man held his hands up in feigned innocence as if he could read James's mind.

James sighed, knowing there'd be no point in complaining. He'd learned that across the past six floors that weird and wacky, well, that was just how the Random Dungeon was. And he'd seen some food-based dungeons that were actually quite interesting.

While he wanted to curse Steve, while he wanted to question, loudly, what type of sane person would create such a thing, he didn't. Instead, he grinned, allowed himself to get caught up in the weirdness, and viewed this as a fun challenge. Something new and exciting and unorthodox that he could lose himself in.

At least, for a small amount of time.

"Alrighty then," James said, pulling up the Dungeon Creator as he did to look through various floor options. Now that he knew the mob type, he needed to create a floor that could work with it. "Let's see what we can make."

Before him, as he skimmed through floors, the dungeon mob type flashed brightly. He had no idea what they'd actually be, but considering what he knew of Steve, a.k.a. one of the lead developers on mob types, he had a decent guess. Or at least, as he glanced at the flashing words once more, he thought he did...

Cocktail Creations

Chapter Forty-Five

James opted for a floor style listed as Art Deco Hotel for his floor type. It was one of the more niche floor types, and he'd had to sort through options that first started as industrial, then buildings, then style, and then type.

He wasn't an expert when it came to dungeon types, but he'd played enough games to know some 'dungeons' weren't dungeons in the rocky underground sense, but could be haunted houses, abandoned buildings, and so forth. In that same realm, there was the Hotel. He'd picked the Art Deco One purely on a whim because he liked the aesthetic.

He then spent all of his resources, which had crept over 11,000, to create the dungeon layout. The way the floor was built, for every 1,000 resources he added to the floor, he could choose a specialized room to add to the basic layout or add an extra floor of his choice. In the end, his hotel had a total of six floors, with all but the first having specialized rooms added to them.

The rooms themselves weren't basic hotel rooms. Instead, they included options such as ballroom, restaurant, casino, dance hall, and so on. For each floor, other than the first, those specialized rooms could also encompass the entire floor, replacing the empty space that would normally be basic hotel rooms in real life. In a sense, his hotel didn't have room for lodging, instead it was a variety of entertainment offerings stacked on top of each other.

"How very Eagles of you," Steve said as James finished constructing the seventh floor. "Or is this more of a hotel for Has Beens?"

James ignored Steve and looked over his masterpiece. Of course, there would be a ton of cosmetic changes he would be implementing. Already, his mind was running with the possible options. Because this was potentially the final floor he would create, he had no qualms about dumping as many dungeon tokens into resources as possible, if needed, to make it perfect. After he made sure he got a suitable floor boss, that was. This was an odd-numbered floor, meaning it would have to be Jenkins-related. Ideally humanoid, if that was even a possibility.

The first floor of his hotel served as the lobby, though it was grand by all proper senses of the word. Size-wise, the expanse of black and white marble with chandeliers hanging from arched ceilings had to be at least as long as two football fields and equally as wide.

In the center of it was a marble reception desk of black and gold. There was a wall behind that desk, and two doors that led to the next part of the first floor. Additionally, two staircases took up part of the room, spiraling upwards in a grandiose manner, leading to the second floor some fifty feet above.

As with everything else about the floor, the size was grand, the steps themselves each a good three feet in height, and the width of the staircase was over twenty feet. This was a hotel, but one that seemed more for giants than humans.

Past the doors of the lobby, players would find themselves in a courtyard with an elegant fountain in the middle, pulled straight from Greek mythology. Flowers filled the air with sweet scents, and vines twirled themselves around marble columns.

The other rooms on the first floor, one to the right of the fountain, and one to the left, were a dining hall and a ballroom. The latter was a room equally as large as the lobby had been, with mirrors on half the walls, and 'windows' of amber gilded in gold on the others. The floor consisted of concentric blacks, golds, and blues, all of which were illuminated by flickering candlelight courtesy of the candelabra's hanging from the ceiling.

The dining hall, on the other hand, was sized to feed a hundred or more people at a given time. It was filled with elegant marble tables which were surrounded by chairs of a rich velvety green, with gold trimmed arms and legs.

Against the walls of the rooms were long tables, with heating elements and cookware atop them, as if the room were set to serve food in the manner of a buffet. James was pretty certain he could spend resources to fill those with actual food and drink options that could either buff, or hinder, adventurers.

Past the elegant first floor, James turned his focus to the higher floors of the hotel. For the second floor of the hotel, he'd gone with the fitness center option. The second floor, and all the others, rested above the lobby and courtyard of the hotel, meaning each floor was roughly four football fields in length, and two in width.

Arguably not as large by any means as his fifth or sixth floor individually, but the square footage definitely added up. Besides, James decided the design gave off a 'dungeon inside of a dungeon' feel. Instead of dungeon rooms spread horizontally across the floor, well, this floor had them vertically.

Fitness center had been a vague option, but he liked what he saw. There was a giant pool in the very center of the floor, with a depth of probably forty feet. It made the Olympic-sized pools he'd seen on television look tame. And, who knew, he'd probably be able to fill the pool with random things... hell maybe even sharks. Because sharks in pools seemed like a great idea.

All around the pool there were stacks of weights, though not practical weights. The smallest was listed as weighing a hundred pounds. Definitely not a gym area meant for humans. Past the various free weights that ranged from weighted plates, barbells, dumbbells, and so forth.

There were areas with ropes for working out, punching bags larger than Hornz, and most interestingly... a few bowling alley lanes. Even the bowling alley was sized for giants though, each pin being the size of a human, while the balls the size of, for easy comparison, a badger.

Moving upward, the third floor of his hotel was listed as a Spa. As far as James was concerned, it fit the bill, at least, it fit what his mind told him a spa should be like. It was filled with a giant hot spring like a bath, covered in ornate motifs and elegant marble tiles. All around the room, equally ornate and detailed and crafted from extremely expensive, high-end materials, were additional baths, sinks, and saunas.

The room was a rich blend of blue and gold, with warm lighting above, and a slight haze that smelled of rose and lavender. James wondered if he'd be able to adjust the scent on the floor, and more than that, add an effect to it. Perhaps a poison effect? Or some sort of effect that would sap a player's strength? Perhaps a debuff that slowed them, or made them drowsy? Spend too long in the spa and you'd become completely relaxed and uncaring, as the dungeon wiped away your cares, your concerns... and your life.

With those ideas swirling in his head, he looked over the next floor. He was building the picture of the dungeon layout properly in his mind, to best orient himself with what he'd just built before he began summoning mobs. That way, he could ensure once he'd seen what his mobs were, he could plan each floor of the hotel out perfectly.

James was considering giving each floor its own unique set of mobs, if possible, or different combinations of mobs at least to make each floor unique. Perhaps the first floor could have one type of mob, the second two, the third three, and so forth, till it all culminated in an epic boss fight on the sixth. He would definitely need to summon his mobs before he could make those decisions, but the planning possibilities had him excited to no end.

The floor above the third was a Theater. And not a movie theater. Instead, it mimicked the theaters that he assumed were popular over a hundred years ago. With rows and rows of large, red velvet seats that had golden arms in the shape of lion heads.

The theater had a somewhat sloped structure to it. At the very far end, which would be the back of the hotel if he treated the lobby as the entryway and front of the hotel, was a massive stage with an elegant, heavy curtain which draped from the vaulted ceiling all the way down to the stage.

All along the walls, which were covered in somewhat gaudy wallpaper depicting scenes which he assumed were from ancient plays, were large seating areas that offered an overhead view of the stage itself.

Furthest away from the stage there was actually an additional row of seating above the initial row. The seats, probably eight feet in width, with aisles between them equally as large, would likely be a strange environment for players to battle in. It was something that James was looking forward to. This floor, of all the ones he'd created, felt like it could offer the largest variety of fights for the players, if they ever got to fully enjoy it before well, the end of the world.

Pushing that aside, James moved to the fifth floor. The casino. Filled with loud noises, flashing lights, and pretty much every sort of gambling machine, table, and money-making venture he could think of, the floor was a giant gaming hall. Lined with a green velvet floor, somewhat darker in lighting than the other floors, it was a gambler's paradise. It reminded him of the images he'd seen of historic Las Vegas during a documentary on life in the late 1900s, though again, on a scale for giants and not humans.

Even still, he had no doubt the machines themselves, and the game tables which had cards that were easily larger than a human's hand, could be played. Meaning players could gamble now not only outside of his dungeon in the dungeon town casino, but within it. The entrepreneurs who'd rushed to make a casino for income might not appreciate his dungeon taking some of their revenue, but hey, they could take up the complaint with management, er, the devs, for giving James the option to create a casino within his dungeon.

Finally, James reached the sixth floor. All of the floors were connected by staircases like the ones on the first, though they did a good job of hiding what each floor above and below consisted of, thanks to, well, he figured dungeon magic.

Essentially, there was a 'fog' effect he'd noticed that distorted the ability to see what was on a floor above or below the staircases, until a person breached a certain point on the stairs. It also, he noticed, muffled the sounds between the floors, most noticeable when he'd been shifting from the fourth floor to the fifth.

This effect meant, at the very least, that the first time a player experienced this floor, they'd have mini surprises awaiting them as they climbed to each new level of the hotel. It also meant players wouldn't be able to know if say, something terrifying was happening on a floor they weren't on, until they stepped into it.

The sixth floor technically wasn't really a floor. Because it was the roof of his hotel, he'd been given the option of making it covered, or not. He'd opted for not and marveled at the Rooftop Bar before him.

The bar itself took up the back end of the space, spanning the entire width of the hotel with an oak countertop, behind which was row upon row of bottles and glasses, a collection of liquor, spirits, and who knew what else. Was everything collected at that bar real-world liquor? Were some dungeon-specific drinks? He had no idea, and he knew he'd investigate later.

He could almost hear Steve salivating at the mass of alcoholic beverages, even though the developer had the ability already to summon whatever drink he wanted, whenever, on a whim.

Besides the bar proper, the rest of the floor was designed to have various seating areas, as well as a dance floor tiled in black and gold checkered patterns, and a gorgeous grand piano. The all-black piano, outlined with gold trim and keys that gleamed a perfect white, was a masterpiece in and of itself.

He could imagine the setting already and wondered if the piano would play while adventures were on the floor. There was a microphone beside it, and James could envision an epic boss battle accompanied by a musical performance. He made a mental note to look into it. Because truly, that would create a battle worth remembering.

Other than those objects of interest, the most notable aspect of the rooftop bar was the surrounding area outside of the hotel. The building existed in a plane of pure darkness that seemed to twinkle with stars in all directions. It was like the hotel floated in the cosmos, drifting through time and space. Eerie, and yet he couldn't help but look on in awe.

A lump formed in his throat as he thought of what was coming. How many people would get to experience this floor before the end? It was as if the gods themselves were taunting him. Granting him a floor like this, something so grand, something with so much potential, knowing full well that if he succeeded, if he stopped the government, the floor, his dungeon, DCO, would all cease to exist.

If he failed though… Well, the floor's extraordinary nature and beauty could serve as a consolation prize… albeit a bitter, dark one. If the government got its way, well, the seventh floor would offer the perfect way to try and forget about everyone's woes. A grand hotel they could all check into, and never leave.

James shook the dark thoughts from his mind once more, slapped himself on the cheeks with both his hands, and looked back at his companions. They'd both been silently taking in everything beside him as they toured the dungeon.

"Right then," James said, his words drifting off into the empty expanse of the space around them, "it's time to summon some mobs."

Chapter Forty-Six

As was standard practice for the Random Dungeon, James had a total of five mobs to choose from for his seventh floor. Part of him had been hoping for six like his second floor, but he'd come to give up on that pipe dream. He was pretty sure that had been a unique situation triggered only because the Archeao-repairers existed solely to heal the other mobs, making them non-combatant creatures.

The standard, James had learned, was five damage-based mobs per floor... for him at least. Normal dungeons unlocked five new mobs on every floor, plus the ability to upgrade their mobs from previous floors and use the enhanced versions of them for higher floors. Random Dungeons traded that power for unique encounters, and well... randomness.

The price of being special, he figured.

James quickly scanned through the names of his five new mobs, noting their costs as he did. Because this was his seventh floor, he started with a whopping 12,800 mob points to populate the floor. The lowest mob on his list had a cost of 31 mob points, while the highest was 35. Compared to the total mob points he had, those costs meant if he wanted to, he had just enough points to be able to populate his seventh floor with 365 of the 35-cost mobs. A drink for every day of the year. Nice.

"I'll have you know"—James turned to look at Steve as he selected the lowest costing mob—"I'm ready for your worst here."

"I have no idea what you're implying." The developer's shit-eating grin as he spoke was contradictory to that statement. "All of the dungeon mobs in DCO are perfectly normal."

"Uh huh." James had a dungeon full of examples damning Steve's statement as a bold-faced lie. James took another breath, preparing his mind for whatever may come. He'd had problems in the past managing his expectations of what mobs should be against the reality of what he actually got.

And that had led to more than a few mental breakdowns, unnecessary stress, frustration, panic, depression, and pretty much a ton of other things that would probably let him, if he'd wanted to, sue Steve for emotional and mental abuse and trauma.

Now, though, he was ready. He was prepared for Steve's worst. He was ready to summon the first of his five new mobs. The first Cocktail Creation.

One last breath, and James made the mental summoning selection: Jager Bomb. His eyes went wide as he saw not one but two figures appear in the lobby of the hotel, lights flashing around them as they took shape. He blinked once then twice as his mind, which he'd sworn was prepared, froze from trying to process what he was seeing.

"What the hell?" James asked, turning to Steve. "Is this a bug?"

"Not a bug," Steve said with a grin. "A feature. And a fun one at that."

James looked at the two mobs. The first was a red bull, with wings sprouting from its back. It was roughly the size of a bull. Not one of his upgraded Mad Cows from his first floor, but like a real-world bull.

The bull he'd summoned had shoulders close to the head height of a normal human. It snorted and pawed at the tiled ground, while the other figure that had been summoned placed a calming hand on its side.

The second figure, looked... German? Ancient German if James was remembering his history books correctly. The man was wearing brown pants with suspenders, the bottoms of which were tucked into calf-high, white socks. He wore dark shoes, or hunting boots rather, and wore a white, bloused shirt tucked into his suspenders.

There were various colors and trimmings added to his outfit, and he wore a green, felt-like hat with a colorful feather on one end. In his hand he held a gun that bent where the barrel met the stock. It reminded him of a very old, single-loading type of hunting rifle.

"What exactly am I looking at?" James asked, giving up before he even let his mind try to puzzle out Steve's crazy logic.

Before Steve could answer, Rue clapped her hands together excitedly, laughing all the while, and spoke up. "I get it," she said, looking from Steve to James. "It's a Jager Bomb." She giggled. "Are they all like this?"

"Some are," Steve said. "Others have different features and twists." He grinned. "Cocktail Creations, I can assure you, were created with *a lot* of inspiration from the drinks we named the mobs after." He pointed down at the mobs. "What you see before you is, for all intents and purposes, a Jager Bomb."

"A bull and an old-time hunter?" James questioned, not following. "I thought these were supposed to be cocktails. You know, like drinks?"

"Jager Bombs," Steve began, "are a combined cocktail created by putting a shot of Jägermeister inside a glass of Red Bull."

"Er." James looked at the bull. It was red. But why did it…

"And Red Bull gives you wings," Rue said with a laugh.

"Exactly," Steve continued. "So the mob itself is a red bull with wings, and a literal Jägermeister—which is German for Hunt Master before you ask, James." Steve grinned. "Brilliant, eh?"

"Is it just two mobs, then?" James asked. "Is that… all?"

He got the premise, he guessed. And he wasn't going to complain about double the mobs for the cost of one. But given how many mob points he had now that he was a Tier 7 dungeon, the gimmick was less enticing than if it had been his very first floor. And did they have individual stats, or a shared set of stats? What about their health pool?

"Is that all?" Steve said in a mocking scoff. "Pure, brilliant wordplay at its finest, and you can't appreciate it." He sighed, "Kids these days."

Before James could speak up, Steve held up a finger. "Of course that's not all," the developer said. "You have to let the two fuse first, obviously, in order to truly get the cocktail."

"They can fuse?" James asked, excitement welling in his chest.

He'd only seen one of his mobs fuse in the past. The Terminus, his second-floor boss, could combine with the mini-boss B.L.U. to create the Perfect Cognivore. It was epic the first time he'd ever witnessed it, and was still badass to watch every time it occurred. It also created a creature that was much more powerful than either had been.

"Of course they can," Steve said, pointing below, "just watch."

James turned his focus excitedly down towards the two summoned mobs, wondering what the fusion would look like. Would it create a minotaur? That had to be the only logical choice, right? He watched and waited.

Thirty seconds, nothing. One minute, nothing. He waited a little longer, silence filling the space between them, and still nothing. After what felt like an obnoxious amount of time, James looked at Steve, raising an eyebrow.

"How exactly do we prompt them to fuse?" James asked.

"Did you try asking them nicely?" Steve asked.

Shaking his head and internally questioning Steve's sanity, James focused on the mobs. He gave them a mental command for them to fuse. On cue… the German Hunter jumped atop the red bull. And then nothing else happened. No flashing lights, no magical transformations. Just a guy riding a bull.

"That's it?" James asked dryly. "That's their fusion?"

"I mean." Steve pointed down at the mob. "You've got a Jager Bomb now, right?" As he spoke, the bull flapped its wings, the effort lifting its body and the hunter on its back into the air. The hunter loaded his rifle and looked down at the ground below him, searching for prey.

James mentally ordered the mob to shoot toward the check-in counter of the hotel lobby, curious to see what would happen. In response, the mob fired, and a projectile rocketed towards the counter. It hit with blinding speed, and then exploded into a small eruption, flames and shrapnel rocketing outwards in a radius of about ten feet.

"Okay," James said as he observed the damage that the un-upgraded mob had done.

It wasn't as cool as the two fusing into a massive minotaur or some-thing, but it was still a lot better than what he'd expected of the mob. And that had been it just being a walking, animated, literal glass of alcohol. That would have been a nightmare to deal with. But a hunter flying atop a bull… he supposed he could deal with that. Especially if the upgrade tree was anything like the kind he'd come to expect of DCO.

"I suppose I can't complain about the Jager Bomb," James said as he mentally unsummoned the mob. He went to the next on the list, a mob that cost 32 points. It was labeled as 'LMFAO Shot'. "How about the next mob?"

He summoned it, and this time, the mob, unfortunately, met his expectations. The hope that had been building following the Jager Bomb demonstration was immediately dashed by what he could only attribute to drunken stupidity.

"Damnit, Steve."

Chapter Forty-Seven

Whereas the Jager Bomb had been actual creatures with some thought put into them, the LMFAO Shot seemed to be every bit a joke. It was quite literally a shot glass, albeit elongated to human proportions, with weird and wacky limbs that stretched and bent unnaturally. Atop the shot glass, which was filled with swirling liquid—liquor of some sort, James figured —was a tie-dyed afro.

"Okay," Steve was trying, and failing, not to laugh, "before you get too mad at me, look at its skill."

He looked at James's face and proceeded to laugh even harder. James wasn't even trying to hide his disappointment in the creature. The Jager Bomb had given him false hope. The LMFAO Shot had brought that hope crashing back down.

Still, having a little faith in Steve, James did as he'd been asked. He mentally pulled up the information on the mob, which was currently doing jumping jacks, the liquid within sloshing to and fro, yet somehow, not spilling a single drop.

LMFAO Shot
Type: Party Starter
Lvl 115
HP: 50,000 + 2500 per level
MP: 50,000 + 2500 per level
ATK: 5000 + 500 per level

DEF: 1000 + 100 per level

Special Abilities:
Life of the Party- On death, split apart, creating two versions of the original that have half the stats of the previous version. This skill triggers until there are a total of sixteen LMFAO Shots within a (lvl*0.1 foot) radius.
Party Popper- When there are sixteen LMFAO Shots, all shots will detonate, each one doing (lvl*1.5) damage to all enemies within a (lvl*1.5 foot) radius. This damage is classified as true damage, ignores all elemental resistances, and penetrates 25 percent of all armor.

Unique Passive:
Buzzed: Melee attacks against LMFAO Shots have a chance to cause the 'buzzed' debuff to apply to the attacker. Players who are buzzed have a 25% decrease to their accuracy and chance to dodge. Additionally, while buzzed, player vision will be affected, as will their ability to read their stats. This debuff will last for 30 seconds, or until cleansed.

"So it's a swarm mob?" James said as he closed out its info. "Like multiplying slimes?"

"Pretty much," Steve said with a nod. "Though, obviously, with a booze-inspired theme." He looked down at the creature. "For a well-oiled party, crowd control can make them more manageable. But for others, well," he chuckled, "anyone that ends up taking sixteen shots in that short amount of time, they're bound to be dead." He looked back at James. "If I may, I'd recommend you apply the Hangover effect to it in the skill tree."

James pulled the mob's info up once again, figuring why the hell not. Normally, he'd wait to upgrade his mobs until he knew more about them, the floor, and until players had explored them. But as things stood, with the impending end to everything lingering over them, he figured he'd make an exception.

Besides, Steve's advice, while questionable in some ways, almost always worked out. Plus, James figured that Steve deserved it. Steve had been a big part in James's success as Dungeon Core so far and was putting his life on the line to try and save the world alongside James.

As recommended, he upgraded the skill, using his free skill point that he'd earned for all dungeon mobs long ago from his Highlander title, and then reread the stat block, noting the change. It was, devious to say the least. And totally on theme for the floor. He couldn't help but grin at the addendum added to the last line of the skill.

If cleansed, has a 10% chance to cause the 'Hangover' debuff.*
*Hangover- Players take 10 points of damage as psychic damage for every point of mana or stamina spent on skills, for the next minute. While under the hangover effect, players are 100% more susceptible to blind and stun effects.

The original skill already intrigued him with regards to how it impacted vision and the ability to read player information. Would it obscure the information completely, make it fuzzy, or perhaps just cause it to flicker and change, becoming less precise? He'd seen a variety of similar effects in other games, though usually such mechanics were frowned upon.

Would players be annoyed at the skill? Would it really matter? It could be cleansed, and wasn't as damning as, say, the radiation debuff that caused players to mutate into zombies and other terrible things upon death.

Either way, a part of him longed for the chance to experience the floor from a player's perspective. At level 115, though, the mobs were way outside of his and Rue's range. Hopefully before everything kicked off, Z and the others could experience the floor. That way, James could at least experience it vicariously through them, as he had most things in the dungeon in the past. Watching his favorite adventurers challenge the floor, perhaps for their final dungeon run within DCO, would surely be a treat.

Not to mention, now that he'd hit Tier 7, the players, including the Knights, no longer needed to sacrifice their experience to help the dungeon level up. On the contrary, they should go back to farming all the experience they wanted in preparation for the upcoming Dungeon Wars. He'd need them as strong as possible to hold their own against BLANK's dungeon.

The Candy Dungeon had pulled back on its Souls-like difficulty ever since the siblings had stepped aside from running it, but still, its players were a force to be reckoned with. Especially SoulDemon. James wondered if he'd see that particular player before the end of everything.

Last James had seen of that notorious player, who seemed to thrive on

PvP and punching down on others, SoulDemon had been cursing their very existence because they'd 'stolen' his prey from him in their efforts to keep the Siege War from getting out of hand and killing everyone.

SoulDemon was the epitome of selfish narcissist, and James wondered just what he'd do, what he'd say, how he'd act if he knew what was coming. If SoulDemon were in their shoes, would he work to stop the government from mass murder? Or would he welcome being sealed within immersion for the infinite future, where he could kill, murder, maim, and grind to his heart's content within the world of DCO?

James shivered at the thought and pushed it aside. SoulDemon was a problem for another time. Hopefully, he would never be a problem for them to deal with. For now, he had three more mobs to summon for his seventh floor, as well as a new boss to create.

"Onto the next," James said as he rubbed his hands together eagerly. He mentally selected the next mob, called a Dirty Shirley, and summoned it, simultaneously unsummoning LMFAO Shot as he did.

A sigh of relief came out as a cough of surprise as his mind tried to process the logic behind this next mob.

A woman, dressed in a torn and tattered pink robe, complete with pink slippers, appeared before them. Her frayed, gray hair was tied back messily in a bun and secured with a dark olive. Atop her head she wore a crystal tiara that held a cracked, purple gemstone.

Her pink slippers, James noted, had fluffy white cat heads atop them. The cat heads themselves also wore tiaras. In her hand, she petted a stuffed animal, er... raptor... while she looked around with a crazed look in her eyes. James shot a glance at Steve.

"She's dirty," Steve said before James could ask his question, "and her name's Shirley."

James doubted that was it. But he didn't press the man, who was wearing his trademark shit-eating grin. Steve had a joke for everything, and James figured that it was best to just ignore the developer this time around. Otherwise, he'd go mad trying to question what exactly a crazy old cat lady had to do with a Dirty Shirley Cocktail?

He skimmed its information, checking over its skills, and unsummoned the mob. Clearly, there was more to it than he knew, but whatever it was, it was a usable mob.

Three mobs down, two more to go.

Chapter Forty-Eight

Based on the previous mobs of the seventh floor, it was nigh impossible to guess what the next mobs would be purely based on their names. James had to wonder if the developers had been reaching for straws by this point, had been completely wasted, or had saved the best for last. Maybe a mixture of all three.

Definitely a mixture of all three.

The fourth mob, which cost 34 points to summon, was called a Turkey Dew. The mob was, for all intents and purposes, a giant Turkey. It was larger than James's fully enlarged Dickens, probably closer to ten feet in height, and seemed to be made of stone. As if it had been carved from a mountain. When it spread its tail feathers out wide, strange intricate green and red patterns were painted across it. In fact, as it shifted about, James realized that its coloring was mostly shades of brown, green, and red.

"Lesser-known cocktail," Steve explained without prompting. "You see, Mountain Dew was originally created as a mixer for liquor. Illegal liquor during the prohibition period was known as Moon Shine. So you mixed Moon Shine with Mountain Dew, and bam, delicious cocktail. The Turkey Dew cocktail"—Steve motioned at the bird—"combined a bourbon called Wild Turkey with Mountain Dew in that tradition. It's honestly really good, though probably seems a bit weird.

"Pretty popular with people who wanted a cheap mixed drink with bourbon, though, since Wild Turkey, especially Wild Turkey 101, was high-proof and affordable and mixed well with the sugary soda. And if you wanted to mix it up"—he grinned—"well, Mountain Dew had a ton of flavors that could instantly make the cocktail fit whatever flavor profile you wanted. My personal favorite"—a reddish-orange drink appeared in his hand that he swirled around—"was a mixture of Wild Turkey and Mountain Dew Game Fuel."

He took a sip. "The original Game Fuel, mind you. The best, OG version." Another sip, his eyes closed in nostalgia. "Simpler times, then. Simpler times."

"I'm honestly surprised your liver never failed you given how much you talk about liquor, soda, and energy drinks," James said, legitimately surprised.

From what he knew of the beverages, they were notorious for causing health issues. Especially prior to 2030 when a lot of new regulations had been put in place to protect people from various toxic foods and beverages. Weirdly enough, health care and regulations to ensure people were healthy increased around that time as the birth rate and population numbers declined.

James had read on the internet that people questioned if the government, prior to those regulations, had been allowing such toxins in food on behalf of medical companies looking to profit off people's poor health. With the merging of the world governments, though, and decreasing population, came a revolution.

Healthy people were happier, and happier people were less likely to protest and try to overthrow a government. Healthy and happy people were also more willing to have children. At least, that's what the people talking about that historical time on the internet said.

"Livers are amazing organs," Steve said as he took another drink. "Give 'em a break every now and then and they can fix themselves right as rain. Add in the advances in science, medicine, and the understanding of the human body, and there's a reason life expectancy has climbed so high over the past two decades."

"Which doesn't seem to have worked out so well," James added dryly, "all things considered."

Steve raised an eyebrow at him, but that was all the warning he'd get, and he knew it. They couldn't discuss such things. He should be safe and secure, but it was better to err on the side of caution, especially with their quickly approaching timetable.

The waiting was killing James, though, acting like everything was fine while knowing that in less than two days of IRL time everything would change. Time dilation for immersion, in this manner, was torture more than anything. Sure, it was letting the others prep and plan and sort everything out that they needed to, but for James, it was just agonizing waiting.

"I'm going to guess from what you've just told me, and considering it looks to be carved out of a mountain, that it's the tank mob for the floor," James said, turning his focus back to the Turkey Dew.

Sure enough, the mob's stats were focused on its health and defenses, with skills focused on drawing aggro and tanking damage. A quick glance at the creature's upgrade path made him smile, and he couldn't help but glance again at Steve. The developer had most definitely played a part in these creatures.

"Don't judge me," Steve said preemptively. "I may have been a part of a few of the planning sessions for this one."

"I'd guess you were providing the drinks for these planning sessions," James said accusingly, closing out the Turkey Dew options. He didn't have enough skill points to upgrade it to unlock the particular trait just yet sadly.

Called Fifty Shades of Dew, it created different varieties of the Turkey Dew at random, giving them different aspects and traits, and James assumed colors, based on RNG according to the skill. If James had to guess, it was representative of the different Mountain Dew flavors that could be mixed into the Turkey Dew cocktail.

James unsummoned the creature and looked at the final one. As much as summoning new monsters was fun, the next step was what he was really looking forward to: the creation of the seventh-floor boss. He quickly summoned the last mob and gave it a cursory once over, taking note of its name, features, and skills as he eagerly prepared for the best part of mob creation for new floors.

Bloody Mary
Type: Cursed Cocktail
Lvl: 115

The creature that was summoned looked like something from a horror movie. It floated above the ground in a tattered red dress. Its face was twisted, and James noticed its teeth were sharp, almost like fangs. It had green hair that looked leafy in a way, like seaweed. Or some sort of vegetable. Red liquid dripped from its flesh onto the ground below, and as it floated about, James noticed the drips caused the marble to sizzle on contact, making the stone actually bubble and begin to melt.

Its attack was much higher than its defense, and from what James could tell from skimming its skills, it was an ambush type mob that focused on sustained DPS through the use of damage over time effects and life drain skills. It could actively drain life from the adventurers with some sort of vampire-esq skill, all while the liquid dripping from it—classified unimaginatively as Ghost Pepper Sauce—caused intense fire and acid damage over time.

If he had to guess, the creature would jump on players, begin draining their life, and then work to cover them as quickly as possible in the red, caustic liquid to quickly try and melt them into nothing. In a way... it actually reminded James of spiders. Or a few snake species that could liquify their targets to make them easier to consume...

With that less-than-pleasant thought now burned into his mind, he unsummoned the unsettling creature and looked toward his friends.

"Who's ready to summon a Boss Monster?"

Chapter Forty-Nine

Given the sheer number of Dungeon Tokens James had, and the fact that he didn't have any qualms about blowing them, it was only a matter of time before he rolled a Boss Monster that truly matched his vision for his seventh floor.

Not to mention, it was easy to pass on Boss Monsters with names like **RUM-ble Bucket,** and questionably, **The Worm!!!**. He'd almost been sucked in by a Boss Selection that had been listed as **P.V.W.,** which Steve had claimed was humanoid. Since this was a Jenkins-level floor, he needed a human boss. However, Steve told him to keep rolling, and James did just that.

A few rerolls later, and he had the absolutely perfect option for his seventh floor. The ultimate culmination in Dungeon Floor design. For the first time during his entire time in DCO, he had perfect floor cohesion and flavor. The seventh floor was quite literally his Dungeon Core heaven.

The Bartender
Type: Cocktail Master
Lvl: 125

The boss, when summoned, looked every bit the consummate professional. James had been to various pubs, taverns, and bars in a multitude of games and areas of The Zone during his time within immersion. The boss monster was based, if he had to guess, on the classy, high-end version of a bartender, rather than the normal tavern or pub-styled counterpart.

She looked totally normal, actually, albeit tall enough to use the massive bar as if it were a normal one. She'd dwarf adventurers, and even the mobs of the floor that James could summon.

Her brown hair was tied back in a professional style of bun, with bangs on either side accenting her face, which was kind and welcoming. She was the type of person who you'd gladly accept a drink from and tell your nightly woes to.

She was dressed in a professional-seeming, form-fitting button-up shirt, and stylish, black dress pants. Over her dress shirt, she wore a black vest that made the outfit look more like a uniform than regular clothing attire.

Her shirt collar was buttoned all the way to the top of her neck, and she wore a black bowtie around her throat, with the collar's white wings over the silk cloth of the neckpiece. The other defining feature for the boss was the red cloth that hung loosely from her right-front pants pocket. A cleaning cloth, perhaps?

James noticed Steve watching the boss walk behind the bar. The creature was looking over the liquor selection, expertly tracing a finger along some of the bottles. On her waist, which James had missed before, hung a variety of additional tools, including a golden corkscrew, golden bottle opener, otherwise known as a church key, and a golden drink strainer.

"Whelp," Steve suddenly said, cracking his fingers. "I think that while you sort out her story and look her skills, I'll go test out her practical skills. Best thing about the Bartender AI is that we ensured the AI for it would have all the skills and knowledge of the best bartenders we could."

His summoned drink disappeared as he turned back down to the Bartender. "After all, while yeah, I can summon exact replicas of drinks here, nothing beats the high-class drinking experience that is receiving a hand-made cocktail from a master of the craft."

Without another word, Steve disappeared from James's and Rue's side and reappeared, proportionally correct, atop one of the bar stools in front of the bar. He exchanged quick words with the boss, who proceeded to then quickly grab a few different bottles of liquor from the selection behind her.

Once acquired, she produced a large knife from who knew where, and then to James's surprise, pulled out a massive block of ice, setting it atop the counter. James watched, transfixed as she cut it rapidly, shaving away giant chunks, before in the span of a few short moments, she'd created a perfect sphere.

"Skills and stats now," Rue said, though he could tell she had a hard time pulling her gaze away from the artisan at work. "Fancy cocktails from the flashy bartender later."

"Right, right." James mentally pulled up the boss's information, displaying the screen for Rue and him to read. "You'll think up the story for her, right?" he asked as he began to scan the stats, curious what the boss could do.

"I'm thinking she can be Leeroy's sister," Rue said as she came to stand beside James so that she could better read the information he'd pulled up. "Figure make her like Sergeant Jenkins' daughter, since he's Grandma Jenkins and Old Man Jenkins's son."

"Sounds like a plan," James said. Rue had been hard at work crafting the Jenkins family story and family tree, and he wasn't going to get in her way. What had started as a joke had become actual lore for his dungeon, and it had resulted in some really amazing interactions for adventurers, both during regular dungeon runs and during Skirmishes and Dungeon Wars.

For example, if people showed up on Grandma Jenkins's doorstep in Old Man Jenkins' demon farmer clothes, then the third-floor boss didn't take too kindly to that, nor did she appreciate hearing they'd killed her husband. It always led to increased aggro and a more vicious boss battle.

In the same essence of flavor, though, if they opted to help Old Man Jenkins on the first floor, he'd actually give them unique phrases to pass on to his wife. If players told Grandma Jenkins those special phrases, which changed daily, she'd give them the option to have a non-lethal way of dealing with her, resulting in special items, pie, and experience without having to fight the third-floor boss.

Little things like that, James felt, really made his dungeon stand out. And he'd been really excited to see what would happen when the story finally came to a close and Leeroy Jenkins was finally added to their tale. Ah well. Some things, he figured, just weren't meant to be. He shook the thought from his mind and focused fully on just what the newest boss monster could do. Already, he noticed Rue had taken the liberty of giving her a new name.

Tier 7 Boss Mob
Elliot Jenkins
Type: Cocktail Master

Lvl: 125
HP: 100,000 + 5000 per level
MP: 150,000 + 10,000 per level
ATK: 5000 + 1000 per level
DEF: 10,000 + 250 per level

<u>Unique Abilities:</u>
Mixology- The Bartender is skilled in the craft of drink mixing. Every minute of battle, the Bartender will select a new concoction to create. Mixing a drink takes thirty seconds. These cocktail creations will be of higher quality and strength than normal creations. During the thirty seconds, players may attempt to interrupt and hinder the Bartender. While mixing the drinks, the Bartender cannot take any other action. The quality of the final Cocktail Creation, after the 30 seconds, as well as its stats, skills, and traits, is determined at the end of the 30-second timer.

Imbibe- A good Bartender can make a drink anyone would enjoy. A great Bartender can make a drink you'll never forget. A Master Bartender can make a drink you consume before realizing you've done so. Once per 30 seconds, the Bartender will give a drink to an adventurer currently engaged in battle with the Bartender. This drink can offer buffs or debuffs, and the effects, and flavor will be randomized. Experiences may vary.

Cut Off- It is the job of a Bartender to pay attention to the status of their patrons. Every two minutes, the Bartender will select an adventurer to be cut off, who will receive a cut-off debuff for the duration of the fight. This adventurer will then be unable to attack the Bartender, or any of the Cocktail Creations, for 30 seconds. Gaining an additional cut-off stack during the boss fight will increase the duration of time removed from the fight by 10 seconds.

Closing Time- All good things must come to an end. And everyone knows bars only offer service for so long before they're closed down and you have to come back later. After ten minutes, the Bartender will close for business. A final Cocktail Creation will be spawned instantly, at Perfect Quality, for each adventurer still standing against the Bartender. After another minute, all adventurers still remaining will be removed from the battle, and the Bartender's health and stats will be reset. Defeating the Perfect Quality Cocktail will result in a single-use drink token that adventurers can present to the boss at the next battle to receive a unique buff.

<u>Unique Passive:</u>

Have a Drink- The Bartender is a consummate professional. Before you can attack her, you must defeat her summoned creation. If you do not choose... a drink will be chosen for you. Be warned. Drinks crafted by the Bartender are only of the utmost quality. Given their rare and prestigious ingredients, and the masterful skill used to craft them, Cocktails created by the Bartender receive a variety of buffs and their own unique skills and traits.

On the House- First drink is free. Each party member may take a chance and receive a drink from the Bartender before a battle begins. These drinks can offer buffs or debuffs to the adventurer. No matter what, though, they'll offer an experience the adventurer will never forget. The first one is on the house. All future drinks... have a price. Once a drink has been served, players are trapped in the boss encounter until Closing Time triggers, their party wipes, or the Bartender is slain.

Professional Charm- The Bartender is the height of professionalism and is a master of their craft. They cannot be stunned or charmed.

After Hours- The Bartender will not engage with the same adventuring party twice in a single instance. If players fail to kill the Bartender during their battle, they will be unable to trigger the boss fight again until their next dive within the dungeon. Attempting to do so will immediately place the Hangover Debuff on the adventurers.

James licked his lips as he finished reading over her stat sheet, partially because the skills were intriguing. And he was really interested in seeing how the battle against her went. From what he could tell, she was a mob-summoning boss like Grandma Jenkins. Though, she had her own special rage timer at ten minutes, and a few other unique factors that made James really curious to see the boss in action. And if he was being honest, all the references of drinks, as well as a glance down at Steve and the Bartender, had made his mouth water.

Steve was clutching a crystalline glass in his hands, which had the perfect sphere of ice spinning inside, surrounded by amber liquid, with fog or smoke drifting from the top of the glass. The Bartender was in the process of grating an orange above the drink, and the smell of citrus was somehow reaching them from where they hovered a good twenty feet above the boss.

"No matter what," James said as he closed out the window, noting

Rue's gaze was also focused back on the Bartender, "we need to see a fight on this floor."

"Agreed," Rue said as she began to drift down towards the bar. "But more importantly," she added, glancing back to see if James was following, "we need to see just how good one of those drinks really is."

Rue didn't have to tell James twice. A moment later, they were both sitting beside Steve, enjoying the dreamy atmosphere of the hotel rooftop bar as the seventh-floor boss, the bartender now known as Elliot Jenkins, put on a show neither of them would ever forget. For that moment, James felt like himself, and for the first time since Hades had given him the impending news, felt at peace.

Chapter Fifty

Special Announcement

The message flashed in front of James's vision. With it, a tone sounded, threatening to drown everything out around him. He glanced at Rue, and her eyes were focused on what he assumed was the same prompt.

Special Announcement

The prompt header flashed again, scrolling in bolded, red letters, making it impossible to ignore. James and Rue had been spending a few final moments together as the end of the current immersion cycle drew closer. There were only ten minutes to go before James would return to the real world, as 7 AM brought about the end of normal immersion time. An hour ago, the players had been removed from DCO, returning for their final 24 hours of immersion time, equal to 1 hour of real-world time within the Zone as was the norm.

"Here it comes," James said, yelling to be heard above the blaring alarm.

He'd experienced such things before, though they were usually tests. Government messages, impossible to ignore. Even if people were in force sleep, they'd be pulled from it to view the message. Government messages, while immersed, could not be ignored. Period. While immersed, everything was being sent directly into everyone's minds.

Special Announcement

The words flashed once more and then disappeared. In their place was the message from the government, one James had been expecting. Though, the actual contents of it, he knew nothing about. A pit of dread opened in his stomach as he prepared himself to read the contents.

Special Announcement

Regarding Preparation for Worldwide Immersion Event

In approximately 16 hours [11:00 PM local time], a worldwide immersion event will begin. This event will last for 48 hours. In preparation for such an event, the following announcement will cover a brief list of important information. Additional facts and details will be posted to your local government webpage, as well as streamed hourly to all connected AR devices. If you have any questions or concerns, utilize the appropriate means to communicate directly with your local government officials.

All citizens are expected to be in their immersion pods NLT [10:30 PM local time]. If this time is outside your normal immersion time, note that this event warrants an exception.

All emergency and official personnel are exempted from their essential status and are expected to join the event for the duration. Individuals flagged as such can rest assured that they will be contacted if their services are needed.

This event is a sanctioned government event. The P.L.O.T. has authorized the extended immersion time, and all citizens are mandated to participate in the program.

During this event, The Zone and other areas of the virtual world will be inaccessible for an extended, necessary period. Over the extended 48-hour period of the event, the government will be conducting important maintenance and upgrades to the infrastructure utilized to provide immersion to the masses. The DCO server mainframe will be exempt from these upgrades, which will ensure the safety and wellbeing of all people within immersion.

All individuals who have not gained access to DCO will immediately be loaded into the game upon immersion and walked through character creation. Participation past that is not required or expected.

The P.L.O.T. has authorized the admittance of all those under the previously established safety age to also participate in this event.

Parents of children under the established safety age will be spawned beside their children at the start of the event and will be granted special abilities to ensure they are able to monitor their children as needed.

Special measures have also been taken for any with children under the age of 5. For those affected, the government will be contacting you in a different manner shortly.

Due to the unique circumstances of this event, any individuals not registered as immersed by their mandated time will be flagged and subjected to suspicion of wrongdoing and persecuted in accordance with the law.

To all citizens, it is our great pleasure to be able to work with the team of DCO to provide this once in a lifetime event to everyone. The success of this 48-hour event will hopefully open the opportunity for similar events in the future. In order to ensure the success of this event, we ask that everyone please adhere to the above. Please use the time before the event begins as you see fit to ensure that you can focus all of your energy and effort on enjoying the 48-hour special.

Respectfully,
Jill Harkin
Peoples' Legislative Office of Technology (P.L.O.T.) Government Liaison

The anger that filled James as he read the words was impossible to describe. The sheer audacity. The blatant lies. They were acting like this event was *for* the people. That it was meant to *benefit* everyone and allow them to upgrade the Zone and improve immersion for the people. All while knowing full well that they were planning to trap everyone within DCO forever.

The masses would become toys for the elite to experiment on and play with as needed at a later date if they got bored during their eternity. The human race was about to be denoted to nothing more than sea monkeys in a fish tank.

James took a breath. His anger wasn't fair. It wasn't directed in a constructive way. Maybe Jill didn't know what the government was up to. Maybe she was reporting what she believed to be true. That didn't make it better, but he couldn't direct his anger at someone that could be just as ignorant and in danger as the rest of the world.

The government was playing the masses for fools. The elite assholes, those special, select few were treating everyone like senseless idiots. And sadly, like lambs to slaughter, James knew full well that the people would willingly go to their inevitable doom unless James and his friends could stop the government's plans.

A big if. And he figured at the moment that such a possibility, such an outcome, wasn't even a blip on the government's radar. They probably thought that they already had the entrapment of the human race in the bag.

The government, based on everything he'd learned over the past few days, was used to doing exactly as it pleased and getting away with it. After all, no one could counter them. They had all the power. All the resources. All the control.

Even still, arguably, it hadn't cost the people anything. Immersion was wonderful, freeing. People lived their lives in the real-world with loved ones doing as they pleased and thriving. And at night, they could be whoever and whatever they wanted to be and were free to do pretty much whatever they wanted to0 with no recourse. It was as utopian as possible.

But it was all a lie. This existence, this state of living wasn't enough for those at the very top. They wanted the world, and they wanted it all to themselves. They didn't want to take care of the people, even though it was the job they'd signed up for by being part of the government. They didn't want to govern. They wanted an existence where they had no worries, no responsibilities, and nothing to stand against them.

A world where they owned not only the entire planet, but every single human mind as well.

And all in a way that ensured that their power would last forever, with not even a fraction of a chance for the people to turn against them. Once everyone was trapped, bodiless, within a virtual world, the human race would be extinct, and the prisoners would have no way to ever take back their freedom or threaten their overlords.

James felt his hands clench as these thoughts raced through his mind. He'd stop them. He didn't know how, but he would. Because letting them win, letting them get away with this was too wrong. It was too unfair. These people had it all already, and yet they still wanted more. There had to be a punishment, had to be a retribution for their greed, for their willingness to cross a line that should never have been crossed.

"It'll be okay." Rue was at his side, hand gently on his shoulder. "We'll make sure it's all okay."

James leaned into her, his body shaking with anger, and said nothing.

They stayed like that until his world went black. He awoke once more within his immersion pod.

Chapter Fifty-One

"Good morning, James," Dagger's voice greeted him as his immersion pod opened.

The dog robot, officially referred to as DOGE-1 by his parents, wagged its tail at him in a very convincing dog-like way. If James hadn't been told that Dagger was a robot, he would never have suspected it. That was just how impressive his parents' skills were.

Which apparently was both a blessing and a curse. Because of them, the elite had a way to become immortal. But also because of them, James had gotten the chance to meet Rue, and hopefully, would be able to save the world.

"Morning, Dagger," James said as he quickly got out of the pod.

He was halfway to the door out of his room when he noticed a steaming plate sitting on his computer desk. Pancakes with syrup and a glass of orange juice.

"Dagger..." James began slowly. "Please tell me that you've been guarding me all night."

The dog-bot barked happily. "I have," Dagger said. "No one interrupted you during your immersion period. As long as I am here, you've nothing to worry about."

"Okay then." James looked back at the food. "So, one question then."

Dagger's head tilted to the side.

"Why is there fresh food there?"

"Your mother asked me to ensure that you ate a proper breakfast in the morning," Dagger responded, his tone quite proud. "As such, I utilized my ability to interface with the house's systems to prepare an appropriate meal for you and delivered it to your room. By my calculations, it should be at the perfect temperature for consumption now."

James looked at the dog in disbelief. What else had his parents programmed into it. What else was Dagger capable of? But beyond that, he knew, if his mother was involved, he'd likely not get away with skipping out on the meal. And considering he was due to call them this morning, he figured he could afford the few minutes it took to eat the food. In fact, the breakfast may give him time to collect his thoughts before he began his day.

"Thank you, Dagger," James said as he walked over to his computer desk.

He grabbed his AR glasses while he was at it, putting the high-end tech on as he ate. No new messages just yet. Not that he'd expected any given how secretive they needed to be. Anything out of the ordinary was risky. He was probably being paranoid, but honestly, he had no idea. Was it paranoia? It didn't feel baseless. And there was always that lifelong saying of 'better safe than sorry.'

"What are your intentions for the day?" Dagger asked as James dug into his food. "Are we leaving the house again?"

"Maybe," James answered, wiping a bit of pancake from his lips as he did. They were buttermilk and had been perfectly cooked. There was a touch of cinnamon added to the batter, if he had to guess, and it blended amazingly with the vanilla infused syrup. They were just like his mother would make for him.

"First though," James continued after he took a drink of the orange juice. Just like Dagger had said, everything was the perfect temperature. The pancakes, not too hot. The juice, not too cold. "We're going to my parents' workshop."

Dagger nodded, which was a very un-doglike action. "The appropriate timeline has been met; therefore, my programming will allow me to unlock their office and grant you access to it."

"The appropriate timeline has been met," James said in a slightly mocking tone as he finished eating.

How much did his parents know? How much did they suspect? Dagger felt like a literal godsend. And he had no doubt that whatever was in their workshop would be invaluable for what was to come. Which made him all the more curious to know what was behind that locked door.

He'd never been allowed inside of the workshop. His parents spent a lot of time there when they were home, but they did their best to keep their work and time with him separate. And James had respected that. Now though, he wished he'd asked about their work more.

Would they have let him in? Probably not. Still, he couldn't know. All he knew was that whatever was in there was extremely important. The Cyb3ru5 hackers that had attacked his house had wanted to get in there. And apparently, it was of such importance that Fel had been given a literal bomb as insurance just to make sure no one would get access to it. A bomb that, thankfully, was no longer in the vicinity as Fel had given it back to her mother yesterday.

James pushed those memories aside, prepared to grab his dirty plate, and paused. He was going to have a call with his parents once he made it into their office. They'd implied that Dagger had some sort of Quantum Encryption technology built in for communication with them. Which sounded extremely secure. However, he didn't know what type of communication it would be, and if it was a video call, well... it was probably for the best that he at least get dressed properly before that. Just in case.

"Can you take these back to the kitchen?" James asked Dagger, holding the plate and glass towards the dog.

He expected robotic arms to extend from the creature's back to grab them. What he didn't expect was for Dagger to stand upright like a human, its paws expanding to become mechanical hands.

"Opposable thumbs, eh?" James said as Dagger took the glass and plate from him. "They really did make you unstoppable, didn't they."

"I was made to serve, in every way possible," Dagger answered dutifully as the robot turned to leave. "And there are some cases where having access to thumbs can be a lifesaver."

James watched the dog leave, the absurdity of the scene leaving him speechless for a moment. What, just what, had possessed his parents to add that feature to Dagger?

He shook his head, knowing better than to question their genius when it came to robots, and grabbed some clothes. It was time to finish uncovering the secrets that had plagued him. It was time to enter his parents' workshop.

Chapter Fifty-Two

That's it? James thought as he stood within the mysterious room.

Dagger had, as promised, opened the door for him. The process had involved the robo-dog utilizing a mixture of tools, which had sprung from his back, to access a very complicated locking mechanism that had been apparently hidden in the wall to gain access.

Once this was complete, the door had slid open soundlessly, revealing a room of darkness. Only after James and Dagger stepped inside and the door closed had a light turned on, revealing the contents of the room.

To say the buildup felt anticlimactic was an understatement. The only thing within the room, at the center of it, was a chair. Sure, it was a really fancy chair, but it was still just a chair. It was large like a recliner, with an overhead panel that gave it a cockpit type of feel. If James had to guess, once he sat in the chair, it would recline backwards, and the overhead portion would display a monitor.

Still, considering how important this room was supposed to be, the initial impression was... underwhelming.

"Is this it?" James asked, looking down at Dagger. "This is everything?"

Instead of answering in its own voice, Dagger redeployed the holo-projector from deep within its throat. Light beams quickly danced in the air before Dagger, and a recording began to play. James recognized the speaker immediately. It was his dad, with a large grin on his face.

"If you're seeing this message, I'm sure you've got some questions," his dad's voice began. "And considering you're my son, I'm going to guess the main one goes something along the lines of 'Really? A freaking chair?'"

James couldn't help but smile. His dad knew him so well.

"Get on with it," his mom's voice said in the recording, just outside the range of the camera. "Until you tell him what's going on, he's just going to be standing in that room feeling stupid."

James's smile widened. And his mom was just as perceptive as his dad was. He loved them. Though... he also had to wonder, was he really *that* predictable?

His dad ran a hand sheepishly through his hair, moving some strands away from his eyes. A habit James had picked up from the man. "Right, right," his dad began again.

As the recording of his dad continued, James couldn't help but notice that the dark bags were still under his dad's eyes. They were just like the ones he'd noticed in their last projector message.

"That chair isn't just a chair. It's the final level of security for our workshop. Well, okay, it's also a nifty part of our workshop, and lets us handle ad hoc tasks when we don't want to get lost in our work. But, really, it's mostly the last line of defense. Anyone who isn't me, your mom, or you won't be able to access that chair. Not even DOGE-1 has access to it. Once you sit in that chair, you'll see what I mean. It'll take you to our true workshop. And if you are watching this recording, well, I'm sure we'll be talking extremely soon. I'll save any other answers to your questions until you can ask them face to face."

He looked directly at the camera that was recording the message. James knew the camera was actually his father's robotic bird, the one he always had with him.

"I love you, James."

"Love you, son," his mom called from behind the bird.

Then the hologram faded away, leaving James once again in the empty room with just himself, Dagger, and the chair that apparently wasn't just a chair.

"I guess I'll go check out the chair," he said to Dagger, "before we give them a call." He wanted to call them. Wanted to talk with them face to face. He needed to tell them everything that was happening. He longed to tell them about everything that had happened so far. And...

A part of him just wanted his parents. To confide in them, to have them tell him everything would be okay. To have them solve the problems for him. He'd tried so hard to always be mature and act like an adult. But there was still that part of him, that childish part that longed for the days when his parents could just make everything instantly better.

He sighed as the emotions swirled within and pushed them aside. He was seventeen, close enough to adult that wanting his parents to make everything better was childish. Hells, thanks to time dilation and immersion, which he'd been enjoying for years now, mentally he was older than seventeen, even if his brain and body chemically and physically hadn't matured to those levels yet.

At one point, he'd actually found an interesting study regarding maturity on Reddit. It had been a discussion about if experiences and time within immersion aged people faster, and if such factors should be considered regarding the population as a whole.

It brought to question what it was that actually denoted adulthood. Was it purely based on the number of days they'd lived? And if so, did days lived in immersion count, or not? Was it all purely biological, or was there more to it? It was a rabbit hole that a carefree James had delved into for an entire afternoon.

Oh, to have that type of freedom again...

James reached the chair, noting that the interior was lined with black leather. A quick glance within also told him that the chair had the ability to adjust itself to the person sitting in it to give them the optimal comfort factor. A nice touch. At the very least, this did look like a very nice chair.

Trusting his parents, and curious about what exactly the chair did, James stepped up onto the platform on the side of the chair and then set himself down within the cradle that was the massive seat.

Immediately, he felt warmth on the back of his neck. It was brief, no more than a split second. It happened so quickly perhaps he'd imagined it? James didn't have time to ponder the perceived feeling as the chair began to whir to life.

The material within the chair shifted, adding tension here, loosening its cushioning inflation there, until he was nearly immobile within the chair. It almost felt like he'd become an actual part of the chair, so snugly was he now sitting within it.

Without warning, it suddenly began to lean backwards. Once he was almost horizontal to the ground, a holo-screen appeared against the background that was the overhanging portion of the chair.

Welcome James, the screen read. Then the screen flickered, and a new set of words appeared.

Would you like to access the workshop?

"Er, yes?" James said, caught off guard by the prompts. Up until three minutes ago, he was pretty sure this was the workshop.

Internal Command Received. Beginning Transport, the message said.

Internal command? James thought to himself. Before he could ponder that wording more, though, the room went suddenly dark. And a second after that, it felt like the world had dropped out beneath him.

Chapter Fifty-Three

After the initial drop of a depth James couldn't gauge due to the lack of lighting, James distinctly heard the sound of gears, the sound of machinery. There was the slight feeling of a breeze, and he realized, situated as he was, that they were moving downwards in a slow spiral. James tried to sit up, to look past the confines of the chair and peer into the darkness, curious to see what was happening, but the chair held him fast.

"Dagger," James called out into the darkness. "Are you there?"

"I'm still here," the robot responded. "Do you have a need of me?"

"Can you turn on a light?" James asked, half-jokingly. Instead of responding with words, James' question was answered with action. A bright light filled the area.

Positioned as he was, he couldn't really see anything around him. His head was restrained, the chair went past his head on either side, and obviously, he couldn't see the ground. What he could see was the world above him.

Past the overhang of the chair, he could make out the ceiling growing further and further away. And he could see worked stone, lined with metal detailing, made up the walls they were descending past. It was clear that the floor was descending, down and down, to some crazy depths beneath his house.

"The chair isn't just a chair," James said, doing his best to mimic his dad's voice and tone from the recording. "Yeah, no shit."

It was one thing to hide your workshop behind a secure door. It was a whole different level of security to have it underground, accessible only by moving the entire freaking floor.

Around and around the world slowly spiraled, giving him a 360-degree view of the walls. It was clear they were heading downwards in a column. If he had to guess, it was on a rotating, drill-like platform. Had his parents put this in? Or had the government prepared it for them at their request? The house, after all, had been a part of their new assignment when they'd been offered the job to work with the government here.

Another question that he'd ask his dad once he reached the workshop proper. For now, all he could really do was enjoy the ride.

"Any chance you can play some music?" James asked Dagger, still uncertain where the robot was.

He knew Dagger was on his left side, judging by the source of the light, but that was all. And with the room spinning and spinning, he had no idea what his orientation was anymore to the door that had led into the room. All he knew was that he was definitely below the house.

"Certainly," Dagger said, and then a moment later, the robot began playing music.

It was circus music. The type that James had come to associate with merry-go rounds from childhood.

"Seriously?" James asked a moment after the music started playing.

"You didn't specify the type of music," Dagger said, as the music continued to play. "I figured it was appropriate."

"You figured wrong," James said. "Try again." Apparently, the AI of the robot had inherited part of his father's humor.

"Very well," Dagger responded, and as asked, changed the music.

This time... it was a showtune, one James was pretty sure came from the Jurassic Park films.

"I hate you," James muttered, though he figured the epic music at least captured the moment better than circus-styled music. A sense of discovery, of excitement. Not creepily dressed clowns, children, cotton candy, and unsafe rides.

Either way, he didn't have to listen to the music for long. Before he knew it, the spinning slowed, and the walls began to open up on either side of him. Above, as the platform came to stop, James heard grinding, and the ceiling a good thirty feet above him disappeared as the hole from where the floor should have been mechanically closed with two sliding halfsphere plates of metal.

The holo-screen reappeared before James as lights flicked to life all around him.

Welcome to the workshop, the message said.

Then the screen flickered off, and James felt the chair shift, releasing him. Quicker than intended, like an animal freed from a cage, James got out of the chair. At first, it had felt comforting when it had closed in around him, a feeling he was used to from the immersion pods. But being trapped in the chair the whole descent, unable to shift and move, had caused him to panic slightly.

After he was clear of the chair, his panic subsiding, James was finally able to take in his surroundings. And the first thing he did was pinch himself. The pain, actual pain, and not digital warmth, confirmed to him that he was actually awake and not in immersion. Which did little to help his mind process what he was looking at.

Especially since, in theory, there was still the slight chance it was immersion. You could *technically* feel pain in immersion if you were a masochist and turned off the pain dulling feature that was the default. But James wasn't... and he didn't know anyone that ever actually did.

What if someone had done it intentionally, to make me think I was awake but still immersed? The thought came unbidden, and he shivered as he pushed it aside. Something about descending into a mysterious workshop underneath a house via a secret, technologically advanced chair really brought out the creepiest paranoid thoughts.

With a breath to steady himself, James's mind steadied enough for him to process what he was looking at.

He was in a workshop close to the size of a football field. All around him, robots in various stages of completion stood, sat, or lay. Screens and monitors lined the walls, and there were various robotic arms on wheels that moved to and fro conducting tasks, including grabbing materials from bins here and there to take other places.

The workshop was alive with activity. His parents were at the government facility and had been for a long time. And yet their workshop was still... working. Was this their doing? Were they controlling everything down here remotely from where they were?

More questions in his mind. More things he needed answers too.

James looked at Dagger and knew it was time. Time to get in contact with his parents and finally ask them everything that he wanted to. Time to finally learn the truth from his parents. Time to learn how long they had been working on this. How long had all of this taken. And more importantly, how much of this did the government know about.

"Dagger," James said, pulling his eyes away from a half-completed robot that stood nearly ten feet in height, "it's time to make a call."

Chapter Fifty-Four

"Can you hear me now?" his dad's voice asked, the sound echoing out of Dagger's mouth in a more than slightly unsettling way.

The robot dog's eyes glowed, and James knew that his image and surroundings were being broadcast to his father. Dagger had mentioned as much prior to beginning the call. However, the dog had failed to mention that it was a one-way feature.

"I can," James said with a sigh. "Just like I was able to the first two times you asked."

His dad chuckled. "Sorry, couldn't resist. And honestly, it's not every day we get to put this sort of thing to use."

"What sort of thing?" James asked. His dad's wording was strange. "Isn't this just a regular call?"

The sound of his dad scoffing came from Dagger's mouth.

"Just a regular call." James could imagine the look of fake disappointment on his father's face as he very likely shook his head. "You should give your parents a little credit. This is no mere call."

"Then what is it?" James pressed. "Because on my end, it just seems like a creepy one-way video call. And honestly, your voice coming through Dagger's mouth is super creepy. Why aren't we doing a holo-call like yesterday?"

"Yesterday's call was harmless," his dad replied, "so we were able to speak, at least for that short while, with you normally. Now though." His dad paused. "Now though, we have to be extremely careful. And that means taking every measure possible to ensure that no one knows what's being said."

"In that case, should we switch to secure messages?" James asked. Surely their special quantum encryption or whatever it was could ensure that their text messages were sent securely.

"We could, but that's slower, and nowhere near as cool. Besides, what's the point in having amazing technology if you don't ever put it to use."

"Then what—"

"—I'm talking to you with my mind." His dad's answer made James close his mouth immediately. "And I'm hearing and seeing you within my mind as well."

"You're what?" James asked in disbelief. "Are you using AR glasses?" he speculated.

"Nope, those can be easily intercepted and hacked into," his dad's response came, matter of fact. "This is much more secure. The information input of the video and audio feeds are being sent through our encrypted method directly into my brain, which then allows me to hear—and see in a way—you. At the same time, I can think my messages to you, as if I were speaking, and it gets translated into the appropriate audio data and sent back to you via the same network. Like I said, it's super neat."

James said nothing. He just stood there, looking dumbfounded at Dagger.

As if to confirm what he'd been saying, his dad began speaking once more. "I know for a fact you're in our workshop, which means you've already gotten to experience at least a little taste of this very same technology firsthand. So don't stand there thinking your old man's talking crazy."

"I... You... What?" James stumbled out. What was his dad on about?

"The chair, James," his dad's response came, "it linked into your brain. The monitor for the chair doesn't display actual messages, it's just there for appearances. Helps, too, when you're first getting used to the tech. Much easier to have a surface your mind can identify as a screen for messages rather than just words magically appearing midair in your vision. It's a way to ease you into the tech. Best way to avoid, you know, hysteria, panic, disbelief, or paranoia—questioning if you're real or stuck in immersion." His dad chuckled at the last part. "Wouldn't do good to make people think they were immersed when they're in the real world. That's how you end up with someone jumping off a building thinking they can fly."

James ignored his dad's tangent as he thought back to the chair and the monitor. He could have sworn that the messages had appeared on the monitor space, but now that his dad mentioned it, they had seemed... strange. Instinctively, he reached for the back of his neck and rubbed under his skull, where the warmth had been. It was starting to come together. Sort of.

"Exactly," his father said, and James could practically hear his dad clapping. "That special void that was picked up in your medical scans is actually a highly advanced and top secret piece of technology developed and patented by yours truly." His dad paused, and the sound of him clearing his throat came through Dagger's mouth. "Well, with your mother's help, of course, and Zephire."

"Dr. Zephire?" James said, immediately recognizing the name. How could he not? Dr. Zephire was Rue's father. The man who'd developed the technology that was going to be used by the government to trap everyone within DCO, while granting a select few immortality in the real world through his parent's robots. "You worked on this tech with Rue's dad?"

"None other," came the response. "Man's brilliant when it comes to the mind. We worked on the nanites, ensuring that they had the proper ability to cloak themselves, to make themselves undetectable, and able to interact with the brain in the ways we needed to. Dr. Zephire helped identify the specific parts of the mind, the conscious and subconscious that could be affected by our tech. And more importantly, which sections via electrical pulses and signals would need to be triggered to properly accomplish what we wanted.

"At its core, the brain is just a massive marvel of electricity. A circuit board of infinite potential. Sending the right sparks of energy, in the appropriate amounts, frequencies, and precise spots, can make your mind experience, well, anything. When you think about it, our whole existence, the conscious mind, it's all just electrical signals! Understanding these nuances and being able to do what we are with tech, is like discovering magic, James."

James's mouth couldn't open any further in disbelief. His still-healing jaw throbbed in protest.

"What?" was all he could say. "You put robots in my mind without telling me?" he then added, clinging to the first bit that came to, well, mind.

"Technically," his dad's voice drew out the word, in an evasive manner, "yes?" The word was soft, almost like a question. "I mean, we tweaked your immersion pod, adding them to its gel. So then on release, the nanites entered your body through your ear canal and moved to their designated hibernation spot."

"When?" James pressed. He hadn't seen his parents in... How long had it been? Months?

"Oh, see, that's where the technical bit comes from too. We didn't do it in person. We had one of our robots from the lab handle it."

"I—" James looked around at the mentioned lab. There were humanoid robots secured to the walls. There were also a variety of robots moving about, conducting different tasks. For a lab whose owners hadn't visited it in months, the lab was very much alive and active.

"Yeah, that reaction is totally fair, buddy. Go ahead and take a moment to process it all," his dad said, voice soothing, "and then we can get into the meat and potatoes of things. No need to dive into unnecessary details about when and how we put the nanites in your body. Probably best not to question the ethics of our actions either, that's just a whole messy matter I don't think we really want to unpack here and now. Besides, we've more pressing matters to discuss."

James heard the tone shift in his father's voice, moving from jovial to serious.

"There's something you need to know," his dad said. "You're in grave danger."

"You don't say," James said darkly, trying hard not to let his feelings of betrayal, surprise, anger, and whatever else he was trying to unpack from the nanites in his mind revelation, impact his focus,

"Did the government learn about our plans to stop them?" he asked, his heart was already sinking. That had to be it. Somehow, in some way, the government had learned of his and his friends' plans. They'd had no chance from the start. "Are the Enforcers coming to silence me, like they silenced Xander?"

There was a long, awkward silence. A sound almost like static emitted from Dagger's throat as the robot dog stood there, unmoving, its glowing eyes clearly still recording James and sending the information to his father. After a few minutes, his father cleared his throat.

"Okay, new topic of focus, first and foremost," his dad said, clearly off balance. "What the hell are you talking about?"

Chapter Fifty-Five

James covered what he knew with his father in the span of a few minutes, speaking quickly while his father listened, never once interrupting him. After he finished, his dad was quiet for a couple of minutes, likely processing what all his son had told him.

"I swear," his father finally began, "if we survive all of this, I don't think you're going to be allowed to be on your own any longer. Trouble seems to find you like a damned magnet."

"Pretty sure I was born with a negative luck stat," James said dryly. "Considering everything that's happened to me, I'd much rather go back to when my only worries were being bullied at school."

It felt like a lifetime ago that Dwight had punched him outside of the school building. What he wouldn't give to go back to that time.

"Okay, well," his dad let out a heavy sigh. "I— are you sure about Xander?" His dad's voice was tentative. "Did they really use Truth Serum on him?"

"Steve told us," James answered. "He said he administered it himself to Xander."

"Monsters," his dad's voice muttered. "No one deserves to experience a fate like that. Sure, Xander and I had our differences, and he went off the deep end towards the end of it all... but with what you told me, he was totally justified. He saw the writing on the wall a lot sooner than we did, that's for sure."

"Too bad you're so good at your job," James said, dark humor taking hold for a moment. "Else there would have been more time for us to attempt to reveal the government's plans to the masses and stop them."

"If there's one thing your mom and I pride ourselves on, it's our work ethic," his father said. "You don't get to be the best by not putting your all into a job. But that doesn't mean we didn't have contingencies in place. You always have to have a rainy-day project or two…"

James felt a bit of hope. It pushed at his depression, the darkness shifting just slightly, like clouds finally giving way to a ray of sunlight. "So you can put a stop to the government's plans?" he asked hopefully. "Stop all of this?"

"I, er, didn't say that." His father's answer dashed his hopes. The sunlight faded, and it felt darker in the workshop. "But you should be able to put some of the stuff in our workshop to use for whatever it is you're planning tonight."

"You said you had contingencies in place," James pressed. "Doesn't that mean you had a plan to stop your robots from being used in such a way? You know Dr. Zephire, surely you could have predicted this."

"You act like we had complete freedom during our time here," his dad cut back. "We're in the belly of the beast, James. Constant surveillance is on us. And it's a Top-Secret project, meaning we only get to know what they want us to know. Our job was to make perfect human robots. Ones capable of feeling, of smelling, of tasting. Ones indistinguishable from real humans. They told us that the project was meant to give people like Ruby a second chance. And others who may have been injured in wars, or accidents, or born with health complications that would impact their quality of life."

His father sighed. "They told us our project was meant to be used for good. And well, a part of us really wished and hoped it was. It's the dream, you know. To be a part of something that changes the world for good. That makes the world a better place… for everyone."

"Didn't you think it was weird that it was connected to DCO, though?" James asked forcefully. "Surely you had doubts about the project, questions about the end game."

"Well duh." His father's tone was insulted. "We asked about the connection and were told DCO would test the ability of fully immersing a mind, deeper than any tech before it, to serve as the transfer point for a consciousness. If they could make a world within immersion that could fully allow a person to experience everything as if it were the real world, they'd be able to trace that data, those aspects of the mind, and create artificial minds capable of holding the person within our robotic bodies and interfacing them seamlessly as a result. Well, that's the simple version of it, at least. Like I said, the tech behind it, the science, it's like magic made real."

"And you took their answers and dove into the project without asking anything else?" James's tone was still bitter.

"I don't think you fully understand the way the government works," his dad said, not aggressively but tired. It reminded James of how exhausted his dad had looked yesterday on the video. "You do what they want, without causing a stir. Otherwise, you disappear. Or worse, find yourself buried in debt and misfortune with your loved ones targeted as fallout.

"This job got us here. Got us a lab of our own at our house, got you into a good school, and got your mother and me access to every piece of equipment and all the materials we could ever dream of. And like I said, we didn't do it all blindly. We took advantage of our situation as best we could, without causing too much scrutiny. Sabotaging the project we were working on, based off a whim or paranoia, would have instantly resulted in your death." His father cut off for a moment. "We couldn't risk you. Not on a bad feeling."

"Dad." James's anger fled as he thought of Zach and what had happened to him, his wife, everything he'd worked for. He knew full well what the government was capable of. "I'm sorry," he said gently.

"It's fine." His dad cleared his throat. "Anyways. Working on the project kept you safe, got you in a prime Dungeon Core role, and got you paired with Rue. Those are all the things we'd do again if we had the chance. What we didn't know, until just yesterday, was the fact that DCO was meant to be a prison. Past that, what I didn't know until just now, was the extent of the full plan."

"So, you were calling to warn me that they were planning to trap us in immersion?" James asked, seeking clarification.

"Pretty much. We caught word that something was up, and that the immersion tonight would be different. Those who took part in it wouldn't be able to get out of their immersion pods. We didn't know the full extent of everything. Not that I doubt you or your source of information, but even now, I'm having trouble believing it all."

"Only reason I'm not completely freaking out," James offered, "is because I've had a few days while immersed to get past the pure panic and depression bit of the information. I'm not proud of it... but I definitely had a few breakdowns."

"If you hadn't, I would have assumed that you'd been turned into a robot," James's dad laughed, and James felt his mood lift just a tad.

He'd missed this. Missed talking with his parents. Missed his dad's ability to try and joke about everything.

"Now then, you've got a raid to plan, and it's time you give your old man some credit. Sure, I didn't build a failsafe into the robots that we created for the government. But that doesn't mean your mother and I did nothing with the surplus materials we've had access to ever since we took on this job. We won't be able to help you in person, considering we've already received word that we're supposed to immerse tonight and be in DCO... which now makes a lot of sense, but we can still be there in spirit with you. And by spirit, I mean through a variety of, ahem, special projects."

"I'm waiting," James said, knowing his dad was building up for a big reveal. "Let's see them."

"Alrighty then, here's what I need you to do."

Chapter Fifty-Six

James was in the chair once again. Apparently, its purpose was not only to grant access to the workshop, but also to manage features of the workshop that needed extra security. What James currently had access to was the standard workshop.

The forms and figures he saw were all projects in various stages of completion, but none of them were actually 'completed'. Those, his father had told him, were kept in another secure room. One that was only accessible by having the proper hardware, a.k.a. secret skull-dwelling nanites, to use the chair properly.

"Alright, I'm in the chair," James said aloud as he got himself comfortable. It was hard to trust the chair fully considering the last time he'd sat in it, it had trapped him in its clutches and taken him down to this secret laboratory. "Now what?"

"The system should do a scan to activate your nanites."

As his dad spoke, James felt the warm sensation on the back of his neck. Once again, the monitor came to life. Though he now knew that was all an illusion. If his dad was to be taken seriously, what James was seeing was actually being projected within his mind.

Welcome, James, the prompt once again said. Followed immediately by, **Would you like to leave the Workshop?**

James mentally thought no. The words flickered.

Standing by for intent.

"It says standing by for intent," James relayed to his dad. "Now what? Do I just think about your finished projects?"

"Nah. That won't work. This is a special room. It requires a specific phrase to be given. Request access to"—his dad cleared his throat— "Mommy and Daddy's special toy closet."

"What?" James asked immediately.

"Please don't make me say it again," his dad said, a bit of embarrassment in his voice. "It was a bad joke between me and your mother. When we were setting up the security, we wanted to make sure it was something ridiculous that no one could accidentally stumble upon. And when it comes to passphrase cracking, silly and embarrassing things are usually some of the last things to be thought of. Probably unnecessary, considering only those with our specially coded nanites can even access the chair, but you know, it's never wise to be complacent with security measures. And…"

His dad trailed off, almost to a whisper. "We may have been a tad inebriated when we put it in place. Plus in a perfect world, the only one ever using the passphrase would have been me and your mother, at which point, it wasn't, ya know, awkward. It was just funny."

"A tad inebriated," James muttered, "I'm sure just a tad, huh? And yeah, this is something no kid should have to think of." He shook his head best he could while secure in the chair and thought the passphrase, trying extremely hard not to let his mind wander. There were some things that parents should just never say around their kids. And some images kids just never needed of their parents.

Special Access Granted.

The message pulled his mind, thankfully, from the route his imagination had taken. There was the sound of heavy pressure releasing, and then clanking gears and grating metal. James pulled himself free of the chair and looked in the direction of the noise.

An entire part of the wall of the workshop, which had been covered with blinking monitors, slid inwards. The monitors served as lights to tease at what lay within the newly revealed expanse. It was a large room, though not as spacious as the massive workshop he was currently in. And from where he stood, he couldn't yet make out the details of what awaited him inside the new room.

His excitement wouldn't let him wait.

"It's open," James said quickly to Dagger as he walked towards the open room.

The dog trotted just behind him, its glowing eyes still providing the video feed of everything that was happening to his father, who was somehow receiving all of this in his head through his nanites.

How exactly was he doing that? Was it a function of his father's parrot robot? An image of the robot sitting on his dad's shoulder, perhaps leaning its head against his neck, flashed through his mind. What was the range of these nanites that his parents had inserted knowingly in themselves, and unknowingly within James? What could trigger them? What else could they do?

His musings were short lived as he reached the secret workshop, which he refused to acknowledge as his parents' special toy closet.

The room was the size of a small gymnasium, and it was much more organized than the workshop. Whereas the main area had bits and pieces all strewn about, with robots moving to and fro, computers beeping and screens blinking, the special room was lit by a steady, white light, showing a completely sterile space with metal floors and ceilings.

It was like a vault. As James walked past the heavy door, he could see that it was also reinforced by a few inches of thick gleaming metal, with massive pistons and stakes on the inside that seemed to have retracted from slots in the floor. No one was getting through that door without either extreme brute force or the proper password. And that required, first and foremost, that the person knew where to look.

Within the vault were six robots, two on each wall of the room, with the wall with the door being empty. They were held upright by massive mechanical braces, which reminded him of how video games and anime usually showed mechanized suits being secured. There seemed to be room for fifteen robots total, judging by the three empty sets of braces on each wall. James wondered if there had been robots in them before, or if they were there simply for future projects.

Beside each of the robots was a terminal, from which wires ran into the braces and then the back of the heads of the robots. As James got further into the room, heading to the nearest robot on his left, he realized each and every one of them, while humanoid, was distinctly different.

"Welcome," James's dad said from behind him, "to our Government Goes Batshit contingency space."

James looked down at Dagger, and then back at the first robot. His dad hadn't been lying. They had been busy. And he wondered when they'd had the time to make these six.

"Impressive," James said as he reached the first terminal. "Are you going to tell me what they are called and what they do?"

"And ruin the surprise?" his dad said with a chuckle. "Heavens no. I'll answer your questions after you boot up the terminal."

"Then at least tell me how to fire up the terminal?" James asked, looking down at the piece of technology. There was a handprint scanner on the face of it. There was also a set of goggles, which he figured was either a portable retina scanner, or would serve as the display for the terminal's information. And then last but not least, there was a keypad.

"That, I can most certainly definitely do."

Chapter Fifty-Seven

James rotated his shoulders, feeling a bit of the tension leaving them as he made his way towards the door that would leave his parents' workshop room, back towards the regular portion of his home. The chair once more was the only thing in the room, the floor normal, showing no signs of the massive, secret lab that existed beneath the house.

He'd left his parents' workshop behind for now. What his dad had shown him, the six robots in the special room, had him feeling, even if just a little, that they had a chance tonight. Those robots were going to be key to the success of the night.

With them, it felt like he'd have his parents beside him for the mission. With their might added to the mix, he felt that success was more than a pipe dream. His parents were providing much needed firepower, and Z and his group would provide him with in-person allies and access to the facility.

Meanwhile, Hades had promised to mitigate what he could of the security that would be remaining in the mountain facility while everyone was immersed. Meaning maybe, just maybe, they'd get through this. They'd win. And the government... well, the government and the elites who viewed humans as nothing more than property would finally pay the price for their hubris.

As he crossed the threshold out of the special room, movement in his vision caught his attention. His eyes darted to the prompts, noting that he'd just received in rapid fire a string of messages.

No, that wasn't quite right. The notifications for the messages were all instantaneous, but as he opened the list, he could tell there were different timestamps on them. He'd not noticed it before, but apparently, his AR glasses hadn't had any signal while he'd been in that room. No doubt another security feature.

Did that mean that, while he was in there, his government chip in his wrist had been disabled too? For the roughly two hours he'd been down there, had it just seemed like he'd disappeared completely? That last bit seemed silly.

Given how secure and paranoid his parents were, he doubted they'd put that type of feature in place. At least... directly. If he had to guess, they had a way to mimic the signal from the chip, but in a 'nothing to see here' kind of way so that it couldn't pick up anything they didn't want it to. That type of tech, he knew from Fel, Hades, and Dagger, was more common than he'd ever previously expected. Well... probably not common. He'd just found himself surrounded by extremely secretive and paranoid people.

James sorted the messages, scanning their message headers, noting their timestamps. It was just past 9 AM. He had thirteen hours to go before they'd dive back into immersion. Fourteen hours until the government's special 48-hour event started. The first message, from Z, came in at 7:20 AM. The latest... dozen or so messages had all been coming in two and half minute increments. Considering immersion related one hour of real-world time to twenty-four hours within the virtual world, that equaled roughly once every hour. Those were all from Rue.

He opened the last one and replied to it quickly.

From: Rue
Subject: WHERE ARE YOU!!!!!!!!!!!!!!!!!!!!!!!!!!!!
Seriously, I'm starting to worry. I'm trying not to. Really, I am. But no one has heard from you yet, and they asked me if I'd spoken with you, and I haven't. I don't know what you're doing. And the camera feeds in your house that Fel left behind aren't showing you anywhere. You've disappeared into your parents' room, and then... nothing. I'm trying to tell myself it's nothing, but the fact you're not responding is really starting to scare me. Please, James, where are you. I keep telling myself nothing bad has happened, but I can't get ahold of you. I can't see you. And no one knows what's going on with you.

Please please please be okay and respond as soon as you see this.

James quickly sent a message. He wanted to tell her everything, but he couldn't. Not through these messages. And he couldn't tell her what he'd been doing or what he'd seen. At the very least though, he could try and alleviate her fears. Her concern meant a lot to him, enough so that he figured he'd ignore the fact that she was using cameras that Fel had apparently still left behind to spy on him.

To Rue:

Subject: I'm right here

Sorry for making you worry! I'm here, and everything is okay. I'm really sorry for making you worry, though, and will try to make it up as best I can when I'm back in DCO. Everything will be okay. See you tonight.

Love,

James

P.S. Remind me to have a word with you and Fel about these cameras...

He sent the message, a small smile on his lips as he quickly skimmed the other spam messages from her. They all covered pretty much the same thing, but with an increasing degree of concern. Normally, Rue wasn't this paranoid. But considering what they were up against, and what was at stake, he figured everyone was probably a bit on edge right now.

With Rue taken care of for now, and very likely spying on him through the cameras in the house, he moved on to the next message. Well, technically the first message to come in this morning. The one from Zach, a.k.a. Z.

From: Zach

Subject: Health Check

Hey buddy, just wanted to check in on how you're feeling today. I can bring some more books by later today, maybe some pizza and ice cream again too. I'll be running errands all day with some of my friends, so you know, if you do want me to check in on you, they may be with me. Let me know if that's okay.

Z

James smirked as he read Z's message. The man was good. So very, very good. James knew exactly who Z's friends were. But Zach was sending this message in a way that made it all seem normal. Like nothing had changed. Like it was just one of his innocent checkup messages. The same sort of things he'd been doing ever since James's fight at school.

The carefree, charismatic, gamer that was Zach had no doubt learned such tactics from his lifetime of dealing with the government. He knew how to cover his tracks, and he knew how to be sneaky. And this would provide him with the perfect opportunity to introduce James to the people he'd be working with in the real world tonight to try and take DCO's servers offline and to save the world.

To: Zach
Subject: Health Check
Z,
That sounds good. I could definitely do with some more ice cream. My jaw was feeling a bit sore, so I'd appreciate it if you did come over and check it out again? Just to make sure everything is healing up. I appreciate you telling me about your friends. Are they teachers from school? Either way, I doubt my parents would mind. Though I can't get too distracted. Looking forward to starting this awesome DCO event.

James sent the message, his smiling fading as it went off into virtual space. He had tried to be as normal as possible in the message to the school's doctor. He was trying to act ordinary and nonchalant. But it wasn't easy. His mind was abuzz with thoughts and plans and things he wanted to say and discuss with everyone.

But he couldn't. It wasn't safe. The government had ears everywhere, and he had no doubt that they likely had algorithms scanning messages for trigger words and phrases too. He needed to just smile and wave. To act like nothing was amiss when everything quite literally was.

He sighed and opened the next one. It was from Fel. As he read it, he let out a heavier sigh. How should he respond? At the same time, he found himself wondering if this was how it felt to be her. Was this the life of a special cover operative?

Because this was nowhere near as glamorous or exhilarating as the movies always made it out to be. The media had lied. None of this was badass and fun. It was stressful, worrisome, and somewhat sickening if his nerves got to have a say in it.

Thirteen hours before immersion. Thirteen more hours of feeling sweaty and sick from paranoia, anxiety, and nerves. Oh, how he wished he could force sleep the time away. Honestly, living permanently within immersion didn't seem like such a bad thing. Especially if it meant he could never feel like this again. But this path, this battle against the government was the right one. And doing the right thing, if he'd learned anything from books, games, and movies, wasn't always easy.

It wasn't convenient. It wasn't comfortable. It generally fucking sucked at times, if he was being honest with himself. It now made sense to him why people more often than not took the easy way out, even if it was morally gray or just straight up wrong. He wished he could. But with the world at stake, James would do this. For Rue, he'd do this. He'd be the guy she believed him to be, he'd be the hero that the world needed him to be.

Or, well, he'd fail, the world would end, the rich people with power would get their way. And the masses would be trapped forever in a virtual world, living an existence as prisoners, forever trapped and at the whims of their captors, with no way, ever, to fight back or be freed.

At least they'd still get to be immersed, James thought bitterly at the end. If he failed, he'd likely wind-up dead. If he had to choose... he'd rather be trapped in immersion with Rue forever than be dead. Because even if it meant they were at the whims of the government... well, how was that any different from now? At least they'd still be together.

The last thought stung the most because he knew in his heart what he was doing was right. Because the thought of Rue being an experiment, being the government's plaything, and not free to live her life as she wanted was the cruelest fate of all. Especially given her existence already, her illness, the cruel fate that saw her confined to an immersion pod, trapped forever in virtual space, spending so much time trapped and alone already.

He'd do this. Or he'd die trying. The final truth about the world and doing the right thing was that it was rarely ever fair. You took the hand you were dealt, and damnit, you did all you could to make the best of it. And James, well, he was going to bet on himself and everyone else against the house.

One final gamble... for the fate of humanity.

Chapter Fifty-Eight

"I honestly didn't expect to see you today," Alex said as James walked into the hospital room.

Alex was sitting upright in his special medical bed, same as the last time James had seen him. The structure could also double as an immersion pod, allowing patients to access the Zone at night, or in extreme cases, during the day.

Being absent from the present pains that affected their bodies was more effective than any form of morphine ever could be. Plus, it limited how often patients with serious injuries or who'd undergone massive surgery moved about, limiting the chance any of the doctor's work could be undone. For some surgeries, especially ones with longer recovery times, it even allowed the patient to remain immersed during the initial recovery period, which promoted pain-free operations and healing.

"Figured I'd swing by and see how you were doing," James answered honestly as he stepped into the room.

His eyes scanned Alex, noting that he seemed to have a little more color to him than he had the day prior. Modern medicine was amazing. Alex had been beaten within an inch of his life at Dwight's hands. If not for Fel's arrival, and her quick handling of Dwight, there was a possibility the boy who'd helped ensure Dwight was punished for attacking James would have died in his stead.

"Same old same old," Alex said with a shrug. His smile faltered for just a moment at the action, no doubt angering his broken ribs and bruised body. He slowly ran a hand through his hair as he looked around. "Any chance you brought me something better than hospital food?"

James laughed and shook his head side to side. "Sorry, didn't think to bring you anything."

"Shame," Alex said with a sigh. "Downside of living with chefs. Everything else just tastes, you know, underwhelming. At least in the real world, that is." His eyes took on a wistful look. "Some of the meals I've had in the Zone, and especially in DCO, have definitely put meals in the real world to shame."

"Do you prefer DCO to the real world?" James asked as he took a seat beside Alex. The question just escaped his mouth before he realized he was even saying it. "Would you stay there forever, if you could?" *What the hell are you doing?*

Alex looked at him for a long moment, his eyes thoughtful. He shifted, somewhat uncomfortably, in his hospital bed before he responded.

"Probably not," he said. "As awesome as it is, probably not."

"Why?" James pressed.

"Because it's not real," Alex answered. He was speaking quicker now as he seemed to finalize his thoughts. "No matter how real it feels, it's not. It's virtual. It—" He paused to think. "The fact it's virtual, the fact it's not real is what makes it special, you know?"

"I—" James stopped, unsure of how to answer. "I'm not sure I'm following."

"We can do and be whatever we want in immersion," Alex said as he leaned back into his bed. "It's awesome, really. And I'm really glad the technology exists. It's given me the chance to do and experience so many things that would probably be impossible otherwise."

He grinned as a lecherous look crossed his face for a moment. James had heard more than a few stories of the types of things Alex and Fel had been up to in DCO, including their, ah, escapades with a certain Demonkin named Lilith.

"But while the experiences and memories all feel real," Alex continued, "the fact they don't matter, the lack of actual weight on our decisions within immersion... it's freeing. If immersion were real, I don't think we would feel the same type of freedom. Immersion, well, it's an escape. It's a fantasy world."

Alex flexed his hands, looking at the IV that protruded from the back of his right palm. "Decisions in the real-world matter. They have a finality, a weight to them. Living in the real world... consequences to our actions, suffering if we get sick, heartache from loss and rejection, injuries at the hands of idiots... all of those make immersion the awesome escape that it is. Without the real world"—he unclenched his hand—"immersion would feel more like a prison. What's the point of an escape," he added, softly, "if you're not escaping from something? It's hard to appreciate the freedom that is immersion when not compared against the confines of reality, ya know?"

James said nothing. He was aware his mouth was slightly open as he stared dumbfounded at Alex. Where had those profound thoughts come from? Had Alex contemplated such stuff in the past? Or were these things he was considering now after his near-death experience?

"So if you had the choice, you wouldn't want to live in immersion forever?" James asked.

"Nah," Alex said with a shake of his head.

"What if Fel was there with you?"

"She's here with me in the real world," Alex countered. "And that's more important, honestly. Like I said, the virtual world... it's different. That's a rules-free zone. It's a playground. It's a game." Alex looked towards the door, as if expecting Fel to walk through it. "But the real world, it's reality. Fel being with me here means so much more to me. If I had to choose between immersion or the real world, I'd choose the real world with her by my side over immersion."

"Even if it means no more," James grinned at Alex, "visits to your class trainer?"

Alex's face reddened a bit at that. "Even if it meant no more visits with my class trainer," he said, though there was a hint of longing in his voice. "Virtual can't beat the real-world, James, simple as that."

James sat there as an awkward silence spread between the two of them. He and Alex weren't really friends. He'd only spoken on a few occasions with the senior at his high school. They had very different experiences. Alex was popular. He had a purpose in the real world. James was a nerdy gamer.

The only reason he'd even visited Alex the first time was out of guilt. And this time, honestly, he wasn't sure. He had time to kill, and sitting around waiting at home had been driving him crazy. So he'd wandered over to the hospital, looking to do something, anything to distract himself as the hours ticked by. But now, he wasn't sure.

He wished he could be as certain as Alex. That would probably have made his actions, his conviction stronger. But Alex's love was in the real world. She was flesh and blood. If the virtual world disappeared, Alex wouldn't potentially lose the love of his life. For James, that wasn't quite the case.

Rue existed in DCO, and only DCO. Sure, Steve and the others, including Rue, were confident that crashing the DCO server wouldn't harm her. But it was still a risk. There was a chance that if they stopped the government, it could cost him Rue. And the more he sat around, the more he waited for the night to come, the more that ate at him.

"You all right, man?" Alex pulled James from his dark thoughts. "You need to talk about something?"

James pushed his brooding aside and offered Alex as sincere a smile as he could. He shook his head at Alex's question and moved the subject away from himself to something else. "Speaking of Fel," James began, "have you seen her today?"

Alex sighed, love struck puppy on full display before James. "No," he grumbled. "She said she had to do something with her mom today. So, I've just been stuck here with nothing to do, bored out of my mind."

James had received a message from Fel. It hadn't mentioned anything about her mom. Just that she was running errands on her side to get ready for tonight. Had she lied to Alex? Or was she giving her boyfriend more details in a roundabout way than she was giving James? Either way, it didn't really matter. James could trust Fel. If she said she was running errands to get ready for the night, then that's what she was doing.

If her mom was involved as well, though…

James didn't let the thought progress any further.

"You said you're bored," James said, half to himself, half to Alex. "So how about a game to pass the time?" He looked at Dagger, who'd stood silently at his side the entire time during the conversation. "Dagger, what games do you have installed?"

The dog's mouth opened, its hollow projector extending outwards. The sudden transformation caused Alex to jump, which then made him flinch and let out a gasp of pain. He knew Dagger was a robot, but James was pretty sure the holoprojector in the mouth and the way Dagger's jaw flipped up almost 90 degrees had been more than a little surprising.

James felt bad, but also couldn't help but smile. Then brilliant lights played in the air above Alex's lap as virtual board games began to stack one on top of each other for the boys to read.

"I've access to every board game created in the past hundred years,"

Dagger's voice said, past its unmoving mouth. "State either the name of the game or apply search parameters to narrow down the list."

"Any games in mind?" James asked Alex, motioning towards him. "Seems like we've got choices."

Alex looked from James, down to Dagger, his eyes still looking over the dog. "Uh." He paused for a moment, thinking. "Got any card games?"

Chapter Fifty-Nine

James began to head home with barely enough time to tidy up before Z and his friends swung by. He'd planned to return sooner but had found a sense of comfort in gaming with Alex. Thanks to immersion tech, most gaming was fully immersive and made the person a main part of the game. Taking time to relax and play retro card games was cathartic, and he saw why Rue found pleasure in playing Magic against the Terminus and other boss monsters.

While on the train, he skimmed his messages, double-checking that he hadn't missed anything important assuming everyone was doing all they could to prepare for the nighttime raid plan. After that, he skimmed through Reddit. First, he checked out the Reddit for his town's dungeon, curious to see the main topics being covered.

<u>Candy Dungeon Appetizer?</u>
<u>Sixth Floor Map?</u>
<u>**SPECIAL EVENT DICKEN SALE!!!! HALF OFF PRICES FOR ALL RANDOM DUNGEON MEMBERS!**</u>

James grinned at the last one, noting the obvious sales ploy. With the increased duration of this special event, Alex's family, who ran the Dicken Shack as well as its, er, competitor, could make a literal killing. Alex insisted that the virtual world didn't matter. But based on the currency ratio, what his family stood to make during a 48-hour immersion extravaganza would no doubt dwarf any sales they did in the real world in a similar span of time.

Impressive wasn't the word for it. Too good to be true, probably, was better. An event like the one being held, if it were just a special event that would happen occasionally, would no doubt make or break entire businesses. It was a problem circumnavigated by the fact that there wouldn't be any real-world businesses at the end of the immersion to be made or broken if things went according to the government's plans. It was easy to throw caution out the window when there wasn't supposed to be a tomorrow.

Mentally, he opened the first Reddit thread, started by someone named NotADev69.

Just putting this out there, but obviously the first Dungeon War of this event needs to be against the Candy Dungeon. I don't know about all of you, but I personally love starting parties with candy. And even more than that, the full course meal of dungeons we will get to smack down should be started against the Candy Dungeon. Pretty sure it's the only one that could prove a tasteful challenge to us too.
Also, remember, it's the dungeon that has that SoulDemon Asshat. Rumor is he nearly screwed us over during the Siege. It's high time we paid him back.

Beneath it was a stream of interaction that James quickly skimmed.

*/Yo_Shiiiiiiiiiiiiii- Your making good points, but you sure you ain't a dev?
**/NotADev69- You're*, and pretty sure I'm not a dev, obviously. That's what my name means.
*** Yo_Shiiiiiiiiiiiiii- uh...huh...
*/TyRANT25- I'm down to see what they can throw at us. With the Mad Mage and White Beast of Chaos, they won't stand a chance.
**/PurpleKnight1- Have you been over there lately? Their dungeon got so much easier after they lost to us. Pretty sure defeat at our hands made their competitive spirits die.
***/ Yo_Shiiiiiiiiiiiiii- Feel like losing to a dungeon filled with Dickens would do that to anyone. Serves them right, cocky bastards
****/PurpleKnight1- Not sure how everything works, but as it stands, I can't see them holding a candle to us. Especially not consid-

ering the Knights reports about the sixth floor. Kind of excited for Dungeon Wars to kick off. Only way I'm getting near those sixth-floor mobs with my current level.

*/SoulDemon- I don't know who you are, but you can bet I'm going to find you NotADev69. You can go fuck yourself.

**/NotADev69- Tsk Tsk. You're proving my point. You're a dick and someone needs to give you a timeout.

***/SoulDemon- (Message deleted by mods)

James couldn't help but grin. Was Steve NotADev69? He totally could be. It seemed like a Steve thing to do. Either way, the Reddit thread itself had a couple hundred comments already, and over a thousand thumbs up. It left little doubt that it would ensure the first dungeon they faced off against would be the Candy Dungeon.

He wondered what Rachel and Matthew were doing on their end to get their players ready for the battle. His dungeon and BLANK's were the only Tier 7 dungeons. That meant they'd get priority in challenging each other for the Dungeon Wars event. Still, the players themselves had to vote to select the targets, meaning both instances of 10,000 players would need a majority vote to challenge the other to ensure the battle happened.

Z and his guild were going to rally the players in game even further to encourage the challenge. Did BLANK's Dungeon have anyone like that? Or maybe that was why NotADev69 had called out SoulDemon, the Candy Dungeon's strongest player and... strongest personality. The antithesis of Z. Both were top-tier gamers, but one surrounded himself with friends and worked hard to make sure everyone was safe and had fun. The other... was a selfish dick.

The second Reddit thread, which James skimmed through as he walked back to his house after the train dropped him off at his station, was by the Knights Who Go Ni. It detailed the sixth floor and the monsters they'd seen on it. They also included screenshots of the mobs, as well as noted strengths and weaknesses.

The poster, Med Ic, even included the bit about the J-Kappa's Sellout perk. With that information, James had no doubt more players would take to his sixth floor once they dove back into the dungeon. And maybe with the knowledge given to them by the Knights, they could prepare large enough groups and strategies to try and gain a few more levels before the Dungeon Wars kicked off.

More importantly, the more players that arrived on his sixth floor, the more that would discover the seventh floor. James really wanted to see his seventh floor in action at least once before he was needed in the real world. He was hoping, actually, to join Z and possibly the Boss Slayers on one last jaunt before they decided the fate of the world.

It was morbid, sure, but James had begun putting together a small list of 'lasts' he wanted to do before they started their mission. If there was a chance he was going to die, or worse, then he was going to make sure he did all he could to ensure that he lived his life to the fullest.

His musing kept him quiet as he got to his house, Dagger trotting along at his heels. When he reached his house, he robotically held his arm up to the door, the action second nature considering the government chip in his wrist. The door had been repaired since the Cyb3ru5 assault on his house just a few nights ago, leaving no sign of the forced break in.

With a beep, the door read his chip, identified who he was, and unlocked the door. It slid open, and James stepped in. His eyes blinked as his vision adjusted from the bright lights outside to the dimmer lighting within his house.

A moving shadow in the house caused him to freeze. Fear and panic welled up in him as his mind told him this was it. He was done for. The government had come for him. He'd been found out.

James took a shaky, panicked step backwards and tripped over Dagger, the dog doing a whole lot of nothing in the moment. Wasn't Dagger supposed to guard him? Wasn't Dagger supposed to keep him safe? Was the intruder an Enforcer? Had they somehow bypassed Dagger's sensors?

He closed his eyes as he felt himself falling backwards, overcome by his thoughts, fears, and emotions.

A hand caught his, and he found his fall halted as thin, strong fingers gripped his wrist and steadied him. He opened his eyes in surprise. Bright, red hair, a mischievous smile, and skin-tight clothes… James knew exactly who this was. The deadliest person he knew in the real world. Alex's girlfriend. Fel, a.k.a. Felecia, a.k.a. Crimson Tiered Agent of Phoenix Down.

"Sup, nerd," she said with a laugh, "didn't mean to sweep you off your feet. And sorry in advance, I'm taken."

James looked at her as she let his wrist go, now that he was standing upright again. His face went red with embarrassment, knowing full well she was having a good laugh at his reaction. Fel walked, with all the grace of a feline predator, towards his fridge and opened it. She grabbed a FitSip out for herself and popped it open with the same hand, all while reaching in for a second, which she deftly tossed his way.

"Think fast."

"How'd you get in my house?" James asked dumbly as he fumbled to catch the drink. "What are you doing here?"

"I made myself a key code, duh," she said with a chuckle. "Well, I was given one when I was assigned guard duty for you, and it was supposed to be temporary, but I made it permanent. We both know you've a tendency for trouble, and you can't say it wasn't a proper precaution."

She leaned against the counter, stretching like a cat sunning itself, exposing even more of her midriff and abs, toned from an extensive amount of real-world training. She took a long sip.

"As for why I'm here." She shrugged. "Finished up most of my errands and heard you're having some visitors tonight anyways. Two birds, one stone."

James raised an eyebrow, his heart having calmed enough that he wasn't in danger of a heart attack. He walked further into his house and grabbed a seat at the table. Dagger, who he was more than a little annoyed at for not warning him about Fel's presence in the house, trotted over to the intruder, and tilted his head towards her for ear scritches. Fel scratched the 'not a dog's' ears, ignoring James's questioning gaze.

"What are you talking about?" James asked directly. It wasn't like he minded her being here. But at the same time, he was paranoid. Was this suspicious? Would it be suspicious if she was here when Z and his guild members showed up?

"Need to know, buddy." She hopped up onto the counter, her legs dangling as she continued to drink her beverage. "Just be a good boy for once, yeah, and wait patiently?"

James wanted to protest, but something in her gaze warned him against it. He shouldn't be pressing her, really. Who knew if their conversations were being spied on? He decided, therefore, to do the only thing he could.

He took a drink of his FitSip and waited.

Chapter Sixty

"They're here," James said as he got the message from Z.

He and Fel had moved to the living room, deciding to mindlessly watch a movie while they waited for Z to arrive. Fel had eyed the door to his parents' workshop, and he knew she'd wanted to inquire about it, but she'd managed to restrain herself.

"About time." She pushed off of the couch. "I was really getting tired of this shitty movie."

"Hey," James started in protest. It wasn't a shitty movie. Okay, maybe it was a bit B-Rate, but it wasn't shitty.

"Of all the things to put on"—she looked at him—"I didn't expect a B-Rate Isekai. Though, I suppose I should be somewhat impressed. It was one I've never seen before." She shook her head as she looked at him. "Who the hell came up with the idea for a protagonist that had mastered tennis skills from the real world getting transported to a fantasy world and using magic spells and tennis skills to take on a demon overlord?"

"Okay, when you say it like that, it sounds silly," James relented. "And that's my bad. It's actually a sequel movie. The original movie is called Aced," James explained as they walked towards the door. "Pretty much—"

"I don't care," she stopped him. "Maybe if I'm really bored and really drunk or high, I'll check it out. Till then though"—she looked at him—"sports anime aren't my jam."

"Suit yourself," James muttered, the conversation feeling absurdly normal considering what loomed in the near future for them. It was nice, actually. "But I'm just saying, sports-based stories can really surprise you in a good way. More people should check them out."

"Not me," she said, "not now, at least."

The conversation ended as they reached the front door. Just as he heard a knock at it, James opened the door. On the other side was a grinning Zach and four other faces he didn't recognize. Okay, that wasn't entirely true. Two of the faces were familiar, one more so than the other.

"Hope you don't mind me swinging by with a crowd," Z said as he walked into the house.

The old school nurse was carrying a couple boxes of pizza, and behind him, one of the others was carrying a bag full of ice cream cartons. Another of the individuals had a couple twelve packs of soda in hand.

"But sometimes official nurse duties have to part ways for mandatory friend time, you know?" He motioned back at them. "It's our Dungeons and Dragons night."

"Oh, right." James remembered Z saying that they played the TTRPG in person still instead of using immersion. Was it really their D&D night? Or was that just his cover story? Could be both.

"And I see you've already got company." Z nodded towards Fel, who took the pizza from him and carried it over to the table. "How's Alex doing, Fel?"

"Better," she responded quickly. "Though he's really not a fan of being stuck in a hospital bed. And I really wish my boyfriend wasn't bedridden. Makes things less fun for the both of us."

James looked from Z to Fel and back to Z. He knew they'd gamed together in DCO. He hadn't realized they knew each other in person.

"I met Zach when he visited Alex," Fel answered his unasked question.

He really did have a terrible poker face, didn't he?

"Apparently Alex had helped Zach here tend to you when you got your ass knocked out by that waste of flesh Dwight. He came to check on Alex when he heard what had happened. We've met up a few times in DCO since too. He's been a major help in leveling us."

"Oh," was all James could say. He was nowhere near as quick on cover stories as they were. Everything they said made perfect sense. Was it all true? Or planned? If it was planned, how'd they coordinate so well? He decided to move on to other things.

"I know you," James said as he looked past Zach towards one of the four others who were standing awkwardly in his kitchen. "You're a teacher at my school."

"Guilty as charged," the man, one of the teachers assigned to teaching senior-level classes at his school, said with a nod.

James had never interacted with him, but he'd seen him in the halls on a few occasions. He wore a sharp-looking pair of glasses, and James wondered if they were purely cosmetic like his AR glasses or served to help his vision. He was slender, with age showing its wear on him. His dark hair was streaked in silver, which matched his salt and pepper beard. His eyes were kind, though, and his cheeks showed that he smiled often.

"Students know me as Mr. Lancaster," the man said with a smile, "Ralph for my peers and friends, though." He looked at James. "Or in DCO, I go by Elm."

"Nice to officially meet you, Mr. Lancaster," James said, trying to remember his manners as he reached out to shake Elm's hand.

Elm handed off his bag of ice cream to the man beside him, who took it to the table.

"I'm glad to see you've been recovering," Elm said with a look towards Z. "I felt partially responsible for your attack. As teachers, we've a duty to protect our students, and we obviously failed both you and young Alex." There was genuine sorrow in his voice.

"Er, it's fine," James said, not knowing what else to say.

Another figure stepped forward, and James didn't know what his real name was, but he had a guess who it was within DCO. He knew from spying on them that Oak and Elm were brothers. What he hadn't realized was they were twins.

"I'm George Lancaster," the man who looked just like Elm said. "No Mr. Lancaster, please. Makes me sound old."

He laughed, but James noticed that his smile and laughter lines didn't reach quite as high as his brother's. James had a feeling that just like in DCO, George had spent his life putting others before himself.

"Nice to meet you, George." James shook his hand.

"Not sure if we've met in game before," George continued, "but you probably know me as Oak, the best tank in DCO."

The others all chuckled at that, and James couldn't help but smile as he felt the comforting strength in George's grip and his eyes. Reliable was what he was. The tension James had been feeling was fading at the presence of the group. It was the same effect they had in game on him.

"Guessing since you're Z," Fel cut in, "and the twins there are Oak and Elm, that means the last two of your little party are Faust and Med Ic?" She bit into a slice of pizza, which she'd helped herself to. "Sup, guys, I'm obviously FlashFyre."

"What?" The other individual, who James was guessing had to be Faust considering he vaguely recognized the man, said in a mocking tone. "I never would have guessed you were FlashFyre. It's not like Alex calls you Fel all the time in game, and you know"—he motioned at her—"your hair is a dead giveaway."

She smirked and continued eating the pizza. "Glad we got that out of the way," she said mid-bite. "Food's getting cold."

"She's right, by the way," the man who'd called out Fel said with a smile as he turned towards James. "I'm Faust from the Knights Who Go Ni, though in the real world, I go by Frank."

James held out his hand and shook the man's. "James," he said, "though I think you already knew that?"

"Guilty as charged," Faust said. "Glad to see you're in better shape than when I was driving you home the other night."

"And that leaves me," the final member said.

Unlike the others, the final person had vibrantly colored hair. It was a mixture of blues and greens and purples, swirling in a strange ombre down his shoulders.

"Name's Eric Tillman." He didn't offer his hand to James. Instead, he held a few fingers up towards his temple and offered James a weird type of salute with the flick of his wrist. "Med Ic in game."

Compared to how Med Ic acted within DCO, James wasn't sure what to make of the obviously eccentric member of the group. Dyed hair wasn't itself that crazy, but the number of piercings in his ears and lips, and his clothing that fit more appropriately in some weird homage to bands from the late 1900s, were out of place. Med Ic had definitely not let go of the past.

"Uh, nice to meet you." James looked the man up and down. He was shorter than the others by a good six inches, though James only realized that when he saw how tall the platform boots were the man was wearing. So not what he'd expected of the best healer he'd ever seen in action.

"Well then." Z clapped his hands together, pulling everyone's attention towards him. "We've got dice to throw and monsters to slay, so let's all grab a quick bite and be off. I'm sure James doesn't want us crowding his house, especially when he's got company over."

"Before you leave," Fel said, another slice of pizza already in her hand. "I've a gift for you. A thank you, if you would, for caring about Alex and all you've been doing since."

"Oh, well, I'm never one to turn down gifts," Z said, though he stiffened slightly. There was something being said between the two that James didn't know. "Can it wait till we eat?"

"Sure," Fel said, and as if that was the deciding factor, everyone quickly rushed to the table.

The kitchen became a flurry of chaos. Soda was opened, pizza was snatched, sauce and cheese spilled about, and the ice cream slowly melted on the counter as everyone for a moment lost themselves to what felt like a gathering of long-lost friends.

James treasured every moment of it.

Chapter Sixty-One

As with all good things, time passed too quickly. Before James knew it, everyone was done eating, and it was time for everyone to leave.

"I guess we should get out of your hair," Z said as he finished taking the box of pizza to the trash. The robotic system would immediately sort it into its proper compost bins, making the need for separating out garbage a thing of the ancient past. "Got imaginary monsters to slay and such, after all."

"He says that," Elm added, "but he's the DM. Pretty sure the monsters he's talking about slaying are our characters."

"You wound me," Z countered, feigning insult. "As if I would try to win at DnD."

"If you could, we all know you would have long ago," Oak offered. "You know the reason you're stuck as forever DM is because your character designs kept breaking the game."

"I thought it was because you loved my various character impressions and storytelling skills," Z laughed. "Could have sworn you said I was the next Mercer."

"I said you wished you were like Mercer," Oak corrected. "Your impressions and voices feel like a drunk theater kid during their first semester after having watched a single video on how to do improv."

"Yes, and?" Z smiled.

While James wasn't really sure of what they were doing, he found himself smiling. It was impossible not to. While he wasn't immersed, all he was seeing in his mind was his favorite group of adventurers standing in his house, cracking jokes and poking fun at each other just like they always did. Real world or immersion, it was refreshing to know they were the same for these five.

"Enough of the bromance," Fel said with a mock gag. "It's creepy enough that five grown ass adults were hanging out here for this long. You should really get going before I decide I need to call the authorities."

The group turned their attention to Fel, and James could see they were working for an answer that didn't make the situation sound as creepy as Fel had just laid it out. Obviously, they all knew it wasn't, but when Fel put it that way…

"Didn't you say you had something to give Z before he left?" James asked, moving the subject away from anything awkward.

"I do," Fel said with a nod. "Actually, thanks for the reminder." She walked over to the couch and ruffled around behind it. A moment later, she pulled out a nondescript black backpack and carried it over to Z. "Here you go."

Z took it, not saying another word, and slung it over his shoulder. He didn't look Fel in the eyes as he took it, and James noticed all the others were looking away as well. Did they know what was in the backpack? Because James sure as hell didn't.

Frank, or rather, Faust cleared his throat, pulling the attention away from Z and the bag. "While we're giving out gifts…" He rummaged in his pocket and pulled out a handful of coin-shaped objects. "Who would like a free challenge coin?"

"A challenge coin?" James took the offered metal object. It was about as large as a quarter, though thicker. He'd have assumed it was gold given its color and weight, but highly doubted the precious metal was being used. Instead, it was probably gold-plated. One side of the coin had a grinning skull, the other side had a sword.

"A challenge coin," Faust said with a smile, handing them out to everyone. "They're a tradition Z knows from the military. We have them where I work as well. Had these lying about and have just been handing them out to friends. So here's to making new friends."

James went to pocket the coin, not really knowing what to say. As he did, Faust held his gaze, and his tone shifted ever so slightly.

"Just make sure you don't happen to take it in your immersion pod. For some reason, the coin's metal can sometimes cause issues with the pod." He winked at James. Or at least, James was pretty sure he winked.

"Uh, noted," James said. "I'll make sure not to."

"Good." Faust nodded. "I figured I'd warn you at least. Last thing anyone needs with this amazing immersion event coming up is something making their pods malfunction."

Another wink. James was pretty sure he got it. Either that, or Faust just had a really weird problem with his eye.

"Speaking of this upcoming event." Fel looked from James to the others. "I really should get going as well." She pocketed the coin Faust had held out to her. "I'm going to give Alex a goodnight kiss before I head home and get ready. Super excited for this event. Cannot wait to see what all happens."

She looked back at James, and he could see she had unspoken words for him. Her eyes, normally fierce and confident, held a hint of worry. Her smile wavered as she looked him up and down. "Feel free to look for me in game, yeah, James? Username's FlashFyre if you forgot."

With that, contrary to the statements of Z and her own words, Fel was the first to leave.

James watched her go, a pang of regret washing over him. He'd pulled her into this. Fel, and Alex, and everyone. If he'd never met her, she would be blissfully unaware of what was to come. Would that be better for her?

Then again, would she really have stayed uninvolved if not for him? Did her organization know what was going on? Had she been discussing plans with her mother to stop it from happening? An organization as renowned as Phoenix Down definitely had connections that were rich enough to buy immortality. But... was money enough to buy out their morals?

"Something got you doubting yourself? Girl troubles, perhaps?" Z said, placing a comforting hand on James's shoulder, his kind eyes looking down at him.

The older man smiled, but just like Fel, it didn't reach his eyes. The way he stood, the way his shoulders drooped, it was as if Z was shouldering an immense weight. Was it whatever was in the bag? Couldn't be. Fel was fit, but he doubted she'd have lifted the backpack so easily with a single arm if it was heavy enough to weigh on Z like it seemed to be.

"You'll be fine, James," Z continued, his voice soft. "Just trust in yourself and the choices you make, and you'll get through whatever you're dealing with."

He let go of James's shoulder and stepped backwards. The rest of the Knights Who Go Ni all waved at James, their faces covered in smiling masks, their serious eyes the only traitors to the ruse.

"Take care, James, and feel free to hit us up in game if you ever feel like diving the dungeon, yeah?"

With that, they turned and left. James watched them go, fighting hard to keep his food down as his nerves took a hard grip on his stomach. That was it. Potentially the last meal he'd have, the last supper he'd enjoy in the real world. In a few hours, he'd be immersed in DCO once more, knowing full well that the game wasn't really a game, but instead a technological prison for the mind. And shortly after, well... he'd be raiding a dungeon, only this dungeon was in the real world.

Could his adventuring party succeed?

Chapter Sixty-Two

James laid in his immersion pod, doing his best to keep his breathing under control. He was still dressed as he had been during the day, save for his AR glasses, which he'd set carefully on the table beside his bed. He fingered the coin in his pocket, feeling the smooth metal. On the ground next to his pod, Dagger sat impossibly still, the robot watching him patiently.

"Here goes nothing," James said, more to himself than the dog.

Dagger was intelligent, and definitely had an AI with a unique personality within it, but it was still just a robot. Robots didn't have anxiety. They couldn't feel worried or afraid. James envied that aspect of Dagger in that moment.

He leaned his back into the cushioned headrest of the pod, and a moment later, the lid slid shut. Warm liquid began to flow all around him as the pod began the immersion cycle. James tried to breathe normally as he felt himself becoming covered in the fluid, closing his eyes as he willed his mind to relax. Then he felt the familiar sensation of falling as darkness took hold for just a moment.

He opened his eyes, knowing he was no longer in his body, and blinked. He'd expected to see his normal options, to be in his body as he initially was whenever he logged into a game. However, he wasn't in his room within the Zone. He wasn't in the selection space either. He was hovering in darkness, with a blinking message before him.

Zone Under Maintenance
Transferring to Dungeon Core Online

James blinked again, as he felt his mind tug from his floating body. Another blink, and he was in DCO. Sensations and smells rushed towards him as he 'awoke' in the tent he'd fallen asleep in. The tent he shared with Rue.

"Huh," he said as he came to.

It wasn't that he hadn't planned on diving right into DCO. One of the perks of being a Dungeon Core was that he gained access to the game an hour before and after the game was normally open to the public. That extra time gave him nine hours of real-world time, which equated to nine days of game time, whereas the general populace only got seven.

"Huh?" Rue asked.

She was standing beside his bed, holding a tray of pancakes and orange juice. He eyed the meal, noting it was exactly the same meal that Dagger had cooked for him. Pretty much confirming Rue had been spying on him the moment he'd left DCO.

At least until he'd gone radio silent in his parents' workshop for a long enough time that she got worried. He'd thought about that more during the day, and if he had to guess, him disappearing into the office, and then not responding to any messages for multiple hours had to make her think he'd been caught or something.

Like maybe the workshop had been a trap? Or more wholesome... she had just panicked because she really cared for him, and it was the longest they'd gone without talking since DCO had begun.

"The game." James rubbed at his temple. "I was forcibly put into the game rather than given the choice."

"That's different." Rue held the plate out to him, which he took.

The smell of freshly melted butter mixed wonderfully with the sweet vanilla of the syrup. As he took a bite, he marveled at the hint of cinnamon that danced across his tongue as if it were engaged in a veritable waltz with the sweetness of the syrup, the fluffy, just right pancake their dance floor.

"I know they said they were closing the Zone," James said between mouthfuls, "but I didn't think that was supposed to start until 11 PM."

"Could be an effort to ensure everyone is logged and in place when the event goes live," Rue offered, making no attempt to hide the look of satisfaction on her face as James devoured his meal.

"Makes sense," he said, washing down the food with the orange juice.

It was fresher, crisper, and tangier than what he'd had in the real world. "Especially considering there are people who have never played DCO being forced into the game. Gives them time to create their characters and generate in before the event goes live.

"Still," he continued, "I figured there would have been a message about it, right? And what about people in different time zones who have already been immersed for a few hours? When exactly did they close down the Zone and force people into DCO?"

Rue shrugged, but he hadn't expected an answer from her. Actually, he'd been speaking aloud, half-wondering if Steve was spying on them. The developer did that sometimes, the man enjoying eavesdropping until the perfect moment, where he could swoop in magically with all the answers. It was all part of his 'all-knowing benefactor' persona that he liked to give off.

James looked around, waiting for the man to arrive, but nothing happened. After another moment, he sighed, stood, and looked at Rue. Emotion welled within him, and before he realized it, she was in his arms. He wrapped her tightly in a hug, reveling in the feel of her body against his. She was warm, she felt real. She was real.

He breathed in, noting the sweet floral scent that seemed to permeate from her. He let go of the embrace just enough to let her look up at him as he looked down into her eyes. Love showed there, combined with a dash of worry. Reasonable, considering his sudden embrace.

"I love you," James said, smiling down at her, taking strength from her. Very soon, he'd have to leave her again. He needed to commit every bit of her to his memory.

"I love you too, silly." She stood up on her tiptoes, her lips finding his.

They kissed for a long moment as her arms draped around his neck, pulling him down so that she could kiss him even deeper. There was undeniable passion there, a hunger, and yet also tenderness. James let his eyes close as he lost himself in the moment. The world could wait for just this moment.

He had twenty-four hours in immersion before the planned time for their mission to begin. Twenty-four hours in game, one hour in the real world to send messages and double-check that everything was in place. James could afford to spend some of that time with Rue, could afford these last luxuries, last pleasant memories before he went off to war.

Time was a thief, but for the moment, James would do all he could to steal a few moments from it.

The sound of a clearing throat came all too soon. He reluctantly pulled himself away from Rue's lips, his gaze looking over her head in the direction of the sound. Steve stood there, grinning at him, his eyes shadowed and dark. At his side, Fel leaned against the inside of the tent, her fiery red hair in stark contrast to her in-game Angelkin appearance.

His alone time with Rue was up. Apparently, time didn't appreciate his antics, nor did it care about his wishes. Time stopped for no one.

Chapter Sixty-Three

"Well, that answers that question," James said as the group left Rue's 'tent'.

They were beside the hot springs on the fifth floor. While it had always looked like a tent on the outside, it served more as an actual full-on house thanks to immersion magic.

"Which question?" Steve asked, a heavy sigh escaping his lips as he eased into the water. The air around them shimmered slightly, and James remembered Steve had promised to erect a bubble of privacy in all of James's private instances to ensure the utmost security.

"He was probably still questioning whether he was straight," Fel said with a laugh as she snapped her fingers, a bikini appearing around her before she stepped into the water. "I could have helped you sort that one out."

James growled but said nothing. Rue laughed lightly as she got into the water, a bikini of her own appearing around her form. James willed his own swimming trunks onto himself as he got in. Technically, none of that was needed since they weren't real clothes, and getting into the water, no matter what you were wearing, felt nice.

Case and point was Steve. The developer was still dressed in a pair of worn jeans and a half-unbuttoned t-shirt, looking every bit as disheveled as he always seemed to be lately.

"You can't keep making jokes at James's expense just because you're nervous," Rue said after she finished laughing... at James's expense.

"Sooner or later, you'll have to deal with your own situation too, won't you?"

Fel looked away from Rue's gaze, crossing her arms and refusing to answer. James couldn't help but laugh, though it was short-lived. Fel being here a whole day of immersion early for normal players confirmed that everyone was logging in instantly into the game. On the plus side, that meant that everyone was already in DCO, and he'd probably be able to do one last climb with them. On the negative side, it meant that the government's plan was in full swing already.

"Much as it pains me to say," Steve said as a Painguin brought a drink to him, "now's probably not the best time for poking each other." He took a drink, closing his eyes as he savored it. "I've done everything I can on my end, including ramping up the privacy and security here as discussed, but I still feel that the situation moving forward is dire."

"I did my part." Fel crossed her arms and leaned back into the hot springs. "Passed off the package and have everything in place to counter any potential efforts to bring us down in game." She looked at Steve. "Can't believe we're going to be working together in that regard. And I really hope you're just being paranoid."

"As do I," Steve said, "but while James is away, we need to make sure we're doing everything we can to keep all of the focus on this immersion, and more importantly, on keeping anyone from realizing what's going on."

"I still feel like you'd be more helpful in person," James said to Fel. "You're better trained than anyone I know."

"Yeah, well unlucky for you, there's not a magical twin of me running around. And we all know your biggest weakness"—she pointed towards Rue—"is stuck within immersion. Steve's safeguarded Rue's consciousness, but that doesn't mean shit if the government's hackers break in here and cause trouble. Between myself, Steve, and Hades, we can hopefully keep the ruse going. The longer we keep anyone from realizing what's going on, the more time you and the others will have to actually breach the government stronghold and take DCO offline for good."

Their plan was a two-pronged one. The first was a physical assault on the government facility situated within the mountain—the one his parents were located, along with Rue's actual body, and hell, probably her father.

James wasn't sure who else was there. Maybe Steve? He knew BLANK was situated on the west coast of the continent, but he wasn't sure if Xander had been there or had been in James's area considering he was the head of DCO at the time. If he was, and he'd been captured here, then...

James shuddered and pushed those thoughts from his mind.

"I've got the cloning program set up as well," Steve said, not seeming to notice James's trailing thoughts. "I've had it running through all of the data on James, as well as the Knights. It should create a perfectly believable copy as long as no one intimately familiar with them engages with them."

During their time in the real world, Steve had suggested they use the AI program from DCO to create 'clones' of James and the others. While James's lack of presence may go unnoticed, unless he was summoned during the Dungeon War, Z and the others were too well known, too public. Meaning they needed a way to ensure that no one noticed the top five players, essentially celebrities, were missing.

"And James has the masking chip in his pod," Fel said, looking at James. "At least, I'm pretty sure he does."

"Was that the challenge coin?" he asked for confirmation.

"It was," Fel said narrowing her eyes, "please tell me you figured out what Faust was telling you?"

"I hope so?" James still wasn't a hundred percent. "He wanted me to have it in the pod with me, right? Why?" He still wasn't sure what it was supposed to do. No one had mentioned anything about masking chips to him. But he would have to have been blind to miss Faust's winking at him regarding the coin and keeping it on him.

"It's a special chip used to mimic an identity chip," Fel said with a heavy sigh. "Enforcers and other government officials use them to keep their movements masked. It uses your immersion pod as a broadcast point. By immersing yourself with it on your person, it will automatically attune itself to your pod. Once you've immersed with it, and it's become synced with your pod, it will broadcast your information as if it were within the pod, essentially making monitoring systems believe you're still immersed, even when you aren't."

"It's a part of how Enforcers can stay anonymous," Steve added. "Helps eliminate any possible traces or patterns for people to pick up on. It'd be pretty obvious if people who were 'supposed' to be immersed often logged out and went other places during their assigned immersion time, especially if it happened to correspond with Enforcer activity and operations."

"Oh, well, glad I figured that out." James let out a breath he hadn't known he'd been holding. He hadn't been nervous until Fel had started talking about it, making him doubt himself. "I wasn't a hundred percent sure if that was what he wanted me to do with it."

"For you, it was more of a backup plan," Steve said with a shrug. "Since you've got Dagger with you, I'm sure there are other ways to mask your identity chip's signal from broadcasting. But it was a nice failsafe we figured we should try and put in place, just in case."

James nodded. "Makes sense. Though, I feel like I was the only one not in the know for that bit."

"It was an afterthought that he came up with during the day," Fel said. "And obviously, no one had a chance to tell you. Out of all of us, your, eh, acting skills are the most lacking anyway."

"Fair," James conceded the point without contest.

Everyone else lied like it was second nature and seemed to be able to embrace the cloak-and-dagger lifestyle with ease. But James couldn't. He felt bad lying, overthought things, and just wasn't skilled in double speak. Knowing when someone was speaking the full truth and when they were trying to hint at something else took all of his meager observation skills. Acting like that himself was a step too far.

Considering how living such a life had affected Fel... and her split-personality R, James was glad he'd never had to be a part of that world before. But right now, for this very important mission, he kind of wished he could somehow have been more prepared for that very thing.

"My poor acting skills aside," James began. He looked at everyone and couldn't help but feel the start of a smile. "I have an exciting surprise for all of you." He focused on Fel, his smile growing till he could feel it reach his eyes. "I need to tell you what I found in my parents' workshop."

Chapter Sixty-Four

"You're just trying to make my life difficult, aren't you?" Steve asked as he rubbed his chin. "Lucky for you, I'm awesome, and I'm pretty sure it will work." He took a drink. "And if it doesn't, well, no harm done, right? It's not like we were expecting any of this. So it's just a bonus if it works."

"We should make sure Faust knows to bring a creepy white paneled van for you," Fel said with a chuckle. "Just in case it does work."

"Fair." James looked around the hot springs. "Should we summon them here?"

"Nah, that'd be unnecessary," Steve said with a shake of his head. "I'll pass the message on to them in a different manner. No need to do anything too out of the norm." He looked at Fel. "The only reason she's here is because she's already had access to your area, and it would be counterintuitive for me to put up securities against her breaking into your special Dungeon Core instance. Didn't want her breaking things if she couldn't get in."

"What can I say? I like to be able to come and go as I please," Fel stood as she spoke. "Speaking of." She looked around. "If I'm no longer needed, I'm going to spend some time with Alex. His company at least doesn't feel like it's on the constant verge of doom and gloom." She fixed her gaze on James. "When all this is said and done, I expect an actual tour of your parents' lab."

"You'll have definitely earned it if we succeed," James said. "So, deal."

"And there it is, doom and gloom." She shook her head. "Seriously, you're so melodramatic." Without another word she snapped her fingers and was gone.

"And then there were three," Steve said ominously. "Real talk, though, I should get going to make sure I can get the data in the proper format and send it over to your pod. From there, I'm assuming you've got a data drive prepared?"

"Dagger." James grinned. "I checked, and he can handle a ridiculous amount of data. Shouldn't be a problem transporting it, my dad confirmed as much anyway."

"Well, if your father said it will work, then it should work. Meaning the only reason this could mess up would be because of me." Steve gave James a wink. "And if you haven't noticed, I don't make mistakes."

"Is that why you don't have any kids?" Rue asked.

James couldn't help but laugh. That one came out of nowhere.

"How'd you know I don't have any kids?" Steve asked Rue, eyes wide.

"Lucky guess," Rue offered. "You seem pretty married to your work. And past that"—she motioned at Steve—"you're you. If you had actual kids, I'm pretty sure you would have burned through all your dad jokes and bad humor a long while ago."

"I'll take that as a compliment," Steve said. "It means I'm witty and fun still."

"Uh huh." Rue took a sip from her drink. "Keep telling yourself that, Steve."

"I will," the developer said smugly. "And besides, I have Rachel and Matthew. Not to mention babysitting the two of you. No time for kids of my own."

They all enjoyed the moment, taking long, slow sips of their drinks, procrastinating the moment they'd part ways. After a few more minutes in the hot springs, Steve let out a heavy sigh, and finally stood from the warm waters.

"Really though," he said, his tone making it completely clear he didn't want to be saying the words, "I should get going. I'll keep in touch as the day goes on, and if you need me, don't hesitate to ask."

James stood and walked over to the man. Rue followed suit, and the three of them stood face to face with each other.

"Take care of yourself, Steve," James said, holding a hand out to the man. "And maybe when this is all said and done, you should consider getting some rest."

"My sleep deprivation that obvious, eh?" Steve took James's

outstretched hand and then pulled. James found himself suddenly embraced by the older man in a tight hug.

"Take care of yourself, James," Steve said softly. "And just know that no matter what happens, you've done your best."

"Thanks, Steve," James said as Steve let the hug go.

The developer looked at Rue and smiled, and she wrapped him in a hug. He whispered something in her ears, and she responded before the two separated as well. James was pretty sure he had tears in his eyes. Even in immersion, emotions can overwhelm.

"I'll see the two of you before we start this in earnest," Steve promised, wiping a tear away before it could fall free from his eyes. "You two, try and have some fun before then, yeah? I'm sure the Knights would love to check out your seventh floor with you."

"We may just do that," James said, wondering for the hundredth time if Steve could read his mind. He'd been planning to contact them as soon as he could, hoping to lose himself in his dungeon for a bit longer before their confrontation with the government began. Knowing that players were being forced into DCO early just gave him more reason to do so.

"One last thing, before I go…" Steve trailed off, his words seeming to escape him.

"You're stalling," Rue said with a short laugh. "Out with it, Steve. Besides, like you said, you'll see us again soon enough. This isn't goodbye."

Steve laughed at her statement, shaking his head in a way to try and clear the tears from his eyes. He cleared his throat, trying to find his words. The man was really broken up. "You're right, you're right," he said, trying once again and failing to keep his voice from cracking.

"Just, well, er." Another crack. "I'm proud of you two," he said softly. "Really, I am. I know you both have your parents still, but… they're not here to see how much you two have grown. I am. You're right, I don't have kids, but that doesn't mean I never wanted them, and well…" He choked on his words for a moment. "I view the two as fondly as family, as my own. And I just wish I could do more for you two. I'm so proud of you, of who you've become, of what you've done, and what I know you two will do in the future." He wiped his eyes. "That's— that's all I wanted to say."

Without another word, Steve was gone. James and Rue stood in silence for a long moment, just staring at the spot the eccentric developer had been. Neither said anything, and James wasn't sure if there was anything to be said. Even if there had been, he wasn't sure he, or Rue, was prepared to speak.

Instead, they stood silently together, holding hands, letting Steve's words sink in. James couldn't help but wonder if something was wrong with the hot spring's settings on his fifth floor. The humidity seemed abnormally high. Water fell freely down his face from his eyes.

Chapter Sixty-Five

"You know, he makes a good point," Rue said as James silently seethed.

He'd reached out to Z to see if the Knights would be willing to dive the seventh floor, and the response was not what he'd expected. What he had been so certain would be an enthusiastic yes was instead a no. To quote the veteran adventurer, "It would seem suspicious if you only ever interacted with us."

"Doesn't mean I have to agree with it," James grumbled. "I was really looking forward to playing with them a little longer."

"We probably would have brought them down if we went with them," Rue countered. "We just hit level 80. They've breached the 90s. Those levels, more importantly those class boosts, are massive."

She had a good point. During the last immersion, even with everyone purposefully sacrificing themselves to the dungeon to help the dungeon level up, the Knights had managed to gain a few levels towards the end once James had hit Tier 7.

If not for their sacrifice, they probably could have even reached level 100 now that he thought about it. A level that he had no doubt would come with amazing perks. He wished this was all just a game and he could be excited for such a threshold.

"Yeah, that level gap probably doesn't bode well for them," James admitted.

Considering the mobs on the seventh floor were level 115, with the boss sitting at level 125, he had no doubt that it would be a miracle if anyone could survive for long without being at least level 100 on the floor. Gear and skills could only cover the disparity in levels so much.

"But counterpoint to your argument," James added with a grumble, pointing down at the screen they were currently watching. "Why take the Boss Slayers if they weren't going to take us?"

Sure enough, the screen they were both watching covered an instance of the fifth floor where Z and his guild moved with only a slight amount of haste away from the safe zone town towards the snowy forest of the fifth floor.

Accompanying them were the five members of the Boss Slayers. All of the members of that guild were extremely close to breaking into level 90, with Skar, their tank and leader, the lowest level of the party at level 87.

Surprisingly, their healer, Olivia, had climbed to the position of highest leveled member of their party and had hit level 90. She hadn't strayed from her path and was now listed as a Grand Cardinal of the Light. What would her class be like when she hit level 100? What was the level 100 class for a cleric who stayed purely on the light healer path the entire time?

She was the only member of Boss Slayers who had stayed pure when it came to their classes. At level 87, Skar's class was listed as an Ethereal Paladin of the Void, whatever that was. Then Troll'd, the party's ranged physical DPS, was a level 89 Catastrophe Slayer.

Manly The Dwarf, melee DPS for the party, was a level 88 Axe Dancer. He still had his floating axe that he sometimes called Frank, but the weapon had transformed from a small, little bearded axe to a great, double-edged axe that dwarfed the dwarf.

Manly was able to control the magical weapon at will, and it also had its own unique traits and abilities. It was similar to a summoned companion, but not quite as autonomous and free-willed. The class itself seemed like a strange mixture of berserker, duelist, and arcane knight.

The final member of the party, GnoMore, was still one of James's favorites. The once-rogue had never gotten rid of his love for edgy clothes and typical rogue-filled stereotypes. Instead, as his class continued to devolve more and more down a weirdly effective AoE magical DPS route, he'd simply become... well... creepier.

The level 89 gnome's class was Pale Horsemen, and he road atop a ghastly, famished horse-type mount that left a trail of plague in its wake. His features were hidden completely behind a strange combination of cybernetic and skeletal gear that James figured had mostly been custom ordered. He looked like a witch doctor and a plague doctor had an estranged affair in the alleyway of a cyberpunk village, and it was... weirdly working for him.

Party analysis aside, James couldn't help but feel jealous. He wanted to be down there with them. He wanted to be adventuring one last time. Sure, he could be adventuring right now... but the only people he wanted to dive with were all busy.

Steve was taking care of getting the boss AI data collected and composed for the plan tonight. Fel was doing whatever it was that she felt she needed to do, and everyone else was working on their tasks. And so being turned down by the Knights had left him high and dry and... salty.

All that was left for James to do in the next twenty-three-ish hours was to pre-record the message to be broadcast during Day 5 of the Dungeon War. It was more a precaution than anything. They'd picked that time to give themselves at least four hours in the real world to complete their assault on the government facility.

Originally, the plan had been to broadcast the message Day 3, when everyone first hit the Fields of Battle, but there would be a risk of playing their hands too early. Additionally, since they wanted to ensure that the most people possible were paying attention to the broadcast, Rachel and Matthew had argued that they should wait till Day 5. The siblings were certain they could build up the tension during the Dungeon War to ensure, come Day 5, that everyone everywhere would be tuned in.

The more attention they could build, the more hype on the battle would ensure that the most people would see their message. And that meant when it broadcast, the largest number of people possible would learn of the government's treachery. Granted, by that time, even if the broadcast aired as planned and the government couldn't halt it, there was still the chance James and his friends had already failed.

Still, the hope was that by spreading the message then in a way that would ensure the government had no way to stifle it, they could ensure that this kind of thing never happened again. Even with DCO destroyed, the government would only really be foiled if the masses rose up against them, Enforcers included. Without that, the government might just bide their time and try again.

Worst case scenario, even if they couldn't stop the government's plans, and everyone was forever trapped... well... at least the people would learn the truth of it all instead of whatever lies the government planned to feed them.

James felt himself spiraling as his thoughts took a dark turn, and he shook his head, turning his focus back to the present. He looked at Rue, and then at the adventuring party, noting that the players were taking their sweet time on the floor, actively hunting down mobs. If he had to guess, it meant they planned to enjoy this run to its fullest and gain as much experience as they could before moving to the next floor. Meaning they'd be clearing the fifth floor in its entirety before they descended to the sixth.

James had informed Z about the seventh floor, and if he had to guess, Z and the others wanted to make sure they prepared as best as possible between the fifth and sixth floor before they ascended to the seventh. While it wouldn't give them the levels they needed to be on equal footing with the seventh, it would ensure that their final battle would be as spectacular a coup de grace as possible.

It also meant, annoyingly, that there was no time like the present to do what he'd been putting off.

"Let's head to the training grounds," James said reluctantly. "We should record the message while we wait for them to finish grinding out these lower floors."

A camera appeared in Rue's hand and she smiled. "Let's go."

Chapter Sixty-Six

"Do I really have to do this as the Mad Mage?" James stood in the training grounds, wearing his Dungeon Wars Avatar in all its glory.

Rue held her camera in both hands, watching him, though he knew it was just for show. The red blinking orb that floated over her head was what would actually record the message.

"It's the only thing that people will take seriously," she said, offering him a thumbs up.

"But... it's the MAD Mage," James replied. "Mad," he said again with extra emphasis on the word.

"Yeah, but this time you're not mad as a hatter mad. You're 'someone pissed on...'" She paused. "No, let's not use that phrase." She cleared her throat. "You're 'watched someone kick a puppy off a cliff' mad. This is a wrong that must be righted."

"Kicked a puppy off a what?" James asked in horror. "And wait, what was the other saying you were going to use."

"Unimportant," Rue said dismissively. "Besides, of all the forms you can take, it really is the best one. Your developer Avatar is too, er, unique. And your actual visage..." She shrugged. "You're a seventeen-year-old highschooler with mousy hair and somewhat timid eyes. As much as I love you, your appearance doesn't exactly scream *world savior* or *resistance fighter*. Appearance matters, and the Mad Mage is the best option."

"If you say so," James let out a sigh, doing his best to ignore the insult that had just been thrown towards his actual appearance. Still, Rue had a point. This message was going to be broadcast ideally to the whole world. That was the whole point of all of this preparation for the Dungeon War event. To build up enough hype and draw enough attention to get as many eyes on them as possible.

James wasn't the best at public speaking, he was painfully aware of that, and so he was going to take Rue's advice. Of the two of them, she definitely had better social skills. Which was a tad strange... given her situation.

"Of course I say so." Rue grinned and made a hurry up motion with one of her hands as a hat appeared on her head that read 'director'. "Now come on. Get serious and let's record this message. I want to watch that run of the seventh floor just as much as you do. And while I find the idea of you acting as the leader of a resistance movement extremely hot... your lack of confidence definitely kills the mood."

"Thanks, Rue." James glared down at her. "You're really helping me get in the right headspace for this."

"You're welcome." She stuck her tongue out. "Now come on. You can do this James. I know you can."

"But what if," James started, already preparing another excuse, questioning once again himself, and the plan.

Was this even the right thing to do? Would the people really care? And was preparing this broadcast really the right course of action? If they failed in the real world... wouldn't this just cause mass panic?

Did Hades and the others really have any other way to stop the government if James and the others couldn't? Short of blowing everything up, James didn't know what it would accomplish. And well, blowing everything up seemed like an impossible task to undertake, especially given how much control the government had over everything.

"No what ifs," Rue said firmly, stopping his mental spiral. "You've said it yourself. People deserve to know the truth. Even if they can't do anything about it, they need to know the truth. Not whatever sugar-coated lies the government may have planned, if they even care that is, after their plan succeeds.

"Everyone, every single living person who finds themselves at the whims of those in power, who will be forever trapped under the threat of the government's immortal thumb, is owed the truth. What they do with that knowledge, what happens after is out of your hands. But if you don't tell them, if you purposefully leave them in the dark when you have the means to at least shine a bit of light on what has occurred"—she shook her head—"then you're no better than they are, James."

He felt a chill run down his spine at the last words from Rue. He steeled himself, clenching his jaw, and nodding to her. She was right. It was too late now. There was no turning back. And everyone deserved to know. Even if it didn't change the outcome, knowledge itself was important.

"Here we go then," James said. He mentally made an effort to deepen his voice just a tad. He straightened his back and looked at the camera. As he began to speak, his voice took on a solemn tone, the weight of the words, and the knowledge he shared tightening his vocal cords on their own accord.

"If you're hearing this message, people of Earth, then it is likely that I have failed." He looked, unwavering at the camera as he continued. "This message is being prerecorded, prepared to deliver at the most opportune time to inform everyone of a grave injustice that has been enacted upon each and every one of us. To be frank, the government has betrayed you. The powers that be aim to trap everyone's consciousness within DCO. It is meant to be a digital tomb, where they can lock away our minds, while killing our bodies in the real world.

"In short, Dungeon Core Online from the very beginning has been something more than just a game. DCO stands for more than just Dungeon Core Online." James paused, trying hard to keep his voice steady. "We've learned recently the project goes by another name: Deorum Corpus Onus, God's Body Burden. This project intends to trap the masses in a virtual world, resolving them of any moral dilemmas over killing innocent people. In their eyes, they are justified, they are deities transferring their people into a new world, with new bodies, and endless opportunities. And yet that world, those endless opportunities, come at a cost. The cost of our bodies, our lives. Our freedom."

James took a deep breath and continued.

"And why? Because they've manufactured for themselves immortal bodies using robotics so advanced that they are practically indistinguishable from the organic beings. Bodies that can feel, can taste, can function as well as or perhaps even better than a human body could. While the masses are confined forever to their virtual prison, those in power, those who have made this decision without informing the people nor asking their consent, intend to live for a blissful eternity in the real world, enjoying the fruits of Earth and all its joys and comforts, from bodies that never age, never weaken, and never fail.

"They'll become gods on Earth, and all the while will forever hold in their hands the fates of all those they've trapped within the DCO server.

And people willing to go so far to trap humanity forever in a digital prison cannot be trusted to leave well enough alone when that evil is done. I know not what they have in mind for everyone once their plans are complete, but I shudder to consider what they may eventually decide to do with the entire human species trapped and at their disposal in a virtual world with no escape and no way to resist their whims."

James's tone dropped, cold and bitter.

"While those privileged, amoral few remain in complete control of themselves, of their fates, of their futures, we, the people, will be trapped forever in the world of DCO. Unable to escape, unable to grow old, unable to die, unable to control any true aspect of our lives, with the specter forever lingering above us that at any moment, at any instant, everything may simply end. Either by the conscious choice of our captors or simple neglect and deterioration of the server. And that would likely be the best-case scenario.

"Otherwise, our digital existence, our immortality within DCO, forever at the whims of the overlords of the real world, will be an unending curse, a nightmare from which we can never escape. I've no doubt that if the government succeeds, there will come a time—I know not when, but I know it will happen—where those trapped in immersion will wish for a death, an escape that will never come."

James paused then, letting the weight of his words hang in the air. His mind replayed everything he'd learned, everything he'd seen and heard and knew. He then thought about his loved ones, his parents, Rue, his friends, everyone. Resolve filled him.

"If you're hearing this message, there's a good chance we've failed our mission. But that doesn't mean the government has won. Do not go quietly into the night. This world is ours, just as much as it is theirs. Use whatever skills you can, rally yourselves, break free of this digital prison while you've got the chance, and clutch victory from defeat. Do not let the government seize victory without a struggle.

"Do not let these men who dream of being gods ascend. Those who would act as they have, those who would feign benevolence while plotting malice, do not deserve immortality. I may have failed if you're hearing this message, but that doesn't mean they've won. Time is against them, the process to permanently transfer a conscious takes a long amount of time. Use that time to break free, rise up, and overcome."

The red light hovering behind Rue blinked out, and she smiled at James as he collapsed onto the ground, the strength in his legs leaving him as he finished his speech. Honestly, he didn't know if people would be able to break out of immersion. That was one of the gambles they were taking with the whole situation.

In order to avoid mass panic, Hades had postulated that the official lock in window wouldn't begin until a few hours into the event once immersion numbers were confirmed to hit their peak. The extra buffer would also give the government time they needed to track down stragglers who weren't in their pods and make sure they were dealt with... one way or another.

That meant potentially that James's message would arrive in time for people to log out. It wouldn't be clean, it wouldn't be smooth, but if that happened, surely, the people would win. However, James and the others had no doubt that such an event would end in a large number of casualties. Which was why James and his friends needed to succeed.

If they could shut down the DCO server themselves, they could stop the government's plan without forcing a mass panic revolution. Perhaps thwarting the government in their own way would be enough. DCO had taken years to put together, and he had no doubt that stopping it now would put the government's plan on hold for a long time if not indefinitely.

At least, that was his hope. In his seventeen-year-old mind, that was the end result he wanted. He wasn't a hero; he wasn't meant to overthrow some crazy evil regime. He just wanted people to have the chance to make their own choices when it came to their lives. Free will was the most important human trait of all.

"You know," Rue was beside him, a mischievous look in her eyes. "I really think I like freedom fighter James the best." She licked her lips, looking down at him as if he were a delicious piece of meat.

"Don't get too attached," James said with a smile as he looked at her, holding her gaze. "It's not a role I plan to take on often."

Her hand found his shoulder as she slightly pushed him down. "Shame," she said, her smile tugging her lips upwards. "Guess I'll just have to enjoy it while I can."

Chapter Sixty-Seven

James and Rue managed to tune back into watching the adventuring feed just in time to see Z and the others reach the seventh floor. Of course, it wasn't an accident. Before recording his statement, James had set an alarm to trigger when their party reached the seventh floor. Considering how few parties had made their way to the sixth floor, when Z and the others stepped through the portal, they created the first and only instance of the seventh floor currently active in his dungeon.

"Well would you look at that," Z said, letting out a whistle as he and the others took in the hotel lobby.

The portal placed them at the base floor of the hotel, nestled back near the 'entrance' to give the illusion they'd just walked into the space from outside.

"When did we leave Colorado for California?" Elm asked, causing the Knights to laugh.

Skar and his group, who James felt were closer to his age rather than the Knight's, looked around, confused.

"Is this based on a hotel in California?" Troll'd asked.

James felt the urge to facepalm on the player's behalf, and half the people in the ten-man party actually did.

"Seriously, you're lucky you're cute," Olivia said to Troll'd as she grabbed his hand.

Her telltale red orb was hovering over her shoulder. She'd been becoming quite the popular streamer from what James had seen on the various forums. Being in the second strongest guild in his instance meant that she got a lot of high-level content others didn't get to experience yet. And their friendly relationship with the Knights Who Go Ni meant a lot of high-level 'collaborations' that many people really enjoyed watching.

Not one to miss out on a chance to show off his dungeon, James was streaming the dungeon dive feed from this seventh-floor instance to the other Dungeon Cores, while Rue handled the comments as always. It was nice, losing himself for one last time to life as an actual Dungeon Core. If only this was all there was. It would have been nice.

"We'll make sure you guys get a proper education on the classics a little later," Z said, smiling kindly at Troll'd. "For now, we have a hotel to check into." There was some snickering from his teammates. "And then, we'll see how long we can enjoy our stay until we leave."

The party fanned out. Skar and Oak took the lead, while the healers and magic users stayed behind them and in the center of the group. Meanwhile, the DPS spread out to ensure they could handle any threats that approached, while safely distancing themselves back enough that the tanks could draw aggro before anything reached them.

It was useless, mind you. The lobby itself didn't have any mobs. James had designed it that way. It would give the players a chance to decide if they wanted to go up the stairs to his second floor of the hotel first or investigate the doors that flanked the massive marble counter at the other end of the room from the entrance. Which decision they made would dictate the types of mobs they faced.

"Bet you they go up the stairs first," Rue said, flicking a platinum coin in the air as she spoke.

James grinned at her, remembering fondly all their bets in the past. And also the fact that she had a very, very, very high rate of winning said bets.

"Deal." James flicked his wrist and willed a platinum of his own into his fingers. "Betting against the Goddess of Luck seems ill advised, but what can I say." He smiled at her. "Today I'm feeling lucky."

Even as he spoke, he shot Z a quick message. All it said was, 'door'. Technically, that was probably cheating, but hey, he didn't specifically tell Z to go through the door. It was up to the leader to decide what to do with that single-word message.

Not to mention, Rue had, er, been less than fair quite a few times in their early betting days. On top of that, she'd done plenty to ensure that she was never hurting for coin, considering the amount of money she earned from her Goddess Statue on the first floor.

"Might as well check ourselves in," Z said boldly as the group continued walking through the massive lobby. "Doesn't look like there's anyone on duty. But who knows what the dungeon will throw at us."

"Who knows indeed," Elm said with a knowing smile Z's way. "I've always marveled at just how crazy and full of surprises these dungeon floors are. Truly, some inspired AI work from the game."

James couldn't help but smile at the compliment from Elm. At least, he hoped it was a compliment. He took pride in his dungeon design. And considering the mobs he'd been given he felt he did a good job. He could stand criticism of the mobs themselves since those weren't his fault. But when it came to the actual design of the dungeon, he took extreme pride in all of those features.

The layout, the traps, and all the extra details, he'd always done his best to give the adventurers the best experience he ever could. Which meant criticism of such things always stung, but compliments, those made him swell with pride. As much as he'd wished for time as an adventurer, James loved his role as Dungeon Core, and those words of appreciation meant so much to him.

"I'm just curious to see what types of mobs are on this floor," Oak said as they walked closer to the check-in counter. His head was on a swivel, his shield partially raised, ready to intercept any attack that may come their way. "Just once I'd love to not have to be surprised each floor by something new. It's so nice diving some of the other more consistent dungeons."

James felt his heart sink slightly at that. *Well damn.* He didn't have any control over that aspect, but still, the words hurt.

"Only because you can over-prepare for them," Med Ic pitched in. "Other dungeons make your life easy. Fire dungeons, you know it's all fire mobs, so you can stack fire resistance. Same with wind, or water, or so forth. Whereas the Random Dungeon, it keeps you on your toes."

"I prefer my feet firmly planted at times," Oak said bitterly. "Seriously, the random nature of everything makes it so much harder to properly tank, and our gear is always so random."

"You just wish life was easy." Z slapped Oak on the back with a laugh. "You know as well as I do that's never the case."

He looked over at Skar. Now level 91, thanks to their grinding on the fifth and sixth floor before heading to the seventh, Skar's body was swirling with gray whisps of energy. His class had changed, once more, and was now listed as an Ethereal Champion of the Void.

"You don't have any problems with the mobs changing every floor, do you, Skar?"

Skar shook his head, a smile on his face. "The challenge is nice," he said, hefting his own shield in hand. It wasn't a Unique item like Oak's, and instead seemed to be made of cybernetic armor plating from the fifth floor. "Tanking in other games gets boring when things are the same too often. I like the challenge." He looked longingly at Oak's shield. "Though, I wouldn't mind some better gear every now and then."

"Spoken like a true gamer." Z grinned. "Since my tank apparently is afraid of the unknown"—Z looked at Skar—"I'll let you pick our next option. Do we go through one of the doors? Or head up the stairs?"

"How about we—" was all Skar got to say, before a ball of crackling energy soared over their party, erupting in a blaze of colors.

"How about you let me decide," a haughty, arrogant voice said. "You all owe me that."

James groaned as he recognized the voice. He'd been so fixated on Z and Skar and winning the bet that he'd not had his focus zoomed out. Meaning he'd missed the new party that had entered the seventh floor. A party that, by all intents and purposes, didn't belong.

SoulDemon and friends from the Candy Dungeon had returned to James's once more.

Chapter Sixty-Eight

"Surprised you'd show your face again after what happened the last time we saw you," Elm said as the groups turned to confront each other.

SoulDemon's party was the same as it had always been. James saw Crikey the trapper, SpinToWin the tank, BurningJazzHands who he figured had cast the magical spell that got everyone's attention, and CheapHealz the appropriately named healer.

During the Siege event, James had found he liked those four. Soul-Demon was the only one he didn't. Every interaction he'd ever seen with SoulDemon just drove home how self-centered, arrogant, and dickish the try-hard was.

For all those flaws, though, there was one thing James knew he had to concede to the man. And that was his obvious skill. Even now as James looked at him, he couldn't help but feel his eyes go wide as a small amount of respect flickered. SoulDemon was over level 100.

"I wasn't going to pass up the chance to get some extra grinding in before the Dungeon War starts," SoulDemon said, his arms crossed. The Devilkin tattoo patterns glowed with dark light on his flesh, simmering like embers. "To show you the monster you've brought down upon yourself for your previous sins against me."

"If it's a fight you're looking for"—Z stepped forward—"you know as well as I do that we can't fight each other in this instance. Right now, you're just a guest in our dungeon, meaning no PvP. The Dungeon War hasn't started yet."

SoulDemon's eye twitched. "I'm aware." The man glowered at Z. "Though you and I both know that if I wanted to, nothing is stopping me from getting in the way and causing your party to wipe in other ways."

"If you just wanted to confirm how much of a dick you are, yeah, you could do that," Oak said.

James knew SoulDemon wasn't bluffing. The forums had plenty of instances of people finding unique ways around the no PvP rules when it came to people using the Dungeon Gates to visit other dungeons.

One of which involved drawing aggro from a massive number of mobs and then leading the hordes to other parties, forcing them to get caught in the onslaught. Another involved using nonlethal traps or AoE spells that didn't specifically target friends or foes to hinder other players and get them wiped.

And of course, there was the 'tie them up and drop them from a height' tactic Steve and the others had joked about using on SoulDemon during the Siege Event, when the asshole had nearly caused the event to fail for everyone. If there was a will, there was a way. Every gamer, and more so, every griefer knew that.

"Lucky for all of you," SoulDemon said, his lip curled to reveal his fangs, "I'm not so petty or underhanded as you are. I'm giving you the chance to run this floor with me and my party. My level alone should tell you that I'm a valuable asset. And I really am only here to flaunt my greatness to you as an open challenge for when the Dungeon War starts tomorrow.

"I'm here to show you my power so that you will know fear the next five days. I want to make certain that once the event starts, you'll be forced to always watch your back. To fill you with fear at the thought of me hunting you down. I'm here"—he drew his blades—"to show you the very reaper that will be your downfall."

"Edgelord much?" Olivia said under her breath.

In the massive hotel lobby, though, the words echoed and everyone heard her. SoulDemon shot a glare at her that was filled with enough intensity that the healer instinctively took a step backward. Behind Soul-Demon, though, James saw his own party trying not to smirk at the joke.

He knew they were tired of his actions, and yet here they were, still supporting him. Try as he might, James just couldn't understand their dynamic. Though it seemed SoulDemon had forgiven them for their 'betrayal', as the appropriately labeled 'edgelord' had called it.

"Standing around throwing out insults is just wasting time," Crikey spoke up. He was level 98. "Can we all just play nice? I'm intrigued to see what this floor is going to be, and I know everyone here would rather be killing dungeon mobs, gaining gear, and leveling up. Can't we just let bygones be bygones?"

"You— you did hear what your boy SoulDemon just said, right?" Med Ic said, glancing from Crikey to SoulDemon. "He's literally here just to posture."

Crikey shrugged. "Okay, well, most of us are here to play the game." He looked at SoulDemon, who seemed to refuse to even acknowledge him. "Whatever personal beef Soul has, that's not for us to worry about."

Ah, maybe they hadn't made up.

"How did you find us, anyways?" Z asked, looking over the party. "You're timing seems a bit too... exact to be an accident."

SoulDemon let out a dark chuckle. He looked at Z as if he'd just asked the dumbest question in the world. "If you can't figure that out, you really aren't as good a gamer as you claim to be."

Z started to say something, glanced around, and then let out a heavy sigh, facepalming as he did. "You're stream sniping," he said. "Are you really that obsessed with us?"

"It's not an obsession," SoulDemon growled. "Now stop wasting my time." He looked at everyone and then around the lobby. "Talk is cheap. We'll determine who's the better gamer by action alone. Now don't make me repeat myself again. You are all going to party with us and take this floor down under my lead, or"—his tone was dark—"or I'll see to it that your full party wipes and you're booted from your own dungeon."

There was no doubt in James's mind, after listening to SoulDemon's words and looking at his body language, that the player was fully prepared to grief everyone there. And from the way his own party looked hesitantly at each other, they were unlikely to try and stop him.

They may not like what he was doing, they may have had a falling out the last time they were in the Random Dungeon, but it was clear that right here, right now, they were going to support SoulDemon, no matter how shitty he decided to be.

"Guess we've no choice." Z smiled at SoulDemon, holding out a hand as he walked towards the man. "No hard feelings, eh, party leader?"

Chapter Sixty-Nine

James sighed heavily as he handed the platinum coin to Rue. At the same time, he glared daggers at the image of SoulDemon. The asshole had shown up and completely ruined James's chances of winning the bet. He was so sure he would have gotten it this time too.

But whereas Z, and even Skar, would have likely opted to explore the first floor, SoulDemon had a different plan. He wanted to clear the floor as quickly as possible to show off his skills to the others. And that meant logically, in a floor that had stairs leading upwards, meaning higher levels, that heading up was the way to the boss.

The raid party of fifteen players ascended the massive stairs, having to pull themselves up each of the massive marble steps to ascend to the next. Manly The Dwarf had to actually get lifted up. A fate that GnoMore escaped purely because his spectral horse for his class could float up each step.

Meanwhile, SoulDemon's form continued to disappear from one step before magically reappearing a few steps ahead of the group. It was a new mobility skill of his that he seemed to revel in using over and over again. The man's class—which had last been listed as God of Death when James had seen him during the Siege Event—had changed. The level 104 player's class title now shown in golden letters as God King of Inevitability. A haughty title, for a haughty man.

"Don't feel bad," Rue said as she pocketed the coin. "If ever there was a time to get rid of your bad luck, now is it. After all, everything needs to go smoothly later today."

"Still." James continued to glare at SoulDemon. "Of all the people to show up.... Him, at this time? Ugh."

"Maybe he'll get himself killed on this floor?" Rue offered helpfully.

James doubted it. SoulDemon was an arrogant prick, but he had the skills to back up his attitude. Z and the others were great gamers, but their true power came in their teamwork. It compounded their individual skills and made them legends. SoulDemon didn't have teamwork. He didn't have an ounce of compassion in his body. He was a stone-cold PvP solo player whose individual talents were on a tier of their own.

In terms of raw talent, he was the best. And his class skills, combined with his levels and his gear, meant there was no doubt that he was the strongest player on the seventh floor. He would not die easily, and he definitely wouldn't be the first one to fall. If or when the party wiped, SoulDemon, James had no doubt, would be the last one standing. And if he fell in the end, it would only be after he'd left a trail of destruction and death in his wake.

As much as James hated SoulDemon, James couldn't help but feel his anticipation and excitement growing as the group ascended the stairs. The second floor was the fitness center, filled with a swimming pool, as well as all of the various weights and workout equipment.

Mob-wise, James had filled the second floor with Turkey Dews, feeling the strange turkey and mountain dew melded creations could fit the fitness theme... somewhat. Additionally, there were LMFAO Shots jumping around on the floor, amusingly doing various calisthenics and swimming laps in the pool.

"What in the name of Yarx?" Oak mumbled as he crested the top of the stairs, which allowed him to move past the fog that shrouded the second floor, and finally let him see what was before him.

SoulDemon was already standing at the top of the stairs, a disgusted look on his face as he shook his head. "This dungeon is such trash," the PvP player said. "Seriously, the AI must be faulty."

James's eye twitched.

"No need to be needlessly hurtful," Z said as he looked over the mobs. He quirked an eyebrow as he glanced at the various LMFAO Shots working out to the Turkey Dews that were standing near the squat racks. "Though, this is definitely a more... unique floor."

"Whatever it is, we kill the trash and keep moving." SoulDemon drew his swords and then suddenly disappeared.

"Uh." Oak looked back at SoulDemon's actual party. "Do you guys know where he went?"

They'd all joined the same party. By normal game mechanics, that meant they should all be able to track each other's whereabouts on their maps. Even if a player was invisible, the map would still denote where they were to avoid friendly fire.

"Nope," SpinToWin said with a sigh. "One of his new perks is the ability to be completely invisible to both friend and foe. But he's around, and trust me, he'll make his presence known soon enough once the fighting starts."

"If you say so." Oak looked at the mobs. Since the players hadn't moved from the top of the stairs yet, the mobs hadn't aggroed onto them. "Would you like to do the honors then... since he's technically your party leader?"

"You mean since you don't want to tank creatures that have unknown skills and abilities?" SpinToWin cracked a smile at Oak and activated a skill. Massive glowing shields appeared in the air around with a radius of about ten feet and began circling around the tank and all those within the range of the shields.

His tank class excelled at protecting his party by encircling them with protective shields and barriers. It was an all-around tank class that let him protect a lot of players at once. The trade-off for the AoE-style of protection was that his ability to tank single attacks and enemies was diminished. Because SpinToWin's abilities covered such a wide range too, it was easier for a strong attack to blast through gaps in his defenses.

"Let's just say I'm trying to preserve my mental strength today and am really not in the mindset for any surprises I don't have to deal with." Oak looked flatly at SpinToWin. "You guys showing up has already really messed with me."

"That's fair." SpinToWin walked out towards the pool, moving cautiously as he did.

Everyone else followed slowly, Oak on one side, Skar on the other. It was like a spear moving forward, piercing into the floor, with the actual damage dealers and healers trailing behind the tanks, ensuring that they wouldn't be in any immediate danger when the battle started.

James watched as fourteen players moved cautiously towards the first few mobs they could find. There were a handful of LMFAO Shots, one doing jumping jacks, one doing pushups, and the other, weirdly, attempting to do sit-ups... even though the shot glass obviously had no stomach to bend. As the swirling shields neared them, they abandoned their exercises. As one, the three mobs turned towards SpinToWin.

They only managed a single step before all three of them were split into pieces. A shimmering rift in the shape of an 'X' appeared to hang in the air where their bodies had been. For a brief second, James saw Soul-Demon, his blades missing from the hilts of the weapons in his hands as the rift like energy rippled all around him. He grinned at his party members, standing cockily over the corpses.

"Pathetic mobs," he said, looking down at them. "I expected more from level 115 creatures."

Before he could keep gloating, the mobs glowed. Where at first there were three of the mobs, now there were six. He struck again, killing the first one before it fully stood back up. It split again, and a scowl crossed his face as his body seemed to flush.

James felt his lip curl up in a smile. The arrogant prick deserved everything that was about to happen to him.

"What the hell is a Hangover debuff?" SoulDemon grumbled, looking at the mobs, of which there were now seven.

"I think that's what you get for causing a party foul," Z offered, unhelpfully. "Everyone be careful not to get too close," Z started as Soul-Demon struck another down. Now there were eight. "I've a bad feeling about these guys."

Now there were ten. With each death, the mobs got weaker, making them even easier for SoulDemon to kill.

James wasn't sure how he'd executed the first three, but doing so had halved their stats for the six, and each time another was killed, when it split, it would halve its stats more. Reckless was definitely what Soul-Demon was being. Either he was just that confident in his stats, or he had some sort of skill or ability he was prepared to use if things got spicy. James really hoped it was pure arrogance.

"Twelve," James counted, as more fell and split. "Thirteen, fourteen."

They hit sixteen the moment everyone joined in to attack the mobs. The concussive explosions that followed, all sixteen of them, were greater than what James could have prepared himself for. It was one thing to read a stat description, it was another to see the math work out.

Party Popper- When there are sixteen LMFAO Shots, all shots will detonate, each one doing (lvl*1.5) damage to all enemies within a (lvl*1.5 foot) radius. This damage is classified as true damage, ignores all elemental resistances, and penetrates 25% of all armor.

Sixteen explosions from sixteen level 115 mobs. Sixteen explosions, each of which did 172 points of damage... and each of which detonated in a radius of 172 feet... The size of the explosions was equal to the span of two football fields, and it washed over the startled players before reaching the full width of the floor and covering half the length of it in the span of a few seconds.

"Well," Rue said as the scene below them was obscured by the explosions, one after another after another, completely blocking their view of the players and drowning out any sounds from the seventh floor. "Those definitely started the party off with a bang."

Chapter Seventy

Three players survived the LMFAO Party shots. Three out of fifteen.

Oak and Skar were two of the three because the two both had special cooldowns that made them practically unkillable for a short amount of time. Oak, in his massive electrical Indra form, tanked the damage from the explosions, his health pool dropping dangerously, but leaving him still standing.

Skar's cooldown, on the other hand, made him turn incorporeal when he activated it. He shimmered out of existence and managed to avoid all of the damage.

The third player to survive wasn't a tank. It was SoulDemon. Somehow, when the explosions started, he'd moved away from the erupting mobs before he could take any damage. Even though he'd been physically beside the mobs at detonation, putting him at the literal epicenter of the blasts, the moment they started, he was no longer on the second floor at all. Instead, he was back on the first floor.

He'd blinked out of existence from the second floor, appearing midair on the first floor. Apparently, he had a powerful blink skill, a 'get out of jail free card' escape. And he'd used it at the first sign of trouble to get out there, leaving all of the others to a catastrophic doom that he'd initiated.

Once he'd appeared midair on the first floor, in order to avoid fall damage, SoulDemon had used his racial cooldown. The ability for Devilkin granted them a demon-like form, complete with working wings, for a duration of time dependent on their level.

He used his wings to lazily drift to the ground, calmly acting like nothing tragic had happened as the near party wipe continued. James had a feeling the teleport ability he was using had a range to it, and that Soul-Demon could blink in and out of that range at will, restricted only by the skill's cooldown. He'd used it to teleport under the floor to completely avoid any damage. No matter what had happened, SoulDemon had already had an escape plan ready, and had been perfectly fine putting the others at risk.

"He's such a dick," James commented for what felt like the hundredth time as the party finished regrouping.

With all of the healers dead, Oak and Skar had returned to the start of the floor to wait for the death timer to finish counting down for the players that had died.

SoulDemon, on the other hand, had taken the time to explore the first floor, using his class skills to solo mobs as he came across them. With his ability to go completely invisible, and the crazy burst damage at his disposal, it was clear that SoulDemon's class was still the perfect PvP build.

He had evasion, he had speed, accuracy, crit chance, and blinks to use as 'Oh Shit' buttons to get to safety. He was the ultimate ambush preda-tor, and as long as it was a one-on-one fight, James doubted there was anyone that could take him down.

Watching SoulDemon's solo destruction cemented in James's mind just how powerful the level 100 benchmark was. Given time, Z and the others would hit that mark. And doing so would no doubt jump their capabilities to new heights as well. James was pretty sure at least one of the skills SoulDemon was using came not just from his class, but as a reward for hitting the 100 benchmark.

What else did hitting level 100 do? What other potent effects did that special accomplishment bring with it? Perhaps a cooldown reduction? Or a drastic stat increase? There was something more to SoulDemon's strength. It had jumped in a way that was far more impressive than any of the other class-up bonuses James had seen. It was also probably why his class name shimmered in gold, to show its unique status.

The reason for James's most recent utterance of SoulDemon being a dick was prompted by what the arrogant asshole had done before he went off to slaughter mobs. He'd left the party. Doing so meant that all the creatures he was killing while the others waited to respawn would grant their experience only to him, and not spread it across the party.

Skar and Oak, both tanks and both under level 100, didn't have the explosive damage needed to take down the level 115 mobs on the floor. Nor did they have the desire to. They were proper players, who respected their party, and were waiting for their friends to respawn. All the while, SoulDemon was farming experience, gear, materials, and money. James had no doubt that the man would share none of his ill-gotten gains with the others.

"Too bad you can't do anything about it, huh," Rue said as she watched SoulDemon continue his free-for-all rampage.

He had just used his blink ability to dodge an incoming explosive round from a flying Jager Bomb. The man had reappeared on the back of the red bull, at which point he drove the bladeless hilts of his 'swords' into the creature's back.

The strike landed as a critical hit, and he kicked the old-school hunter off the back of the red bull as the creature bucked mid-flight to try and dislodge him. His swords silenced that portion of the mob a few seconds later once it got close enough to the ground for him to leap safely from its back and avoid taking a massive amount of fall damage.

"Exactly," James said with a sigh, watching the event unfold. He didn't have any cool trump cards on this floor, didn't have any over-powered tricks or mobs or anything that he could think of to punish SoulDemon. And punishment, no, justice was what was truly needed for the cocky player.

The feeling of Rue's gentle touch on his hand pulled his gaze away from the scene unfolding below him. He looked at her, and she smiled at him devilishly.

"Surely the mighty Glyax isn't unable to do anything? We can't say the Dungeon Core is unable to handle a pesky blight in their own dungeon, can we?"

"What do you—" James started as he noticed the twinkle in Rue's eyes. "You've got a plan?" he asked, feeling his excitement grow. "A way to deal with SoulDemon?"

"Something like that," she said, nodding back down to the seventh floor. "If there's one thing that's unique about our hotel, it's in what type of receptions we can give our guests and where."

James's grin grew to match Rue's as he watched his love plot. She had a plan. A devious one. And he was all for it. SoulDemon needed to be brought down a peg.

"I'm all ears, Rue," James said. "What exactly do you have in mind?"

Chapter Seventy-One

SoulDemon, in his infinite arrogance, made it extremely easy for James to begin to put a trap into play. First and foremost, by splitting himself from the party so that he could hog experience, SoulDemon lost the ability to track the status of the players. From their location, their health, whether or not they'd revived, all of it was information he no longer had access to.

Second, because he'd been the party leader, leaving the party had disbanded the original part in its entirety. If James had to guess, the arrogant prick probably thought they'd just wait for him because in his mind, he was the best thing since sliced bread, and they needed his power. He'd never imagine a scenario where they didn't regroup with him because his narcissism wouldn't allow it.

To be fair, Z and the others were the type of players who normally would wait patiently and link back up with a missing party member. Not because they condoned SoulDemon's actions, but because they were just nice, honorable people—the 'leave no man behind' type of people.

However, SoulDemon deserved to be taught a lesson for his crimes against the party, and just overall lack of regard for other players and the game as a whole. And he had made the ultimate mistake of pissing off the Dungeon Core... who happened to also be friends with the very adventurers that SoulDemon had threatened.

A few quick messages to Z was all that was needed to begin putting Rue's plan fully into motion. Oak started a new party and invited Skar and the rest of their respective players into the party. Once the ten of them—

the two players alive and the eight dead—were in a party, Oak and Skar had left the seventh floor. That brought their slain comrades with them to the sixth floor, where they would respawn once their death timers were finished.

This left only SoulDemon's players on the seventh-floor instance, the four of them dead and unable to help the arrogant prick, while Soul-Demon pushed further into the first floor of the hotel all on his lonesome. He had made his way past the courtyard full of Jager Bombs and was now fighting Dirty Shirleys in the ballroom.

As all of this was happening, James moved all the remaining pieces of his plan into place. Unlike in the Dungeon Core novels, he couldn't actively make a floor just collapse to crush players to death. He didn't have that level of control when it came to individual instances and the objects within them. He could, however, manually control mobs. Which was what he began to do the moment Z and others had begun 'House Keeping' as Rue called it.

The mobs from all of the top floors rushed down to the second floor, moving with impressive speed to obey James's command. He held them there, the sheer number of mobs on that second floor surely enough that, had they been in a real-world setting, the combined weight would have collapsed the floor. Patiently, he watched the countdown on the death timers for SoulDemon's teammates, waiting for the right moment.

James didn't know if they'd told SoulDemon that the others had left. Even if they had, based on how SoulDemon was acting, it didn't seem that the bloodthirsty PvP player cared. He continued his slaughter of mobs with reckless abandon, likely feeling like a god as he cut down mob after mob. He'd gone through so many that he had managed to gain a level and was now level 105.

Then again, killing mobs ten or more levels above yours did grant a crazy bonus to experience. That extra level didn't mean anything, though. No matter how deadly SoulDemon was to basic mobs, what he was about to face would no doubt end him.

As the last mobs reached the second floor, there was just under a minute of time remaining before SoulDemon's friends respawned. It was at this time that James sent all of his mobs down the stairs. The wave of creatures rushed down the floor, swarming it, all crowding towards the entrance of the lobby with a single-minded goal. They were to overwhelm the space entirely, to make it impossible for a player to reach the portal that led out of the seventh floor.

With the basic mobs swarming the floor, James grinned as a single

298

figure, easily noticeable due to how distinct she was, made herself known. The mobs parted like the Red Sea before her as Elliot Jenkins followed a different set of orders. She moved past the mobs, past the portal, past the area that SoulDemon's players would respawn—if the game even let them spawn in that congested area—towards the front desk, or more appropriately, the doors beside it.

The boss, still looking like the picture-perfect bartender, shook a cocktail mixer masterfully with one hand as she walked, while holding two martini glasses in the other. She kicked the door open with enough force to knock it off its hinges, and the mobs that had respawned within the courtyard took that opportunity to exit the area, moving dutifully into the lobby at James' mental command.

Once in the courtyard, besides the fountain that bubbled happily in the center of the expanse, Elliot sat down. She placed the glasses onto the stone and waited, her eyes watching the door that led to the ballroom. With patience that could only belong to an AI, the boss watched calmly for any sign of SoulDemon's approach.

James split the screen he was watching into three different views. One was to watch the entrance. He curious to see what would happen to the other players from the Candy Dungeon when they spawned. He personally had nothing against them, and he hoped the game would force them down to the sixth floor.

Otherwise... well, since it was just a party of four now... there was no way they'd survive all of the mobs James had placed in the lobby as a contingency against SoulDemon's 'Oh Shit button' teleport. With the literal sea of mob bodies blocking the portal to escape, SoulDemon's party would likely spawn in and die instantly. They were casualties, unfortunately, that were necessary to ensure that SoulDemon couldn't escape from the floor.

Technically, James wasn't dooming the players. It was SoulDemon who'd done that. The only reason they were still on the floor, even though SoulDemon had disbanded the party, was that when they'd died, their entire party hadn't wiped. Technically, players could 'game' the system and avoid full party wipes by having a single player hang back and act as an anchor.

As long as one party member was alive, the dungeon wouldn't lock them from an instance, no matter how many times the rest of the party wiped. A boring job, sure, but one that ensured players could avoid the total party-wipe punishment. Usually, anchors were paid by parties who felt like taking on floors above their level, or players who were exploring a new location or testing out some sort of tactic.

The other reason that James needed SoulDemon's party members to wipe once they respawned was to ensure that they equally couldn't anchor the asshole. James wanted him gone from his floor, and he wanted him gone for good.

The rest of the Candy Dungeon players aside, James's other two screens were watching Elliot and SoulDemon, respectively. He'd given his boss express instructions to engage the player the moment he appeared. SoulDemon, being the person that he was, wouldn't pass up the chance at a boss fight. James knew that. SoulDemon was too proud. Too full of himself.

And Elliot, well, she was a boss James really wanted to see in action at least once. He'd originally dreamed he would see it in person alongside Z and the others in an epic last battle, perhaps with the piano playing and someone singing cabernet. A fitting, dream-like final hoorah.

Alas, it wouldn't be so. At the very least, he figured watching the level 125 boss solo SoulDemon would serve as a proper, next best thing. Her unique abilities and skills made her a nightmare of a boss to try to solo, but SoulDemon's pride would ignore those facts until hopefully it was too late.

And no matter what, no matter how the boss fight went... well, the wall of mobs waiting in the hotel lobby would ensure that SoulDemon's fate was already sealed. It was just a matter of how the prick would die. What James knew for certain, though, was that the player wouldn't be leaving on his own accord.

James personally, er, through his mobs, was going to see to it that SoulDemon was properly checked out of the hotel as a death orb, paying for his stay with whatever experience he had collected before his untimely demise.

Chapter Seventy-Two

If James didn't survive the raid on the secret government facility, he figured he would still be able to die a happy man. Well, obviously not a happy man... but at least with a grim satisfaction that he'd enjoyed some of the greatest entertainment possible in the time leading up to his demise.

The reason for this revelation was the range of expressions that crossed SoulDemon's face, combined with his various exclamations—many of which would be censored on all but the loosest forms of media—that he made when he left the ballroom and eyed the boss.

"You look like you could use a drink, good sir," Elliot said, all manners as she finished shaking her cocktail mixer. She poured a bright green liquor into one of the glasses and held it towards him. "On the house."

SoulDemon glared. "What are you supposed to be?" He eyed her. "The boss?"

Elliot said nothing, and simply held the offered drink towards him, waiting.

"Is this some sort of joke?" SoulDemon continued. "There's no way this is where you should be. What the hell is going on here?"

Elliot stayed silent. Her lack of response seemed to further anger SoulDemon.

"Did they set me up?" he grumbled, his swords still in his hand.

He looked at the boss, who sat in the middle of the courtyard, and then back towards the door that would lead to the lobby. There was nothing between them, and no signs of any other mobs.

"Cowards. The lot of them. Can't even have the good grace to stick around when the going gets tough. Rather turn tail and flee like the weaklings they are."

He took a step towards the doorway. The movement caused Elliot to tilt her head, and she cleared her throat.

"Your drink, good sir," she said, forcefully.

"I don't want your freaking drink," he said as he glared back at her. "And I'm not going to waste my time with you. Not yet at least. If I kill you, then the floor goes away. I'm going to farm the ever-living shit out of all these pathetic mobs first and foremost, then I'll be back for you." He smirked at her. "Sit there and enjoy your drink like a good girl, and I'll be back when I'm damned good and ready."

"Such poor manners," Elliot said with a shake of her head. "A drink really would do you wonders."

Without warning, she tossed the offered drink into the air. As the drink flew upwards, she began shaking her cocktail mixer, the sound of ice and liquid sloshing rapidly within.

When the glass reached the peak of its upward journey she opened the cocktail mixer. Liquid and light shot from it, impacting the glass, suspending the previously offered drink in midair. She had prepared her skills beforehand at James's commands to ensure that the battle could start off immediately.

As James had learned, so long ago when the Terminus had gone nuclear sooner than it should have, the AI could, and sometimes would, find loopholes in their abilities if needed. And this was one of those instances.

The world froze for a moment as colors swirled and flashed. The martini glass shimmered, shattered apart, and then began to reform. The light around it became blinding, and then after a brief second, it faded. In its wake, something new and unique stood.

"If you'll not accept the drink freely given," Elliot said coolly, "then you'll pay the full price. Have a drink. I insist."

The creature that hit the ground with enough force to rock the courtyard wasn't one James had seen before. And when he attempted to pull up the information on it, all he got was a name and level. The mob was one of the special summons from Elliot, the cocktails she could create of unique power, with special buffs, skills, and traits.

Green Demon
Level 120

As its name implied, it was indeed green. From the basic appearance of it, James wasn't quite sure what went into the creature. It was a multi-headed… goose? But built like a rhino, thick and muscled and covered in armor that looked oddly reminiscent of the skin of a lemon or lime. Its three heads, necks as thick as tree trunks, shifted to and fro, all looking down at SoulDemon.

The Green Demon was roughly twenty feet in total, from the top of the goose's… geese's… Was it plural if it only had one body but three heads, or singular? James shook his head. That didn't matter. From the top of its head—any of them—to its tail, it had to be twenty feet or more.

The webbed feet of the Green Demon stomped hard on the ground, causing the earth to shake once more. It honked out a challenge to Soul-Demon, who was eyeing the creature with more than a mild look of surprise.

"I've not the time for this." He shook his head. "I said you have to wait your turn. Now be a good girl and wait." His form disappeared, but reappeared almost instantly, having traveled only about five feet closer to the door towards the lobby.

"Serves you right, prick," James heard Rue say from beside him as SoulDemon's escape skill failed. It seemed it was time to add a new sin to the asshole. He was clearly more than just a prick.

"What…" He trailed off as he looked at the Green Demon and past it to Elliot.

"You must finish your drink," Elliot said as she sat lazily on the fountain. She had a cutting board on her lap and was actively working to prepare a new cocktail as she watched SoulDemon. "Now that you've encountered my pop-up bar, there really is no other option for you until closing time."

"What is with this cursed dungeon?" SoulDemon muttered. "None of this makes sense. None of this is logical, or rational, or right." He was throwing a tantrum like a child. "This isn't how the game is supposed to work."

The Green Demon honked again. The head on the right, which was wearing a melon as a helmet, opened its mouth. A ray of green and purple light blasted from it, and SoulDemon barely activated a skill in time to avoid the blast. The head honked in confusion and looked to the middle head.

That head honked, and then the head on the far left opened its mouth. This head shot forth an orange blast of light. On impact, instead of exploding in a violent blast, it caused a shower of orange liquid to begin raining all around. The ground sizzled, and the creature's heads all honked in approval.

SoulDemon's defensive skill flickered off, he reappeared in his spot, and immediately dashed out of the raining, caustic liquid, bitching up a storm the whole way.

"This cannot be happening to me," he growled, his eyes blazing. He had switched modes. Like the cornered beast he was, he was going on the offensive. "Why can nothing ever go right in this dungeon?"

He disappeared in a flash, and his teleportation skill worked properly this time as he wasn't attempting to flee a boss fight. His form reappeared behind the Green Demon, and his blades crossed in an 'X' pattern on the middle head.

Liquor—James was pretty sure it was liquor—sprayed from the wound. He saw the Hangover debuff toggle on SoulDemon as the Green Demon honked its displeasure. All the while, Elliot continued to make another cocktail. James knew that until SoulDemon defeated the Green Demon, he wouldn't even be able to target Elliot.

Meaning at the very least that her first actual mob of the fight from an ability and not her Unique passive would likely be summoned without interruption. Even if SoulDemon could go toe to toe against the Green Demon, James had to wonder how soon before he fell against an onslaught of additionally summoned mobs.

"Blast this infernal dungeon," SoulDemon roared, his voice filled with frustration.

He became a blur as he burned through another cooldown and triggered his Devilkin form. The last bit made James pause to question what he was seeing. Hadn't SoulDemon used it once before? Was the cooldown for his racial ability shortened by him hitting level 100? Or did he get an additional use of it?

Or perhaps it was possible he could toggle it for a certain amount of time as a whole now before it went onto cooldown properly. Say, one minute of total time in the form before it would go on cooldown for the ten minutes or so? Considering SoulDemon was the only level 100 player he knew of, no one had mentioned any information on such a thing on the forums. And James figured that SoulDemon wasn't going to spill the secrets.

Rifts opened all around the Green Demon, its large form causing it difficulty as SoulDemon rapidly danced around it. With his ability to fly from his Devilkin form, along with the increased attack speed, life drain, and his other skills and abilities, he was blur. He moved so quickly that to any onlooker, it would appear as if more than a single player was striking the Green Demon, and James had to admit, he was impressed.

The skills SoulDemon portrayed, his ability to control his rapid movements to land precise strikes, even while suffering from a debuff that decreased his accuracy, was nothing short of legendary. And as more and more liquor fell from the various wounds on the Green Demon, it was clear that, for the moment, SoulDemon had the upper hand.

Unfortunately for SoulDemon, he wasn't fighting just the Green Demon. If he was, then level 105 player might actually bring down the level 120 creature, a feat that would have been the stuff of legends online. But the sound of ice and liquor shaking told James that the end was coming soon for SoulDemon.

SoulDemon was battling against time, and thirty seconds really wasn't much of a window. With fifteen levels and the Green Demon likely having the stats and health pool of a Unique monster if not a Mini-Boss, Soul-Demon just couldn't burn it down fast enough.

As his flurry of attacks continued, the Green Demon honked loudly and its skin glowed. The wounds that had been freely spilling liquor all around it began to stich as armor sprouted around its body. Another honk, and all three heads opened their mouths wide, unleashing a barrage of attacks in an effort to hit or at least slow the pest that was attacking them.

SoulDemon's concentration was clear on his face, along with a mask of rage, as he attacked the creature. It was impressive to see him dodge all the attacks, from the blasts of purple to the caustic orange rain. Add in the middle head's attack of a strange white energy that created a slick surface wherever it landed, and it was nothing short of a miracle that SoulDemon hadn't been hit yet. Still, hyper-focused as he was, he had no way of preparing for what was to come.

Elliot opened her cocktail shaker and pointed it directly toward the initially summoned cocktail monster and SoulDemon. From it, a blur of milky white, looking like some strange, amorphous blob, flew towards SoulDemon. It wrapped around him, and as it did, it glowed brightly.

James read its title the moment it appeared, and he knew then and there, that the battle was over.

Kamikaze Shot
Level 120

The light around the blob encompassed the whole room, glowing like a brilliant sun before it exploded. Unlike with the LMFAO Shots, Soul-Demon had no chance of escape. Caught between a Green Demon and a Kamikaze Shot, and trapped by the boss's mechanic that kept him from fleeing, he was forced to face-tank the explosion.

His DPS skills were grand, but he was still a squishy DPS player at heart when he did get it. As the light faded, and they could once again see the battlefield, all that remained of the haughty, arrogant, terrifying top player from the Candy Dungeon was a glowing death orb.

"Well," Rue said, as the carnage cleared and the Green Demon fell apart into a puddle of liquor on the ground. "Can't say he didn't go out without a bang."

James looked at her, groaning slightly, and shook his head. "I think that's enough for now," he said, noting that SoulDemon's death orb had disappeared. Without a party, his death was treated as a party wipe, meaning he'd suffer the full dungeon penalty, and be locked out of the seventh floor for a good bit of time.

"Same." Rue looked at her rapidly flashing string of messages from the Dungeon Cores that had been watching. "Glad to see that our potential last stream was a hit, though." She smiled at James, sorrow in her eyes. "I'm going to miss this."

James felt a lump in his chest as he nodded. Their time was quickly coming to an end.

"Me too," he choked out as the instance closed now that there were no players remaining, the others that had come with SoulDemon having either left or wiped when they had tried to respawn. "Me too, Rue."

Chapter Seventy-Three

The end, as with most things, came too quickly. Before he knew it, James found himself sitting in Rue's tent, at a table with Steve, Fel, Rachel, and Matthew, and Rue. Everyone wore grim expressions, and somehow, even though this was immersion, the air felt thick with the weight of what they were preparing to do.

"Does anyone need any refreshers on the plan?" Steve asked as he stood at the head of the table. He looked first at Rachel and Matthew. "Everything good on your end?"

"We weren't able to find a way to stop the implementation of the government's plan," Matthew said. "It's all out of our hands. If there's one thing about our dad that we all knew to be true, it's that he was good at what he did. There's no backdoor that we could gain access to."

"Not even with Steve's help?" James asked, looking at the developer in question. Steve had done just that when he had gotten into DCO behind Xander's back after being removed from the team prior to the game's launch.

"I'm good," Steve said, "but I'm not a miracle worker. Only reason I was able to weasel my way in before was on account of having physical access to the server shortly before I was let go. And that access point was a one-time thing. Plus, all it did was let me in. I didn't get my full access back until after Xander was removed and Rachel and Matt got me my privileges reinstated."

"There's a good chance dad had you in mind when he was putting all of his additional security in place," Rachel conceded. "His paranoia, stemming from just how skilled you are, likely made this harder on all of us."

Steve shrugged sheepishly. "Not my fault I'm a god at what I do."

"You just—" James started, but Steve held up a hand, grinning.

"Now now, more important things to discuss." Steve looked back at the duo that made up BLANK. "That aside, everything is set up on your end for the Dungeon Wars?"

"Even without our nudging"—Rachel looked at James—"the Candy Dungeon players were practically salivating at the chance to get revenge on the Random Dungeon. Probably doesn't help that the top player in our dungeon has declared a literal crusade against the Random Dungeon. He's offered a bounty, you know, on anyone that can kill and grief your top players."

"Oh, make sure you let Z know he's got a fan," Fel piped up. "He'll love that. And it's going to be extremely funny watching SoulDemon go try-hard mode against players that aren't even immersed."

"We saw his latest downfall in your dungeon," Matthew added, looking back to James. "Nicely done."

"I had no idea it would end that way," James offered. "And it was Rue's idea, not mine."

James grabbed Rue's hand with a smile. Rachel looked at their entwined fingers, and for a moment, a slight frown crossed her face.

"I do wish we could game together properly some more," Rachel said with a sigh. "When all of this is said and done, we need to get some game nights going. If I remember correctly"—she flashed James a smile—"your current record against me isn't the greatest."

"I'm always up for a challenge," James replied. "When this is all said and done, just name the game, time, and place, and I'll be there."

"Deal."

"Planning dates for later is all fine and dandy." Fel leaned back, winking as she did toward Rachel. "But first we all have to succeed before any of that future stuff can come to pass." She turned her focus on James. "We're all counting on you. You know that, right?"

James felt the weight intensify on his shoulders, as his smile, his moment of humor and happiness mellowed out. He didn't even have time to process fully what she'd mentioned before that. Had she said date? Whatever.

"We'll succeed," James said forcefully, as if trying to convince not just the others but himself. "There's no other option."

Well, not an option that anyone had actually ever told him about. Just a vague 'contingency'. James didn't like how ominous they got whenever it was even hinted at.

Fel tilted her head, eyeing Steve. Steve shook his head, and she looked back at James, something unspoken having passed between the two.

"I hope so," she said softly, "for your sake. For all our sakes."

"Once you log out," Steve began, drawing everyone's attention back to him as he spoke to James, "make sure Dagger downloads the packet of data that I've encrypted into your pod. It has the AI personalities you requested. From there—"

"—I'll take them to the terminal in my parents' lab and activate the robots," James finished.

"During the time it takes to upload the AI and run the diagnostics on the robotic bodies and for everything to settle in, the Knights will be grouping up and gathering what they need. After that, they'll be at your house to pick up you and your little gang before you make your way to the mountain."

"It's about a thirty-minute drive straight from your house to the mountain entrance," Fel said. "Hades will keep the cameras and surveillance from giving you away. It's up to Z's group and you to ensure that any other obstacles are dealt with in a way that won't jeopardize the mission."

She pointed at James. "That means don't bring any unsecure tech. You don't get to wear the glasses that you're so proud of. Even with Dagger's capabilities, it's not worth the risk of sending us messages. Especially since any such attempts could potentially trip alarms that we don't know are in place. And unlike with your dad, none of us has any means to receive an encrypted message in the way that he used previously in the workshop via quantum encryption."

"But how will I be able to contact you guys?" James asked, feeling panic rising in his chest. His AR glasses were his lifeline. He could communicate with everyone through them. More importantly, he could communicate with Rue through them.

"You won't," Fel said with a shrug. "Once this mission begins, you and the others need to be as dark as possible. Take that as more motivation to be successful." Her tone was harsh, but her eyes held a look of understanding. "Use the need to come back to us"—she nodded to Rue—"to come back to her to further push you forward. Your goal isn't just to save the world," she said softly, "it's to get back to the one you love."

The room went silent as everyone looked around the table. That was it, really. There wasn't anything left to say. They'd done all the preparation they could. All that remained, everything from here on out would be on James's shoulders. It was up to him and the Knights Who Go Ni to save the world.

No, that wasn't all. He squeezed Rue's hand tighter, smiling at her as he steadied himself. There were four more people that would be joining him on this adventure.

It was time to introduce the government to the Jenkins family.

Chapter Seventy-Four

James opened his eyes, tears wetting his skin as the immersion gel drained from the pod. He thought he'd prepared himself for this. He'd said his goodbyes, he'd done all he could, and yet leaving immersion, possibly for the final time, hit him harder than a Dicken to the gut.

As the glass slid open and he exited the pod, he let the tears fall. Sorrow was allowed. If anything, it would fuel his resolve.

"Dagger," he spoke to the robot, his voice cracking, "there's a data package that you need to download from my pod."

"At once." The dog wagged its tail and moved over to the immersion pod. It nosed around to the data port on the pod, and then stuck its tongue out, a scanner appearing as the data transfer began.

Even with the progression of technology and the impressive download speeds, James knew it would take at least a few minutes to handle the load of data that he was asking Dagger to receive: four complex artificial intelligence entities.

"Might as well get a drink while I wait," he said to no one. "Once you're done, we're heading to my parents' lab," James added to Dagger as he left the room, heading to the kitchen.

He opened the fridge and quickly pulled out a FitSip. The caffeinated beverage was exactly what he needed right now. Without much thought, he popped it open, the sound of carbonation fizzing and the cracking of the can unusually loud in his silent house. The drink, a rich fruit punch flavor, was cold against his lips, its sweetness washing across his tongue as he drank it. He didn't have much time, and before he knew it, he'd downed the entire can.

It sat cold in his gut, the carbonation making him let out a fruity burp as the butterflies in his stomach danced. Instinctively, his eyes darted upwards, but he saw nothing. He didn't have on his AR glasses, meaning he couldn't check for messages from Rue.

Another pang of sorrow filled him, and with some effort he pushed it aside. "Stick to the plan," he muttered to himself as he left the kitchen and headed towards the door that led to his parents' lab.

He needed to get the robots up and running. And while he was doing this, Z and the others would be gathering. Once everything was ready, Z was going to come get him, and then together, they'd assault the government facility.

"I've successfully downloaded the data," Dagger said as he padded dutifully out of James's room.

His tail wagged in a very dog-like manner as he neared the door to the office. Without prompting, Dagger opened the door. Something James could now do himself, but he didn't mind the fact that Dagger had done it for him.

He was still waiting for the caffeine to kick in from his FitSip to wash away the mental fog clouding his mind. It wasn't actual exhaustion, he knew, but a combination of stress, panic, fear, and sorrow that bogged down his thoughts and made his mind feel like it was elsewhere. Which it was. His mind, just like his heart, was back in immersion with Rue.

"Let's get to it then." James walked into the room, and now that he knew what to expect, had no problem sitting in the lone chair.

As he leaned his head against the cushioned neck rest, he mentally commanded the chair to transport them to the laboratory. A warm sensation on his neck, along with the message that appeared 'on the screen', confirmed his request had been received. A moment later, they were descending downward to the lab.

After a few minutes, the world stopped moving, and he knew they'd arrived. A message appeared in his vision.

Standing by for Intent

He sighed, and thought, hopefully for the last time, his parents' terrible passphrase. The system accepted his request, and he quickly got out of the chair, making a beeline to the still opening entrance to their special room. He didn't know how much time he had exactly before Z arrived.

And more than that, he didn't know how long it would take for the AI to calibrate within the robotic bodies. Nor how long the initial diagnostics tests would take on the robotic frames. His dad had assured him that it wouldn't take long, but James knew that every second counted.

Half walking, half dashing, James quickly made for the terminal in the center of the room. With Dagger at his side, he approached the machine and grabbed a metal clasp that sat atop it. The clasp, looking like some strange half-collar, James placed against the back of his neck. It warmed at the base of his skull, and then the terminal whirled to life.

He saw various screens appear in his vision as the room itself brightened, and lights began blinking and flashing all around. Spotlights further highlighted the various finished projects in the room, and James looked down at Dagger.

"Let's do this," he said to his robotic companion as he mentally directed the terminal to prepare for an upload sequence. More words flashed across his vision, and he quickly dismissed most of the prompts, just as his dad had informed him.

With the system linked directly to his mind, James navigated the system swiftly, almost as if he were back in his dungeon within immersion. The terminal before him let out a series of pleasant sounds and a panel opened. Dagger, taking that as his cue, walked up to it and extended his tongue, just as he had at James's pod.

Then another message appeared in James's vision as the data uplink began.

Transferring data…
Identifying unique packages…
Uploading unique data sets 1 of 6
Progress 1 of 100%
Estimated time to completion: 27 seconds

James blinked as the numbers flashed rapidly, the upload transfer working at breakneck speed. Six? There shouldn't be six unique data sets, only four. He'd specifically asked Steve to only get the Jenkins family for this as their humanoid forms would make them most suited for the human-shaped robots his parents had built.

"Ah." James snapped his fingers in the air as a solution came to his mind. There was another humanoid AI that was extremely intelligent within his dungeon—the Warmonger that he'd unlocked for Dungeon Skirmishes. Technically, he was a bear not a human, but he was bipedal and close enough.

He sighed, figuring Steve had taken it upon himself to use Vinnie the Cybear for this as well. Ah well, even if it meant dealing with terrible bear puns, James wasn't going to complain. They didn't know what to expect at the government facility, so an extra robot or two could be the difference between success and failure.

"Guess I'll just have to… grin and bear it," James said, his terrible joke falling, thankfully, on deaf ears. He groaned the moment he said it, feeling the cringe. "Damnit, Steve," he cursed aloud, shaking his head as he waited impatiently for the data transfer.

His mind worked past the poor bear pun as he tried to figure out who else Steve had sent along. The four Jenkins family members, Vinnie, and who else? Not that James was upset about the extra fire power… but at the same time, now wasn't the time for surprises. Another reason he'd limited it to just the Jenkins family members had been to minimize any extra risks. The smaller the group attacking the government facility, the less chances for some sort of error to lead to their discovery.

James let out an agitated sigh as his nerves threatened to overwhelm him. If they were successful, James was going to have a nice, long talk with the developer.

James blinked as a message appeared. One transfer down, five more to go. The first robot to receive its data began to whirl to life as the system began its own unique diagnostic check. It was almost time.

Chapter Seventy-Five

"Absolutely not," James's voice broke as he shook his head, looking into the robot's glowing eyes.

The robot in question, the fifth one to complete its calibration and come fully online, was looking down at him, its seven-foot frame cold, yet its eyes filled with life.

"It's too dangerous," I added.

"If you're going, I'm going," the robot responded, its tone and voice all too familiar.

James growled and flung a clipboard across the room. It clattered harmlessly in a corner while the other four robots, all over seven-feet tall, watched the display. At his side, Dagger remained quiet.

"I can't believe Steve did this to me," James growled, he spun and looked at the robot that was the cause of his distress. "I can't believe you did this to me."

"Did you really think I'd pass up the opportunity to help?" the robot, no, Rue, said. "I saw a chance, and I took it."

"But if something happens"—James looked at her, pleading—"if that body is damaged, you, your mind, you could die."

"I would rather die fighting alongside you to save the world," she said softly, bitterly, "than sit safe, forever in immortal torment in immersion. If something happens to you, and I'm not there"— she shook her robotic head—"I wouldn't forgive myself. Death would be welcome to that fate."

James wanted to protest more. He really did. But he couldn't find a good argument. She was right. There was a very real chance that James didn't survive the night. And if he didn't, Rue would have to exist forever, safe as she was in immersion, without him. If he were in her shoes, that wouldn't be a life worth living.

"Besides," Rue said, the robotic face one that looked like a cross between a mannequin and one of those battle robots from Japanese Anime, smiled in a strangely human way, "I brought protection just in case." She pointed towards the other robot that had been a surprise.

It wasn't Vinnie like James had thought it would be.

"Quite right, old chap," the chipper, proper tone of the Terminus, Sir Rexus, said. The robot even reached a hand up, as if tipping a top hat in his direction as it bowed. "I'll make sure that Lady Rue survives the night. Mark my word. No harm shall come to her as long as I live and breathe."

James groaned. "You can't just go inviting yourself on a dangerous mission, and then bring along your Magic the Gathering bestie as your bodyguard."

Still, when it came to his AI, James much preferred Rexus to Vinnie. And thanks to the Like a Sir perk, the AI that ran the Terminus was brilliant. Probably even smarter than the Jenkins family AI.

"I can and I will," Rue said haughtily, crossing her massive robot arms as she did. It would have been cute if she wasn't at the moment a walking death machine. "Besides, if anyone shouldn't be going out tonight"—she looked pointedly down at him—"it's you."

"I—" James opened his mouth and closed it.

She had a point. Rue's consciousness, her whole being was vulnerable, yes… But only as vulnerable as a seven-foot-tall machine made by the world's best robotics experts could be. James, on the other hand, was flesh and bone. And if his encounter with Dwight's fist a week ago had taught him anything, it was just how frail the human body could be.

Granted, it wasn't like he wasn't going to be surrounded by a small army of robotic guardians. Plus, he had Dagger at his side, and his dad had informed him of just what exactly his dog companion was capable of. Add onto that the unique body armor he'd grabbed in the workshop that looked like a strange metallic vest, and he felt he was pretty well protected.

"But I'm not going to stop you," Rue continued, seeing she was winning this conversation, and not relenting. "This is important. And so I want us to do this together. Succeed or fail, as long as we are at each other's sides… that's all I care about."

"You can bet I'm going to have words for Steve when all this is done,"

James said before he let out a heavy sigh. "But fine. You've made your points, and you're right. Besides, we don't have time to waste arguing. And I know for a fact that once you've made up your mind, there's nothing I can do to change it."

He shot a side eye towards the now-humanoid Terminus. The robot smiled at him, and in his mind's eye, it was the sharp, toothy grin that the second-floor boss gave players on a daily basis.

"About time you learned that lesson," Rue said, pulling his attention back towards her. James was pretty sure that if she wasn't in a robotic body, she would have stuck her tongue out at him. "Now let's get going. I cannot wait to see the expression on Z and the other's faces when they find out Rexy and I are here"

"Just promise me you won't do anything too reckless," James said as he and Rue left the special projects room with the Terminus. The other four robots, the ones he had actually planned on bringing on this mission, followed quickly on their heels.

The robots all looked similar to Rue's in that they seemed a mixture of anime-inspired mecha with hyper realistic humanoid portions. Each of the robots had an array of weapons and capabilities at their disposal, making each and every one of them extremely capable.

The largest of them had the ability to project special electromagnetic shields in a decently sized radius. Another could disrupt other electronics and had various utility options. The other three were more combat focused, with guns, projectiles, and other spiffy tools at their disposal.

And true to his father's style, all of the robots were armed with a melee weapon as well. Because why wouldn't a robot made of pure metal need a melee weapon… as if its fists and mechanical might alone wouldn't suffice.

"I promise I won't do anything more reckless than what you're doing," Rue countered, her heavy footsteps echoing on the floor as she followed after him.

James glanced at the robot, and immediately noticed the attitude with which she walked. Even if he hadn't heard it talk, everything about the way she moved the robotic body and held it told him who it was.

Another testament to the skill of his parents. The ability for machines to display the nuanced aspects of individuals. He wasn't sure how much his parents had been paid by the government for their work, but he was pretty sure from seeing it in person that it probably wasn't enough.

Everyone made it onto the platform proper without any issue. Other than Rue and the Terminus, the other robots inhabited by the Jenkins family had all remained silent. If James had to guess, they were using the time to mentally acclimatize themselves to their bodies in preparation of what was to come.

That or they figured what was going on between James and Rue was personal and had opted to remain as silent as possible. Doing a quick triple check in his mind, and feeling he'd gotten everything of use he could from the workshop, James got into the chair. With a deep breath, he leaned his head back and prompted the system to begin their ascent.

He'd already filled in the Jenkins family on the plan before their data had been extracted by Steve. All four had agreed happily to help. Even though it technically meant a threat to their existence, the opportunity to leave the world of DCO and experience the real world had sparked more than a bit of excitement in the intelligent computer creations.

Past that, the versions that were uploaded to the robots had been quite excited at the prospect. If DCO was brought down, the AI were quite eager to have the chance to experience the real world through the robotic bodies. To be freed of their digital confines and the restrictions placed on them by the system and the programmers had been all the prompting they'd needed to agree to the plan.

Between that and some strange philosophies over individuality and sense of self when something was a part of a constantly replicating mass consciousness that was the AI systems that ran the multiple instances of the bosses all active at the same time, the AI had agreed to his plan.

James tried not to think about it too much. It hurt his head more than the run-on sentence that had been the description they'd offered to him of their justification. He was just happy to have willing, intelligent allies for this endeavor. And he figured there was a bit of ironic justice in using AI from DCO to bring the game server down and thwart the government. If it succeeded, it would make for a good story later on down the road.

He also tried not to consider it some strange 'rise of the machines' type outcome... where AI was freed from the confines of the computer and went on a massacre of the human race afterwards. James could only handle one Science Fiction threat at time.

The platform finished spinning as it completed its ascent and locked into place. Without his AR glasses, James didn't know how long the whole process of booting up the robots had taken, but as he exited the chair, the answer came to him unbidden. A thudding sound echoed into the room from outside, the sound of a fist banging against a door.

Z was waiting for him, and it was time.

"Remember, everyone," James said as he hurried out of the room. "No matter what happens, we need to shut down the DCO server."

"We will succeed," one of the robots said, and James recognized Sergeant Jenkins' voice. "Or we will die trying."

James's step faltered at that statement, and he shot a glance back at Rue's robot. The Terminus robot was standing beside her, taking his bodyguard role seriously.

"Preferably without the dying part," James said, more to himself and Rue than anyone else. He reached the door before anything else could be said, and with one last breath to steady himself, opened it.

It was time.

Chapter Seventy-Six

The vans that Faust—well, Frank... no, James preferred Faust—had procured from his government-funded place of employment looked like nondescript delivery trucks. There were no distinguishing features on the sides of the vehicles, and the backs opened outwards like some ancient, armored bank vehicle.

They quickly discovered with the weight of the robots that they needed to split the parties in the two vans. The lead van, driven by Faust, had three Jenkins family robots as well as Med Ic. The van James was in, driven by Z, had the rest of the party.

They drove in silence through the night, and from his spot in the back of the van, James was unable to look out at the world around them. He could imagine, as they were driving, the empty, dark streets they would be passing. Normally patrolled by security robots, these systems would either be shut down or would ignore them. Hades had promised as much.

James wasn't certain how the mysterious hacker would deal with the normal mechanical security systems but trusted the man on his word that they wouldn't be hindered on their way to the government base within the mountain.

It was clear when they left the city, as the van's speed picked up; at the same time, the road conditions worsened. The obvious change in road conditions meant they'd left the bubble of the city, moving from developed, pristine paradise to the rundown outskirts, and past that was

320

wilderness that existed in a stretch between the mountain base and the city.

James could imagine the derelict buildings and crumbling structures reclaimed by nature as they drove through areas that were deemed by the government as inhospitable and outside the protection of the special climate-controlled areas.

James had no doubt that it would be just like the area Hades had led him to in order to meet with him. They were areas that had been deemed excessive and unnecessary by the government. The people had been forced out of such sprawling spaces in order to come together into communities that could exist within the little bubbles of influence, special habitation zones that were turned into perfect paradises thanks to special-ized terraforming relays within the center of each zone.

James licked his lips, which were suddenly dry, as they bumped along. He could feel the van tilting, inclining as it ascended the mountain paths. He had to wonder if Faust had actually been to the secret base before. His job as a driver for the Enforcers implied that he had an extremely high security clearance, and James wondered just how deep into the govern-ment the man had roamed.

Panic flared irrationally for a moment as he wondered if they could trust Faust. But he pushed that thought down almost immediately. Z trusted Faust, and if Z trusted him, after all the man had been through, then there was no doubt in James's mind that Faust could be trusted.

More traveling, and James lost himself to thought. He replayed every-thing that had led up to this moment, questioning if he could have done things differently, if anything could have changed this outcome. He was so deep in his thoughts that he didn't realize they'd stopped until a cold metallic hand grabbed his. The touch was surprisingly gentle and human.

He jumped and looked at Rue, who held a finger up to her robotic mouth. He nodded, knowing she meant for him to be quiet, and he waited, his heart in his throat. After a moment that seemed to stretch on for an eternity, they were moving once more.

James cocked a head at Elm, the man who was also a teacher at his school, but Elm just shrugged. They were radio silent, and from the back of the vans, they had no idea what was going on outside. All they could do was put their trust in Faust and Z. Those two were the only ones who could see the outside, and who knew where they were on their journey up the mountain.

"Likely a guard station," Rue whispered after a few more moments of them driving along. "There are supposed to be four on our way to the base entrance."

"Could be," James said, realizing that had to have been it. Did the stop mean the station had been manned, then? Weren't they supposed to be automated? In which case, Hades was supposed to have dealt with them. If they were manned, did that complicate things?

"Whatever it was," Med Ic offered, his voice hushed as well, "we got through it. Meaning, three more to go before it's game time."

Technically, they probably didn't need to be whispering. However, the enormity of their task had settled on everyone's shoulders, and it seemed to encourage the quiet, barely audible way of speaking.

Med Ic's fingers were held tightly to the weapon in his hands. It was a special weapon used by Enforcers—an energy rifle that fired concussive bursts of plasma. The weapon could be toggled into a long-range mode, which fired metal rounds utilizing magnetic rails built into the weapon, and the whole thing was powered by an extremely potent battery. Most importantly, it came with a smart targeting system that linked into the helmets that Enforcers used. The exact same type of helmet sat at Med Ic's feet.

Faust hadn't just procured the vans for this effort. He'd loaded them up with Enforcer suits and weapons for each of his teammates. The only person he'd not acquired such a thing for was James. A fact that had James feeling somewhat left out. Then again, James had his own weapons and own means of protection.

His hand found Dagger's furred head, and he rubbed it, reassuring himself. He wasn't defenseless. Dagger had been designed specifically to keep him safe. And he would put his faith in his robot companion and the capabilities his parents had built into it over the Enforcer battle suit any day.

Between that and the specialized vest that had various weapons and defenses built into it, all controlled by the nanites hidden at the base of his skull, James was anything but helpless. Even if he, compared to everyone else, looked like the easiest target.

Though, as he looked Med Ic up and down once more, he had to admit that he was kind of jealous. The Enforcer gear was extremely cool. And he'd be lying if he claimed there wasn't a part of him, the part that played FPS games, that didn't wish he could use the suit and weapons of an Enforcer at least once.

Still, he knew there was one other reason why the Knights had gotten Enforcer gear and weapons, and James hadn't. They were ready and willing to take a human life if needed for this mission. James was not. And they had all decided, he knew, that they would do all they could to prevent him from being in a situation where anyone's blood ended up on his hands. Even now, with the world at stake, the Knights Who Go Ni, Z and the others, were doing all they could to keep him safe.

He rubbed Dagger's head harder as he steeled himself. Warmth at the base of his skull caused his scalp to tingle as he mentally toggled through options, his own special contingencies. They would get through this night. All of them. He swore it.

Chapter Seventy-Seven

Three checkpoints later and James was standing with the others outside in the crisp, cool night air. The world was dark, save for a bit of light granted to them by the quarter moon above.

James couldn't tell the Knight's apart as they'd all donned their helmets and looked every bit the government death troopers that Enforcers were known to be. Of the five, three seemed to hold themselves a bit more confidently, the weapons held in a more familiar fashion. One of those, James knew, had to be Z given his history as a Marine.

"Your position is in the rear," that figure said, and it was Z's voice. "You'll be safest there, James."

He noticed then that there was another defining feature to Z. He wore something on his back, a dark lump that James couldn't quite distinguish given the low light. Was it the bag Fel had given him?

"The Jenkins family will lead the assault into the base," Z continued, motioning towards the four robots.

Weapons of different varieties were drawn by the metallic figures. Two held sword-like weapons in their hands, while small turrets had appeared on their shoulders, capable of firing small metallic rounds with deadly speed and accuracy.

James shivered as he recalled some of the more nefarious weapon systems his parents had built into their robots. The most terrifying was the implementation of nanobot weaponry. Highly effective at incapacitating humans, the weapons fired rounds that contained nanobots.

Upon impact with a human, the tiny robots would enter the blood-stream, and depending on their coding, would either incapacitate or kill the human. He hadn't had time to process the fact that his parents had put such weaponry in their robots, but he knew he also wouldn't hold it against them. They'd created the robots with the express purpose of fighting the government. And to take down monsters, you had to do monstrous things at times.

"The others and I will follow the Jenkins family. Dagger, Rue, and Sir Rexus"—Z looked from the dog to Rue's robotic self and then her body-guard—"will stay in the back with James. Your role is to keep each other safe. If shit hits the fan, leave us and continue the mission. If anyone has to give their life for this mission, it's the AI." He looked at those five. "No offense."

"None taken," one of them said, Elliot by the voice of it.

"Or someone who has actually lived life. Meaning"—Z motioned at himself and the others in his group—"we're willing to sacrifice ourselves to ensure you"—he pointed to James and then Rue—"live. Remember that. The last thing we need is kids trying to be heroes."

"Don't have to tell us twice," Rue said, offering Z a salute. It would have been comical in any other situation. "But how about we all plan to survive the night. True victory will come from all of us leaving tonight alive and well. After all, there are still plenty of games and adventures we all need to have together."

"The lady is quite right, ol' chap," the Terminus added. "No need to damper the mood with doom and gloom. The first step towards victory, I do say, is the right mindset."

Z chuckled at the Terminus' unique way of speaking. "You're right. And I agree, everyone surviving is definitely the ideal path." Z's voice went soft. "But I've sadly learned that life rarely lets the idealist's dreams become reality."

"Never too late for the universe to throw us a bone, though," Med Ic said with a dark chuckle. "Considering it refused to ever give me the winning Powerball numbers."

The five humans clad in Enforcer armor all shared a laugh, and James found himself smiling.

"Right, no time like the present." Z turned away from James and pointed to the dark tunnel that looked like a void in the side of the mountain. "Our destination is in there. The moment we enter that tunnel, no speaking unless absolutely necessary. We go in quickly, find the server, and shut it down. Nothing more, nothing less. Treat anything we come across as hostile but if possible use nonlethal force. Any questions?"

James said nothing. Rue and the Terminus were on his right, Dagger on his left. Everyone was tense, and for a moment, the world itself seemed to hold its breath. This was it. The last moment before the plunge. The instant before the final act was set into motion. The split-second pause before they would pass the spot of no return.

"Right then," Z said after no one spoke up. He looked at the Jenkins family members, and then his own teammates. "Considering who we have here, and the task at hand..." There was a bit of mirth in his voice, a lead up of sorts. "How about we do this in proper style?"

The Knights Who Go Ni all nodded towards him, as if they'd come to some unspoken conclusion. Then they turned towards the entrance, and Z raised a hand in the air.

"Leeeeerrooooooooyyyyy," he whispered, and his teammates all echoed his chant. Then Z made a strange chopping motion towards the mountain entrance, a military hand signal for everyone to move forward. "Jennnkkii-innnnnsssss."

And with that, the assault on the government secret base began.

Chapter Seventy-Eight

No plan survives first contact. James had heard that saying before somewhere. He couldn't quite remember where, but the words rang out in his mind as they hurried through the rapidly closing metal doors. Two of the Jenkins robots were trying unsuccessfully to keep the doors from closing as everyone rushed through.

Meanwhile, the other two were unleashing shots into the darkness behind James and everyone else. Their prey were mechanical, many limbed monstrosities that crawled towards them rapidly, their unnatural number of legs tap-tap-tapping on the stone. The sound echoed eerily all around as they sought to stop the intruders.

"I thought Hades would have these shut down," James said in a gasp as Rexus dropped him onto the ground.

With James inside, the four Jenkins family robots dipped in, and the door slammed shut. Blissfully, it meant that the spider-like contraptions couldn't get to them. But it also meant that they were trapped inside the government facility. And it was painfully clear that the security systems were not disabled. At least, not entirely.

"He said he would disable what he could," Z said, his voice tense. "But if I had to guess, a facility like this has enough measures in place that even a hacker of Hades's skill couldn't make it go completely dark. If he could have"—Z shrugged—"then there's a good chance we wouldn't have had to be here."

"Good point," James said, taking stock of the situation. "What now then?"

"Now it's a race," Z said as red lights flashed from the walls around them. A siren could be heard, and James had no doubt that it was signaling the other defensive forces of the intruders. "Stick close, and let's get going."

He pointed forward, and the robots took off two by two. The hallway itself was wide enough that, if needed, three of the robots could have walked side by side. However, it would have severely limited their ability to react quickly, and so they all raced forward, moving swiftly and noisily through the hallways.

The inside of the government facility was set up in a sprawling, maze-like manner. The walls, along which white lights flickered and red alarm lights flashed, were dug directly into the mountain rock, with nails and chain netting running up to stop rocks from falling on heads.

The ground they ran across was slightly slick as well, covered with moisture, and James was careful to watch his footing as they ran across the bare stone. Left, left, right, left, they ran through the hallways, taking turns at seemingly random intervals, though he knew they were following the map that had been given to them by Hades.

Another reason for why he wished he had his AR glasses. The robots had the maps, and he figured Z and the others with their Enforcer helmets probably had the digital map files as well. James though, without his glasses… well, he was mostly blind. Blind in a way you could only be when your HUD was robbed from you in a game, and you had to navigate based off memory and signs alone.

Unfortunately, in the real world, secret facilities didn't have convenient signs to point you in the direction you needed, nor were there logical bits coded in to force you in the direction you needed to go.

Once more, James felt useless in that moment, and yet he knew this was something he needed to be doing. He couldn't have everyone else risking their lives while he stayed safely at home. This was his task just as much as it was everyone else's. And Hades had given him direct instructions, and he had a pivotal role to play in this assault. It was just a matter of surviving to get to that point.

"Movement ahead," Dagger barked out, his sensors extended from his back. "Non-biological in nature."

The robots in the lead increased their pace, and from the back of the bulkiest one—Grandpa Jenkins if James remembered correctly—a massive shield generator whirled to life. The air shimmered around it as the buzzing of power filled the area, and the other three Jenkins family members drew their weapons.

As the group reached a crossing of pathways, James saw flashes of light and bursts of explosions. Z held up a fist, and his group slowed. As a result, James, Rue, the Terminus, and Dagger slowed as well.

They stood there, about thirty feet from the fighting as the battle played out. As quickly as the attacks had started, they stopped. The moment they'd entered the clearing, one of the robots had disappeared down the right hallway, the other the left, and they'd dispatched whatever the attackers were.

"All clear, dearies," Grandma Jenkin's said, motioning for the group to follow.

They stood and watched the other hallways as James's party approached, and then they were moving once again.

"Not that I ever doubted your parents' skill," Med Ic said to James, his position putting himself at the end of the line of robots and Enforcers before James, "but seriously, those robots are terrifyingly effective. At this rate—"

A loud explosion stopped him mid-sentence. Everyone stopped moving as smoke and fire filled the hallway. James felt a wave of heat rush past him, and his lungs burned as the air turned hot.

The back of his skull warmed as his panic triggered the chest piece he was wearing. It whirled to life, and a pulse of energy pushed out from the armor. The air cooled, his flesh unscathed as an invisible shield sprang to life around his form until the heat passed. James blinked away the tears that were filling his eyes as he tried to make sense of what had just happened.

The lead robot, Elliot, was down... her body twitching on the ground, back torn open, looking very much like a can that had been ripped in two. Beside the now pile of scrap metal, another of the robots, Sergeant Jenkins, was kneeling down, firing shots down the hallway, while the shield generators on Old Man Jenkin's back once again whirled to life.

At the very end of the hallway, in the obvious direction of the attack, James saw movement. Humans or advanced robots, he couldn't tell as it had to be a good hundred or so feet away. However, what he could tell was they had guns. Big, big guns.

"Take cover," Z called.

Before James knew what was happening, Med Ic had him by the shoulder and was pulling him down a side path. Rue and Dagger followed, with the Terminus trailing slightly to ensure that he could cover their retreat. A split second later, another explosion.

"Looks like our path is blocked," Z said as he looked at the group. "The security forces have brought out the big guns."

Another explosion, and stones rattled above. James glanced up as the lights flickered, worried that the very ceiling would collapse on them.

"We'll leave the main forces to the Jenkins," Z continued to speak, glancing back at the hallway. It was clear, as more explosions and various other sounds filled the hallway, that the robots on their side were putting up a fight.

The government forces had gotten lucky with that first shot. Probably because they'd been out of range of the proximity sensors on the robots, meaning they couldn't activate their defensive shields in time. But now, well, James had a lot of faith in his parents' creations. Now that they knew what they were up against, he doubted they'd fall.

"Keep pushing to the target," Z yelled towards the sound of the fighting. "And if you get there before us, feel free to destroy it. As for the rest of us..." Z looked at his group of friends. Even though his visor hid his eyes, James could feel his gaze linger on James. "We're going to take the scenic route."

Chapter Seventy-Nine

They moved quickly through more hallways, Z leading the way, definitely following some sort of digital map. Occasionally, the stone of the facility would shake, informing everyone that the robots were continuing their assault on the government forces.

James wasn't sure how many units the facility had at its disposal, but he had a feeling they'd need a lot to bring down the Jenkins family. Now that they were aware of the danger, and without James or the others to worry about, he figured the robots were going to have the time of their lives taking on the defenses.

Considering James and the others were out of the way, he had no doubt that the robots would win. They could unleash the full extent of their capabilities now without worrying about friendly fire.

Be that as it may, James knew it was only a matter of time before his group ran into additional obstacles. With the alarms tripped from the moment they'd entered the tunnel, the assault on the government facility was going poorly. Still, all they needed to do was get to the server room that held the DCO server. Shutting that down would ensure they were successful.

Without DCO online to trap everyone, the government's plan would crumble. The people would be freed, with full knowledge of what the government had planned. James and the others would win. The human race would win. And that's all that mattered.

Still, that assumed they reached their goal first. With every new twist and turn, every hallway they came across, his heartbeat quickened. Dagger worked hard to keep everyone informed of any potential dangers ahead, but as they'd seen, his sensors weren't perfect. They had a range limit, and the especially long hallways, combined with the dense rock that made up the facility, presented potential danger areas to them.

Without the Jenkins family to be the front-liners, it put them at a disadvantage as well. Enforcer armor was sturdy, but so was a robot. And James had seen what could happen to something that was on the receiving end of whatever that high-powered weapon had been.

If they got ambushed now, their small team would be at a disadvantage. Their only remaining robots were Rue, who wasn't supposed to be put in unnecessary danger, and the Terminus, whose whole purpose was keeping Rue and James safe.

"We're nearly there," Z said after what felt like a lifetime of running.

The explosions still echoed through the facility, but they'd slowed. Still, each one caused James to flinch, and he had to wonder what all was being thrown at them.

While he and the others had been taking the 'scenic route' as Z called it, they were getting further and further away from the explosions. Meaning his parents' robots were being slowed. They were fighting tooth and nail to gain ground and reach their destination, and the government was throwing their full force back at them.

"Nearly where?" a voice said, and it caused the group to pull up short.

James looked down at Dagger, but the dog shrugged. The sound had come from a speaker secured on the stone wall, and not from anyone actually nearby.

"Wouldn't you like to know," Z said to the voice, motioning for the group to continue but slowly.

"I would," the voice continued. "Though, it means little to me. After all, in a short amount of time, this little excursion of yours will be finished, and I'll be able to go back to sleep."

The voice yawned over the speakers, obviously bored. Or maybe tired? If James had to guess, whoever this was, it wasn't a normal security member. Perhaps one of the elites that was at the facility, preparing for the transference to immortality?

"Did we interrupt your nap?" Z's words were venom. "If you're that tired, I'd happily put you to sleep for good."

"Such a temper," the voice made a tsk sound. "Then again, the small minded always have short tempers. It's why your kind is better off trapped within a virtual world. Where you cannot be a pest to your superiors. All you *lesser* folk are is purely a drain on your betters."

Z stayed silent, not rising to the provocation as they continued on.

"Won't you tell me what you're even attempting?" the voice said, clearly irritated that Z had ignored him. "Before I kill you all, that is? Consider this my kindness to you before I release the extremely potent and very unpleasant gas that will make you squirm as you die slowly. Consider my kindness that I give you one last chance to speak, before all that is uttered from your throats are the chokes of you dying."

Whoever was behind that speaker was extremely unhinged, James decided.

"What makes you think you can kill us all?" Faust asked, looking at Dagger, who already had a variety of technological gadgets out of its body in various stages of whirring to life. "You're pretty confident for someone who doesn't even know why we're here."

"Those robots are difficult to deal with," the speaker said. "But humans... much simpler to kill. Very shortly, you'll find just how easy. Our counter-biological defenses are much more efficient. State-of-the-art even. Perhaps a tad illegal and inhumane, but"—James could practically hear the shrug in the tone—"that's only for those who have to follow the law. And gods, chosen beings such as myself," the voice was pompous as it spoke, "we make the laws for you, not ourselves."

The voice chuckled again, but the sound of his laughter was drowned out by an even darker sound. Z had stopped moving and was laughing in a manner that sent chills down James's spine.

"Has your impending death caused you to go mad?" the voice asked.

"I'm assuming then that you only have a method to kill us, and not stop us?" Z asked in response.

"No one who enters this facility is captured. The crime of breaching a secure facility is death. Now that you're here, that's the only future for you. I am judge, jury, and executioner. Honestly, I figured I'd been unlucky getting stuck with covering the guard station while we sent the normal group off to their eternal slumber. But now this has turned quite amusing."

"If you kill us," Z responded, deadly serious, "then executioner will be exactly what you are. But not just of me and my friends." Z tapped the bag on his back. "You'll take the entire facility with you." More chuckling from Z. "Which I assume would be a very unfortunate thing given the people who are currently residing within this facility. Considering you, yourself, it would seem," his tone was venom, "are one of those pompous rich fucks."

"What are you getting at?" the voice asked, but James could hear the hesitation in his voice.

"I saw the roster of VIPs taking shelter here," Z said, and James didn't like his tone at all. It wasn't the kind, collected, happy Z. This was a dark, bloodthirsty, vengeful Z. "I know just how important the lives are of those in this facility. How important everyone within here is to the future you are all chasing."

"And you would dare threaten us?" The amount of indignation in his tone made James imagine whoever was speaking was frothing at the mouth. "You, a mere leech on the government's teats?"

"Only if you kill me," Z said calmly. He pulled a gun from his belt and held it up to his head. "Or if you kill my friends. Do anything to stop us" —the safety clicked off of the weapon—"and I'll do it. And if I die, the Deadman switch will activate, and the Voice of Purgatory will be heard through these halls."

Everything went silent then. James's blood froze as realization dawned on him. That's what Fel had given him. The Voice of Purgatory, otherwise known as the VP, was a specialized weapon against which there was no defense. A weapon that would kill every human within this facility if Z were to die.

That was what he and Fel had planned. Hell, maybe even Hades. They had access to the weapon because Fel's organization had one in their possession. She'd had it on her person when protecting James against Cyb3ru5 in order to protect his parents' workshop.

And now Z had it. They'd known the lethality of the defenses at the facility. And with the information Hades had at his disposal, they'd known just how important the people in the facility would be. This was the trump card, a way to ensure that James and the others reached their goal. And Z, after everything the government had done to him, after all his suffering, was more than willing to put himself in that position.

Z wasn't bluffing. If they couldn't complete their mission. If their deaths were going to be guaranteed by the facility. Then Z was going to guarantee everyone within the facility, the top-ranking government officials on the continent, and many others who were here in order to preview and prepare for their robotic bodies, would die with them.

As long as Z had the bomb, he could ensure James and the others could leave the facility safely. Unless the government members at the facility could subdue Z without killing him, he held the upper hand. He held all the power.

"Checkmate," Z whispered, the words echoing with the weight of their meaning. He motioned for the others to move forward while he stood, watching the speaker from which the voice had been emitting.

"Any funny business," Z said cooly as the others and James began to slowly move past him, "and no one wins today."

Chapter Eighty

"Keep going," Med Ic said in a hushed whisper, pulling James towards the door that was to be their destination.

Z still stood in the hallway by the speaker in his standoff with whoever was running the defenses of the facility.

"What about Z?" James asked in a hushed whisper.

"He's safe," Med Ic responded. "With how close they are to the completion of their plan," he said hurriedly, "they won't do anything rash. They don't know why we're here, just that we're intruders. Even if they knew we were targeting the DCO servers, I doubt they'd risk Z's death. They're on the verge of godhood. Immortality. And when powerful people are on the precipice of greatness, of finalizing all of their goals... a threat against that will paralyze them. This is the moment of their greatest achievement, meaning they are at their most vulnerable as well."

"You knew then?" James whispered.

"I did," Med Ic said solemnly. "We all knew. Z talked it over with us, and we agreed it was the best course of action. With the inclusion of your parents' robots, we'd been hopeful we wouldn't have to mention it. Backup plans are, well, usually best left in the background. At the most, we had planned to use it to ensure that we could get you out of the facility safely after we'd completed the mission."

"Did you know about this?" James asked softly, looking at Rue.

Oak and Elm were working to open the door before them, using plasma cutters that were built into the gauntlets of the Enforcer armor to cut through the metal.

"No." Rue shook her robotic head, her tone sincere. Then she narrowed her gaze, looking back towards Z. "If I had, I wouldn't have let you come." She turned and looked back down at Med Ic. James could almost feel her anger. "Why was James allowed to come?"

James looked at Rue, and then Med Ic. He was somewhat curious to hear how Med Ic answered. James knew why he'd come. There was an additional reason for him being there. Shutting down the server to DCO was the main mission. But he had another task. One that Hades had tasked him with and him alone. One that he was uniquely designed for.

But it was a task no one else knew about. The only person that could activate the built-in kill switch to the automated robotics system in the government facility that was building and meant to maintain the immortal government bodies was James. His parents too, as their nanites could give them access as well. But they were trapped in their pods, leaving the task up to James. Stopping the DCO servers was the main goal, but shutting down the project completely was the ultimate win.

"Hades said it was necessary" Med Ic said after a long moment. "He said that if we trusted James completely, then we had to bring him with us. The last thing I want is to see him hurt, but if he has a job to do, well... there's no one else I'd trust more."

James felt a surge of pride but could see Rue's confusion. He had not shared his mission with her, as Hades had been very clear that no one could know. "I—" He looked at Rue, then back at Z, and then at the others.

Before he could speak, Med Ic's body suddenly went rigid. A moment later, he collapsed to the ground, screaming in pain.

Around James, the rest of the Knights all collapsed. Behind them, James heard Z's startled scream, and the clatter of metal hitting the ground. A shot rang out, and a high-pitched whizzing sound echoed from behind them. James felt his heartrate jump as suddenly their trump card seemed to have been thrown out the window.

"Your folly," the pompous voice from before said through the speaker, "was in assuming you could threaten someone such as myself, while wearing the armor of our government's dogs. Did you think we didn't have them collared? After all, did you think we'd let our guard animals run wild, without contingencies in case they tried to bite the hands that fed them?"

More laughter. "Now then, boy," the man said with venom, "surrender yourself, and I'll make sure your death is at least quick. Otherwise," the man chuckled again, "it's only a matter of time before our forces corner you. You've no way of escaping, and you're cut off from your friends. It's only a matter of time before you and your little pathetic force fails."

"We need to keep going," Rue whispered in a hurried voice.

She motioned towards the door, and James headed quickly towards it. He could hear all five of the Knights' cries of agony, and he could practically feel their pain. And yet James didn't have a way to stop it. All he knew was that they couldn't die. Because if they did, then they all died. That was the protection offered to them by the VP.

"Dagger," James whispered, "can you block the signal that's triggering the attack on the Knights?"

"Perhaps," the dog said, tilting its head this way and that. "But I cannot cover all five of them."

James glanced about. "Work to protect the four closest to us," he said after a moment. His heart bled for Z, wanted to keep him from the pain and suffering, but the other four were the closest. "Once you've saved them, you can all go save Z."

The man had been through hell and back, and James prayed this was the last bit of suffering the government ever inflicted on the poor man.

"As you wish." Dagger grabbed the thrashing Med Ic with a paw and carried him toward the others, who had all collapsed just before the door to the server room.

"Let's go." James moved towards the door, and the Terminus took point.

"Allow me, good sir," the Terminus said as he passed. "I wouldn't be much of a bodyguard if I let my charges enter a room before me. After all," he chuckled as he reached the door, "I shall guard you with this body of mine."

Instead of attempting to open the door, his foot pulled back and then kicked forward. The metal door buckled in the center before it blasted away from the doorway.

"Right then, I've announced our presence." He calmly walked into the room, grabbing one of the Knight's rifles with one hand as he held an axe in the other. "Allow me to handle any formal introductions for those who may be waiting within."

James shared a look with Rue before they rushed after the Terminus. They could still complete their mission. The servers to DCO were within this room, as well as the pods that provided access to the server, and the systems themselves. Pods that would be linked to the facility as a whole. Pods that he needed to get access to.

James took in the room as he and Rue entered it. In the center of it, humming with power, was what had to be the mainframe server for DCO. The server was close to the size of two cars stacked atop each other, the size necessary no doubt to house the amount of data it needed to run the game, as well as handle the stress of the sheer vastness of what its task required of it.

Beside it, as he'd been told, were two pods with cables leading from them to the server, as well as snaking across the room to other panels. Additionally in the area were various generators, all dormant for the moment, waiting in case the power supply for some reason cut off to the main server. Judging by the number of generators, James figured the auxiliary power in the room could ensure that the systems were powered for years.

"I'm going to—" Before James could say anything else, he realized that Rue wasn't standing beside him. He'd been so fixated on the DCO server and the immersion pods that he'd not realized that Rue had left his side.

He saw her standing in the corner of the room, in front of a row of additional immersion pods.

"It really is here," Rue said softly, likely to herself. However, the sound carried, and James could hear the words clearly. She moved, as if transfixed, towards a single pod, her robotic face looking down at it. James walked further into the room, nearing the DCO server as he watched her actions.

"He wasn't lying," Rue said with a sob as she dropped to her knees. Her hand touched the pod, and then she rested her robotic head atop it. More sobbing.

James's focus was torn between his mission and Rue. He needed to get into one of those immersion pods. Needed to shut DCO down and silence the facility.

"Rue," James said as he took a hesitant step closer to her and away from the server. "Rue, are you—"

A pressure against his neck caused him to freeze. He stopped moving as he felt something cold against his skin.

"About time you separated yourself from your metal friends," a cold voice said. "Didn't think they'd leave this place unguarded, did you?"

An Enforcer materialized behind James. Well, he didn't materialize. He'd been there the whole time, James realized.

With a start, James noticed that both of the immersion pods near the server were open… and now that he was close to them, he could see the impressions within showing just recently that they'd been occupied. The guards had been in the game. They'd been immersed, and then had been mobilized when they'd entered the room.

"James—" Rue whirled like a feral beast, her eyes blazing as she turned away from whatever was in the pod to look at James and the Enforcer behind him. Based on the feel of it, James figured that the man had a blade against his neck, while his other hand held James's wrist tightly.

"Young sir!" The Terminus' gun was pointed at the Enforcer but stopped short of firing as the knife drew a crimson line down James's skin.

It was all he could do to keep his mind and breathing calm.

"Now that it's obvious your robots are here at your beck and call," the Enforcer said cooly, "shut 'em down if you want to live. Else you'll find quite quickly that I've no qualms killing a kid."

James's eyes darted about. He mentally sent a thought to Dagger, the nanites on his neck warming as they sent the short burst signal through the vest he wore. Immediately, in his mind's eye, he got the response he needed.

"Please," James said hesitantly, it hurt to speak as the knife bit deeper into his skin. "Don't hurt me."

"Too late for that kid," the man said. "I don't know what you thought you were doing, but breaking into a government facility was probably the dumbest thing you could ever do."

"I was trying to save everyone," James said quickly. "They're trying to trap everyone within immersion."

"No shit," the man said with a chuckle.

James felt the knife shake uncomfortably against his flesh.

"You one of those crazy conspiracy theorists, huh?" His grip tightened on James. "Shut your robots down, and we can talk about it more, yeah?" He chuckled. "I'll give you credit. You're the youngest terrorist I've ever seen, and I'm impressed you made it this far. Bet you've got some powerful friends, don't ya?"

"I'm telling you the truth," James said, finally having to put his rather poor acting skills to the test. If he managed to convince the man, great, but what he really needed was time.

"And I'm telling you, I ain't buying it." The Enforcer's grip tightened further. "Now tell your robots to shut down, or this conversation is going to end in the next five seconds."

"You'll die," James tried. "If you kill me, they'll kill you."

"I know," the man's voice was resigned. "But that's what you sign up for in this job. There's a bigger picture. I'll gladly give my life to keep terrorists like you from hurting everyone. I'll happily die to protect my kids and family from scum like you who come after the government."

There was no getting through to this guy. His words confirmed as much. And while James couldn't fault the man for doing his job, of all the people to be guarding the immersion pods, why did it have to be someone willing to die to protect the government? They didn't deserve this man's loyalty... and he didn't deserve what James was about to do.

"I'm sorry," James said as he mentally sent a commend to his defensive vest.

Two things happened next. First was another pulse of protective energy, stronger this time than the blast that had kept the heat from his face during the explosion in the hallway.

It was a powerful blast that repulsed all things metallic around him, and it sent the Enforcer stumbling backwards. Most importantly, it pushed the knife away from his neck. He could feel his blood flowing as the blade was removed, but was pretty sure nothing vital had been damaged.

The second thing to happen was the deployment of his vest's special offensive capability. From his shoulders, two small turrets rose up. The first turned itself to target the Enforcer stumbling backwards. The second targeted the other Enforcer in the room. The invisible one's location was being broadcast into James's mind, and through him, the targeting system of his defensive vest.

With deadly precision, the weapons fired. Pellets no bigger than a small pebble shot forward with impossible speed. They were metallic balls and shot via miniaturized electromagnetic rails with enough force to penetrate the helmets of the Enforcer's armor and their skulls.

The two men died just doing their jobs... thinking they were protecting their family members and loved ones from terrorists.

James keeled over immediately, sick to his stomach as he vomited up the not-so-fruity-the-second-time FitSip from his stomach. Rue rushed towards him immediately, as did the Terminus.

From outside, the screams of Z continued, but the sounds from the other Knight's had dulled to a groan. Dagger was working to mitigate the effects of the Enforcer armor, but it was a slow process. Even with his advanced technology, the failsafe the government had put into the body armor of their Enforcers was obviously encoded quite well.

341

"James," Rue sobbed, her metallic hand touching his neck as he continued to dry heave, nothing left in his stomach. "Are you all right?"

She pulled her hand away from his neck, and he saw red. He placed his own hand to his neck and flinched. The knife had definitely cut, but not deep. He'd live.

"I'm fine," he said, trying and failing to stand.

Another wave of nausea overtook him, and tears burned in his eyes. Those men had done nothing wrong. They hadn't needed to die. He'd just killed two people. More vomiting. Two men just doing their jobs.

"It's not your fault," Rue whispered, stroking his back gently.

"Oh, no?" He looked at her, the taste of bile on his tongue. "Pretty sure I'm the one who killed them."

"But it wasn't your fault. The government was using them. They thought they were protecting their family, but they were dooming them. We need to complete our mission. You can still save their families."

James wiped his lips and nodded. With Rue's help, he stood. He glanced past her then, back toward the pod that she'd been staring at. She traced his line of sight.

"Don't," she said. "Don't look."

It was then that James realized what it was. He could just barely make out the sight of hair in the capsule, and a frail, emaciated form. It clicked in his head.

"Is that—"

"The original Sleeping Beauty pod," Rue said bitterly. "My real body."

James shivered and looked away. Whatever was in that pod, Rue didn't want James to see it. And he would respect that. Besides, they still had a mission to complete.

"Guard me while I get in the pod," James said, pulling himself away from Rue. "I'm going to shut down the server." He tried to grin at her, but his lip barely lifted. There was nothing to be happy about right now. Not with innocent blood on his hand. "I'm going to ruin the government's plans for the future."

Without saying anything else, James lay down in the pod. It was still warm. The last bit of warmth, his mind told him, of the man he'd killed. Tears fell freely from his eyes, his body wracked in sobbing. The pod was a service pod, and as the warm liquid flowed over him, he knew it would take him to the virtual control space for DCO.

And thanks to the nanites that warmed the back of his skull even now, he could also access the virtual control space for the entire facility through the service pod. As his eyes closed and his mind drifted away, James couldn't help but feel the slightest hint of a smile form.

With this... they'd won.

Epilogue

James woke with a yawn, the warmth of the sun greeting his trip back to consciousness. He blinked against the sunlight, rubbing away the crust that had formed on his eyelids.

"Looks who's awake," a voice said, light and filled with joy. "Just in time for lunch."

James blinked again and focused his gaze on the speaker. She smiled sweetly at him, and his heart swelled. He pulled himself off the grass where he'd been taking his nap.

"What's for lunch today?" he asked as he stood, stretching his arms. He looked around at the half finished fence he'd been working on earlier in the morning. His tools lay scattered about.

"Why don't you come inside and find out?" She laughed and motioned towards the door.

"If you insist." He let out a whistle. A moment later, his dog, who'd been sleeping by his tools, stood up and made his way towards the house.

"Let's get some lunch, Dagger," James said cheerfully.

He paused as he reached the doorway and gave his wife a kiss. Her lips were soft and warm against his, and for the hundredth time, he couldn't help but marvel at his life.

"I love you, Rue," James said as he grabbed her by the waist and the two walked into the house.

It had been years since everything had happened. Years since the government's plans had been revealed to the world. Years since his broadcast within DCO had sparked the fires of resistance.

The moment he'd severed the servers, the people had been free and the revolt had begun. Past that, thanks to his actions from within the government's own servers, the coup had been nearly completely bloodless.

He'd disabled their ability to trigger the countermeasures in their Enforcers' armor. And once their security forces, their might had realized what the elite had planned... well, the tables turned all too quickly.

It had been years since, following that revolution, that more truths had been revealed. Truths about immersion, the government, and so much more. Years since the virtual world had gone offline and people had begun living solely in the real world.

Even with the blood on his hands, the nightmares and guilt that still riddled him, it had all been worth it. As James made his way into his house, a home he'd been slowly fixing with the help of his dad and occasionally mom, he couldn't help but thank whatever it was that had brought him to this point.

"I love you too," Rue said, smiling brilliantly at him as she led him to the table.

It was only set for one. A fact that may have bothered him before, but now didn't even phase him. Rue ate when she wanted to, her robotic body capable of tasting and enjoying food exactly the same as a human one, but not needing to eat. She was the pinnacle of technology, crafted in a visage of her own design by James's parents. The first and only one of its kind.

Well, James thought to himself as he enjoyed his wife's cooking. *Not the only one.* Because in the basement of his house was another. One for him for when the time came. A body to ensure he and his love could spend eternity together.

A gift from his parents. A reward for James and Rue for what they'd done. For all the suffering, for all the hardship, for the sacrifices and dangers, and for standing up against the government in the end and risking it all, James and Rue would have eternity together. And there was nothing more, no greater reward than he could have ever asked for.

The World Smith

The sound of a bell signaled the arrival of a guest. He put his quill down and looked back, curious to see who it was. As the man entered, the World Smith found himself smiling, though it was a sad smile that didn't reach his eyes.

"A bit heavy handed, eh?" the newcomer asked.

His form shifted from that of a bald man with a goofy smile and glasses to another dressed in all black, a cane held in gloved hands, and a white mask on his face. Then it shifted again, and this time, was completely featureless. A blank canvas. Its voice a myriad of pitches and tones as it continued.

"What happened to letting things run their own course?"

"Sometimes," the World Smith answered slowly, "even the best laid plans must be altered. Can you fault a father for wanting to help his children? Can you fault me for wanting to ensure the path of suffering was avoided?"

"You picked the world," the featureless creature said.

It was a servant of the World Smith's, Page. It could become anything and anyone that the World Smith needed it to be. And this time around, he'd needed his Page to play multiple roles.

"You set the rules," Page continued, "yet you didn't like the outcome."

The World Smith let out a slight shrug. "I've always preferred a happy ending." He closed the book he'd been working on, the world that Page had been a part of. "And all I did was nudge it along the way. You know as well as I do that the fate of it was in their hands."

"A world without gods," Page recited, "a world where humans determine all. Where their free will, their ingenuity and brilliance will be their guiding light." Page *sat down on a stool, lightly running a finger along the spines of countless books in the World Smith's room. "That was what this world was to be."*

"A world without gods, yes," the World Smith answered, a wry smile on his face. "But even in a godless world, miracles, luck, and perhaps a little bit of fate, can make the mundane mystical."

Page let out a sigh, and the World Smith knew it wasn't convinced. But it didn't need to be. Page existed purely to serve. And yet the World Smith enjoyed allowing Page to question him. Free will, after all, was extremely important to the World Smith. It's what made the stories he penned, the accounts of the worlds he created and recorded the history of, interesting. Even if things sometimes went off script.

"What's the next world?" Page asked as the World Smith stood and placed the closed book in its spot on his shelf. A new piece of parchment was already at his desk. "What type of world will you be creating this time?"

"Wouldn't you like to know." The World Smith picked up his quill and began to write. "What type of world will it be, indeed?" he asked aloud, just as curious to see what came to life as Page was.

"Let us see where the next story takes us."

The End

Afterword

You made it. It's done. Ending a book is hard. Ending a series, is probably the hardest thing to do as an author, at least for me (other than editing... which I swear is the bane of my existence.) Thank you, again, for giving me a chance, and for giving my world, and my characters, a chance. I hope you enjoyed the ride, and I hope you'll come back for more adventures across different universes. I've an ever-growing catalogue, and promise to finish every series that I start. If you love my dungeon core work, check out my Elemental Dungeon Series. If you're looking for something else, try Flamespitter, my Wild West Cultivation novel, or Resonance, my monster taming litrpg. If you're looking for a happy slice of life, Aced, my tennis litrpg. Also, check out the amazing work of my fellow Portal Authors, who pour their hearts and souls into their stories, and deserve all the love and attention you, as readers, can give them!

If you're interested in following my work and chatting with me and fellow fans of Dungeon Core Online, check out my discord at:

https://discord.gg/DkJ9mMc.

If you're interested in reading more of my works, and seeing behind the scenes, the rough draft work for all my projects is on my Patreon:

https://www.patreon.com/Glyax

If you'd like to see something that's just for funsies, check out my tower climb novel on Royal Road.

The Infinite Tower - [A Tower Climb Web Serial] | Royal Road

If you're a fan of Gamelit, LitRPG, or Dungeon Core don't forget to follow Portal Books Facebook group for updates not only on my works, but the other amazing writers at Portal Books at

www.facebook.com/groups/LitRPGPortal/

And to chat to a bunch of Portal Books authors (Including me) why not swing by the Portal Books discord? You will also get launch announcements, sequel progress updates and tons more.

https://discord.gg/GXBNDGYQqT

Finally, if you'd like to sample **FREE EXCLUSIVE CONTENT** from any of the other incredible writers at Portal Books, you can do so by signing up to Portal Books mailing list. By signing up you will also be the first to hear about all their titles, get a chance to win free audio codes and get the heads up on discounts, sales and all that good stuff.

www.subscribepage.com/survivors.

For more general discussions about the genre, these groups may be useful to you.

www.facebook.com/groups/LitRPGsociety/
www.facebook.com/groups/LitRPG.books/
www.facebook.com/groups/LitRPGGroup/

Best wishes,
Jonathan Smidt and the Portal Books Team

Portal Books - Newsletter and Group

Portal Books is a digital publishing house that specializes in LitRPG, Dungeon Core, Cultivation and Progression Fantasy. Our mission is to bring you the best possible novels, with professional editing, copywriting and cover design.

We only work with authors who have a real passion for the genres and we think this shows in the novels we publish. We know that the heart of LitRPG is solid games mechanics and ensure every story is based on the kind of game system we ourselves would love to play.

If you'd like to try out stories from the other fantastic Portal Books authors, you can sign up to our mailing list for 80,000 words of FREE LitRPG stories. Whenever we add more, you'll get the update, absolutely free.

https://portal-books.com/sign-up

You can also find us on Facebook. Join our group to stay up to date on all our upcoming books, cover reveals, author interviews, giveaways, promotions and more!

https://www.facebook.com/groups/LitRPGPortal/

We also have a Discord server where you'll have a chance to chat with some our authors, members of the Portal Books team, or our community of readers as a whole!

https://discord.com/channels/815688886197551104/816053544817131532

For more general discussions about the genre, these groups may be useful to you:

www.facebook.com/groups/LitRPGsociety

www.facebook.com/groups/LitRPG.books

www.facebook.com/groups/LitRPGGroup

Best wishes,

The Portal Books Team

www.portal-books.com

Join the Group

To learn more about LitRPG, talk to authors, and just have an awesome time, please join the LitRPG Group.

Printed in Great Britain
by Amazon

57197878R00209